DISASTER AND THE DUKE

Brides By Chance
Regency Adventures
Book Nine

Elizabeth Bailey

SAPERE
BOOKS

DISASTER AND THE DUKE

Published by Sapere Books.

24 Trafalgar Road, Ilkley, LS29 8HH,
United Kingdom

saperebooks.com

ISBN: 978-1-80055-327-9

CHAPTER ONE

The basket was almost full, tiny blossoms jostling one another for space. Henrietta examined her finds, poking them apart. It would not do if the petals were damaged, and wildflowers were particularly delicate.

She ought to be thinking of turning back, only the woods were so pretty and peaceful, the day so fine. Henrietta sighed a little, looking up into the filtering branches. She would not give in to melancholy. She had agreed to carry out the plan Silvestre had come up with and she must do her best to remain cheerful.

"There is no use our pining for what cannot be, Hetty. We are destined to remain upon the shelf and that is all there is to it."

Henrietta's eyes had filled. "But poor Papa. How will he manage? He cannot afford to keep us forever, Silve."

"Don't start, Hetty!" Her twin had produced a pocket handkerchief and thrown it at her. "Dry your eyes at once! Crying will not mend matters."

Henrietta had struggled to suppress her sobs. Her sensibility was the greatest trial to her family and she made every effort to be more like her robust sister. She admired Silvestre's ability to take their misfortune in her stride and wished she had her resilience.

"What we need," Silve had said impressively, "is A Plan."

Henrietta's tears had been effectually arrested. "A plan? What kind of plan?"

"We must each think of a way we may turn our skills to advantage. We must earn our keep."

She blinked. "But we have no skills."

"Poppycock, of course we have. We have been well educated and we have all sorts of accomplishments."

"Those?" Henrietta had sighed again. "Of what use are such things as playing the pianoforte and singing when we are not going to be married? Besides, I am not like you, Silve. I play horribly, and you know Aunt Angelica always said my voice is too thin." She thought of the only possible use such accomplishments could have, if not to entertain their acquaintance. "And pray don't suggest we should go out as governesses, for you know very well Mama would be shocked at such a notion, and Papa would never permit it."

"I wasn't going to suggest it. Nor am I thinking of singing or playing the piano."

"What then? It is just like you, Silve, to be coming up with impossible schemes."

Her twin had twinkled at her. "This is not impossible, Hetty, truly. Only think! What is my secret hobby?"

Horrified, Henrietta stared at her. "You are not thinking of those dreadful gothic tales? Silve, you can't!"

Her twin bridled. "Why not? If Mrs Radcliffe and Mrs Fossebridge can be published, I can too. You need not look like that. Of course I shall not write as Silvestre Latimer. No one will know." She frowned. "Except perhaps Aunt Angelica. I am depending on her to help me find a publisher."

Henrietta dropped the handkerchief in her agitation. "Silve! If you were found out! Papa would be furious, you know he would. And Mama would be mortified."

"I shan't be found out. Aunt Angelica would never betray me, and I know you won't."

"No, of course I would not, but still." A hideous thought entered her mind. "You are not expecting me to write stories, are you? Heavens, Silve!"

"I wish you won't be so absurd, Hetty," scoffed her sister. "But you too have a hobby, have you forgotten?"

"Pressing flowers? It is you who are absurd, Silve. How in the world can I earn my keep pressing flowers?"

But Silvestre had been adamant. "You make the most beautiful pictures with them. I could not do so; I would not have the patience. But everyone loves the ones you have given them as gifts."

Henrietta's head began to whirl. "Yes, but I could not sell them … could I?"

"Why not? If Aunt Angelica could persuade people to participate in that auction, I am sure she can persuade them to buy your pressed flower pictures."

If Henrietta was doubtful of their godmother's abilities in this direction, there was no doubt of Silvestre's persuasive powers. Henrietta had risen rapidly to enthusiasm and begun upon the scheme immediately.

"Say nothing to Mama or Papa, Hetty. Not until we have secured our first sales."

As nothing would have induced Henrietta to confide in their parents, she agreed to this with alacrity. Although she had entered a caveat. "But we can't do it in secret, Silve. I will need to invade Papa's library if I am to press flowers."

Her twin was prepared for this. "We will let them think we are making the best of things. When Mama does not need our help, we will spend our time on The Plan."

For Henrietta's part, the necessity to take enjoyable summer rambles to collect the flowers she needed made her task a deal easier than she had anticipated. At least she had not to crouch over the writing slope for hours, getting ink stains on her fingers like poor Silve. Aunt Angelica, when applied to by the twins, had not only given The Plan her whole-hearted approval, but also promised to make a list of interested parties for Henrietta and to write to publishers on Silvestre's behalf.

"For I dare say it cannot hurt to be seen to have a fashionable patron," the redoubtable Mrs Summerhayes had said.

She had been dismayed when the auction she had carried out on behalf of the Latimer twins failed of its purpose. Just as Henrietta had feared, the truth had leaked out. The party being the talk of the town meant little, when Papa's unfortunate situation made it common knowledge that his daughters could bring nothing at all to a marriage. Their potential suitors sheered off in a hurry and the sisters returned to Moss House, unbetrothed and with no hope of attending another Season.

Henrietta did not mind being a spinster. At least, not much. She did struggle with the thought of dwindling into an old maid when she had looked forward to having a family and children of her own. But it was worse to know she and Silve must be a charge on Papa for years and years. What was to become of them — and Mama too — when he died at last was too dispiriting to contemplate.

Throwing off the thoughts, she peeped into her basket. The collection of foxgloves, willowherb, wild roses of pink and white, purple orchis and yellow wild iris, among others she could not name, made a delightful multi-coloured splash. It was a pity the colours faded so with drying, but a careful arrangement of the images she had in mind would still create a pretty effect.

Satisfied, she was just turning for home when a gunshot cracked into the silence of the woods. Startled half out of her wits, Henrietta almost lost her balance. The basket went flying and she grabbed at the nearest tree to steady herself. Her heart began to hammer as she glanced about for the shooter. Was it a poacher? No, not in broad daylight. Perhaps the neighbour's gamekeeper? She must have strayed too far into the woods and crossed the boundary into the duke's lands.

Before she could think what to do, a second shot rang out. It sounded a good deal closer. Heavens! Someone was out potting rabbits or birds. What should she do? She dared not venture forth without warning them she was there. Her limbs were trembling under her, but she moved away from the tree and set her hands either side of her mouth to increase the sound.

"Hallooo! Pray don't shoot again! Halloooo! Help! Help! Hallooooo!" Her cries sounded in her own ears like a thin shriek, but she kept it up until she heard an answering shout.

"Hallo? Who is there?"

Henrietta could not see anyone, but she stumbled towards the sound, crying out again. "Pray don't shoot! Hello! Hello! Don't shoot, sir!"

Thumping feet were now to be heard above her shouts and a couple of running figures came into sight through the trees. Without hesitation, Henrietta made towards them, lifting her petticoats and calling out in breathless dismay.

"I am so sorry! I did not mean to stray so far, only pray don't shoot me!"

She stumbled to a halt as a man came hurrying towards her, another at his heels. He was dressed in country wear of frock-coat, boots and breeches, a beaver hat on his head and he was carrying a long firearm. He called out again. "Are you all right? You are not hurt, are you?"

As he neared, Henrietta saw that he was young and very obviously a gentleman. The man behind him seemed to be a servant, one who looked familiar though she could not place him. "No, indeed I am not hurt, sir. But I was afraid you might shoot me if I did not warn you of my presence."

"A good thing you did," said the young man as he reached her, handing his gun to his fellow. "But what are you doing wandering about in my woods?"

"I am very sorry, sir. I didn't realise I had strayed so far. I was collecting…" She faded out as she remembered her basket. "Oh, no! My flowers!" Turning at once, she looked to where she had been standing when the first shot startled her into dropping the basket. She caught sight of it lying on its side and hurried up, exclaiming as she saw that her collection of wildflowers were scattered and disordered. "Oh! They are half ruined!" Forgetting everything but the effort she had expended on selecting the prettiest of the blooms, Henrietta sank to the ground, upending the basket, in which a few of her collection remained. Most of the scattered blooms were crushed and mangled. Tears sprang to her eyes as she picked through them, trying to find any undamaged. "Now it is all to do again and I haven't the heart."

From above her, a scornful voice came. "You are crying over a few paltry wildflowers? Good God, girl, what is the matter with you?"

Stung, Henrietta reared up. "How horrid you are! I have spent ages picking them out, if you wish to know."

"Yes, in my woods. I suppose you know that is stealing."

Springing to her feet, Henrietta confronted him in a fury. "It is nothing of the kind! You do not own the wildflowers."

"I do if they are in my woods."

"Well, I didn't get all of them in your woods! I picked them on common ground."

The young man raised his brows. "Indeed? Which ones did you pick on my lands, then?"

"How should I know? In any event, you may have them all back, for I can't use them in that state."

He set his arms akimbo. "What do you suppose I'm going to do with a lot of squashed wildflowers?"

"I don't care what you do with them," raged Henrietta. "You may shoot them, for all of me!"

"I've no wish to shoot wildflowers. I am trying to shoot rabbits, if only silly girls weren't wandering about my lands and trying to get themselves shot instead."

Incensed, Henrietta could only glower at him, unable to think of a suitable retort. He stared back, and she became aware of a glimmer of laughter in his eyes. She let her breath go in a whoosh of relief. "Oh! You are teasing me!"

His lips twitched, but he disclaimed at once. "Nothing of the sort. You've ruined my sport. I ought to string you up from the nearest tree."

Henrietta's mouth dropped open as she fluctuated between disbelief and a bubble of amusement. But she entered a protest nevertheless. "You c-can't go p-punishing people without — without trial, even if you are a duke."

His brows flew up. "You know me?"

"You said this is your land, so I suppose you are the new owner. Of course I know His Grace of Charlton died last year. Only he didn't have a son."

The new duke eyed her, a slight frown creasing his brow. "Who are you? A neighbour, I suppose?"

"Hardly that. I live at Moss House in the village."

"Sinsham village?"

"Yes, but we are not your tenants, if you were thinking you have a right to complain of me to Papa."

He looked her up and down. "Why should I complain to Papa when I can perfectly well complain to you, Miss Wildflower Thief?"

Henrietta's cheeks grew warm again, along with her temper. "It is not stealing to be picking wildflowers. If I had been shooting your rabbits, you might with justice complain. But you have already said you can do nothing with the flowers, and the plain truth is that I cannot either because of you making me jump half out of my skin with your horrid shooting. It is all your fault!"

To her further annoyance, he grinned. "In that case, I give you permission to pick all the wildflowers you wish. Only don't go doing it while I'm out shooting."

"But how shall I know if you are out shooting?"

"Use your ears!" With which, he turned away and started to walk off, his attendant behind him.

Henrietta felt abruptly alone and obeyed her instinct. "Wait!"

He stopped and looked back. "Well, what?"

She hesitated, fiddling with her petticoats. "I-I am not sure which way to go."

"To get back to Sinsham, you mean?" He glanced at the man with him. "You know the country, Beattock. Which way should the lady go?"

The fellow Beattock, a stocky individual of middle years, pointed. "East, your grace. She'll hit the lane if she heads away from the sun."

A thread of apprehension crept into Henrietta's bosom. She felt quite disoriented after the encounter and was sure she might get lost. "You won't shoot again, will you, until I'm out of the woods?"

The duke made a sound of exasperation. "I suppose we'll have to escort you. I don't want to be finding your corpse lying across my path. Lead the way, Beattock!"

Henrietta's relief was tempered by his utterly unchivalrous attitude. She was about to turn to follow the servant when she remembered her flowers. "Oh, my basket!" She flitted to where it lay on the ground and picked it up, observing that a small collection of wildflowers had survived. She poked them apart. "I may still be able to use some of these."

"Will you come on?"

Hastily she moved to join the young duke, who was waiting in ill-concealed impatience.

"You are the most tiresome girl! First you steal my flowers. Next you insist on my giving up my sport. And now —"

"I didn't insist on anything. You offered to escort me!"

"I was forced to it because you obviously haven't a clue. I'm astonished you manage to get up in the morning without falling over."

"I don't care if you are the duke," Henrietta burst out, incensed, as she stomped along beside him, "you are the rudest young man I have ever met in my life!"

"That's position for you, Miss Wildflower Thief. I can do whatever I like."

"Good heavens! You mean you think your situation gives you the right to ignore common courtesy? Well, you will not be very popular around here, then."

"Good. I've no desire to be popular. The more people leave me alone, the better I shall like it."

"Well, you won't then because nobody is going to leave you alone once they know who you are. Besides, you can't just ignore everyone. They will start paying calls on you when they know you are out of mourning."

A groan escaped the duke. "Thank you for the warning. I'll put it about I'm still in complete shock. Which, I don't mind telling you, is not far from the case."

Henrietta regarded him curiously. "Why are you in shock? Didn't you know you must inherit?"

"Oh, someday possibly. I certainly didn't expect my uncle to go dying on me just when I was about to embark on an adventure."

"What kind of adventure?"

"None of your business, Miss Nosy."

Henrietta bridled. "What a beast you are! There is no necessity to speak to me in that horrid way."

He grinned. "Yes, there is. You'll tell everyone how beastly I am and they won't plague me."

"You are mistaken. You don't know people very well, do you?"

"Don't I?"

"No. If you mean to be curmudgeonly, they will be more eager. People love a curiosity, that's what Aunt Angelica always says."

The young man frowned. "Who the devil is Aunt Angelica?"

"She's not really an aunt, but Silve and I call her so because we have known her forever and she is our godmother. She is Mrs Summerhayes and lives in Barkham and she is bound to call on you."

"Oh my God! I shall depend upon you putting her off."

"I won't. Besides, you can't put Aunt Angelica off when she has made up her mind, and in any event I need her help with my wildflower project."

"Indeed? I suppose I may look next to have her prancing about on my lands and stealing my wildflowers instead."

The notion of Mrs Summerhayes doing any such thing was so comical, Henrietta let out a giggle, which immediately drew the duke's irritation.

"Do you mean to share the joke?"

She gave him a haughty look. "Not with you."

He was silent for a moment. "Who is Silve?"

"My twin sister."

He stopped dead, staring at her in horror. "There are two of you? When one is more than enough?"

To Henrietta's own astonishment she dissolved into giggles. "Oh, you need not fret. Silve is quite different. She would have sent you about your business in a trice."

"Ah, Miss Bossy Boots, I apprehend?"

"She is a bit. In fact, it was her notion I should make wildflower pictures to —" She broke off. What was she about, confiding The Plan to a complete stranger?

But the duke chose to take it up. "So it's her fault you've been traipsing about on my land and nearly getting yourself shot?"

"Yes — at least, no, of course not. I wish you would stop teasing me about it."

She was spared any retort he might have made by the gamekeeper.

"This is the lane, your grace. If the lady follows it that way, she will come to Sinsham."

The duke nodded and turned to Henrietta. "Know where you are now?"

She glanced up and down the lane. "Yes, I think so. I didn't come this way. I think I crossed it further up."

"But can you get yourself home from here? I mean, even you can't get lost on a familiar lane, surely?"

Henrietta eyed him with resentment. "What do you mean, even me? I've been living here for years, I'll have you know."

"No one would think it."

"I can't help it if I don't have a very good sense of direction."

"Or a very good sense of anything."

"Oh!" Her cheeks warmed all over again and tears sprang to her eyes. "You are quite abominable! I th-thought you w-were t-teasing, b-but now I s-see you are n-nothing but a b-brute."

His brows drew together as he dug a hand into a pocket of his breeches. "You're not crying again, are you?"

"I c-can't h-help it when y-you're so b-beastly…" Henrietta faded out, struggling to control the rising sobs.

The duke's hand reappeared, flourishing a pocket handkerchief. "If there's one thing I can't abide," he said in fierce tones, seizing Henrietta by one shoulder, "it's a weeping female!" Then he was wiping at the leaking tears with his handkerchief, looking perfectly furious as his eyes, of a startling light grey, bored into Henrietta's. But his ministrations with the handkerchief were gentle, belying his words and his tone. "There! Now, will you please stop before you drive me out of my mind and my handkerchief gets utterly soaked?"

She let out a watery chuckle and sniffed back the tears. "I didn't mean to cry."

"No, you couldn't help it," he said, still wiping her cheeks. "So much I understood."

Somehow his hand had slipped behind her head and Henrietta's pulse speeded up as she found he was suddenly very close, the handkerchief resting against her cheek as he studied her face.

"Not too bad. Your cheeks haven't gone blotchy at least."

Henrietta could not utter a word. She found herself staring into the grey eyes, which became intent. The question came softly.

"What's your name?"

She found her voice, aware it was husky. "Hetty."

He smiled for the first time, a perfectly charming smile that transformed his face to friendliness — and more. "I'm Theo."

A sound, which had been growing in the vague background of Henrietta's mind, resolved into hoofbeats. They stopped abruptly and an expletive rent the air.

"Good grief! Henrietta?"

Shock brought her back to reality. "Papa?"

The duke released her and turned just as her father reined in.

"What in the devil's name is going on here? Who is this young man? Has he assaulted you?"

Before Henrietta could disclaim, the duke cut in swiftly. "I don't know who you are, sir, but I take leave to tell you your assumption is an insult!"

"Insult, is it?"

To Henrietta's horror, her father swung himself out of the saddle. He thrust his reins at the gamekeeper. "Hold these for me, Beattock!"

"Papa, pray!"

But she was forestalled by the gamekeeper. "This is his grace, the Duke of Charlton, Mr Latimer."

Papa appeared even more incensed by this intelligence. He seized Henrietta's wrist and pulled her away, glaring at the duke. "It is, is it? Well, if he means to try and dally with my daughter, he will find himself at the thin end of my whip, duke or no duke!"

Horrified, and perfectly agonised at the instant rise of hauteur in the young man's features, Henrietta tried to intervene. "Papa, it was nothing of the kind, I promise you!"

But Papa was in no mood to listen. "I'll deal with you when I've dealt with this whippersnapper. How dare you, sir? Explain yourself at once!"

For a moment, the duke said nothing, looking from Papa to Henrietta and back again. He was perfectly white and she saw a muscle twitch in his cheek. His eyes narrowed dangerously. His voice was silky, redolent with a fury that had nothing to do with the bantering protests he had adopted with Henrietta earlier. "I see how it is. My dear Mr Latimer, if that is who you are —"

"Don't you patronise me, young man!"

He ignored Papa's belligerence. "My dear Mr Latimer, if you imagine I am to be caught by such a trick as this, you have mistaken your man."

Papa's face became thunderous and his grip on Henrietta's wrist tightened so that she winced. "I beg your pardon? What in Hades are you getting at, sir?"

An unpleasant smile curled the duke's lip. "I may be, in your words, a mere whippersnapper, sir, but I am not without experience. I have kept aloof from Society ever since I discovered my expectations opened me to precisely this sort of manoeuvre. Rest assured, you and your daughter's stratagems, while I admit they are novel, can have no effect upon me."

His words fell upon Henrietta like a fountain of ice water. She hardly heard Papa's outraged response for the painful knot that lodged itself in her bosom. "Stratagems? Stratagems? You dare to suggest —"

"You need not dissemble, Mr Latimer. Your scheme is blown. I do not look for a bride as yet, and if I did, it would not be one who descends to trickery to gain her point. I will bid you good day."

With which, he executed a neat bow, turned and strode off into the woods, leaving Papa standing in fuming silence.

Henrietta was in no better case, and matters were not helped by the gamekeeper, who shifted close, holding out the horse's reins.

"Begging your pardon, Mr Latimer, but he don't know the village as yet, nor its people. I've to follow at once, sir, if you'll be so good as to take your reins."

Papa received them with a brief word of thanks, still staring after the duke. Henrietta quailed as he turned on her instead.

"And what, may I ask, miss, have you to say for yourself?"

CHAPTER TWO

Theo trod blindly through the woods, scattering leaves and debris, together with an occasional small creature that skittered off at his approach. It was just as he knew it would be. That hurly-burly girl! Who could have supposed such a seemingly scatter-brained creature had taken a deliberate path to intercept him? As for her father —!

He ground his teeth, gripped by consuming fury. If the scheme had not been so obvious, he wouldn't have minded the way the fellow addressed him. Better than the toadying note he had come to expect. But Latimer had an end in view, that was certain. Though he would not have thought it of the girl. Hetty, did she say? She had seemed very innocent. The more fool he for being deceived.

"Your grace!"

He broke stride, slowing as he threw a glance at Beattock, hurrying along in his wake. "What is it?"

"You're heading for the lake, your grace."

Theo stopped abruptly. Ahead through the trees he glimpsed a trace of silver where the ornamental water was situated. He had no desire to ruin his boots in the wetlands around it.

Beattock waved the rifle. "The house is this way, your grace."

Theo grunted and changed direction. He had lost all desire to pot rabbits and his eye was annoyingly drawn to the plethora of wildflowers dotting the ground. The reminder threw him into speech. "Who is that fellow Latimer? You evidently know him."

The gamekeeper caught up, though his breath was a little short. Feeling faintly guilty, Theo moderated his pace.

"He's not a gentleman of account, your grace. Unlucky, though."

"How so?"

"He was heir to Baron Horwood, but seemingly he was cut out of the succession last year. Rumour has it he lost his allowance into the bargain. It's why he's a trifle short-tempered, your grace."

This was said on a note of apology. Or was it explanation? Did Beattock think his supposition mistaken? "I dare say he may be, but it doesn't give him the right to take me to task."

"No, your grace."

There was silence for a space, but Theo could almost feel the man itching to speak. He glanced round. "Well?"

"Your grace?"

"If you've got something on your mind, spit it out."

A deprecating expression overspread the gamekeeper's features. "Well, it's this way, your grace. Always found him a good sort, Mr Latimer, friendly like. But since this come upon him, he's been different. What with them twins of his left on his hands and he can't do nothing for them."

Which, in Theo's view, argued in favour of his assumption of a scheme of entrapment. If his daughters were portionless, Latimer might well be driven to stratagems to get them married off. "In that case, he would do well to aim for lower game."

"Yes, your grace."

The fellow sounded subdued. Exasperated, Theo halted, turning on him. "Well, what? You think I had it wrong back there? Much you know!"

The man disregarded this rider. "It's just as it ain't the kind of thing Mr Latimer would do, your grace. A very correct gentleman I always found him. Protective of them twins of his."

Protective enough to try to foist one of them off onto his neighbour? Theo remained unconvinced of Latimer's innocence as he started off again. His arrival was too pat. That silly girl had pretty well forced him into escorting her to the lane. What's more, it was a damned sight too convenient to be turning into a watering pot just at that moment, driving him into acting like an utter fool. A sight too chivalrous, Theodore Oliver Lionel Devenal. He ought to know better.

Except that he didn't. He kept forgetting his exalted blasted station, that was the trouble. Life was much easier when he was merely Theo Devenal. His uncle had not bothered to confer a courtesy title on him, convinced his much younger second wife would produce an heir of his own loins. Nor had he made more than a cursory effort to initiate his actual heir into the workings and demands of the estates during his occasional visits, for which Theo had been thankful. No more than his uncle did he suppose he would inherit. Nor had he wanted to. Those who supposed a dukedom was a blessed sinecure were mightily mistaken. More like a prison. A luxurious prison, but still a prison in the sense of tying him to inescapable duties he could well have done without. Not to mention the sort of matrimonial trap to which he had just been subjected.

They were approaching the edge of the woods and the house was within sight. It was a fair-sized house, but nowhere near as substantial as his principal seat up north, a vast mansion set next to the ruin of a dour and looming castle after which it was named. Theo much preferred Whisley Park, and had escaped to Berkshire as soon as he decently could once the obligatory year of mourning was up.

He was enjoying the rare days of freedom before the family joined him for the summer months. Even potting rabbits provided a welcome distraction from the daily grind, grappling with the burden of work that had come upon him on succeeding to the title. All well and good for his aunt to say he could leave it to his agent, who seemed capable of holding the damned place together. The duchess had no notion how enormous was the work to maintain the whole estate. Whisley Park was bad enough, but Devenal Castle was a nightmare. He was already growing to loathe the place.

He parted from Beattock on the curve of the drive and entered through a side door, slipping into the main corridor where his ears were at once assailed by the sounds of unusual activity. Thumps, bumps, shouts and hurrying feet.

Good God, were they here already? Bang went his freedom, then!

Sighing, Theo swallowed the rise of frustration and went forward into the hall. He entered upon a scene of organised chaos, catching snatches of instruction and comment out of the murmuring cacophony.

"Take the trunk first! No, that big one, Thomas."

Old Flint, the Whisley Park butler, obviously enjoying himself hugely.

"I'll take the other end, Tom."

"That's right, Robert. Now, John, her grace's dressing case."

The footman grappled one of the boxes out of the jumble of luggage as the shrill voice of Cecilia's dresser cut in.

"Take care with that, my man. Don't drop it! There are bottles in there."

Theo could not but feel sorry for the unfortunate footman, harried up the stairs by the redoubtable Miss Mohr, herself burdened with the duchess's outer garments, an umbrella and a small valise.

"Will you not come into the parlour while Flint disposes of all this, your grace?"

Mrs Oughtibridge, with what looked like every maid in the place at her beck and call, fussing about Cecilia and the rest of her entourage. Besides the dresser, Theo spotted her companion, Mary Eddleston, two nursemaids, one carrying Baby Pru, Ellie's governess — as if she needed one at five years of age — and little Ellie herself, rummaging in the luggage in search of the Lord knew what. With a groan, Theo noted Cecilia had brought her blasted steward as well. He ought to have known she would not set forward on such a hazardous journey without Swarland's escort.

He remained thankfully unnoticed for a few minutes while the duchess performed her usual panic-stricken flap at any untoward occurrence, trying to handle fifty things at once.

"No, Ellie, don't do that, you're in the way. What, Oughtibridge? The parlour? In a moment, I must see to — Mary, don't let that girl take the smaller portmanteau, for I am sure my smelling salts are in there. No, Ellie, darling! For heaven's sake, Miss Jurby, stop her! Flint, where is his grace? Why is he not here to greet us? Well, Swarland must find him at once. Oh, only look at poor Pru, she is exhausted! Oughtibridge, is the nursery in order? Milk! Tell Cook to heat some warm milk for the children. Take Baby, Nurse, and put her to bed at once. If she wakes, give her the milk. Now, Swarland — Swarland, where are you?"

"Here, your grace. I believe his grace is —"

"Theo! Theo!"

Leaping over the luggage, Ellie bounded across the hall and threw herself at Theo. His mood lifted at his little cousin's enthusiastic greeting and he caught her up, throwing her into the air and laughing.

"Hello, monkey face!"

"I'm not monkey face," she protested in time-honoured fashion, grabbing him around the neck.

"I bet you are! Don't tell me you haven't been in mischief, because I won't believe you."

She giggled into his shoulder as he settled her into his arms. "I haven't really, Theo. I've been very good." She lowered her voice to a whisper. "Miss Jurby don't let me make mischief."

"Oh, don't she?" he whispered back. "We'll soon fix her."

She giggled again, but the reunion was interrupted.

"Good heavens, Theo, don't encourage her! She has fidgeted us all to death the whole journey. I declare, I could readily have strangled her!"

"She's strangling me," Theo said, grinning at the culprit, who beamed and kissed his cheek.

"I wouldn't. I like you too much. Will you marry me when I grow up?"

"Ellie! Don't be ridiculous, child. Put her down, Theo!"

"Marry a monkey? You must be joking!" Which set the child off into giggles again. "Off with you! We'll play later."

"Take her upstairs, Nurse."

Theo set her on her feet and she scampered off with her nursemaid, who hustled her up the stairs.

"Oughtibridge, pray show Miss Jurby to her room. Oh, and tea in the parlour at once, if you please. I am positively gasping. Mary, have you found my smelling salts? Oh, Theo, don't run away! I must talk to you. Swarland, see to all this jumble, will you? I cannot cope with such a shambles in the hall. Oh, for some quiet!"

She drifted into the parlour where a maid was holding open the door, Mary Eddleston twittering behind her. Suppressing a groan, Theo followed, but he lost no time in trying to escape.

"I need to change, Cecilia. I've been out shooting."

His aunt, who was ridiculously a mere six years his senior, waved this away as she sank her willowy form into a sofa. "So must I change, but not now. This cannot wait."

"Can't it?" Theo tried again. "Surely we can talk later. I can see you need a good rest after the journey."

Cecilia brushed a weary hand across her forehead. "I do indeed. It is a miracle I have not developed the headache. But I must have tea before anything else."

"Well, why don't you enjoy your tea in peace and we will —"

"No, no, no, Theo! I know you too well. You will be off heaven knows where and I shan't see you until the dinner hour. You are dining at home, I trust?"

He bowed to the inevitable, throwing himself into a chair removed from the women. "Of course I'm dining at home, Cecilia. Did you think I'd be off doing the pretty?"

His widowed aunt, who was lying back among the cushions with one hand at her brow, threw it in the air instead, sitting up in a bang. "That is just what I need to discuss with you, Theo. We must pick up the threads again, and the gentry are bound to call once they know I am in residence. But have you prepared the way as I begged you to?"

Guiltily conscious he had utterly ignored the plethora of instructions she had heaped upon him before he came south, Theo grabbed one of his timely excuses out of the air. "I haven't had a chance. I've been buried in papers since I got here."

Cecilia's large eyes fixed him with a reproachful stare. "No, you haven't. You've just said you were out shooting."

"For the first time in weeks."

"You haven't been here for weeks."

"Well, I haven't had a chance to go poking about the neighbours and exposing myself to the sort of —" He broke off, suddenly reluctant to mention the encounter in the woods and Latimer's subsequent ploy. Why that should be so he could not imagine. It was not as if that idiotic girl deserved his sympathy.

Fortunately, the duchess was too taken up with his iniquities to notice. "If that is not just like you, Theo! I was depending upon you to have broken the ice." She gave an elaborate sigh, collapsing again. "It is all of a piece. Now I dare say I must perform the introductions as well as run the gamut of their expressions of sympathy. I declare, I wish I had come down with you. I knew you could not be trusted to do what is right. What my poor departed Oliver would have thought of you I dare not think."

Theo was tempted to protest he did not give a fig for his dead uncle's opinion, adding a rider that as he was now the duke the only opinion that mattered was his own. But as he knew Cecilia would treat him to a display of lachrymose despair if he did, he held his tongue. Adept at getting her own way, was his aunt. Uncle Oliver had himself complained of it to Theo often enough, if only she knew. But he was not going to pander to her unscrupulous methods.

"Don't fret, Cecilia," he said instead. "You know very well you will thoroughly enjoy touting me about the neighbourhood. In fact," he added, warming to his theme, "I deliberately refrained from spreading the news of my presence so that I would not deprive you of the pleasure."

For a moment the issue hung in the balance while Cecilia eyed him in something of a dudgeon. But then her sense of propriety in quarrelling before her companion evidently overcame her irritation and she laughed. "Teasing creature! Is he not an utter beast, Mary?"

While Miss Eddleston predictably disclaimed, Theo found an echo ringing in his head, in quite another voice. *What a beast you are!* An image of a pair of pansy eyes drowning in tears flipped into play. Theo banished it, springing up from the chair.

"I'm going to change. We'll make some plans at dinner, Cecilia."

"But, Theo —"

He exited the room at speed, closing the door on her protests. He negotiated the remaining bandboxes and trunks still strewn about the hall and almost collided with Flint, staggering under the weight of the tea tray. Irritation claimed him. "Why the deuce are you carrying that, Flint, when you've a coterie of able young men to do it?"

"They are still dealing with the luggage, your grace," panted the elderly butler.

Theo threw up his eyes. "They could have done this first, couldn't they? Here, I'll open the door for you." He crossed back to the parlour. "I suppose all the maids are busy preparing rooms as well." He thrust open the door, taking care not to be seen by the women within, adding in a low voice as Flint passed him, "Don't you overdo it, old fellow. This place won't run without you."

The butler looked gratified, but he tutted nevertheless. "Never did know how to keep a proper distance, sir, did you?"

"No, and I'm not going to start now. Get in there before my aunt sees me and calls me back. I've only just managed to escape."

"Master Theo! I mean, your grace…"

Theo grimaced. He could wish he was still merely Master Theo, but it would not do to say so to old Flint. He closed the door behind the butler and retraced his steps, running lightly up the stairs and managing to make it to his apartments before anyone else could waylay him.

He rang for his valet and began to strip off his clothes, his mind dwelling on Cecilia's determination to parade him before the local gentry. A certain expressive face and a basket of scattered wildflowers popped back into his head. Would she include the Latimers? That was liable to be deuced embarrassing.

CHAPTER THREE

Smarting from her interview with Papa, Henrietta wept out her misery on her sister's shoulder.

"It is not the scold I mind, Silve, but the injustice," she complained when she'd had her cry out and was sniffing into a damp handkerchief. "I told him he had it wrong, but he would not listen. And now the duke thinks I am a designing wretch, and I'm not, Silve, I'm not!"

Her sister patted her in a consoling way. "Of course you are not. You couldn't carry out a scheme of that nature if you tried until you were blue in the face."

This way of looking at it did little to cheer Henrietta. "You mean to imply I am perfectly bird-witted. You are as bad as Theo!"

Silvestre's brows shot up. "Theo? Is he the duke?"

"Yes, and he would keep teasing and making me out to be idiotic when it was his firing his gun that made me drop my basket." The memory of those dreadful last moments returned. "Only he became horridly stiff and sarcastic when Papa accused him and I don't blame him in the least for that, for I was never so mortified in my life!"

"Don't fret yourself to flinders over it, Hetty." Silvestre rose from the little sofa where she had been perching beside her twin and plonked back down in the chair in front of the bureau. "Papa will come round and then he will be even more mortified at having misjudged you."

"It isn't me he misjudged, but the duke. Of course Papa became utterly infuriated at the accusation he made."

"Well, of course, and if this Theo of yours knew him better he would realise his mistake. Papa would never stoop to such a despicable trick." Silvestre, who had been discovered scribbling at her novel in the little upstairs room, once the twins' nursery but now their private den, began to tidy her sheaf of ink-spattered paper, opening the drawer where she kept the growing pile that constituted her story.

Henrietta at once felt guilty. "I've interrupted your labours, Silve. At least one of us was making progress."

Her twin sighed. "As a matter of fact, I was not getting on at all." She held up the top two sheets to show the plethora of crossings-out. "I seem to have reached an impasse at the moment, so I am glad of the excuse to leave it. Besides, Mama wants me to help her sort jam in the still room."

"Well, she won't now because she isn't there," said Henrietta on a gloomy note. "She met us in the hall and of course she knew at once something was wrong. Papa sent me off and I expect he is telling her everything in his library."

Silvestre wheeled on her stool. "Good heavens, why did you not say so in the first place, Hetty? If Mama is closeted with him, we may expect an invasion at any moment."

Hardly were the words out of her mouth than a knock on the door was followed by the entrance of Mrs Latimer, who poked her head round in the way she always did, her round and bespectacled countenance looking perfectly perturbed.

"There you are, my poor darling."

Henrietta could not refrain from bursting out. "Oh, Mama, is he very angry still?"

Mrs Latimer tiptoed in, putting a finger to her lips and closing the door gently behind her. She spoke in a hushed tone as she came across to Henrietta. "Poor Papa has the headache. I've sent Dinah for a tisane from Cook."

"But is he still furious with Hetty, Mama?"

Mrs Latimer waved agitated hands. "Keep your voice down, Silve. He needs peace and quiet and we must not disturb him. You know how upset he becomes when he has been obliged to rebuke one of his beloved daughters. Poor Papa is not at his best, as you both know very well. It was remiss of you to provoke him, Hetty."

This was too much, even for Henrietta's rising conscience. "But I didn't, Mama. It was all a terrible misunderstanding."

"Hush, my dear. Not so loud."

"But, Mama —!"

"Papa knows, my love, and it is that which has distressed him so." Mrs Latimer took Henrietta's chin in her hand and examined her face. "Just as I thought. You've been weeping your heart out."

"She's cried buckets, Mama, she's hopeless." Silvestre rolled her eyes at her twin, who bridled.

"I can't help it. I do try not to cry, but P-papa…"

"Don't start again! Mama, tell her, for heaven's sake."

Squashing down the urge to weep again, Henrietta looked up at her mother, who was patting her cheek. "I'm not starting again, Mama, only…"

"I know, my love, I know. I am afraid you too closely resemble Papa. He does not break down, of course, but he feels things very deeply just as you do, my darling Hetty."

"Yes, he gets headaches instead," put in Silvestre on a resigned note.

Mrs Latimer tutted at her. "You must not be unkind, Silve. We are not all made the same, you know." She gave her curious little laugh. "Indeed, it would be a dull world if we were. If Papa and Hetty have a great deal of sensibility, you and I, my dear, have perhaps too little."

"Not you, Mama," Henrietta broke in. "You feel things deeply too, for you are always in a worry."

"I worry for Papa and my girls, my love, and just try to make the best of things. Besides, I have my dear Angelica to talk to if I am troubled. She is such a comfort. Poor Papa has to bear his trials alone."

Silvestre gave a scornful snort. "Poppycock, Mama! He has you."

"Not that indelicate expression, my love, pray." She sighed a little, settling beside Henrietta on the sofa. "Of course I do my best to support Papa's spirits, but he is finding it very hard, poor man."

"Yes, we know." Silvestre frowned. "It is a pity one of us did not take Wintringham last year when he was so desperate. And now Lynchmere has gone and married Felicity, who was even poorer than we are…"

The thought of marrying the dissolute Earl of Wintringham, who had ended by marrying a penniless girl of no account, or indeed her godmother's cousin, the Marquis of Lynchmere, had the curious effect of filling Henrietta with revulsion. The image of a pair of light grey eyes with a tease at the back of them intruded into her mind and she was glad when Mama took up her twin's words.

"That will do, my dear. There is no sense in repining over what cannot be helped. Besides which, at the time Papa would not have countenanced Wintringham, although it is rumoured he has become a very model of propriety since his marriage."

"Yes, and neither of us had the least wish to marry Lynchmere," Henrietta reminded her sister, "even though Aunt Angelica hoped he might pick one of us."

Mrs Latimer shook a decisive head. "No, my dears, you are quite wrong. Angelica was always firm on the point. She knows her cousin too well and she told me privately he would not do for either of you. She says he has met his match in that girl, though, for which she is deeply thankful."

Silvestre waved an airy hand. "I did not mean I wished to be married to either, Mama. Indeed, if it was not that Papa is left with us on his hands, I should be decidedly relieved not to have been obliged to accept any of the gentlemen who might have offered for us."

Mrs Latimer adjusted her spectacles. "You must not suppose Papa minds it, my loves. He would have liked to see you settled, but not at the expense of your happiness." She patted Henrietta's hand. "Do not be wallowing in misery, Hetty. Papa will be distressed to think of you in tears. Show him a cheerful face at dinner, if you please."

"I'll try, Mama." Although how in the world she was to look Papa in the face she knew not.

"I shouldn't think she'll succeed." Her twin cast her a sceptical glance. "But don't fret, Mama. I will draw him into literary discussion. We will talk of Shakespeare. That will divert him at once."

Mrs Latimer laughed and rose. "There, I knew I could rely upon your good sense." She smiled upon both. "However, as regards your futures, don't despair. Angelica is confident you may yet come about, and so am I." With which, she departed, saying she must check on poor Papa again and reassure him that his dear Hetty was none the worse for the contretemps.

"Which is perfectly nonsensical," said Silvestre the moment their mother was out of the room. "Anyone can see you are cast down and Papa won't be fooled for an instant."

But if truth be told, Henrietta found the thought of her next meeting with Papa far less troubling than the hideous possibility of meeting the duke again. If he was intending to remain at Whisley Park, he was bound to appear in public at some point. Recalling his assertion that he didn't wish anyone to like him, or indeed to pay him a visit of courtesy, Henrietta revised her ideas. Perhaps she need not fear a meeting after all.

Oddly, this possibility was even less welcome. Why in the world it should make her feel deprived Henrietta could not imagine. Theo — or rather, the duke — had been perfectly rude and dismissive, and obviously believed her to be a creature of no brain and less ability. What had he said? He wondered how she managed to get up in the morning without falling over.

A hint of amusement almost made her laugh out. Until she remembered he had said it before he was wrongfully accused of dallying with her and took the beastly notion into his head that she had done it all on purpose. In which case, he did not think her bird-witted at all. He thought her as vile and grasping as a harpy. Indignation consumed her all over again and she was hard put to it to refrain from blaming Papa for spoiling everything. If only he had not come riding along just at that instant!

But when, later, she joined the family in the back parlour where they habitually foregathered, she was at once disarmed when her father, who was standing by the mantel, instantly referred to the distressing scene.

"Ah, Hetty, my child, come here to me."

She went forward, a little hesitant, unsure of his mood since his forehead was creased with a frown. "Papa?"

He held out a hand and grasped hers as she reached him, drawing her close and dropping a light kiss on her brow. "There. I did not mean to upset you. Am I forgiven?"

Henrietta's eyes pricked. "Oh, Papa, don't!"

He retained his hold on her fingers and smiled, though it looked forced. "Your mama tells me you were in tears, my dear, and I wish you won't dissolve again. It grieves me to see you weep and to know I am the cause."

Henrietta valiantly sniffed back her tears and smiled. "I am not weeping, Papa."

"Excellent." He lifted her hand to his lips and kissed her fingers and then released them, turning instead to his wife. "Shall we go in, my dear Margaret?"

"Of course, my love."

Mrs Latimer set her hand on his proffered arm and they proceeded through the side door into the dining-room. Henrietta found Silvestre at her elbow and a low-voiced murmur reached her.

"Well done. He's ripe for a reconciliation, so don't say anything. I will draw him out."

Only too relieved not to be obliged to speak, for her throat ached with the effort of holding back her tears, Henrietta accompanied her sister and took her seat.

"Mmm, is that pease pottage?" said Silvestre in an enthusiastic tone. "I do love Cook's recipe and I'm devilish hungry."

"Not that unbecoming word, Silve, pray," said Mrs Latimer as Papa's brows rose. She did not allow the matter to grow, at once instructing their only remaining footman to serve the master with the bread rolls.

Silvestre threw a comical grimace at her twin, mouthing "Oops!" and made up for her lapse by embarking upon her promised diversion. "Papa, I have been meaning to ask you. I have been struggling with the *Dream*. So much obscurity in that scene with Titania and Oberon, where she speaks of the forgeries of jealousy. I cannot make it out at all."

Mr Latimer's brow cleared and interest gleamed in his eye. "Ah, you are falling into the trap of looking for too much inner meaning, my dear. To say truth, it is nothing but a quarrel over the changeling boy. Once you see that as the crux, the rest will become clearer. Consider the complaints Titania makes."

In the blink of an eye, Papa became immersed in explanatory discussion, which occupied him for the duration of dinner and buoyed his mood so that he became expansive and cheerful, almost like his old self.

Deeply thankful, Henrietta contributed a question or two, as if she was also interested, and retired into remembrance of her fateful ramble. The abrupt curtailment of what she must confess had been an exhilarating interlude, however, could not but mar the memories. She fell instead to wondering what in the world might happen when she was obliged to meet the duke, if she did, at some social gathering. At best, he would ignore her. At worst…

Henrietta's heart sank. Any possible worst was too painful to contemplate. Only one thing was certain. She would never again see that intent look in the grey eyes as they contemplated her face, nor hear the soft tone when he asked her name. A moment of intimacy that refused to be dislodged, no matter how sternly Henrietta dismissed it.

Sunday came, with its attendant dutiful visit to St Stephen's. In the intervening days, Henrietta had replenished her stock of wildflowers, keeping to the meadows around Sinsham. Try as she might, she could not enjoy the excursion for the intrusive memories. It was easier when she came to selecting which flowers and leaves to press, but the entire procedure, which she was wont to enjoy, had turned into a chore. It was hard to keep her mind on the purpose of the task when the village was buzzing with talk of the arrival of the widowed Duchess of Charlton.

It was rumoured the new duke was also in residence, but none of the Latimers confirmed it, despite their special knowledge. By the time she was obliged to take her place in the pew, Henrietta was heartily sick of hearing *the duke* and *the duchess* on all sides. Worse was to come as the Reverend Netherwitton personally ushered in the ducal party from the vestry end of the church just as the locals were settling into place in the pews.

The size of the party was staggering. Although the duchess was known to Henrietta by sight, since the old duke had been in the habit of spending some part of the summer months at Whisley Park, she could by no means identify the other women. Two must be nursemaids, she realised, for they were each in charge of one of a pair of children, one a bouncing little girl, the other a toddler in arms. That rather severe creature near the infants might be a governess?

Whispers carried across the pews.

"She is left with a very babe. Such a tragedy."

"A pity it was only a girl."

"They ought to be in the nursery, why bring them to church?"

"A pretty child, isn't she? Lady Ella, I believe."

Although the children excited interest, no one spoke of the other adults. Was the older woman the duchess's mother? And who in the world was the older man?

So startled and intrigued was Henrietta that it was a moment before she noticed the principal member of the group, who appeared to be lagging behind the rest. But the instant she spotted the duke, standing in the aisle and looking at the stained glass window above the altar, her gaze became riveted, her heart bumping uncomfortably in her bosom.

He was dressed with a good deal more propriety than he had been in the woods, and in a fashion which might have been designed to leave him unnoticed, with a plain snuff-coloured coat and matching breeches, a lighter waistcoat beneath, his neckcloth neat but unremarkable, his hair tied back. Was it deliberate? From his attitude that day, Henrietta could readily believe it. He seemed determined to remain in the background, taking no interest in the complicated seating arrangements being undertaken behind him in the ornately carved reserved pews to the east of the nave. Henrietta was aware of the murmuring and the necks craning all around her, and could only be glad the Latimers were several rows back in the main part of the church.

"Is that him?"

Silvestre's whisper startled Henrietta out of her abstraction. She looked round. Her twin nodded towards the lone figure, now the only one standing as the pastor turned from his conversation with the duchess and moved towards the duke.

"Yes, it is." Henrietta sank down in her seat as she saw Theo turn at the vicar's approach. "Oh, heavens, he must not see me!"

"In this assembly? I shouldn't think he'll notice you, Hetty, don't fret."

Her sister was mistaken. The duke nodded to the pastor as the reverend spoke to him, but his glance swept the now silent pews, hesitated over the Latimer family and shifted away again. Henrietta shrank, but she could not look away. As the duke moved to enter the side pew at last to join his party, his gaze once more ran across the congregation and then lighted on Henrietta.

It was the briefest exchange, but she could swear his eyes met hers for an endless moment. She felt it as a wrench when he looked away, slipping into position next to the duchess and giving rise to a murmur of talk again all around.

"So handsome!"

"So young!"

"A heavy responsibility for him."

"Why have we not seen him before this?"

"He does not look very amicable."

Henrietta gripped her fingers together and looked down into her lap. Her pulse was unruly. But from the whispers no one appeared to have noticed, thank goodness. Recalling Papa, she sneaked a glance across her mother to where he sat nearest the aisle. His gaze was trained upon the pulpit, where the pastor was now climbing up the little stair. His jaw was set, but he appeared otherwise unconscious. He meant to ignore it, if indeed he, or anyone else, had seen how the duke's gaze found hers. Henrietta breathed a little more easily.

The Reverend Netherwitton took time to welcome the august addition to his congregation before starting his sermon, but it was noticeable that although the duchess inclined her head when he spoke of the little church being honoured by their presence, the duke's gaze remained steadfast upon the wooden panel before him.

Henrietta, remembering his attitude towards his inheritance, felt a twinge of sympathy for him. What had he said? He had been about to embark upon an adventure. Then had been thwarted by his predecessor's untimely demise. Snatches of that stolen interview in the woods kept churning in her head and she heard little of the sermon. Her twin nudged her suddenly and Henrietta realised she was sitting like a dumb thing when everyone around her was rising for a hymn. Under the first booming notes of the organ, a child's grizzling sounded, together with mutters and a plethora of hushing.

Attention became centred upon the principal pew and Henrietta could not resist stealing a glance at the duke. His attention was engaged with the duchess, who was turning between Theo and the nursemaid behind, now cuddling the infant close.

She saw the duke half turn where he stood, speaking to the women in the pew behind. The duchess was evidently arguing and Theo's voice came clearly to Henrietta's ears.

"Let them take the girls out, Cecilia, don't be ridiculous! Off you go."

This last to the nursemaids. Upon which, a commotion of shuffling and movement held the congregation spellbound, still singing but, Henrietta would swear, with almost every eye on the interesting activity going forward.

The duchess was clearly still arguing with Theo, both voices muted, as the whimpering infant was carried out, the little girl following with alacrity and almost skipping by her nurse as she was led away from the depleted party. The children and their minders vanished into the vestry.

The hymn coming to an end, the parson cleared his throat loudly, which put an end to the muttered discussion as the duchess turned her gaze on the pulpit. Henrietta thought she looked decidedly disgruntled. The duke, on the other hand, looked merely resigned. He cast a glance across the congregation, which created an instant flutter of heads turning swiftly to look at the parson instead.

But Henrietta could not look away. Once again, his eye caught hers. Was that the veriest twitch at the corner of his lip? She could not judge, and it was gone in an instant. He dropped his gaze to the wooden panel again and became, to all intents and purposes, apparently divorced from the proceedings.

The sermon began to seem interminable. Henrietta tried to concentrate, but the little contretemps had been all too reminiscent of the duke's earlier conduct in the woods. Was he quite as bossy and unconventional in his dealings with the duchess? Cecilia, he called her. And he had got his way. One could not but wonder why she had brought such young children into church. The little girl perhaps, but the babe? Evidently the duke thought it inappropriate. Had he argued against it in the first place? Henrietta could well imagine it. He was very decided in his views, that much she could vouch for.

She was still pondering the question when the pastor at last came to his conclusion, bidding his flock look not for the mote in his brother's eye but in his own. Although people were rising, none showed any disposition to begin filing out of the church. Neighbour began talking to neighbour, low-voiced, but with eyes on the pastor as he went down at once to the ducal party. He spoke to the duchess, who exited the pew and stood talking to him in the aisle. Henrietta was recalled by her father's voice.

"Come, my dears. Let us go while we can."

Mr Latimer was leaving their pew, his arm encouraging Mama. He did not mean to wait upon the ducal party. At once the memory of the dreadful end to her encounter with the duke superseded everything else and Henrietta's pulse went into disarray as she followed Silvestre out of the pew.

Casting a look back before she turned, she was unable to see the duke. The two older acolytes were waiting patiently behind the duchess, but Theo had vanished.

The Latimers were immediately followed by one or two locals, but most hung back. Henrietta felt all too conspicuous, walking out before the duchess. One or two disapproving looks were cast upon Papa, which was mortifying. But Henrietta bridled too. How dare they judge him? If they knew what had been said, how Theo had behaved towards him…

But such thoughts could only be painful, and she tried to banish them as she came out through the church door behind her parents and Silvestre. Papa looked to be about to stride off, but Mama held him back, whispering.

"Oh, very well, my dear," said Papa and turned off to stroll beside the church a little way.

Silvestre leaned in. "Mama thinks it will look too particular if we leave before the duchess comes out."

"Did you hear her, then?"

Her twin nodded. "Papa didn't want to meet the duke, of course."

"He won't, for he wasn't waiting with the duchess."

"Hetty! Were you watching him?"

Henrietta sighed. "A bit. I think Theo must have slipped out the back."

Silvestre threw up her eyes. "You and your Theo. Really, Hetty, you are hopeless. Are you smitten with him?"

Warmth crept into Henrietta's face, but she disclaimed with some heat. "Of course not. I hardly know him."

"Then you shouldn't be calling him Theo."

"He told me to," said Hetty in some dudgeon. "At least, he said, 'I'm Theo,' which is the same thing."

"Well, you had best keep your distance, or Papa will be upset again."

"I can hardly do anything else, can I, after he said such things?"

"Hush, he'll hear you!"

To her shocked surprise, Henrietta discovered she was angry. Not with Theo, but with Papa. She had been about to retort that she did not care if he heard her. Confused, and a good deal ruffled, she turned away, only to see that the duchess had come out of the church with the parson and was being gracious as he presented her to members of the congregation filing out in a line.

The sycophantic smiles and the deep curtsies made Henrietta feel quite ill. Theo would loathe all that! The thought threw her into worse dismay. How could she think in such a way? What was the matter with her? A strong desire to get away overcame her. She could not bear this. Turning to her sister, she grabbed her arm.

"Tell Mama I am going home by way of the graveyard."

Without giving her twin a chance to object, she darted away from the family group and slipped along the lee of the church, keeping to the shadow until she reached the back where the cemetery was situated. She slid through the opening in the fence and began to walk along the path which led through an avenue of trees to the wide expanse of the graveyard with its stone sentinel memorials to the dead.

She had just come within sight of the first row of gravestones when a childish shriek erupted from a point along one side. Henrietta halted and looked in that direction. The little girl from the ducal party was jumping up and down between a couple of graves, protesting in a childish treble.

"Beastie! Where are you?"

But she was laughing. The nursemaids were standing off to one side and Henrietta noticed the infant was on the ground, watching her elder sister and catching at the air in a gleeful way. A sudden roar came and a figure rose up from behind a gravestone in an attitude of attack, adopting an animalistic pose. With a stab of surprise, Henrietta realised it was the duke.

The girl shrieked again, half laughing, and began to run as Theo emerged from his hiding place and came after her, shuffling along like a demented animal and roaring again.

The infant joined in the chase, likewise shrieking. Theo turned and caught her up, throwing her into the air, laughing and roaring as yelps emitted from the little one. He bent to set the infant down, whereupon the little girl leapt on his back.

"I got you, I got you, beastie!"

Roaring again, he rose, catching her legs so she was safe and turning, he galloped clumsily along a row beside the gravestones while the girl shrieked in delight.

Henrietta, amused and astonished, had a sudden fear for the unseen infant who began to run along behind and involuntarily she called out. "Oh, have a care! The little one behind you!"

Her intervention caused several things to happen at once. Theo stopped in his tracks, turning. One of the nursemaids uttered a cry and leapt after her charge. And the infant cannoned into the duke's legs and set up a whimper.

In the ensuing pandemonium, Henrietta, feeling horribly guilty, rushed in a zigzag path through the intervening graves to help. But by the time she got there, the nursemaid had snatched up the wailing infant and Theo had set down the older girl, who was instantly accosted by her own nurse, fussing about her and tidying her rumpled clothing as she scolded in a falsetto that only added to the cacophony.

The duke, arms akimbo, ignored the fracas and laid his wrathful gaze on Henrietta. "I might have known! Your propensity for causing disaster wherever you go is in no way mitigated, I see."

Henrietta caught up an indignant breath. "I saw the child behind you and was afraid of an accident."

"Which would not have happened if you hadn't distracted me."

"Oh, you are impossible!"

Henrietta turned abruptly and walked off she knew not where, seething, her thoughts utterly askew. Horrid creature he was. Thoroughly unpredictable. Playing with children like that? Then to be so rude to her all over again! She had wasted too many guilty feelings about him, and for what? He deserved no regrets and she would henceforth —

"Miss Latimer! Hetty!"

A hand grasped her shoulder and she came to a stumbling halt. She was turned perforce and found herself staring up into the light grey eyes, which were studying hers. "What do you want?"

His brow cleared of a frown. "Ah, you're not crying? That's a relief."

Henrietta let fly. "Of course I am not crying. Why should I, you rude, horrible, beastly person? And I don't care if you are fifty dukes!"

Amusement leapt to his eyes and he let out a snorting laugh. "I thank you, it's quite enough being one."

He was still holding her by the shoulders and Henrietta shrugged off his hands, shifting away. "If Papa sees you touching me, he will be upset all over again and you have no idea how uncomfortable it is."

His brows snapped together. "What, does he beat you?"

"Beat me? Heavens, no! Papa would never use his daughters so cruelly." The memory of her father's distress and anger leapt back and she stuttered as she tried to explain. "It's just that — he feels things deeply and — and he hates it when he's been furious with us and — oh, I can't explain!" Recalling what had happened between them, she took another step back. "I don't know why I'm trying to explain anything to you after the way you behaved."

At that, the frown returned. "The way I behaved? What about your father attacking me? Not to mention your utter stupidity — if it wasn't a deliberate ploy."

Henrietta fired up at once. "Are you at that again? How dare you suppose I should stoop to such a low trick? As for Papa, he would see me a spinster for life before he perpetrated any such scheme. But, no. You made an instant assumption based upon no evidence at all."

His brows rose. "It wasn't evidence enough that he accused me of dallying with you? No, of assaulting you, wasn't it?"

A thread of discomfort went through Henrietta. "He is not himself lately. He — he wouldn't normally react so — so blindly."

"Well, that's not my concern, is it?"

Henrietta sighed. "You are as pig-headed as he is. He wouldn't even look at you in the church and he made us come away so he would not have to be presented to you in form."

"Ha! Ashamed of himself, is he? So he should be."

"No such thing! He — oh, it is no use talking!" She sketched a curtsy. "Good day to you, my lord duke." About to turn to leave, she was startled when he grabbed her arm.

"Not so fast, Miss Latimer. You and I have a throw or two more yet, I think."

Henrietta looked pointedly at his hand. "Release me, if you please, sir."

His brows rose, but he did not let go. "Haughty! There's a deal more to you than meets the eye, Miss Disaster."

The spurious dignity fell. "Don't call me that! You're so rude!"

"And you're —" He broke off and his fingers dropped from about her arm as he stepped back a pace, an odd expression coming into his face.

Henrietta felt suddenly breathless, with no idea why. She eyed him, feeling uncertain and vulnerable as she had not throughout this exchange. From nowhere she whispered his name. "Theo…"

His lips closed tightly together, and he shook his head, throwing his palm up. Then he turned from her without a word and marched back towards the group of nursemaids and children.

For a moment Henrietta could not move. Then a flood of feeling swept through her, dismay and shame both. Her eyes prickled as she turned quickly towards the main path through the cemetery that would lead her to home and safety.

CHAPTER FOUR

Theo decided he must have taken leave of his senses! Thank the Lord he'd managed to stop his tongue on the words. *A delight?* Had he really been about to tell her she was a delight? What in the world had possessed him? She was nothing of the kind.

A walking disaster, yes. A hurly-burly interfering nincompoop. And, to crown all, a watering pot. Though admittedly she had not wept on this occasion. He would not bet against the chance that she was weeping now, though. He shouldn't have walked off like that. Only when she spoke his name it felt abruptly dangerous to be in her company. He had almost persuaded himself of her innocence. She played it well, he had to give her that.

A voice in the back of his mind protested he was maligning her, but Theo ignored it. In the position he now occupied, he could not afford to let down his guard. He must not forget how pat had been her father's arrival. Of course she would defend him. Not that her explanation had been in any way believable. He was not himself? That was it? Fine. Let him be whoever he wished, and if Mr Latimer was determined not to meet Theo, that suited him down to the ground. He wished to have nothing to do with the man. Or his idiotic daughter.

"Who was that lady, Theo?"

He had been only half aware of Ellie's chatter, but this penetrated. He toyed with deflecting her, but chose instead to answer. "She's called Miss Latimer. She lives round here."

"Why was she cross with you?"

Damnation. He might have known the child would pick up on the one thing he did not wish to discuss. "I don't know."

"Will you play bears again?"

At which, Pru piped up. "Pay bears! Pay bears!"

Theo groaned. "Now look what you've started. No more bears. Your mama will be wishing to go home."

He ignored the chorus of protests, nodding at the nurses to take over the children. "Later, Ellie. No more bears now. Look, there's Swarland coming to find us. We'll have to go to the carriage."

His aunt's steward was indeed walking up the path, and hailed him the moment Theo noticed him. "Your grace! Her grace is ready to go and is asking for the children."

"We're coming! Ellie, dignity, you rascal! You're Lady Ella Devenal, remember, when there are people watching. Take my hand."

She became prim at once, enjoying playing the game as she'd been taught. Theo never had the least difficulty getting her to behave properly, which annoyed his aunt. He knew Ellie did his bidding only because she had become attached. The children were one of the lights in the dim days of taking up his inheritance and he knew he had shamelessly used them. If Ellie had become too affectionate he had only himself to blame. He liked the child and was guiltily aware of encouraging her in unconventional behaviour and exploits as Cecilia was wont to complain.

But Theo could not stand the imposition of his dignities and refused to allow them to alter his conduct. If Cecilia thought he was going to partake of the studied graciousness she employed among her acquaintance here, she could think again. He was not surprised, however, when she took him to task at the first opportunity.

"How dared you disappear like that, Theo, and leave me to explain your disgraceful conduct? I was never so mortified. If this is how you mean to go on, there is little to hope for."

Having rid herself of her retinue upon entering the house, despatching them about various errands and sending the children up to the nursery, Cecilia had adroitly made it impossible for Theo to escape by declaring an urgent necessity to have speech with him and ordering coffee to be brought to the parlour. He had followed her in with reluctance and the attack began the instant he closed the door.

But Theo was in no mood to pander to his aunt's megrims. The end of the episode with that wretch of a girl had put him out of temper. He snapped back. "As I have no notion what you hope for, it scarcely matters, does it?"

"Theo!" She threw a hand to her head. "Have you no conduct? Oliver would turn in his grave to hear you speak with such impertinence."

"No, he wouldn't, Cecilia. He was used to my ways. Moreover, he told me when I was the duke I might do as I pleased."

"Only to ensure you behaved properly while he was alive, you wretched creature, as you know perfectly well. He never meant to imply you should turn into a regular boor."

A twinge of conscience attacked Theo, but he quashed it, moving to the fireplace where he chose to prop himself against the mantel in an attitude of studied casualness. "What do you want, Cecilia? An apology? Very well, I'm sorry. There."

She made an explosive sound, looked daggers at him for a moment and then threw herself into the sofa. Not much to his surprise, she abandoned anger for despair. "There is no doing anything with you, Theo. If you don't take care, you will grow into one of these crusty care-for-nobodies who drive everyone away and end up a recluse."

"Which would suit me down to the ground."

Cecilia's tone became irritable. "Don't be stupid. You are only four and twenty and you are highly eligible. None of the dames with a daughter to dispose of will care how crusty you are, more's the pity."

"Then what are we arguing about?"

She looked up at that, her large eyes reproachful. "You embarrassed me, Theo. It was not well done of you."

He had the grace to feel ashamed and was upon the point of making a real apology when the door opened and one of the footman entered bearing a tray with the makings of coffee. Cecilia at once reassumed her public face, directing Thomas to set the tray down on a convenient table and bring it to the sofa so that she could pour.

Theo groaned inwardly. She was wearing the duchess again, which was precisely the hypocrisy he loathed and did not intend to emulate. People would have to take him as they found him or not at all. But he could not deny the justice of Cecilia's complaint.

"Coffee, Theo?"

He nodded and she poured. He went across and took the drink from her, dropping into the opposite chair and sipping at the black brew. The door closed behind the footman and Theo spoke before his aunt had a chance to start on him again.

"I apologise, Cecilia." She was adding cream and sugar to her own cup, but she gave him a doubtful look. "Truly, I mean it. If you want the truth, I saw how they all stared and I just could not bear to run the gamut, so I slipped away."

Cecilia gave an elaborate sigh as she stirred her drink. "I admit it can be difficult. But you will become accustomed, Theo. You have only to smile and nod and ask after —"

"Yes, I'm aware of how you do it, Cecilia," he interrupted with impatience, "but it's not my style. I couldn't keep it up."

"But you can't ignore people, Theo. It's terribly rude."

The word repeated in his head, in Hetty's voice. She had called him rude several times. He had not minded it from her and it merely goaded him to tease her the more. But Cecilia's criticism rankled.

"It's rude of me to ignore them, but it's not rude of them to stare? To ogle me as if I am a freak? What, is it some kind of duty of the position, to be obliged to endure their avid interest with complaisance?"

She cut in without ceremony. "Yes, that is it precisely, Theo. You have a duty to —"

"Why? Why is it a duty? They are not my tenants. At least, half of them can't be. I know the Latimers aren't, for a start."

He regretted saying the name the instant it was out of his mouth, but it was too late. Cecilia pounced. "The Latimers? You are acquainted with the Latimers?"

"Hardly that."

Cecilia set down her cup. "Theo, they cannot add to your consequence. Not now. I have it on the best of authority that Latimer's expectations are blasted and they are as poor as church mice. I am sorry for poor Margaret Latimer, of course, left with the twins on her hands, but —"

"Wait!" Despite himself, Theo's interest was aroused. Had not Beattock said something of the sort? What was all this about poverty? "What expectations, Cecilia?"

She picked up her cup, leaning in a little as the love of gossip Theo knew she cherished kicked in. "Oh, it was the talk of the

Season, so I've heard. I was not in Town, of course, as you know, but it seems Horwood's young wife delivered herself of a boy just before Christmas, which quite cut out poor Henry Latimer."

"She was luckier than you, then, Cecilia," said Theo, quite unable to refrain from the taunt. He knew well his aunt would have much preferred to produce his uncle's longed-for direct heir.

"That is unkind, Theodore. You know very well I am content with things as they are."

He gave her a wry look. "Or you would be if I would only behave conformably."

She gave a little laugh. "Well, that at least is true, horrid creature. But I have been thinking, you know, how wretched it would have been to be worrying over his future forever as he grew and to be concerned with how the estate was being run while he remained a minor." She shuddered. "I should not have known a moment's peace, and I must say I feel quite sorry for Lady Horwood, for Silvester Horwood is a great deal older than Oliver was when he…"

Theo turned the subject in haste as Cecilia's features crumpled. She had been sincerely attached to his uncle, he knew, despite the wide disparity in age. "How is it Latimer is so poor, then? Has he no competence of his own?"

Cecilia was at once diverted. "Oh, a pittance. It seems Horwood made him an allowance and he ceased to pay it upon the birth of his son. As dear Angelica says, it is such a pity for his girls, left on the shelf as they now will be."

Unless one of them managed to ensnare a duke with a trumpery trick. But this Theo kept to himself, instead picking up on the name that had stirred a vague memory. "Who is Angelica?"

"Mrs Summerhayes. She is cousin to Lord Lynchmere and a friend of mine. They are both half-French, you know. You will like her enormously, I am persuaded. Indeed, I shouldn't think anyone could possibly dislike Angelica."

"She sounds like the sort of gossip I despise."

Cecilia's cheeks took on colour. "Nothing of the sort. It so happens Angelica is very close with the family. She and Margaret Latimer have been friends for years and the girls are her god-daughters. I expect she hoped Lynchmere would take one of them, but it was not to be. I cannot imagine anyone offering for either now since their portions must be negligible."

Theo said nothing, his mind obstinately presenting him with a plethora of images of a tear-stained face looking perfectly indignant and berating him for being rude.

He was recalled by Cecilia requesting him to pay attention. He took another sip of coffee and regarded her over the rim of his cup. "Yes, what?"

"I am saying, Theo, that I mean to invite Angelica to bring her children here."

He was startled. "To stay? Good God, why?"

"Not to stay, stupid creature. For a visit merely. I hope her Sally may become friends with poor Ellie. It is so melancholy for the child to have no companion of her own age."

Theo snorted. "Anyone less melancholy than Ellie I have never met. But by all means find her a few friends. No doubt she'll lead them into mischief, but I dare say this Angelica of yours won't mind that."

His aunt was not in the least affronted, though she gave him a darkling look. "If certain people did not encourage her, she wouldn't be nearly as mischievous."

He laughed. "Meaning me. Have done, Cecilia. Ellie's a bouncing handful and you know it. She'll get into all sorts of trouble without the least encouragement and thank God for it. We don't want her growing up into one of these namby-pamby girls who bore every male into a stupor."

His aunt sighed. "You would say that, of course. Oliver was just as bad. She will grow up so hot at hand no gentleman will have her."

"Now who's being stupid? They'll be queuing up at the door. But don't fret, Cecilia. I won't let her marry anyone who can't appreciate her better qualities. But for pity's sake don't try and turn her into a pattern-card of virtue."

Cecilia waved a dismissive hand. "All this is scarcely germane. I am not now concerned with Ellie's marital prospects, but yours, Theo."

He spluttered into his coffee and emerged with his eyes watering, indignant and dismayed both. "My prospects? So that's why you're so cross I didn't stay to be presented. I might have known!"

"Nothing of the sort." His aunt sipped delicately but did not meet his eyes. "I have no notion of your finding a bride among the gentry here."

"Just as well!"

"You will of course review the most eligible females when we go to Town for the Season next year."

Would he by God? Not if he knew it! What, run his eye over a plethora of likely debutantes with the purpose of saddling himself with exactly the sort of female he detested?

"But it makes perfect sense," his aunt continued, apparently oblivious to his hostility, "for you to make yourself known locally and —"

"Parade myself around like a prize bull? I thank you, Cecilia, but no. I had rather retire to Devenal, and I will if you mean to force me into —"

"I am not forcing you into anything, Theo, but you must think of the future. It is your duty to marry and beget heirs. It would be shocking if the dukedom were to pass even further away from the direct line."

Theo groaned. "There's time enough for me to do my duty, for heaven's sake."

"Theo, you are already four and twenty —"

"A moment ago you were saying I was *only* four and twenty."

"— and the longer you leave it, the harder it will be for you to settle down."

"I don't want to settle down!"

"Moreover," his aunt went on, unheeding, "the more you delay, the more you will be subjected to just the sort of attention you profess to loathe. Once you are betrothed, it will be pointless for the mothers of hopeful damsels to be setting traps for you, and you know, Theo, you can be distressingly naïve in these matters. You have no notion how wily some of these women can be."

Not only women, if his instinct was not at fault. Cecilia's words could not but rake up the memory of that first encounter. Yes, he did need to be wary. But he had no intention of being jockeyed into matrimony by his busy aunt either. He set down his coffee cup and rose. "I have more gumption than you suppose, Cecilia. It's of no use to badger me on this subject. I'll marry when I decide to marry. And it won't be to a female of your choosing."

With which, he stalked to the door and threw it open, ignoring her indignant protests. He found Mary Eddleston hovering in the hall and stepped out, gesturing her to enter.

"You'd best go in and comfort her, Mary. Then the two of you can abuse me in my absence to your heart's content."

Leaving the creature staring, he flung across the hall and sped to the library, where he found Swarland in possession, his secretary not yet having come down from Devenal.

"Your grace? Would you wish me to leave?"

Theo threw up a hand. "Never mind. Stay where you are."

Cursing inwardly, he left the room, traversed the corridor and ran up the backstairs usually used by the servants. Arriving on the first floor, he made his way to the private sitting-room adjoining his chamber and began a restless pacing, his frustrations rising to the surface. He had been prepared to inherit, but not yet. Indeed, it had seemed too remote to worry about and he'd told Oliver as much when his uncle thought he might be disappointed.

"What, that you've married Cecilia in hopes of a direct heir? You jest, sir! Nothing could suit me better and I wish you a dozen sons."

Oliver had bent his kindly gaze upon him. "Are you certain, Theo? You've been brought up to the notion, for I told my brother to prepare you when my Alicia died and the infant with her."

"My father knew better, sir. He said you'd try again when you recovered from the blow and warned me not to think of it. Not that I had any more desire than he had to step into your shoes, which he knew."

But the blow had fallen nonetheless with Oliver's sudden and fatal illness. Theo recalled the weeks of anxiety that mingled with his grief while they waited to learn whether Cecilia was again enceinte. The day she had tearfully declared herself free of any hope was the worst in Theo's living memory. He had clung to a certainty that proved void. In a bid to deflect his doom, he had besought the doctor to deny it.

"I regret I cannot, your grace —" shocking him with the unaccustomed address "— for there can be no doubt. If the duchess had been pregnant, the shock might well have caused a miscarriage."

Even when the authorities had confirmed him in the title, he dared to wish Cecilia and the doctor would both prove to be mistaken. Only to his mother had he confided his secret hope. Lady Lionel Devenal had not encouraged him in it.

"Resign yourself, my dearest one. Cecilia would have known by now had she been with child."

He signally failed to do so, but as the months passed and the bonds tightened, Theo's dreams of escape faded. He had perforce turned his energies to the task at hand. But underneath, despite every effort to put away that other life he might have led, it surfaced in useless regret.

He went to the window and stared out at the surrounding woods. At least he liked Whisley Park. Or he had liked it. But if Cecilia was determined to cut up his peace, he was sorely tempted to run back to the huge rabbit warren of Devenal Castle where it was easier to avoid anyone he didn't wish to see.

A sigh escaped him. There was no going back. Cecilia would take it as a studied insult. He would have to buckle. At least he need not anticipate finding the Latimers on his doorstep. That ridiculous female had made that abundantly clear.

CHAPTER FIVE

Enough was enough. Abandoning any further attempt to arrange the dried flowers into her chosen design, Henrietta slid them back into the box with the rest and brushed off the parchment. She examined her lightly pencilled drawing with a jaundiced eye. It was of no use. She would have to start again.

With a sigh, she picked up the stale bread roll and rubbed at the marks, wishing she might rub away the sting in her bosom as easily. It revived every time she heard the dratted duke spoken of, which was all too often. Each of Mama's acquaintances seemed intent upon reporting their courtesy visit to the Duchess of Charlton, who had been receiving calls all week, from which the duke had been noticeably absent.

"Cecilia told me in confidence that he is shy," said Aunt Angelica when she came to report to Mama.

Henrietta almost snorted aloud. Shy? Of all things, Theo was not shy. Anything but. Boorish and rude, yes. Bossy, hatefully teasing and cruelly unkind to be chasing after her and then repudiating the tiniest overture she had stupidly made. But such thoughts had the effect of reviving the hurt which had ended in a bout of tears, and she must not arouse suspicion. She had not even confided that last encounter to Silve, avoiding her twin's too observant eye until she could command herself again.

But it was impossible to withhold herself from the visitors, Mama insisting upon the twins being present. "We must show a united front, my dears. Nothing could be more damning than to hide ourselves away from prying eyes. Hold your heads up, my loves, and do not appear conscious."

Sage advice, when the world and his wife kept wondering aloud why the Latimers did not choose to pay their respects at Whisley Park. The question was not voiced too obviously, of course, but the hints, if delicately couched, were unmistakeable.

"Such a gracious lady, the duchess, as I am sure you must remember, dear Mrs Latimer, when at last you are privileged to be received."

Or, from another source: "She seems to welcome everyone, dear Mrs Latimer, regardless of their particular circumstances. I am persuaded no one need be concerned to be thought in any way inferior."

That one had set Silvestre off into a fury the moment their neighbour had left Moss House. "Inferior? How dare she? Merely because we are poor. It is too bad!"

Only to Mrs Summerhayes had Mama confided the real reason why the Latimer coach, now so rarely used, had not been seen at Whisley Park. This close family friend had taken a light view of the matter, recommending Henrietta to put it out of her mind.

"A simple misunderstanding, my dear child, which you need not regard since your Papa knows there was no improper conduct. It is immaterial what the duke thinks, since he is destined to marry high."

Silvestre had thrown an admonishing look at her twin and asked the question burning on Henrietta's lips. "Is he betrothed, then, Aunt Angelica?"

"Good heavens, no! Under the circumstances, nothing had been arranged for him. Had he been the direct heir, of course, it would be different. No doubt Oliver Devenal would have sorted out a suitable match while he was still a boy. But Cecilia says they were hoping to the last for a son of their own. However, she is now determined and conceives it to be her duty to find him a worthy match. She intends him to go to Town for the coming season and look about him for a suitable bride."

A plan which left Henrietta both scornful and agitated. Really, could one see Theo submitting tamely to his aunt's dictum? It was plain that he was being recalcitrant, refusing to meet the neighbouring gentry, just as anyone who knew him might expect. On the other hand, he was duty-bound to marry high, like it or not. A thought Henrietta found distinctly unpalatable. Not that it was any of her business. Only she could not imagine the unconventional Theo she had met, twice now, joined to the sort of conformable female his aunt no doubt had in mind. He would crush the poor thing into a jelly. Indeed, any female foolish enough to marry a man who did not scruple to stigmatize innocent females as tricksters or disaster-causing idiots deserved everything she got.

Well, she was thankful she was out of the running. Thoroughly so. Portionless, accident-prone and a watering pot. Everything the duke despised. At least, he despised her as a female he suspected of trying to entrap him. Arrogant beast. She would rather entrap a spider.

At which point, Henrietta discovered she had been scrubbing so hard at her pencil drawing she had rubbed a hole in the parchment. With a cry of frustration she threw the crumbling bread across the room just as the door opened.

"Hey!" Silvestre, entering only to receive a splatter of breadcrumbs in the face, brushed them off and regarded her twin with astonishment. "What in the world is eating you, Hetty?"

Henrietta, busy tearing her ruined sheet across and across, gave her twin a black look over the top of it. "Nothing! I have only ruined my picture, that's all."

Her twin tutted as she shut the door and came into the room, picking at an errant crumb. "Don't say you've wasted the ready flowers?"

"Of course I have not. They're in the box. Not that I care."

Silvestre plonked down on the bureau stool. "It is of no use to pretend, Hetty. You've been behaving like a sulky kitten for days. It's that duke of yours again, isn't it?"

"He's not *my* duke. I wouldn't want him if he was." Henrietta rose from the old school desk where she had been working and flung the torn fragments of parchment into the empty grate. She turned to find her twin desperately trying to keep a straight face and regarded Silvestre's dancing eyes in some dudgeon. "What are you laughing at?"

Her twin bubbled over. "You, Hetty! You aren't making sense."

Henrietta found herself growling like an angry cat, pawing the air in annoyance as her twin laughed the more. "Stop it, Silve! I hate you!"

"No, you d-don't," said her twin, hiccupping on her merriment. "You don't hate me any more than you hate this Theo. It's my belief you've developed a *tendre* for him."

A flood of feeling rushed into Henrietta's bosom and her eyes filled. Her sister's amusement was instantly quenched. Silvestre jumped up and caught her into a stifling embrace.

"Oh, don't, Hetty! I'm sorry, I'm sorry, I should not have said it. Don't cry, for goodness' sake!"

"I'm n-not c-crying." Her voice muffled, Henrietta struggled to suppress her sobs. "It's just that — just that…"

Silvestre released her and whipped out a handkerchief from her sleeve. "Here! It's just that what, Hetty?"

Henrietta dabbed at her eyes and sniffed, then shoved the square of linen back at her sister. "I don't know. Everything is topsy-turvy and I wish I had never consented to your famous Plan."

"You were happy enough with it before you met this Theo."

Henrietta sighed. "I wish you wouldn't keep mentioning his name. And it's ridiculous to suggest I have a fondness for him. I've only met him twice — *once*."

But her too shrewd sister had noticed the slip. "Oho! So there was another meeting? What happened to make you as cross as crabs all this time?"

"Nothing happened." Henrietta made a business of shaking out her skirts, avoiding her twin's eye. "It was an accident, that's all, and — oh, I don't want to talk about it!"

Her twin had no chance to respond as the front door bell clanged. Silvestre threw up her eyes. "More visitors. We had best go down and support Mama. But don't think I'm satisfied, Hetty, because I'm not."

The thought of enduring another half hour of the duchess this and the duke that was more than Henrietta could bear. "Make my excuses, Silve. I'm going out."

Her sister paused on her way to the door. "Going out where?"

"To pick more flowers, what else?"

Before Silvestre could object, she rushed past and headed for her chamber to don a bonnet and spencer. It was warm but looked a trifle blustery when she cast a glance out of the window and saw the upper branches of the trees caught in the wind.

Hurrying down the back stairs to avoid running into the visitors or a member of the family, Henrietta picked up the basket from its accustomed place on the cluttered shelf at the rear of the hall and left the house by way of a side door into the garden. She had no notion where she was going, but the urgent need to escape drove her across the grounds and onto the common beyond.

Avoiding the path that led to the cemetery which she had used on Sunday, she went in the opposite direction, heading for the woods that ran along the road to Barkham where the Summerhayes residence was situated. She might hope to avoid meeting anyone from Sinsham, even if she kept to the edge of the woods. She had no desire to stray into the duke's lands again.

She made no attempt at first to gather wildflowers, intent only upon getting away. But the sight of a bank of purple orchis within the trees impinged upon her consciousness and she exclaimed aloud.

"How lovely!"

An image leapt in her mind. Could she not make a lake? Then some greenery interspersed with colour around it, perhaps. Rapidly losing herself in weaving a design in her head, she began to pick the orchis.

It became a tricky juggling act, holding her basket and grabbing at her bonnet as the wind threatened to whip it off each time she dipped down to grasp a stem. Fortunately there were so many blossoms, in the end she dropped to the ground where the wind bothered her less, set her basket down, and concentrated on gathering. She was going to need Papa's largest books for this project. She might try for those dusty and hefty tomes on the lower shelves which he hardly ever took out to read, as far as Henrietta knew.

She was just deciding she had more than enough for the task when the plaintive mew of a cat caught her attention. Henrietta sat up, looking along the ground and between the leafy trees, branches shifting with the wind, but she could not see any feline in the immediate vicinity. The sound came again, more urgent, as if it sought to attract her attention. It was definitely a cat in distress.

Leaving her basket, Henrietta pushed up from the ground and looked with more intention, peering into the undergrowth, calling to it. "Where are you? Kitty! Kitty!"

An immediate response came, louder, the plaintive note pronounced. Agitation and concern slipped into Henrietta's bosom, and she forgot everything but the need to find the animal.

"Oh, dear, the poor thing! What is the matter? Where are you?" She cast about, calling out in between the cat's intermittent cries. "Kitty! Kitty! Where are you hiding?"

All at once she realised the mewing was coming from above. She looked up into the shifting trees, moving from one to another. The cat mewed again and it occurred to Henrietta to go back to where she had heard it first. The moment she reached the place where the basket lay and looked up, she spotted a ginger cat perched in a high branch of a large elm.

"There you are! Goodness, what are you doing up there? Can't you get down, poor thing? Oh, dear, what is to be done?"

Holding on to her bonnet, she contemplated the tree. The cat had evidently negotiated the lower branches easily and then climbed up the trunk to that higher one and was now afraid to come down. The trunk was sturdy enough, but the surrounding branches were shifting in the wind. Was that what had frightened the animal? She regarded it, head upturned, and it looked back at her, no longer crying, apparently satisfied to have captured her full attention.

"I suppose you are expecting me to rescue you," she told it, addressing the cat in a caressing tone. "Well, I'm afraid I am not very good at climbing trees. You will have to come down by yourself."

The cat gave a mew, furled its tail over the branch and sat down, its stare fixed upon Henrietta's. She sighed.

"Now, come on, don't be silly. The trunk is not moving, you will be perfectly safe." She put up an encouraging hand and called to it. "Come! Come on! You can get down by yourself, I know you can. Come on!"

The cat continued to stare, the tail now curling around its body.

"Goodness, you are stubborn! You realise you are giving me a crick in the neck?"

As if it understood, the cat rose onto its paws, dipping its head towards her.

"There now, you see. You can do it."

It mewed a protest, looking from Henrietta to the tree trunk below, up to the shifting branches high above and back down again. She dared not drop her gaze, but rubbed her neck instead, at once dislodging her bonnet. Ignoring the inconvenience, she called encouragement.

"Come along … come, come, come… Good kitty, down you come…"

The cat continued to hesitate, shifting to and fro in an uncertain dance, an orange splodge against the drifting leafy background. It mewed again, as if to say it dared not make the attempt.

"Oh, for goodness' sake," cried Henrietta in frustration. "I cannot leave you there, can I?"

She brought her gaze down and looked in all directions for help. A labourer, perhaps, or a yokel going about his business. She had passed a fellow carrying a sack and then a boy as she walked by the lane. Both had touched their hats to her, but now there was no one in sight and no sound of a carriage or horse. She was on her own and the cat was still mewing above her.

Uttering a soft drat, Henrietta untied the strings of her bonnet and set it down by her basket. With a quick glance to check there really was no one by, she lifted her petticoats at either side and kilted them into the drawstring at her waist, freeing her stockinged ankles and legs in a manner that would scandalise Mama. It could not be helped. She could not go away and leave the cat stranded up there. She looked up and found it watching her preparations. It mewed at her as if in approval.

"I am coming, Kitty, though whether I can reach you there I don't know."

Approaching the tree, she grasped the lowest branch and, with a feeling of reckless abandon that she had not experienced since she was a child, swung herself up. Steadying her foot on the branch, she felt for the next one, looking for a higher handhold. Encouraged by the cat's mews, she managed to get herself up into the topmost of the lower branches and paused, her hands now on the trunk.

She glanced down and felt abruptly dizzy. Clinging to the trunk, she closed her eyes briefly. The tree seemed a good deal higher from this angle, the ground far below. No wonder the cat was afraid to come down. Henrietta looked up and her heart sank. She could climb no further. There were no more convenient handholds.

Could she reach the cat from where she was? It was a great deal nearer, regarding her from its branch, its head shifting from side to side as it looked from Henrietta to the ground, still emitting the odd complaint. With a horrible sinking feeling, she realised her efforts were to no avail. The cat was still out of reach. Knowing it was futile, she put up her hand as far as she dared and called to it.

"Come … please come down, or we will both be in difficulties."

Indeed, she did not know if she could get down herself, let alone get the cat down. It was completely ignoring her blandishments. She would have to try and climb down. But this now proved impossible as she tried with one foot to locate a safe landing below. It was all very well when she could see where to go above her, but now her kilted petticoats obscured the branches she had used and she could not see her way down. Despair gripped her. A mewl brought her head up and she looked at the cat.

"It is of no use to cry at me now, silly thing. We are both stuck."

Her legs were beginning to tremble with the effort to hold her balance on the branch. With infinite care, she sank down until she was sitting in the crook against the trunk. Grasping the branch with one hand, she managed, with some difficulty, to shift to a position where she was sitting on the branch with her legs dangling. She tried to pull her skirts around, but her situation was decidedly improper.

Then the sound of hoofbeats caught her ears. Rescue! Without thought, forgetful of the invidious nature of her position, Henrietta yelled at the top of her lungs. "He-e-e-lp! Help me, please! He-e-e-lp!"

The hooves stopped abruptly and she shouted again.

"Over here! Whoever you are, please help me! I'm stuck!"

A voice, horribly familiar, called out. "Where are you?"

Oh, no, it couldn't be! But this was no time to be worrying over what could not be helped.

"I'm here! I'm up this tree!"

"Up a tree? Good God! All right, I'm coming!"

She heard the swish and soft clop of hooves through the grass and a figure on a horse became visible through the branches. Just as it appeared below the tree, there was a scrabbling sound above Henrietta and the cat descended with a rush and cannoned into her, dislodging her from her precarious perch.

She shrieked, grabbing at the nearest branch with both hands. The feline leapt away, scrambled along the branch and descended swiftly from the tree, leaving Henrietta hanging like a desperate monkey in its wake.

Under the panic, she heard an amused voice below.

"At it again, Miss Disaster?"

CHAPTER SIX

Dipping her head between her arms, Henrietta peered down. It was indeed the duke. Sitting on his horse and laughing himself silly! A mixture of relief, fury and embarrassment added a flurry to the panic in her breast. She was panting with the effort of holding on.

"Theo, for goodness' sake, stop laughing and help me, you beast!"

He continued to sit there, as calm as if she was not in danger, a wide grin on his face. "I'm much too beastly to wish to end this farce too soon. I'm enjoying it."

Henrietta was in far too much distress to put up with his teasing. She was all too conscious of the hideous impropriety and exposure of her limbs, and her arms were beginning to ache. Desperate, she pleaded, "Theo, I'm going to fall!"

"No, you're not, I've got you!"

To her astonishment, he stood up in the stirrups and in the next instant she felt strong arms grasping her around the legs below the knees. His voice came a trifle muffled.

"Let go on three, Hetty! One … two…"

Her fingers lost their grip and she came down in a bang, falling over Theo's shoulder, her hands flailing for a purchase. She heard him grunt with the impact as she grabbed at the edge of the saddle, feeling him half collapse under the burden of her weight.

"Whoa, there! Steady, boy!"

The horse was in motion! And Theo was cursing. The breath was knocked out of her and she could do nothing but hold on. She felt tugging and resisted on instinct.

"What are you doing, idiot girl? Let go so I can get you right way up."

Obedient to the curt command, Henrietta released her hold and in a moment found herself sitting before Theo on the horse, gulping for breath. She ached everywhere, her clothes were in total disarray and her rescuer was rolling his shoulder as he regarded her in high dudgeon.

"On three, I said!"

"I … slipped," she croaked. "Lost my … grip. I'm sorry."

"So you should be, wretched female. What in Hades were you doing up there?"

The wholly unsympathetic tone was so typical Henrietta gathered her strength and reared up, pulling away from his supporting arm and grasping the pommel instead. She matched him for annoyance, meeting the grey gaze that was far too close. "I was trying to rescue the cat!"

"What cat?"

At that moment, there came a familiar mew. Henrietta looked back at the tree and there was the ginger feline, once more perched in a branch, but this time in one almost at eye level with the humans on the horse.

"That cat," said Henrietta in triumph and at once addressed the animal. "If you go up again, you need not expect me to come after you, little horror! Why have you not gone home? Do you realise you nearly had me falling out of the tree?"

The cat, dipping its head on one side, gave her a tentative meow.

"Yes, you may well say so now. I told you to come down by yourself, didn't I?" She stretched out her hand to it and the cat rubbed its head on her fingers. "Yes, that is all very fine, but it would have been well if you had done so in the first place."

A stifled sound made her turn her head back to Theo. The light grey eyes, all too close, were dancing and he was grinning again. Henrietta's pulse began thrumming as she became abruptly conscious of those parts of her body which were in close contact with Theo's. She felt her cheeks grow warm. Thankfully, the duke took it for embarrassment.

"Don't mind me. Carry on with your conversation with the cat. It seems anxious to continue."

The feline was indeed chirruping, furling its tail around Henrietta's wrist. She could not help stroking it and the thing began to purr.

"I think it knows it put me to great inconvenience and is sorry for it."

Theo's expression changed. "You're blaming the cat? It didn't tell you to go climbing the tree, which any fool could see would get you into trouble. Why didn't you go for help?"

"I couldn't see anyone around at the time." The unaccustomed warmth she had been experiencing in strange places began to dissipate. "You would not have had me go off and leave the poor thing stranded?"

Theo regarded her with a half-smile on his lips. "No, I'd expect you to do precisely what you did, Miss Disaster."

"Don't call me that!"

"I shall call you anything I choose. You're on my horse, after all."

"Which gives you the right to insult me?"

"I'm not insulting you. I'm stating a fact."

"Oh, for goodness' sake!" Patience at an end, Henrietta prepared to jump, setting her hands behind her and beginning to push her rump off her portion of the saddle.

"No, you don't!" Theo seized her around the waist, holding her fast. "Next thing we know you'll sprain your ankle and I'll be obliged to carry you home."

"I will not sprain my ankle! I know how to get off a horse."

But Theo was urging his mount away from the tree. He stopped him after a few paces, released Henrietta and dismounted from behind her in one smooth movement. Then he held up his arms. "Come on! I'll catch you."

She felt like the wretched cat! Well, there was nothing for it. She slid off the horse and Theo did indeed catch her, holding her tightly against him and keeping his balance by a miracle.

Flurried and hot, Henrietta waited for him to let her go. He set her on her feet, but kept his arms fast about her, looking down into her face. Heat swept through her body. She could feel his limbs against hers and the contact torso to torso was positively stifling. The breath caught in her throat and she could not utter a word.

For an eon he held her thus, the light eyes staring into hers. The soft voice came, the one he'd used on that first occasion. "Hetty … it won't do, though, will it?" He released her so suddenly that she almost fell and had to grab at the horse's girth to steady herself. His lips were tight, his voice clipped. "You'd better tidy yourself before anyone sees you like this."

Her heart racing, Henrietta untucked her petticoats and pulled her clothing into place, not looking at him. His words were echoing in her head and the question ran around her mind. What would not do? What had he intended? Had he been about to — to kiss her?

The shocking thought sent a flitter of yearning through her. Oh, goodness! She wanted him to kiss her. Wanton creature that she was. Dreadful thought.

She dared a look and found him watching the cat, who was engaged in getting itself down from the tree again.

"Your friend appears to be keen to fraternise."

His voice was normal again, all trace of the earlier husky note gone. He sounded relaxed, where a moment before he had been obviously holding back on resentment. Her mind flew to the churchyard, when he'd thrown up a hand to stop her from speaking and walked away. He had rejected her then. And again, just this moment past. The hurt, intensified now, welled in her bosom and her throat ached.

To hide it, she cast about for her bonnet and found it crushed. She leapt to seize it. "Oh, no!"

"What now?"

The impatience in Theo's tone sprang a flood of resentment and she turned on him. "Your horse stamped on my bonnet. See, it's all squashed!" She held it up and the duke regarded it with a hint of exasperation in his features.

"Really, does it matter? Would you rather be up the tree still, waiting for rescue?"

"Of course not, but I —"

His brows snapped together. "If you start crying over a bonnet, I won't be answerable for the consequences."

"I'm not crying over the b-bonnet!" Her voice broke as a wave of misery engulfed her.

"Well, what are crying over, then?"

There was aggression in his tone now. She could not tell him she was crying because he was being so beastly. Because he had so very nearly kissed her. Because she wanted so very much for him to catch her back into his embrace and to hell with the consequences. Why she should like him so much when he was such a hateful creature she could not imagine.

The thought gave her strength and she sniffed back the threatening tears. "I am not crying at all, so there."

"You can't fool me, Miss Watering Pot!"

But before she could retaliate, she felt the cat weaving about her ankles. Glad of the distraction, she bent down and picked it up, cradling it in her arms and crooning as it began to purr. "You're a terrible cat, you really are. Where is your home, then? Where do you live? Is it around here somewhere?" She looked up and found Theo eyeing her, that half-smile back on his face. She forgot the intervening argument and smiled back, just as if she was in perfect charity with him. "I will see if I can find where he lives. Thank you for rescuing me, Theo, but don't let me keep you any longer."

He hesitated, glancing from the cat in her arms to the basket lying on its side. A quick frown came. "More flowers? Are they wrecked again?"

She sighed. "Probably. It doesn't matter. I can't leave the cat to roam. I must find its home."

He rolled his eyes. "I suppose I had better help you, then."

"Oh, no, I can manage."

But although the duke had his hand on his horse's bridle, he did not budge. The familiar tease came into his eyes. "If there's one thing more certain than another, it's that you'll come to grief if I leave you to your own devices. You can't be trusted to put one foot in front of the other without making a mess of it."

Though she knew perfectly well he was being deliberately provocative, Henrietta could not help snapping. "Don't start! I've managed to get by every day for nineteen years without your help, I thank you."

"Lord knows how you managed it," he said, turning his mount towards the road. "Stick that pestilential cat in the basket and come on."

With a flurry of irritation he found hard to control, Theo watched as Hetty tried to persuade the recalcitrant animal to get in the basket. Really, she was the limit. Why he found her so damned alluring was a mystery. He ought to have left her as she bade him, but he could hardly go now, having pledged himself to help the creature. Amusement returned as he listened to her talking to the cat again.

"Stay in there, silly, I'm not going to hurt you. What, do you think I'm trying to kidnap you? I just want to help you get home."

As if the animal couldn't find its way by itself if it chose to. He ought to intervene, but she was so ridiculously funny, carrying on as if the feline understood everything she said, he didn't want to stop her.

"Oh, drat," she cried as the cat jumped out of the basket again.

Theo lost patience. Letting go of his mount's rein, he bent and seized the cat, which squirmed in his hold, fighting and scratching. "Damn you, stop biting!" He held it out to Hetty. "Here, take it!"

She fairly grabbed it out of his hold, cradling the thing against her breast in a way that Theo found distinctly unsettling. She showed him her indignant face. "You frightened him! You should always treat animals gently, and cats have a great deal of dignity. They are easily offended."

Struggling with the unprecedented effect she had on him and the amusement once again bubbling up, Theo chose what he knew must provoke her. "Easily offended? Like to like, then. You should find him perfect company. If it is a he."

She blushed adorably. "I don't know and I'm not going to look."

He had to laugh. "You'd best carry him. I'll take the basket." So saying, he picked it up and retrieved his horse's reins. "Come on, Columbus, walk on!"

"Why did you call him Columbus?" Hetty asked as he led the way back to the lane.

"He's well-travelled. We toured the Continent together."

"Not France, surely?"

The anxiety in her tone made him glance round. She was wearing a troubled expression, as if she was truly concerned for his safety. A ripple of tenderness slid through him. He banished it. He was not going down that road. "Of course not France in these times. There's plenty of Continent free of the War." He knew his tone was repressive, but it did not seem to affect Hetty.

"Italy? Did you go there?"

"Yes, why?"

"No reason." She hesitated, standing in the lane as she looked at him, the cat still cradled in her arms. "Is that what you meant by adventure?"

Taken aback, he stared at her. "Adventure?"

She looked anxious again. "You said you had been going on an adventure when your uncle died."

She remembered that? Had he spoken of it? The reminder jolted him back to the harsh reality of his position. What in Hades was he doing? He had no business encouraging this girl's interest. "No, I didn't mean that."

Hetty recoiled. He had not realised how his voice had changed. He fought the impulse to retract. Better she regarded him as a beast, as she put it.

"I d-did not m-mean… I was not p-prying."

To his intense dismay, her eyes filled. He wanted to catch her into his embrace, cat and all, but he must not. He took refuge in scolding. "Must you start crying again? Really, you are the most tiresome girl. Dry your eyes at once!"

As he'd hoped, the tears receded as her eyes kindled instead. "You are the most unsympathetic creature on God's earth! How dare you treat me so? What have I done to you that you should be so horrid to me?"

Relief caused him to seize on this. "What have you done to me? Well, if it's not enough to fall on top of me and nearly knock me off my horse, then I don't know what is."

"I slipped! I told you that at the time."

Good. She was thoroughly indignant again. This he could deal with. But before he could retaliate, he was forestalled as the cat began wriggling in her hold. She uttered a cry of alarm as he struggled free and sprang to the ground, running off along the lane. Not much to Theo's surprise, Hetty turned on him.

"Now look what you've done! You upset him!"

He raised his brows. "If you ask me, it was your berating me that upset him."

She raised clenched fists to heaven. "Oh, you are impossible, Theo! I hate you! Everything is my fault according to you when you know perfectly well you have behaved like a boor and a beast. I can't imagine why you wanted to stay and help."

"Can't you?" said Theo before he could stop himself. Within an ace of saying he liked her company, he bit off the words and chose differently. "Not that I actually wanted to. I told you I felt obliged."

"Well, feel it no longer!" She grabbed her basket from his hands, dropped a curtsy and lifted her chin. "Good day to you, my lord duke. I wish you a very pleasant day."

The combination of indignation with the haughty note was too much. Theo burst out laughing. She gave him a scorching look, turned on her heel and walked swiftly off along the lane. He watched her go, the unconscious sway of her hips half mesmerising. If he obeyed his instinct, he would go after her, pull her about and seize her into a violent embrace.

Theo shook himself out of it. She was not a village maiden to be flattered by the attentions of the great man of the district. Besides, such usage was abhorrent. He despised men who took advantage of their position. But Hetty was a different proposition altogether. She was walking with purpose, and she had not looked back. He would swear she knew he was still watching her. Lord, but she had pride! He had to give her that. She was bumbling and ill-behaved, and a cursed nuisance besides. Soft-hearted little pest. Rescuing a cat, for pity's sake! It would be a great deal better for his peace of mind if that was all she was. But Hetty was…

He eyed the diminishing figure, his mind's eye presenting him with the girl in all her guises: indignant, infuriated, frowningly puzzled, tender, tearful and far too sensual for Theo's good. Unconsciously so. He would swear she had no notion how she gave off such a strong allure. She was far too innocent.

He recalled his first stunned realisation that she was anything but, when her father had arrived so fortuitously to find Theo holding her all too close. If Mr Latimer had seen what occurred today, he might have grounds for his accusations. Still half inclined to believe it was a trap, Theo could not reconcile the notion with the Hetty he had met since. Especially today. There was no purpose in her actions. It was sheer chance he rode by at that moment.

He became aware that Hetty had stopped. She was standing still where a pathway crossed the lane, and she had turned, watching him standing like a fool in the middle of the lane.

He raised a hand in salute, but she did not respond. Shrugging, Theo turned away, put his foot in the stirrup and mounted up. On impulse, he put Columbus at a fast trot and caught up with Hetty, still standing at the entrance to the path. She looked up and met his gaze, her own unfathomable.

Theo knew not what to say. He ought to find a way to end this — whatever this was — but he could not think of anything that would adequately convey what was in his head. He seized something out of the air. "What are you going to do with those flowers?"

Her voice came out flat and dull. "Make a picture." She curtsied again and turned away.

Something broke in Theo's chest and he uttered words from the heart. "It was an ill day you crossed my path, Hetty Latimer."

She glanced back, a look of hurt in her eyes that pierced him to the core. Then she picked up her skirts with her free hand and ran as for her life.

Theo, a curse in his head and a coil of guilt in his breast, urged Columbus to a canter.

CHAPTER SEVEN

"Charming, Hetty, quite charming."

Aunt Angelica turned the picture this way and that, while Henrietta tried to feel gratified. She had brought it down at her godmother's request when she dropped in at Moss House on her way to another engagement. Frank, knowing Mrs Summerhayes to be almost a member of the family, had shown her directly into the back parlour where the twins were sitting, a fire having been lit there on Mama's orders to cheer up the miserable day.

The front parlour, a dark-panelled chamber typical of houses dating from Cromwell's day, was rarely used except for formal occasions. As children, the girls had managed to partake of goings-on there by means of a hatch in the wall which remained forgotten from the days of espionage common between cavaliers and roundheads. But their godmother was never subjected to the formality of the front parlour. She had swept in, reverting almost immediately to asking how their schemes of bringing in a little income were going.

Henrietta was at least able to produce the one picture she had lately finished in an attempt to divert her mind. Using flowers that had already dried, she had made the image almost at random, beset by uncomfortable memories.

To her consternation, her twin, who was seated next to their visitor on the chaise longue, butted in, pointing to a spot on the picture. "Don't you think that looks just like a cat, Aunt Angelica? There, you see. As if it's sitting in the tree."

Mrs Summerhayes peered closely at the splodge Henrietta knew was plonked at a point near the topmost branch. She'd used a red bloom which had dried to a dullish orange. "Oh, yes, I see." Aunt Angelica looked across to Henrietta's chair opposite. "How clever you are, Hetty! What made you think of putting a cat there?"

She felt warmth rising in her cheeks, but Silvestre fortuitously again intervened. "It's her excess of sensibility, of course. She is quite as dopey over animals as she is over people."

"That is unkind, Silve," chided Mrs Summerhayes.

Her sister grinned across at her. "She knows I mean nothing by it. She adores animals, don't you, Hetty?"

Seizing on the excuse, Henrietta nodded. "I do, yes, only they make Papa sneeze, so we cannot keep a cat or a dog."

"Yes, I remember your mama saying as much. That is indeed a pity. But this is excellent, Hetty. I am sure I can find you a buyer for such an unusual piece."

A few short weeks earlier, this would have gladdened Henrietta's heart. Now, however, it did little to raise the low spirits from which she had been suffering for more than a se'ennight. She tried for a note of gratification. "I'm so pleased, Aunt Angelica. That would be wonderful."

Even to her own ears, the words sounded flat. Her twin threw her a frowning glance, but Mrs Summerhayes seemed too intent upon the picture to notice.

"Yes, I know just who to try with this." She looked up, smiling. "I shan't say anything more until I've secured the deal. But do another as soon as you can, Hetty. What have you in mind next?"

Since she had no idea at all, Henrietta found it hard to answer this. She prevaricated. "I never really know until I start, Aunt Angelica. Besides, I must wait for more flowers to dry, so it will be a little while before I can do another."

"Well, as soon as you can, then. If you can do something as unusual as this, I guarantee your work will become very much admired. I should not be surprised if you receive requests in due course."

She knew she ought to be thoroughly elated by the praise, but Henrietta's stubborn heart remained subdued and as crushed as it had been upon the day depicted in the image. She thrust the thought away. She must not allow herself to remember. The pangs would fade in time, she was persuaded. Her efforts to appear cheerful were making her worse, however, and she knew Silvestre was suspicious.

Her twin had tried once or twice to probe, but Henrietta, unable to bear the slightest touch upon her wound, had managed to deflect the questions and change the subject. As long as she did not think of those fatal words, she would be fine. *It was an ill day…*

Thrusting the memory off, she focused her attention on the discussion going forward. To her relief, Silvestre was engaged in talking of the possibility of approaching a publisher for her novel, which was now coming along in leaps and bounds. Aunt Angelica, as fashionable as ever in a round gown of lemon muslin, topped with a hussar jacket of nankeen, wondered aloud whether it would help to have her cousin Lynchmere's assistance.

"I might ask Raoul to agree to lend his name to a subscription list. If we can find a few others as well, a publisher would be bound to take interest."

"But why would the marquis agree to help me?"

"Because you sheltered Felicity, of course. I shan't approach him directly, but talk to his wife first. He dotes on her, you must know, and will do anything she asks, I dare say."

The last thing Henrietta wished to hear about was the utter happiness enjoyed by the newly married pair. Her godmother was apt to dwell upon it, declaring over and over her astonishment and delight at her cousin's having fallen head over heels at last.

"It just shows how a man may be stubbornly aloof for years, and then fall victim to the tender passion just when he least expects it."

Henrietta managed to smile, avoiding her twin's narrow look. She spoke in a bright tone which she knew sounded a trifle false. "Luckily for him, Felicity liked him too. It is f-fortunate when such f-feelings are reciprocated."

Aunt Angelica evidently took this at face value, thankfully missing the slight tremor Henrietta could not control. "Too true indeed, my dear. I've seen far too many lovelorn creatures suffer because the object of their interest does not return their affection. I could wish there were some other way for debutantes to meet potential suitors than the dreadful parade of the Season. There are bound to be disappointments."

"Well, fortunately for us," said Silvestre with a reassuring glance at her twin which did nothing for Henrietta's peace of mind, "we are no longer in any position to be disappointed. I am glad of it now, for I dare say I should never have begun writing in earnest had I been obliged to get married."

This drew a tutting response from Aunt Angelica. "Obliged? My dear, there is no greater joy for any female."

"What, in being subject to the whims of a husband with whom you are barely acquainted? Poppycock, Aunt Angelica!"

"Don't be silly, Silve. One of the joys is getting to know him — provided the gentleman is of good character and disposed to be indulgent. That goes without saying."

"Yes, but how many of them are? The whole thing is a lottery, if you ask me. We are well out of it."

"As far as I am concerned, you are not out of it." Ignoring Silvestre's snort of derision, Mrs Summerhayes set aside the picture and rose, shaking out her petticoats. "I have my eye on one or two possibilities. We cannot be too ambitious, but there is still hope."

"Don't trouble your head over me, I beg of you," said Silvestre, rising too and going to pull on the bell. "I don't want a husband, I thank you. But by all means do what you can for Hetty. A distraction is just what she needs."

Henrietta could have strangled her twin as she came under the beam of Mrs Summerhayes' questioning gaze.

"Why, how is this, Hetty? I thought you were looking a trifle peaky. You are not ailing for anything, I hope?"

"I am perfectly well, Aunt Angelica." She cast a reproachful glance at her sister as she spoke, but Silve merely raised her eyebrows.

"It is this wretched rain, I dare say," said Aunt Angelica, patting her cheek. "Enough to give anyone a fit of the dismals. Now, where did I put that picture?"

Henrietta hastened to pick it up for her, if only for the opportunity of escaping from the dangerous question of her mood. "Shall I wrap it?"

"No, no, give it to me as it is. I am going directly to see if I can dispose of it suitably. I am sure my quarry will be at home on a day like this. Unlike dear Margaret and I, she hates going out in the wet. Not that I like it much myself, but I refuse to allow the weather to deter me."

A knock at the door produced the footman and Silvestre asked him to alert Mrs Summerhayes' coachman.

"Mama will be sorry to have missed you," said Henrietta mechanically as the twins escorted the visitor out into the hall where the maid Dinah helped her into her pelisse. The footman was by the front door, armed with a large umbrella.

"Mama insisted on making her duty visit to old Mrs Fiskerton," Silvestre was saying, "though I tried to dissuade her. She could well have gone another day."

"Mama knows Mrs Fiskerton expects her every week. She would not wish to disappoint her, Silve."

"Well, it would drive me batty to be obliged to listen to her twittering on about the *old days* and how things have changed for the worse while she dithers over which card to play. Mama is a saint to put up with it every week."

Aunt Angelica laughed. "She is a bit of a complaining chatterbox. Cecilia is just such another, but I believe she has reason enough. I shall be sympathetic today, since I wish to interest her in Hetty's picture."

Startled and dismayed, Henrietta almost cried out. She could not mean to offer the dratted picture to the Duchess of Charlton? Before she could think how to object without giving herself away, the sound of hooves and wheels on the gravel signalled the arrival of the Summerhayes' coach. Frank opened the door and held the umbrella ready while Aunt Angelica made her farewells.

Hardly knowing what she said, her mind flitting this way and that, Henrietta stood in the porch with her sister and waved, feeling quite sick.

To her dismay, her twin tucked a hand in her arm as they re-entered the house and Frank shut the door behind them. "Do come back into the parlour, Hetty, for I have something particular I wish to talk to you about."

"But I was going to —"

Silvestre ignored this, turning to the footman. "Frank, please bring coffee to the parlour. Mrs Summerhayes would not take refreshment, but I am gasping."

"Certainly, Miss Silve. The master will be wanting his in the library, so Cook should have a pot boiling by now."

The footman vanished into the domestic quarters and Henrietta was drawn, protesting, back into the parlour.

"Can we not go to the den? We'll be sitting ducks if anyone else visits, Silve."

"On a day like this?"

Thrust into the sofa, Henrietta's heart sank when her determined twin sat down beside her and patted her knee. "Now then, enough prevarication, my girl. Aunt Angelica said you are looking peaky, but she doesn't know the half of it. You've been moping and miserable for days and it's that wretched duke of yours at the bottom of it, or I'll eat my novel."

This threat could not but elicit a faint giggle from Henrietta. "You'll be as sick as a dog if you do."

"I won't have to," retorted her twin. "I'm right, aren't I? What happened? You met him again, didn't you?"

The combination of accusation and anxiety in her twin's voice proved too much for Henrietta's resolution. She sank her elbows on her knees and dropped her face in her hands with a despairing sigh. "Oh, Silve, I am so dreadfully unhappy."

An arm came about her and her sister crooned. "Hush, now, hush, Hetty. I knew you were, I just knew it. Come now, you may as well tell me. What did he do to you?"

"Nothing at all," declared Henrietta, rearing up again. "It's only what he s-said at the end, and I dare say he m-meant nothing by it and I have t-taken it too m-much to h-heart, but it *hurt*, Silve."

Her twin whipped out a handkerchief. "Here. Try not to cry, dearest, or you won't be able to talk. Besides, Frank will be here in a minute with the coffee."

"Well, it's your fault," snapped Henrietta, seizing the handkerchief and dabbing at her eyes. "You would badger me to come in here."

"Just tell me what the hateful creature did to you."

"He's not hateful! At least, of course he is rude and a beast and horridly teasing, but…"

"What did he *do*?"

"He rescued me."

Silvestre stared at her as if she had taken leave of her senses. Henrietta took refuge in the handkerchief, pleating and unpleating its folds. Her twin opened her mouth and shut it again, shaking her head.

Henrietta blew out an overcharged breath. "I knew it was of no use to tell you about it."

"So far you haven't actually told me anything, Hetty. Well, nothing that makes any sense. He rescued you? From what?"

"I was stuck in a tree," said Henrietta in a small voice.

"*Stuck in a tree?*"

"I know it sounds silly,but there was this cat, you see,and—"

Silvestre's expression changed at once. "The cat in the tree! Hetty, what have you been about?"

Fortunately for Henrietta's shredding nerves, the footman came in at this moment with a tray, which he set down on the table by the window at Silvestre's request. Her twin got up and busied herself pouring the coffee and Henrietta struggled to pull herself together. Silvestre caught up a small table to set between them and brought over the filled cups in their saucers.

"Now then, drink up and tell me everything."

Henrietta took a sip and cradled the cup in her hands as she began haltingly to tell her sister what had happened on that fateful day. Silvestre fell into gales of laughter upon hearing of her predicament, which oddly made the telling easier. By the time she reached the point at which she and Theo had parted, she felt a good deal better.

But the sting of his last utterance still lodged in her bosom, and she could not bring herself to repeat it. "And then he … he rode off and I came home," she finished lamely.

Silvestre, sober again by this time, shook her head over it. "Honestly, Hetty, you are incorrigible. Why could you not have told me this days ago?"

Because she had not even now told her twin the worst. Nor would she. She was also guiltily aware of omitting that startling embrace when she had been convinced Theo was wishing to kiss her. He had not. He had said it wouldn't do, and that, in combination with those fatal final words, accounted for her woe. Theo had made it abundantly clear that there was no possible hope for her. Not that she supposed he felt anything more than the sort of passing fancy any man might indulge. He was amusing himself, that was all. But he clearly still thought her designing because he had warned her off in no uncertain terms.

"A penny for them?"

Henrietta started and found her twin's penetrating eye upon her. "What?"

"You were deep in thought. And none too pleasant by the looks of it."

The stern tone had the effect of stiffening Henrietta. She picked up her empty cup and got up. "Nothing of the sort." Moving to the table, she lifted the coffee pot and shook it. "Do you want a refill?"

Her twin was on her feet. "No, I want to know what there was in this ridiculous story of yours to make you feel so wounded." She came across and took the pot out of Henrietta's hand, setting it down.

"I wanted another cup, even if you don't."

"You don't want another cup at all. You are just trying to evade the issue."

Something snapped in Henrietta. "Leave it, Silve! I know you only mean to be kind, but there is nothing you can do. Nothing anyone can do."

Her twin's eyes softened. "As bad as that, is it?"

Henrietta tried to smile. "I will come about."

"Yes, when the moon turns to green cheese. Oh, Hetty. You've fallen for him and he rejected you, is that it?"

The blunt truth was like a slap in the face. For a moment, she could not answer, the violence of her reaction quite shocking to her. As if her heart was on fire, burning in her breast.

The sensation died down presently and she was astonished to realise Silvestre apparently had not noticed anything untoward.

"Well, Hetty? Have I hit it?"

"Oh, there is no denying I like him." Surprised at the calmness of her own voice, she felt oddly separated, as if she was two people. The one who had taken the blow, and the other who had absorbed it. "But Aunt Angelica said it days ago. He is destined for some female of rank."

Silvestre looked dissatisfied. "I suppose so. Such nonsense. As if two people who care about each other cannot bridge such gaps. Only look at Felicity. She is a nobody, yet Lynchmere cared nothing for it. He married her in the teeth of convention and he is a marquis."

"Aunt Angelica says he fell in love. Besides, he has been on the Town for years."

Theo was young. He had only taken the title a year ago. One could not expect him to think of settling into marriage yet. When he did, he would undoubtedly please himself. And his plans would not include Hetty Latimer. That had been made perfectly plain. *It was an ill day…*

No, she must not allow herself to dwell on it. Her twin was right. She had been moping long enough. "I've got a mountain of white work upstairs, Silve. I must get back to it. And you need to finish your story."

Restless, Theo prowled the library while his secretary and Swarland went over the arrangements for Cecilia's upcoming soirée, as she insisted on calling it. His secretary Hathersage had arrived a few days ago, armed with a plethora of matters concerning the Devenal property requiring Theo's sanction before he turned his attention to matters pertaining to Whisley Park.

For a few days he had thrown himself into the work, feeling it as relief from the intolerable burden of his conscience. Not to mention his aunt's incessant attempts to force him to socialise. His secretary's needs had provided him with an excuse to absent himself from the saloon, so that he was able to avoid meeting callers. But Cecilia's latest scheme to involve him was inescapable. He could hardly refuse to appear at a blasted party held in his own house. To make it worse, his secretary was necessarily dragged into the business along with Cecilia's steward.

"Will you cast an eye over the guest list, your grace?"

He turned from the window where he had ended up, absently staring out at the rain-drenched grounds, and glanced across at his secretary. "Whatever for, Hathersage? I don't know any of these people."

The steward Swarland's expression, just short of reproachful, gave him to understand that he had only himself to blame. Theo threw up a hand.

"There's no need to say it. I know I could have met the half of them by this time."

The steward took the list from the secretary and came across. "Her grace the duchess was most insistent that you should vet the names, your grace."

Cursing, Theo snatched the sheet and ran his eye down the list. In fact they were familiar, his aunt having mentioned most at some point or another, although he could not have put a face to any. It struck him that the one name that hammered in his head was not there. "There's an omission." He looked up with a frown. "Why are the Latimers not invited?"

Swarland reddened and glanced across at Hathersage, who was looking puzzled. He was not acquainted with the gentry hereabouts either. Theo had hired him on the recommendation of his predecessor's elderly secretary, who had retired due to ill health several months ago, and this was Hathersage's first visit to Whisley Park.

"Well?"

The steward cleared his throat. "Her grace believed you would prefer not to entertain Mr Latimer, your grace."

"Oh, did she?"

Theo's grim thoughts matched his tone. He had not told Cecilia about his contretemps with Hetty's father. How the deuce did she find out? Or was it that idiotic assertion that the Latimers could not add to his consequence? Whichever it was, there was no possible excuse for leaving them out.

Ignoring the coil of anticipation at the notion of seeing Hetty again, and indeed the promise of appeasing his conscience, he concentrated on the social implications. "Put them on the list.

It won't do to exclude them." He handed the sheet back to Swarland, who hesitated.

"Er — your grace, I fear…"

"What, for pity's sake? Spit it out." Aware of snapping unnecessarily, Theo nevertheless stared the man out, daring him to contradict his order.

"Much as I desire to do your bidding, your grace, I fear I must refer the decision to her grace the duchess."

"Oh, you must, must you? We'll soon see about that." Theo stalked across to the door, throwing a command at his secretary as he went. "Get those names on that list right now, Hathersage. And don't forget the two daughters."

Aware his fury had little to do with Cecilia's lapse, he was yet unable to refrain from feeding it with mental animadversions. How dare she presume to judge the family unworthy? Which she clearly had done, as sure as check. He knew she was high in the instep, but this was the outside of enough. An intolerable insult. To be inviting the whole county and leaving out one family because they could not add to his consequence? Outrageous. Disgraceful conduct. And so he would tell her.

Driven by the image of Hetty's stricken face, which had haunted him ever since, Theo reached the hall and flung into the parlour without ceremony. "Cecilia! What in Hades do you mean by —?"

He stopped short as he realised his aunt was not alone. He should have expected Mary Eddleston, but who the devil was the fashionable female of matronly aspect sitting beside Cecilia on the sofa? She did not customarily entertain in the family room.

The stranger was regarding him with interest while his aunt's companion looked apprehensive. Cecilia, whose face had shown instant annoyance, concealed it swiftly under her company face.

"Theo, how fortuitous! Pray allow me to present Mrs Summerhayes. Angelica, this is my nephew, his grace the Duke of Charlton."

Taken unawares, Theo appraised the woman as she rose and dropped a graceful curtsy. Was this the female Hetty spoke of as Aunt Angelica? Of necessity he bowed, grudgingly murmuring words of greeting. "Glad to make your acquaintance, ma'am."

She smiled in a self-assured fashion. "And I yours at last, your grace."

Theo felt warmth rise to his cheeks, but he was damned if he would apologise for his reluctance to parade about and be stared at like a freak at a fair. Yet the consciousness of the woman's closeness to Hetty could not but affect him. Did she know anything of those farcical encounters? How far did Hetty trust her? Enough to confide his unutterable meanness in saying what he had? She did not look reproachful or angry, as she surely would if she knew. Indeed, she was regarding him in a positively roguish manner.

"We have all been eager to meet you, my lord duke. I feel quite privileged."

"Oh, you are, Angelica," Cecilia chimed in, "and rightly so. Mrs Summerhayes is a particular friend of mine, you must know."

"So I perceive." Theo eyed the woman. "You would not else be invited into my aunt's private sanctum, ma'am."

She gave a merry laugh. "Oh, but we are mothers together and that creates a bond. I have a trifle the advantage for my boys are older, but Sally and Lady Ella are much of an age."

"Yes, and they have taken to each other, I am happy to say."

At which point Cecilia's sycophantic companion rushed to corroborate the statement. "Indeed that is true, your grace. The little girls played so happily together the other day. It was a joy to see her ladyship enjoying your Sally's company, dear Mrs Summerhayes."

Uttering an inward groan, Theo prepared to retreat. He was glad for Ellie, but this was precisely the sort of inane conversation he loathed. Besides, he could scarcely mention his errand in front of this particular visitor. "Good. However, I did not mean to interrupt you, Cecilia, and —"

"Don't go, Theo. Only look at this delightful picture Angelica brought." She lifted a framed image that he had not noticed resting in her lap. "I have bought it for Ellie. Is it not exactly what she will like?"

With reluctance, he went forward to peer down at the picture she was now holding out towards him.

"See if you can spot the little orange cat in the tree, Theo. Such an unusual idea. Ellie will be in raptures, I am persuaded. She loves cats."

Theo swore he could not have heard aright. Cat in a tree? He felt light-headed, disoriented. Without realising what he did, he took the frame out of Cecilia's hands, staring at the picture depicted therein. A picture made up of dried, pressed flowers.

A plethora of moving images crashed through his mind and he felt as if his chest was being squeezed. He spoke in a constricted tone. "Who did this?" As if he didn't know!

Cecilia gave a merry laugh. "Oh, that is the delight of it, Theo. Angelica will not reveal the identity of the artist. She is acting for her —"

"It is a female, then?"

Of course it was! A hurly-burly wretched female who must needs throw him into horrible confusion with this travesty of a damned picture. Was it meant for a reproach? Had she sent her blasted Aunt Angelica to stick this abominable reminder in his face and make him writhe?

"Oh, yes, she is a very talented female," said the merchant of doom, "but I intend to keep her identity secret for the time being."

Not from Theo, she couldn't. He knew exactly who had made the thing and he could willingly strangle her. How dared she? Blazoning forth her folly for the world to see. Not to mention dragging him into the business, as she always did. Climbing trees to rescue cats! Idiotic girl. What would have happened if he had not come by, he dreaded to think. Of course she would have fallen off that branch. Broken a limb in all likelihood. It was a miracle she was still in one piece, the way she behaved.

"Is it not a clever piece, Theo? I find it quite charming."

"Charming!" Catching himself up, he altered his tone, still staring at the damned splodge that was supposed to be the fateful cat. "Charming, yes. Very."

"So unusual."

To which the visitor added her mite. "I venture to say my protégée is an unusual lady."

To say the least! Theo gave the frame back to his aunt, though the image remained imprinted in his mind. He pulled himself out of the infuriating preoccupation. "I expect Ellie will be pleased."

"Her ladyship cannot fail to be delighted, I am persuaded," said Mary Eddleston, adding with a sigh, "I wish I might produce something half as unusual, but alas, my efforts are quite ordinary."

The visitor looked at her with apparent interest. "Do you make flower pictures too, Miss Eddleston?"

Was she being polite? Or was it a kindly impulse to include the companion?

"Oh, no, ma'am. But I embroider. Flowers too, but in a perfectly mundane fashion, I am afraid."

Theo moved to lean against the mantel, hardly aware of doing so as a thought occurred while a tedious discussion of feminine employments was going forward. Cecilia said she had bought the picture. Which must mean this Summerhayes woman was acting as a kind of agent between the artist and potential buyers.

Theo was abruptly gripped with a memory of Hetty weeping over the loss of her flowers that first day. He had scorned her tears. In a teasing spirit, it was true, but that was scarcely the point. She had been genuinely distressed and the reason for it leapt to the eye. This flower picture business must be a means to augment her income.

Everything in him balked. Cecilia had said the Latimers were purse-pinched and he had pooh-poohed it because he was angry with the fellow. Surely he could not be so poor that Hetty must use this means to live? The thought appalled him. She was infuriating and impossible. But to be obliged to eke out a miserable few guineas by slaving over dried flowers…

He cut into the discussion without ceremony. "How much did you pay for that thing, Cecilia?"

She blinked at him. "What thing?"

"The picture, of course. What did Mrs Summerhayes ask for it?"

She looked bemused. "Two guineas, was it not, Angelica?"

"Two guineas! Is that all?" Wrathful, he turned on Mrs Summerhayes, who was gazing at him with raised brows. "She is asking for a measly two guineas?"

The woman's cheeks flew spots of colour. "Well, no. It is left to me. I did not think we ought to start high. One does not pay much more for such things in a shop, you know. And Cecilia is a particular friend, besides being the first customer."

With difficulty Theo refrained from blasting her where she sat with a stream of invective. He turned to his aunt. "Pay five, Cecilia. Or better yet, ten. It's still paltry."

All three females were staring at him in varying degrees of astonishment. Theo stared back, hunting for words with which to explain a dogmatic attitude he abruptly realised was utterly inexplicable.

"It's inadequate. Two guineas, I mean. She's an artist, isn't she? Do you expect her to live on bread and cheese?"

Mrs Summerhayes' expression cleared and she broke into a gale of laughter. "Good heavens, your grace, are you thinking of some poor soul starving in a garret? It is nothing of the sort. Merely, my protégée seeks that little extra, you know, for those trinkets and small pleasures that might otherwise be beyond her reach."

She was lying. Theo was convinced of it. The airy note did not fool him in the least. She knew, better than anyone probably, the Latimers' circumstances, but she chose not to advertise it. Or was it Hetty's doing? Too proud to let the world know her predicament?

No, Hetty was not proud. Far from it. He was the one with too much pride to admit of being affected by her more than somewhat, driven by the voice at the back of his mind that spoke of duty.

"Mind you, there is something in what Theo says, my dear Angelica. Two guineas cannot truly compensate for the work involved."

Surprised and gratified, Theo turned his attention to his aunt. "Exactly so, Cecilia. She must first collect the flowers…" He faded out as he realised where his words were leading him. But Mary, to his relief, took it up.

"Yes, indeed, and they take weeks to dry. Very often too they break when you try to use them. I have done the same with the occasional choice bloom, in a bid to keep it, you know. Sadly, they often fall apart."

"Yes, and I dare say it is a chore to glue them without damaging them." Cecilia grew enthusiastic. "Besides, we ought to encourage her if she is capable of such work as this. I will give you five guineas, Angelica. You must ask for as much from others too."

Secretly satisfied, Theo approved this decision. "Excellent. And now I must leave you, or Hathersage will be coming to find me." He began to cross to the door.

"Stay, Theo!"

Halting, he turned to look with question at his aunt.

"What was it you wanted to ask me?"

Oh, lord! This was no moment to be mentioning the Latimers. With the Summerhayes woman in the room? He would infallibly give himself away. More to the point, he might open Hetty to speculation and censure. "Later will do, Cecilia. Good day to you, Mrs Summerhayes."

He left with alacrity before Cecilia could find anything else to keep him in the room. It was no longer urgent. Hathersage would not dream of disobeying his orders and the Latimers were undoubtedly already on the guest list. Which meant he would see Hetty in short order. Unless she withheld herself?

Would she refuse to appear? After his despicable comment, she might well. At the time, he had spoken his mind without a thought for how his words might be received. He had not meant to inflict the pain he perceived in Hetty's eyes. He could not blame her if she did not wish to meet him again.

Another thought intervened. Worse, if anything. Would Latimer accept an invitation from the *whippersnapper* who had accused him of trickery?

CHAPTER EIGHT

"Indeed, we must go, my dear Henry. Not to do so will create particularity for the girls which I know you would not wish."

This argument stayed Mr Latimer's erstwhile determination. Henrietta, a knot of anxiety in her bosom, watched him glance from her to Silvestre and back again.

The invitation, written on crested paper, had been awaiting Papa on the breakfast table. The first intimation of what the letter contained was Papa's violent snort of derision, exploding out of him just when Henrietta was taking a sip of coffee. She had fallen into a fit of coughing and by the time she had been restored by her twin, who applied several judicious slaps to her back, the discussion was already going forward between their parents.

Since Frank and Dinah were never these days required to remain once the breakfast accoutrements had been set upon the sideboard and table, the customary privacy prevailed. The family served themselves and rang the bell if any refill was required.

"A soirée? What, I ask you, Margaret, does this duchess mean by such an affair? In the country, of all places."

Mama's tone had been soothing. "I expect it means a conversable evening, my dear, with perhaps a little music. The purpose must be to allow time for her and the duke to exchange a few words with everyone."

Henrietta fairly jumped in shock, casting a wild glance at her twin. But Silvestre merely grimaced and shrugged as Papa's cheeks darkened.

"I have no desire to exchange words with that impertinent young man."

"No, of course you have not, Henry, but —"

"We are not going, Margaret. I refuse to set foot in the fellow's house."

From this Henrietta gathered an invitation had been issued and this time she threw an anguished look at her sister, who rose at once to the occasion.

"What is this, Papa? Do you mean to say we have been invited to Whisley Park?"

He snorted again. "To a soirée, if you please. No doubt we should consider ourselves honoured." Papa flicked a glance at Henrietta. "You need not be in a quake, Hetty, my dear. I am well aware you must be embarrassed to encounter that young man."

Indeed she would, but not for the reason Papa supposed. She tried to think of a response and failed, but Mama intervened before she could speak, maintaining all her usual calm as she set down her cup.

"Hetty's embarrassment notwithstanding, my dear, I believe a refusal to attend must do more harm than good."

"How so? Have I acknowledged the fellow's presence in church? We have not even spoken to the duchess since her arrival."

"Which is remiss of us, Henry, as well you know. It is not as if we are not acquainted with her, and I have been thinking that we ought to call. Or I should at least. But this —"

"Margaret! I will not have you subjected to that fellow's rudeness."

"I very much doubt the duke would find occasion to be rude, especially when he must play host. I cannot suppose his manners to be uniformly bad."

Except that they were. Henrietta began to seethe all over again. He *was* uniformly rude. He cared nothing for what anyone said of him, and he did just as he wished upon every occasion. Why Mama should imagine he might be different merely because he was the host — if he could be persuaded to act the part in the first place.

The seethe dropped out, to be replaced with an unseemly desire to giggle at the thought of Theo's likely conduct in such an assembly. He would stare people out, make inappropriate comments and in general make himself objectionable to the entire company.

"…as I am sure you will agree."

Lost in her thoughts, she had missed what Mama was saying, hearing only her soothing and persuasive tones. A heavy sigh from the end of the table brought her gaze around to Papa. Silvestre was eyeing him with a look of expectancy, though she had wisely refrained from re-entering the lists. When Papa was in this mood, it was always best to leave Mama to handle him.

"While I appreciate your sentiments, Margaret, I still feel reluctant to yield. You really think this invitation may be an olive branch?"

"I do, my dear. It cannot be but that these rumours of our recalcitrance to call have reached the duchess's ears."

"She therefore extends this invitation? I tell you, my dear, I don't wish to go."

At which point, Mrs Latimer played her ace, pointing out that his daughters must be most affected by his refusal to attend. Henrietta endured Papa's searching look with difficulty, abruptly realising that if Mama won her point, she would be obliged to look Theo in the face again. Her spirits plummeted and her heart rate went awry, pattering in her breast.

"You say nothing, my child." Papa's gaze held on Henrietta's face. "Do you feel you can bear to meet the duke? I am aware the contretemps between us must have rendered your acquaintance with him an unpleasant memory."

More unpleasant than Papa would ever know. But not from that day. Besides, there had been moments so uplifting they made the last one hideous.

"I am content to do as you desire, Papa," she managed, knowing full well this merely allowed her to abrogate any responsibility in the decision.

"Well, I agree with Mama," Silvestre said unexpectedly. Henrietta's gaze flew to her sister's face, but her twin was looking at Papa. "We ought not to appear aloof in this way. You have not been present when our neighbours have twitted us, Papa. It has not been pleasant. I have said nothing, for I have no wish to raise spectres for you, but I believe this is a valuable opportunity to set matters to rights." Her glance flicked to Henrietta in a swiftly reassuring look. "To refuse must be taken by the duchess for a studied insult."

Papa looked taken aback. "As bad as that?"

"Exactly so, Silve." Mama's eyes twinkled through the spectacles. "Let us bury the hatchet, my dear Henry. After all, whatever your quarrel with the young duke, the duchess is always gracious. Angelica is friendly with her, you know, and she speaks well of her. It is unjust to be including her in your dismissal of the boy."

Another sigh came and Papa threw up his hands. "I am outnumbered. Very well, we will accept. But I must beg no one to expect me to do more than nod to that perfectly abominable young whippersnapper."

"No one supposes you will, my dear. Drink up, Hetty my love. There is nothing more efficacious than coffee for soothing the nerves."

Shocked that Mama had noticed her state, Henrietta took immediate refuge in her cup, avoiding her twin's eye. She could not wait for the meal to be over and was thankful for Papa's habit of leaving his correspondence until he had broken his fast.

She took no part in the animated discussion between Silvestre and Mama as to which gowns would be suitable to wear to the event, her mind fixed upon the dread moment of meeting Theo's gaze. She could think of nothing else through the intervening days and deprecated the continuing dull weather that prevented her from sallying forth in search of wildflowers, which would at least have provided a diversion.

Except that, with fate against her in the way it seemed to be, she was almost bound to run into Theo. Had it been anyone else in the world on horseback that day, she need never have been spit upon the end of his sword. *It was an ill day you crossed my path, Hetty Latimer.*

The words were burned on her brain. How in heaven she was supposed to keep her countenance when they met, in his house where she was anything but welcome, she could not imagine.

But he invited you, protested a small voice.

He *invited no one. The duchess invited the family, of course.*

But he must know you will be there.

Poppycock, she returned, borrowing the expression from her twin. She would wager he neither knew nor cared who was on the guest list. Indeed, it was a question whether he would appear at all.

But deep down she knew this relief must be denied her. Even Theo could not be so crass as to absent himself when his name had been on the invitation. Or had it? A burning desire to see the sheet of paper Papa had been holding that morning overcame her for a space. But it was no use. Papa had in all likelihood thrown it on the fire. In any event, she could not draw attention to her state of mind by asking to see it. She toyed with the notion of sneaking into the library to see if she could find it in Papa's desk, but the consequences should she be caught deterred her. Papa would be severe upon her for her sneaking deception and all would end in a horrid upset again.

By the time the day came, Henrietta's nerves were so shredded she was obliged to beg her twin's help to dress in the India muslin robe with silver-spotted trim around the neck which she failed to arrange on her own.

Silvestre, herself attired also in a muslin robe but crossed in front with scalloped edges, eyed her with affectionate derision. "I see what it is, Hetty. You are embarrassed by that cat episode. He won't laugh at you in company, silly."

"I'm not afraid of him laughing." Far other, if she was honest.

"Stop fidgeting while I pin this curl up or it will fall."

Henrietta managed to sit still as her twin deftly stuck pins in her hair, but she dared not meet her gaze in the mirror.

"If you're not afraid of him laughing at you, what are you afraid of? It's of no use to protest you are not in a quake, so don't try."

Henrietta drew in a taut breath and let it out again, pressing her fingers on the dressing commode to still their trembling. "It's just … I don't think he will be expecting to see me."

"Poppycock, why wouldn't he? He must know you are coming. Mama wrote to accept the invitation days ago."

Yes, she knew that. Knew also that Mama had done it because she suspected Papa would prevaricate until it was too late, since he did not wish to go. She could readily have cried off herself. Especially because she was sure Theo would not be expecting her.

"I should doubt if the duke knows who is coming. He won't care either."

"Don't be silly, Hetty. He can't be as dismissive as all that."

"You don't know him."

"No, and the more I hear of him, the less I wish to know," retorted her twin.

This remark, rather to Henrietta's surprise, shot her into a spirited defence. She turned on the stool to confront her twin. "That is utterly unfair, Silve. Theo is not a bad person. It's just his way. He hates being coerced and he wasn't expecting to be obliged to take up this inheritance. He finds it irksome and it makes him irritable, that's all. At least … he can be odiously teasing and he never curbs his tongue," she amended, recalling some of the duke's infuriating remarks.

Silvestre's brows were well up. "You need not eat me. If you are so well acquainted with him, I don't see why you are in such a pother about meeting him at Whisley Park."

Henrietta did not enlighten her. Fortunately, Mama called for them to hurry, upon which her twin uttered a shriek and sped off to her own room.

Rising from the stool, Henrietta went to the long mirror and looked at her reflection with a critical eye. Her hair was dressed high, with ringlets in front and a curling bob atop. She could not help wondering what Theo's reaction might be to seeing her looking respectable for once, instead of the disorder in which he had found her hanging from the branch of a tree.

She could see again the light grey eyes, so close as he continued to hold her when he'd caught her as she slipped from his horse. Their message had been so clear. But then… *It won't do…*

No, it would not do. She was being utterly ridiculous. Wasting her thoughts on a man who deserved none of them. Silve was right in not wishing to know him. She lifted her chin and straightened her shoulders.

No more cowering, my girl. Face him down with pride.

The stream of guests seemed endless with Flint's announcement followed by Cecilia's gracious introduction.

"Delighted you could come. I believe you have not met my nephew, the Duke of Charlton."

Theo was growing tired of the bobbing and bowing, of having to return the courtesy with an inclination of his head, of having to murmur a greeting. Intolerable to repeat the same words over and over. He amused himself by changing them, throwing in deliberate remarks calculated to break through the barriers of politesse he loathed. "Oh, yes, I saw you in church on Sunday," he said to an elderly codger. "You were snoring."

The fellow's bewhiskered face grew red, but his wife, a formidable dame, gave a crack of laughter. "Correct, Duke. He always falls asleep in the sermon."

Liking her at once, Theo grinned. "And who shall blame you, sir?"

But the old fellow harrumphed and passed swiftly along with his helpmeet, leaving Theo to reflect that at least one person in this ghastly assembly was disposed in his favour. He had received, as well as curiosity, so many indications of offense having been taken that he was obliged to realise his reluctance to run the gamut had been taken in bad part.

"So pleased to meet you at last, Duke." A remark that made its appearance several times.

"Likewise, ma'am," he returned to each.

"We had not hoped for this honour so soon," was said with an ironic inflection by one matron.

He responded to this impertinence coolly. "I have been positively agog with anticipation, ma'am."

The matron looked taken aback. Did she think him serious? She was obliged to move on before he could follow it up. But he earned a hissed reprimand from his aunt the moment there was a lull.

"Try for a little conduct, Theo. You are embarrassing me."

He balked. "For God's sake, Cecilia, I'm here, aren't I? What more do you want?"

She was unable to answer, another announcement producing the next guests. But she gave him a minatory look before turning her shoulder.

Theo's conscience awakened, but he forced it back. He was in no mood to placate Cecilia. Not after she had taken him to task for having the Latimers put on the guest list without her sanction. He had gone into the attack at once.

"Why do I need your sanction?"

"Because it's my party," she retorted. "You didn't want to hold one at all."

"No, I didn't, but as long as there's a party going on in my house —"

"It's my house too, Theo. I have not yet been supplanted."

"Granted, but that has nothing to do with the case. I have a right to invite whomever the deuce I choose."

"Very well, but —"

"And while you're taking me at fault," he pursued, riding over her, "why did you leave the Latimers off the list in the first place?"

Cecilia's brows rose. "Because they have not had the courtesy to pay a call on me, of course."

He was brought up short. Then she did not know about the contretemps in the lane with Hetty's father? He hedged. "Well, that's no reason to insult them by leaving them out when you've asked the rest of the world."

Cecilia stared at him with a look of bemusement. "But why do you care? What are the Latimers to you?"

"Nothing at all. But they ought to be something to you. After all, isn't Mrs Latimer a bosom bow of your friend Angelica?"

Astonishment superseded the puzzlement. "How in the world do you know that?"

Cursing his blunder, Theo sought for an excuse and found none. "Never mind how I know it. I've had Hathersage send them an invitation and that's that. And I'll thank Swarland not to go running to you and telling tales."

With which, he had left her flat, knowing Cecilia would be diverted by this slur upon her steward. Nor was he mistaken. She made a point of giving Swarland her instructions for the conduct of the soirée in Theo's presence at the breakfast table, speaking with more warmth towards the fellow than she usually expressed.

"Such a comfort, Swarland, to have your hand upon the reins. I know you will see that everything is done to my satisfaction."

She threw a meaningful glance at Theo as she spoke, which he ignored. He was still at outs with his aunt when the day came, but the thought of seeing Hetty and what he could say to her, should he get an opportunity to speak to her at all, had driven all else from his mind.

Rather to his surprise the Latimers had accepted the invitation, as he'd seen on the final list presented to him by Hathersage. But they had not yet made an appearance, although the upper saloons were already teeming. He stood with Cecilia just inside the Yellow Saloon where she customarily entertained, with Flint stationed at the entrance, awaiting those climbing the stairs.

The line had thinned and he could see none waiting in the gallery when he turned his head. Were they not coming after all?

"I think we might with propriety abandon our position, Theo."

What about the Latimers? It was on the tip of his tongue, but he held it back. "You mean we've got to mingle now?"

His aunt eyed him with a hint of exasperation. "If you behave as you ought, you will take a little time with each of your guests but show none the preference." She gave a little sigh. "Not that I have the least expectation you will do as I desire you to do."

"Good. Then I may do as I choose."

Her tone changed. "Theo, pray … be kind for once, will you?"

His conscience pricked, but he threw up his eyes. "I'll try, Cecilia."

She smiled and seemed about to speak when Flint's sonorous voice cut in.

"Mr and Mrs Latimer, Miss Latimer and Miss Henrietta Latimer."

Despite himself a slight tattoo attacked Theo's chest as he spied the fellow Latimer. He had seen him but once more in church since the fatal day, but his original impression of the man lingered. He'd thought him a blustering martinet, yet although he looked a trifle pained, his features were pleasant and his eyes as open and expressive as his daughter's. Within them Theo read the rapid changes of his thoughts and realised, belatedly, that the embarrassment was mutual.

Latimer merely bowed in response to Cecilia's spurious welcome and indicated his wife as he moved on to Theo. Their eyes met. Latimer inclined his head. "My lord duke."

"Mr Latimer," Theo said, following suit.

Latimer gave him a grave look and moved on. Theo was confronted with Hetty's mother, who smiled at him and popped a pair of spectacles on her nose, through which she inspected his features as she spoke.

"How do you do, Duke? It must be strange to be meeting so many new people all at once."

The unexpectedness of the remark made him laugh. "It is, ma'am, but I am growing accustomed."

To his further astonishment, she gestured towards the two girls behind. "I believe you are acquainted with one of my daughters, but I'm afraid I must plague you with another introduction. This is Silvestre, the elder of the twins."

She moved aside and Theo found himself looking into a face which was not quite a mirror of Hetty's. This girl was taller and her features were more sharply delineated than Hetty's softer countenance. He was acutely aware of Hetty still standing talking to Cecilia and wished he had leisure to hear what was being said. But his attention held on the sister — Silve, was it? — whose smile seemed a trifle forced.

"We are not wholly alike, your grace."

Had she divined his thought? She spoke boldly and with a degree of coolness. How much did she know? He matched it.

"So I perceive, Miss Latimer." A glance told him the parents had moved out of earshot and he lowered his voice. "It is not your habit to climb trees after stray cats, then?"

Surprise was swiftly followed by an amused look, but the tone was minatory. "My sister has a tender heart, sir. I consider it a worthy attribute."

She nodded in a curt way and moved on, leaving him to face Hetty at last. He had half expected her to avoid his gaze, but she lifted her chin at him, looking positively defiant, her eyes a challenge.

"Good evening, my lord duke."

Theo's tongue, which had been obedient throughout the ordeal of greeting guests, betrayed him at this crucial instant. Though thoughts crowded his mind, he remained dumb, unable to utter a single one of them for the presence of his aunt. He could feel Cecilia's impatience and the moment appeared to him to extend into hours as he met Hetty's bold gaze, and his insides churned at the memory of their last meeting.

At last the words his aunt had been using surfaced in his mind and he stole them, merely for the sake of saying something. "Delighted you could come."

A trace of colour seeped into her cheek and a flash of something in her eyes pierced him. Then she was moving on, joining her sister, and Cecilia's voice was jarring in his ear.

"Thank heavens! Flint says there are no more waiting. Any stragglers must find us within. Come, Theo, it is time to circulate."

He was still staring after Hetty and the rest of the Latimers, who were heading for the adjoining saloon.

"Theo!"

He jerked back, staring at her. "What is it, Cecilia?"

"I declare, I don't know what has come over you. Is it those Latimers? I wish you will pay attention, my dear."

An urgent impulse to go after Hetty was swamping his ability to think, but he forged a spurious excuse. "Those twins distracted me. They are very alike."

"Are they? I did not notice. I was too anxious to be making the rounds. Now, Theo, will you promise to do your duty?"

"Go round the blasted room and speak to everyone, you mean? Good God, must I?"

She set a hand on his arm, her tone beseeching. "It is expected, Theo. Oliver always took the trouble to include everyone. You won't wish to tarnish his memory."

He was nettled. "That is below the belt, Cecilia."

She did not appear chastened. "But will you behave?"

What else was there to do? Common sense dictated he could not pursue his one desire in this assembly. Besides, the last thing he wanted was to subject Hetty to gossip by singling her out. That would be crueller than the last sin he'd committed.

"I'll do my best. I won't promise to be uniformly polite because I know I'm unlikely to keep it."

She sighed. "Well, try, Theo. I suppose I ought to be glad you are honest."

That drew a laugh from him. "But you're not glad at all. I can't spout platitudes, Cecilia, even for you."

"You're going to end with the horridest reputation, you know."

He shrugged. "They'll have to take me as they find me. I really don't much care what they think of me."

Except he did care very much what Hetty thought of him. At least, he cared for having hurt her and he wanted to erase it. But he was unlikely to find an opportunity tonight.

CHAPTER NINE

Relieved she had managed to keep her countenance, Henrietta yet found her heart pattering in her breast and the world around her misty and seemingly unreal. She smiled and nodded at faces as her twin urged her on in the wake of their parents, but in her mind's eye she saw only the expression in Theo's clear grey eyes.

What was he thinking? He had not spoken for an age, merely staring at her in the oddest way. She was not sure what he had said in the end, so focused had she been on holding her head high and facing him down, despite the tattoo in her breast.

"Come now, Hetty, the worst is over. You need not address him again."

Silvestre's whisper did little to cheer her, though it pulled her out of the peculiar distrait feeling, bringing the world back into focus. They were still moving purposefully through the crowd.

"Where is Papa taking us?"

"As far away from the whippersnapper as possible, I should think."

Henrietta's pulse was growing steadier but her heart sank. Papa meant to avoid Theo. And it was certain he would not seek her out while she was thus guarded. An instant wish to escape attacked her, coupled with the contrary notion that she was safe from any further unkind remarks as long as she remained with the family. Not that she supposed Theo would say anything untoward. Or would he? It was not as if he cared what anyone thought, was it? Indeed, she must count herself astonished he had been persuaded to stand tamely with the duchess for the purpose of greeting guests.

She became aware of what people were saying in the immediate area.

"A good-looking young man, I thought."

"If only his manners matched his face."

"Oh, I found him polite enough this evening, my dear, did not you?"

"Well, it depends if you concede his sarcasm or not. In any other young man, I should have felt obliged to call him to account for impertinence, saying he has been agog with anticipation or some such thing. When we know perfectly well he has gone out of his way to avoid being introduced." The speaker was a formidable dame who Henrietta recognised as one of the prominent wives in the area. She fanned herself in a bored fashion as she continued. "For my part, I am sorry for Cecilia. He must be a trial to her indeed."

"Did she tell you so?"

"Good heavens, no. The duchess would never commit such a breach of propriety. Besides, she is obliged to put up with her nephew, and I imagine she must be anxious to remain upon good terms with him. He is guardian to her daughters, after all."

Guardian to those two little girls? Gracious! Henrietta remembered how he'd been playing with them in the churchyard and her heart warmed to him all over again. He was not uniformly unkind. This horrid matron clearly had no notion how much affection he had for the daughters. Indeed, he could be very kind — if he liked a person. Stray memories flittered through her head. If only…

But she must not think in those terms. Thankful they were no longer within earshot of the disparaging matron, Henrietta realised Papa had found a resting place at the far edge of the last saloon. He was urging Mama to a seat.

"I will see if I can find a waiter, my dear. I spotted a couple of them walking among the throng with trays."

He went off and Henrietta turned to survey the room as her twin dropped into a chair beside Mama and engaged with her in low-voiced conversation. Within a very few moments it was borne in upon her that she was searching for a glimpse of Theo. Irritated with herself, she lifted her gaze above the crowd and instead found herself staring at a bank of portraits all along one wall. Without thinking, she threaded a way through several knots of chatterers and inspected a large depiction of a family group, dressed in the fashions of an earlier time. A Gainsborough, was it? No use looking for Theo there, then.

The thought swung back at her and she balked, chiding herself. Was she so obsessed that she sought him in portraits the moment she ceased looking for him in life?

Turning her back on the pictures, she made her way to one of the windows. It was still light, although the blaze from the chandeliers dulled the view of well-kept lawns and the extensive woodlands beyond. Instant images leapt in Henrietta's mind and she flinched away. Was there nowhere in this place where she would not be reminded of the duke? Well, of course there was not. It was his house. What else did she expect but to be plagued by intrusive memories?

"Come, Hetty."

"Papa! I did not see you."

"I have procured a glass of lemonade for you, child."

She took the glass in nerveless fingers, feeling all too conscious. What would he say if he knew the trend of her obstinate thoughts?

"Better stay close to Mama, my dear, where you are protected."

Protected from what? Or was it from whom? Did he suppose Theo might pounce on her?

"Yes, Papa."

He moved in the direction of Mama's chair and Henrietta dutifully followed, feeling rebellious and guilty both. If her father knew all! She gave an inward shudder. At best, she would be in disgrace for days. At worst? Her mind shied away from the possibilities. Papa was quite capable of seeking Theo out with a whip in his hand.

Not that there was the least occasion for punishing him when he had rescued Henrietta from a horrid predicament. But Papa would be horrified by the indecorous coupling that ensued, however innocently done.

Only it was not innocent, was it? Theo meant to … what? Kiss her? *It won't do, will it?*

She felt a flush creeping up her cheeks and hastily unfurled her fan, waving it in front of her face as if she was suffering from the heat of the room.

"Drink your lemonade, my love, it will cool you."

Shocked to think Mama had been observing her, Henrietta lifted the glass to her lips and drank deep. Indeed, she was thirsty. Or was it the heat within that made her feel so? She was uncomfortably hot, that was certain. She must escape!

She finished the glass and looked about for a place to set it down. A footman magically appeared with a tray and proffered it.

"Thank you," she said with a smile.

The fellow looked surprised but bowed and began to move away.

On impulse, Henrietta put out a hand. "Stay!"

The man looked back. "Miss?"

Henrietta lowered her voice to a murmur. "Can you direct me to the ladies' retiring room, if you please?"

A discreet look came over the footman's face and he gave an infinitesimal nod. "If you will follow me, miss."

"One moment." She looked quickly to the family and saw, with satisfaction, that her parents had been accosted and were engaged with Mrs Waterbeck. That particular neighbour of theirs would keep them talking for an age. She sidled close to her twin and leaned to whisper. "I've got to use the facilities, Silve."

Her sister eyed her. "I'll come with you, shall I?"

Good heavens, no! "I'll be all right on my own, Silve. I don't need an escort."

She received a narrow look. "You're not off hunting for that Theo of yours, are you?"

"Of course not, don't be ridiculous. I'll be as quick as I can."

With which, she turned and nodded to the footman, who set off in a discreet way, slipping neatly between the knots of guests and picking up empty glasses along the way. Henrietta followed him, trying to look inconspicuous. If accosted, she would say she was trying to find Aunt Angelica. But none questioned her or even took interest beyond a slight nod or inclination of the head.

Recalling their reduced circumstances, Henrietta was forced to the recognition she and her family were of insufficient account in the district to be taken particular notice of. She was glad of it, though she could not help the sneaking question of what the matrons would say should they know of her encounters with Theo.

Aware he must be somewhere in the saloons through which she passed, she took care not to glance about, but kept her gaze on the footman's back. At last she recognised the door through which they had entered and she thankfully slid out into the gallery.

The footman stopped and pointed to the stairway leading on up. "If you turn left at the top, miss, there is a room designated for the ladies immediately past the gallery. The door is on the right."

"Thank you." It was a relief to be away from the oppressive assembly and she blew out an overcharged breath. Henrietta saw the footman hesitating. Did he think she needed more help? She smiled. "What is your name?"

He looked surprised, but a twitch at his lip showed he was near smiling back. "Robert, miss."

"Thank you, Robert."

He did smile then. "You are welcome, miss."

He straightened suddenly and gave a formal bow. Henrietta caught movement in the doorway and glanced across. The elderly butler had loomed up, looking a question. Not wishing to get the footman into trouble, she moved away to the stairs and tripped lightly up, holding on to the banister rail. The designated door was easily found. She was about to enter when a stifled sound caught her attention.

Henrietta looked about. At first she could see no one. Releasing the door handle, she took a step or two towards the stairs, looking up and down the passage. Nothing. Yet an eerie sensation of being watched remained. Should she call out? Or was she being fanciful?

She tried a hushed question. "Is someone there?"

An unmistakeable gasp came from above and she looked up. The stairway continued and her glance caught on a little face peeping through the banisters in the curve. She could only just see it in the gloom up there, in contrast with the well-lit passage.

"Goodness, who is this?"

A giggle came, hastily choked off. Then a whisper. "I'm Ellie."

Lady Ella Devenal? She recalled Aunt Angelica mentioning the name, but the memory of the churchyard came into her head. This was one of Theo's wards.

Without thinking, Henrietta sneaked up the stairs towards her. The little girl rose, but she did not run away, regarding the intruder with a look of wary mischief.

"You won't tell on me, will you?"

Henrietta gave a soft laugh. "What, that you are up? I am very sure you ought to be in your bed."

Ellie, who was dressed only in a nightgown, giggled again. "I know, but I was watching the people. Then I saw you and had to run up and hide." She regarded Henrietta with interest. "You're the lady who was cross with Theo."

Thoroughly taken aback, Henrietta felt warmth rising to her face. She hardly knew how to answer and chose evasion. "You are fond of Theo, aren't you?"

She nodded with fervour. "He's my best beau."

"Oh, have you many beaux?"

"Silly! I'm only five."

She was evidently a confident child. Intrigued and forgetful of her gown, Henrietta sat on the top stair, inviting the girl to join her with a gesture. Nothing loath, Ellie plonked down beside her, leaning against the banisters and watching her face.

"Why were you cross with Theo?"

"I can't tell you that," said Henrietta, matching boldness with boldness. "Is the baby your little sister?"

"Pru is. But she's asleep. I couldn't sleep. It's too exciting. There hasn't been a party for ages and I'm not allowed to come. I like to see the ladies' dresses. When I grow up I'm going to be a belle."

Amused, Henrietta smiled at the child. "Is that your ambition?"

"No, because I can't dance, but Mama says I will be because my papa was a duke and Theo is too."

"I dare say your mama is right. But I am sure you would be a belle even if you weren't a duke's daughter. You are very pretty."

Ellie made a face. "I don't want to be pretty. I want to be fierce and fight duels and have adventures. But they won't let me."

Trying not to laugh, Henrietta made a sympathetic noise. "It is too bad, is it not? That is the difficulty with being a female, you know. One cannot have adventures."

"But it's not just females. I know, 'cos Theo isn't allowed either. He has to be a duke instead. He's very cross about it. He can't go off to China anymore."

Startled, Henrietta blinked at her. "China! He wanted to go to China?"

Ellie nodded, adding as if it was the most natural thing in the world, "He was going to see the Emperor and the tea. Yes, and he said he would run all the way along the Great Wall and sit on an elephant and look in the face of a tiger."

Caught between amusement and fascination, Henrietta, dredging up her scanty knowledge of geography, could not but wonder if Lady Ella had got muddled. Or perhaps Theo had teased her with nonsensical stories. "I had not heard of elephants and tigers in China."

"The tigers are in India. And the elephants too. Papa has prints from India and Theo keeps them in his library 'cos he says they remind him of his adventure." She added on a note of pride, "He shows them to me because I like adventures too."

"Have you had many adventures?"

Ellie's face lit. "Yes, because we live in a real castle with turrets and everything."

"Good gracious, do you really?"

The little girl frowned and amended this. "Well, we don't ackcherly live in that bit. There's a proper house too 'cos the castle is old and crumbly and Mama doesn't like me to go in it, but Theo isn't stuffy like the rest and he lets me 'long as I have Bunny with me."

"Who is Bunny?"

"My special groom. He teaches me riding and everything and he's my bestest friend after Theo."

At which point, the voice Henrietta dreaded cut in from below.

"I might have guessed! What, may I ask, are you doing out of bed, monkey face?"

Henrietta's heart bumped as the little girl uttered a squeal, something between fright and delight.

"You won't catch me!"

Before Henrietta could think or act, Ellie was scrambling up the stairs on all fours, just like a monkey. Rather to her surprise, Theo made no attempt to chase her, instead turning his gaze upon Henrietta.

"Did she inveigle you into aiding and abetting her? Graceless child!"

For a horrid moment, she thought he meant her rather than his ward. It would not be the first disparaging remark he had made of her. Pushing up from the stair, she tried for a measure of calm, though her pulse was jumping. "No, indeed. It was I who invited her to sit with me and talk."

With the light behind him, she could not properly see Theo's expression, but his tone was warm. "Like to like, eh? No less than I should expect from you. Cats, children. What else?"

She glanced up to the floor above and saw no sign of Lady Ella. "She must have gone back to bed."

Theo gave a scornful laugh. "Not a hope. She'll be hiding up there and listening to every word we say —" his voice rose in volume "— won't you, Miss Mischief?"

A choked giggle answered him from above and Henrietta had to laugh.

"You'd best come down, Hetty." His voice had dropped to a near murmur and he jerked his head to emphasise it.

Perforce, she lifted her petticoats with one hand and descended, shaking them out as she reached the passage where he was standing, one hand on the baluster rail. Embarrassment crept in and she could not look at him, glancing instead at the door where she had been about to enter before hearing the child. "I came up to … I mean, I was going…" She faded out, fiddling with her petticoats. Heavens! Her tongue was tying itself in knots. Inspiration came. "I hope I have not dirtied my gown sitting up there."

"Turn around."

The command was curt and Henrietta obeyed before she could think what he would be about. She glanced over her shoulder to see him casting an eye down her person. Warmth rose to her cheeks.

"I think it's all right. You can brush it in the retiring room. There's a maid, I expect. She'll help you."

Henrietta turned back, giving him a fleeting look. "Thank you." Needing to escape, she moved to the door and grasped the handle.

"Hetty!" It was softly said, but imperative nevertheless.

She turned, fingers still gripping the door handle. She dared to raise her eyes. The light was on him now and she found Theo looking solemn. "Yes, Duke?"

A spasm crossed his face. "I deserve that, I suppose."

Confused, she eyed him. "What?"

His face softened. "You called me Duke."

"Did I?"

He grimaced. "You didn't even realise it. That makes it worse."

"I don't understand."

"Never mind." He gave a slight sigh. "I saw you come upstairs and followed you. I wanted to apologise, Hetty. I didn't mean to hurt you — that day."

Her stomach fluttered. The sting of the words he'd used then revived and her eyes pricked. No. She would not weep. Pride came to her rescue and she lifted her chin. "You need not regard it, Duke. I assure you it is nothing to me."

His gaze narrowed. "So that's how it's going to be, is it? Where's the Hetty I know? What have you done with her?"

A spark of anger lit in her bosom. "It's not what I have done, Theo."

"I know and I'm sorry."

"It doesn't matter, does it?"

"It matters to me."

"Oh, stop. It won't do, remember? Let it go, Theo, please."

He seemed to hesitate, his expression shifting as he watched her face. Then he fell back. "I had best go and take that little monkey back to bed before her nurse catches her."

Henrietta gave a small smile, but she could not speak for the sudden hollow in her heart.

Theo took a step towards the stair and turned back. "Ellie loves your cat in a tree picture, by the by."

With which, he ran lightly up the stairs, leaving Henrietta in shock. She heard a girlish squeak and Theo's voice.

"Ha-ha, got you! Back to bed with you, Miss Mischief!"

"Oh, Theo, must I?"

"You don't want old Jurby after you brandishing a hairbrush, do you?"

Another shriek and the voices became muted, disappearing down an upstairs corridor.

Henrietta quietly entered the ladies' retiring room, torn between relief and a hot cloud of disappointment.

The family had been joined by Angelica and her husband Hugh by the time Henrietta had squeezed her way back to the saloon where she had left them. Mr Summerhayes greeted her in his usual friendly spirit, obviating any comment on her absence from her parents.

"Ah, young Hetty, there you are. Angie has been telling me your pictures are selling well."

"Only the one so far, sir." Must he remind her? As if it was not bad enough knowing Theo had guessed her to be the creator of the dratted thing.

"Soon be more, I'm sure."

He turned away to address a remark to Papa and Henrietta found herself accosted by Aunt Angelica, who drew her a little apart, lowering her voice. "My dear Hetty, I have not had an opportunity to tell you, but the most extraordinary thing. I have five guineas for you and all at the instigation of the duke."

Henrietta's pulse went into instant disarray. Had Aunt Angelica betrayed her? "The duke? You told him?"

"Heavens, no! As if I would tell anyone! No, indeed. But he came into the room when the duchess and I had just agreed terms and she showed him the picture. Would you believe it?

He became perfectly autocratic and insisted the duchess should pay five guineas instead of the two we had agreed. Indeed, he spoke of ten at one point."

Stunned, dismayed and secretly gratified, Henrietta stared at her. He had guessed. No one had told him. He had taken one look at the picture and known at once. Of course he had. What else could one expect? Yet his thought for her circumstances could not but touch her deeply, though her embarrassment increased.

"Was it not kind of him, Hetty?"

Kind? Theo, kind? He could be. Sometimes.

"Yes. I mean, how very odd. I had not thought he would ever see it."

"Nor I, for the duchess meant it for her daughter. Cecilia says Lady Ella was delighted with it."

"Yes, I —" Biting off 'know' just in time, Henrietta made a rapid amendment in her mind, seizing something at random. "I expect she — any child … must like cats."

She came under the beam of Aunt Angelica's intelligent gaze. "Dear me, Hetty. Is it distressing you to be here? I thought you were over the embarrassment of that little contretemps."

She seized on the excuse. "Yes, but it was awkward meeting the duke again. Especially as I know Papa did not wish to come."

"But it has broken the ice. Your mama did right to insist upon it. I dare say you will all be included in any further invitations. Cecilia was talking of a picnic. They have very pretty woods in Whisley Park."

Heavens, no! In Theo's woods? She could not endure it. "Silve and I don't expect to move in these exalted circles, Aunt Angelica."

"Nonsense, my dear. We cannot have the two of you becoming hermits. You must be seen if you are to catch a suitor. There are a couple of options, never fear."

The thought of any suitor was repulsive. She was relieved Mrs Summerhayes turned away on the words to greet a passing acquaintance. She soon flitted off, leaving her fateful pronouncements behind to plague Henrietta.

At least she was no longer puzzled as to how Theo had come to know about the picture. He had raised the price too. For her sake. He must also know of the fall in the Latimer fortunes, then. And how unworthy that made her to be associating with the Duke of Charlton.

She had reminded him it would not do. Theo had not argued. Of course not. He was the one who said it in the first place. But he had apologised. For hurting her, he said. Yet he had not withdrawn the words. They stood. It was an ill day he met her because it would not do.

Light dawned in both mind and heart. Theo liked her. He was fighting an attraction. She had guessed he wanted to kiss her. Only she had not supposed it was any more than a passing fancy, brought on by the unaccustomed closeness of their bodies. Yet he followed her upstairs, only for the purpose of apologising. And he had raised the price of her picture the moment he guessed she'd made it.

Was she making something out of nothing? Did these things show more than simple kindness? For he was kind, more than Aunt Angelica realised. Witness the way he behaved towards the girl Ellie. Also, though he couched it in rude terms, he had come to her rescue. He need not have done. Especially after the way Papa had behaved towards him.

Her ruminations had taken her to the window. It was growing dark outside and the reflections in the glass of the room behind showed the shifting groups, a familiar figure moving from one to the next. Henrietta turned, the beat of her pulse increasing again.

There he was, dutifully exchanging a word here, a smile there as he passed through the guests. Making himself agreeable? Oh, heavens, he was moving closer to the coterie that included her parents. Where was Silve? She caught sight of her sister some distance away, laughing as she chatted with a young married female they both knew. She at least had escaped Theo's polite round. Would he actively seek another encounter with Papa? She could not credit it, although he was certainly including everyone as far as she could see.

Panic began to overtake her. If she remained by the window, Theo would not approach her and she need not speak to him. He would not single her out in public.

He was turning, his gaze travelling across the group where Henrietta could see Papa's eyes firmly on Hugh Summerhayes' face. Was it deliberate? He meant to discourage Theo. Dismay and rebellion rose up. Without thinking, Henrietta walked out of the shadow of the window and joined her parents, casting a glance at Theo. He caught it. A faint twitch attacked his lip. Then his eyes left hers and he moved across.

The group fell silent, even Papa perforce turning to look at the whippersnapper.

Theo gave a smile that failed to reach his eyes. "I trust our people have served you?"

To Henrietta's unalloyed relief, Mr Summerhayes took this.

"Very well indeed, Duke. Most assiduously. A very pleasant evening."

Theo bowed in a fashion as formal as it was cold. "Our house is honoured by your presence, sir. Enjoy the remainder of the evening."

He included the rest in an inclination of his head, but did not again look towards Henrietta. Then he was gone, moving swiftly along to the next group.

"Well! At least he has remembered his manners."

Papa's mutter elicited a shushing whisper from Mama, and burning resentment in Henrietta's bosom, but Mr Summerhayes saved the day.

"An unusual young man, but sound, I believe. Oliver Devenal spoke well of him, I remember." He lowered his voice. "Said his nephew was a poor hand at social chitchat, but he could not fault him for integrity. Trusted the boy implicitly to do his duty, if it came to it. As we see it did in the end. Though Oliver hoped to the last his young wife would give him an heir in the direct line. Not to be, but there it is."

Papa had nothing to say to this, his mouth turned down in disapproving lines, but Mama, to Henrietta's relief, took it up.

"Well, it must be hard for a young man to be thrust into a position of prominence. I cannot think it a sinecure. I dare say he would prefer to be doing something quite other."

Of course he would. China and India. But Henrietta refrained from bursting out as she wished to. It was plain Papa could not see beyond that fatal day. She could only be relieved nothing of her further encounters with Theo had reached his ears.

"May we not with propriety depart, Margaret? We have been honoured now."

"My dear, the duchess has not yet been by. It would be a solecism to leave before she has spoken to us."

Papa's low groan reached Henrietta's ears, but Hugh Summerhayes gave a bark of laughter.

"You'll be lucky to get out before midnight, Henry. By Angie's account, the duchess is exceptionally talkative. She can make a dozen of her nephew's effort in a minute."

"God help me, then!"

Mr Summerhayes took his arm, his tone soothing. "Let us go and hunt down a glass, my friend, and leave the ladies to manage the duchess."

Mama beamed through her spectacles. "An excellent notion, my dear Hugh. I will gather Silvestre and we will see if we can find Angelica. She may perhaps shorten poor Henry's purgatory by pushing us in. Then we need not wait for the duchess to come to us."

Henrietta did not know about Papa's purgatory, but her own was acute. She could not help catching sight of Theo, still doing the rounds, as she followed in the wake of Mama and Aunt Angelica. Her arm was taken by her twin as she joined them.

"How have you fared, Hetty? Has it been horrid?"

How was she to answer that? Horrid? No. The opposite, if anything. She hugged the little interlude with Lady Ella to herself, cherishing the details that gave her knowledge of Theo. Even the brief moments with him up there in the passage were not to be regretted. "Not too bad, Silve. I am managing. It is Papa who is still finding it difficult."

Her sister gave her a narrow look, but she appeared to accept this, glancing ahead to where the duchess could be seen in discussion with one of the older dames of the county. "For my part, I am enjoying it excessively. I had not thought I would, but I have been secretly studying how everyone toadies to rank and it has given me an idea for another story."

Diverted from her own troubles, Henrietta regarded her twin with foreboding. "Silve, you are not going to delineate people we know, are you?"

Mischief twinkled in Silvestre's eyes. "Shocking, is it not? Oh, don't fret. They will be suitably disguised."

There was time for no more as Aunt Angelica caught the duchess's eye. "Mrs Summerhayes! I was wondering where you had got to. I have just been telling Lady Alvingham here about the dried flower picture."

As the elderly dame raised a lorgnette to her eyes and peered through it, Henrietta shrank a little behind her twin, fearful of being pointed out.

"Such an interesting idea, to be making a scene of it. Most of these things are perfectly dull and one is expected to admire them."

"That is just what I thought," declared the duchess. "I have sent for the picture to be brought down, Mrs Summerhayes."

Barely had this horror registered, than another hit Henrietta as Lady Alvingham cut in. "Yes, I should like very much to see it. An entertaining subject. I am thinking of my granddaughter."

The duchess waved her fan at Aunt Angelica. "Do you suppose your artist friend might consent to make something similar for Lady Alvingham?"

The 'No!' was screaming in Henrietta's head, but Aunt Angelica answered without hesitation. "I am very sure she would be delighted."

"But not a copy, if you please. My little Ellie's cat in the tree must be unique. Can she think of something else? Similar, perhaps?"

"Oh, of course it must be different. My granddaughter will like to think she has the only one of a kind."

Oh, no, pray. How was she supposed to create something similar that was yet unique? Despair gripped her as the discussion shifted to include others, clamouring to follow the duchess's lead. Henrietta glanced at Mama, who was looking decidedly pleased and gave her an infinitesimal nod of approval as she caught her eye. Then Aunt Angelica had told Mama?

Silvestre's amused whisper came in her ear. "You will be kept busy for weeks, Hetty. Where the duchess leads, the whole world follows."

"What am I going to do, Silve? I can't possibly make —"

"Hush, or they will hear you."

"But how am I to —?"

"We will talk of it later. Here is a footman with the article in question."

Her stomach was fluttering with nerves as Henrietta caught sight of the same fellow who had directed her earlier — Robert, was it? — threading through the throng, carrying the familiar frame. And attracting a good deal of interest. Oh, horrors!

Instinct sent her glance shooting around the room in search of Theo. She could not see him and, half desperate, she gave place as people craned and crowded to see the wretched picture now held up in the duchess's hands.

Aware she ought to be gratified, flattered and pleased by the oohs and aahs and comments coming on all sides, she could only feel utterly dismayed and panicked. Worse was to come.

"Aunt Angelica is taking orders, Hetty. Everyone wants a clever picture to gift to a favourite little girl."

"Oh, Silve, what in the world shall I do?"

"Do? You'll make pictures, of course. Lots of them. It will mean another excursion to pick flowers, I should think. If not several. You'd best ask this Theo of yours for permission to go into his woods whenever you like."

The teasing note was pronounced, but Hetty saw nothing funny in the notion. Although, if she could conjure Theo at this instant, she would do it in a heartbeat. He could put a stop to this, couldn't he? Though why she was being so ridiculous she did not know. She truly ought to be glad. She was uncommonly fortunate, if there really were going to be commissions.

"I suppose it is what we wanted from The Plan, Silve."

"More than I ever expected, I must say. You will be able to help Papa in no time, and then perhaps he will forgive your Theo and all will be rosy and light."

Aware that her twin was merely joking, Henrietta yet allowed the thought to roam her mind. She looked to where Aunt Angelica, in the middle of a vociferous group, had taken to writing names in a little notebook unearthed from her reticule.

Feeling quite overwhelmed, she slid quietly away from the commotion. Thank heavens no one knew her for the unknown artist. She felt besieged enough as it was.

"Miss Latimer!"

Theo! His voice was muted. She looked round and found him standing in the shadows by a wide window. He appeared to be temporarily alone, although a couple of knots of people either side were clearly aware of him. She saw two ladies glance from him to her and back.

He beckoned and the rhythm of Henrietta's pulse went awry. He was going to speak to her in public? He must be mad!

But she could not be seen to refuse the duke, could she? Lowering her gaze, she glided towards him, only too conscious of following eyes. She kept her distance and dropped a curtsy. "Duke?"

He raised his voice to be heard by those within earshot. "I have just met your father and I believe he is searching for you. May I lead you to him?"

Good heavens! This must be nonsense. But she tried for a neutral tone. "How very kind, Duke, thank you."

He held out his arm and she put the tips of her fingers on it, allowing him to lead her away from prying eyes and through to the far saloon where the crowd had thinned to leave only one elderly gentleman nodding in a chair and a couple of gossiping females who had eyes and ears for nothing but their animated cose. There was no sign of Papa.

Henrietta broke out in a scandalised whisper. "What did you do that for?"

"I could think of no better excuse," he returned in the same manner. "We can't be more than a moment or two."

She eyed him, utterly unable to think what he would be at. "What do you want with me?"

It came out gruffer than she intended and he winced, his jaw tightening. "I was merely concerned that my aunt may be putting you to an impossible inconvenience. Do you want to make all these infernal pictures?"

His thought for her was disarming. "It is a little frightening, but I must if I can."

His frowning gaze raked her face. "Is it the money?"

Warmth flooded her face. "You know about Papa's situation?"

He shrugged. "I've been told, yes. How bad is it?"

"Not — not as bad as all that."

The frown intensified. "Come, Hetty, this is me. Don't fib!"

Indignation leapt in her bosom. "But it's got nothing to do with you, Theo — I mean, Duke." Shocking herself by using his name she looked quickly round, afraid she might have been overheard.

"Don't panic. No one is listening." He looked almost fierce, in that way he had on the first day they met, when he had dried her cheeks and complained of her weeping at the same time. "I'm worried about you, Hetty. I don't like to think of you slaving over these damned pictures just to make a few measly guineas."

Stung, she hit back. "They are not measly to me. I'm not like you, Theo, able to think of trekking off to China at a moment's notice."

His head snapped back. "How the deuce did you find that out?" Then his face changed. "Ellie! Wretched child. You can't tell her anything. She brings it out at just the wrong moment."

"She's only a child. What do you expect? Besides, she thinks it's exciting and she wants to have adventures."

"Don't I know it. Drives me batty, the little imp." He seemed to catch himself up, glancing swiftly across to the other saloon. "But this isn't getting us anywhere. Do you want me to stop this business of the pictures or not?"

She blinked at him. "Can you?"

"Of course I can. Cecilia is a tricky customer, but she'll do what I want if I insist. She wasn't going to invite your family merely because you hadn't called on her, mean piece as she can be, but I gainsaid her and put you all on the list."

Shock, hurt and bewilderment chased one another through Henrietta's breast. But one issue superseded everything else. "You did this?"

"Of course. I wasn't going to have you insulted. Or your father, though he clearly can't stand the sight of me."

She felt both faint and embarrassed all over again. "I — I don't know what to say."

"Don't waste your breath. Tell me only this. Are you going to do these pictures?"

She could hardly recall what he meant now, she was so bemused. "Yes, I think. I must."

He let out a sigh. "Very well. On your own head be it." He began to move away. Some instinct gripped Henrietta and she touched his arm to halt him. He looked back.

"Thank you!" He nodded, but she was seized with urgency. "May I pick flowers in your woods, if you please?"

A sudden grin lightened the grimness in his face. "If you promise not to climb any trees after stray cats." She gave a giggle and his features softened. "Hetty … sweet Hetty…"

Then he turned and left her, his figure misting in her vision. It was some time before she could compose herself sufficiently to re-join the family.

CHAPTER TEN

The deliberate policy Theo had adopted these last weeks was paying off. He had stayed out of the woods for the most part, confining his excursions to the area near the lake where a certain roaming flower picker was unlikely to venture. He chose a dull day when it looked like rain to take out his gun, but could not bring himself to risk shooting anything, just in case. Today, however, he was obliged to accompany his gamekeeper, who wanted to show him evidence of poachers operating in the Park.

"There's birds gone missing, your grace, and I found a broken net that day I chased off a scrawny lad I caught loitering."

Theo had perforce consented to come and see, though he secretly hoped Beattock would not catch anyone. Especially some boy, likely starving, whose lot could scarcely be improved by a sojourn in the county gaol. He'd seen enough of the effects of poverty during his early tour of the Continent to become both ashamed and glad of his privileged status. More so now. He was irked by the burden of the dukedom, but there was no denying its advantages. Nor its drawbacks, which effectually barred him from following his inclination. Although he was sure he was by now cured of a most foolish *tendre*. By dint of dwelling on the less endearing aspects of Hetty Latimer's character as well as holding aloof, he had succeeded in ousting her from where she had begun to lodge. He could and would remain in control.

It had provided a convenient excuse to evade, for the most part, Cecilia's attempts to draw him into her social circle. She sulked and threatened, but he paid no heed. He had escorted her only to such establishments where, he guessed, the Latimers would make no appearance. Given the father's reduced circumstances, and despising his world, Theo knew the family would not grace the more exclusive engagements. What was more, he had vetoed Cecilia's plans for a picnic on the score of the unreliable weather.

To his chagrin, today the sun was not recalcitrant and he could not help scouting between the trees as he followed Beattock. Surely by this time she must have gathered all the flowers she needed. What had possessed him to give her blanket permission to roam his woods? Well, if she did happen to be there, he must avoid her, that was all.

"This way, your grace. There'll be a nest of abandoned chicks just along here, if I'm right."

Theo followed. As well Hetty didn't know anything about abandoned chicks. As sure as check she would be climbing up to get them. And weeping buckets when they died, as of course they would without parents to feed them.

Snatching his thoughts back, Theo cursed himself. What was he about, letting that wretched girl's ridiculous sentimentality roll around in his head? He tuned back in to the gamekeeper's words, hearing only the tail end of whatever he was saying.

"…I've found three already and they're what I particularly wanted you to see, your grace."

Three what? But before he could ask, he caught a flash of colour in his peripheral vision. Theo turned his head. Through the intervening trees he glimpsed snatches of a figure a little distance away, bending and moving. Halting, he grabbed Beattock's shoulder to stay him.

"Hold a moment! Someone's there." Peering, he tried to make it out. Yes, it was female. He could see a pale gown and a straw bonnet. Damnation. "We've got to go another way."

"But, your grace, that's just where —"

"Turn about, man! I can't risk it." Theo started off in another direction, but the gamekeeper did not move.

"Your grace!"

He halted again, impatience riding him. "What the deuce is it?"

"Thing is, your grace, we had ought to warn —"

A loud crack followed instantly by a hideous howl interrupted him. There came the sound of a fall, a whimper like that of a wounded animal. And then nothing.

Frozen for a few seconds, Theo's mind shot into high gear. "What the devil —?" As he began to move towards the disturbance, the gamekeeper's earlier words crept in.

Beattock began to hurry beside him. "It's what I was trying to tell your grace. She were walking near one of them traps."

"Traps?"

"The ones I've just been telling you about, your grace."

Realisation coincided with Theo's first glimpse of the body on the ground. "Oh, my God! *Hetty*!" He was running, crashing through the undergrowth, leaping obstacles, his eyes on the fallen girl, horror in his breast. He barely heard Beattock thundering at his back, calling as he came.

"It's one for rabbits, your grace. She'll have caught her foot in it, if I'm not mistaken."

She was in full sight now and he could just see her face under the bonnet, horribly pale. She was alarmingly still. Had she swooned? God send it was no worse!

The trouble became visible when Theo was yards away. The trap had snapped on her foot, catching the edge of her petticoat which was already red with blood.

"Hetty! Dear God, Hetty!" A horrified murmur as he dropped to his knees beside her still form, his gaze going at once to assess the damage, though his stomach churned in revolt.

"Looks like it's across the ankle, your grace." The gamekeeper was down by the trap, inspecting the caught foot.

"Open the trap, man! We've got to release her!"

"Easier said than done," Beattock grunted, shifting his gaze across the mechanism.

Theo knew panic inside and tried to suppress it. Thank heaven she'd fainted! "Get a stout stick! We must prize it open."

"That's not the way, your grace."

"How, then? There must be a way! Is it some trick?"

The gamekeeper was working at a lever along the edge of the trap. "This ought to do it."

Theo's frantic gaze slid up to Hetty's face as he waited for her to be freed. So pale she was. Likely both pain and shock had done for her.

A loud click sounded and the ghastly teeth of the trap flipped open. A low groan came as Theo lifted the injured foot free.

"Hetty?"

Her eyes fluttered open. She seemed to look round in bewilderment. Then her face contorted and she uttered a cry, lifting her head.

"Keep still, Hetty! I've got to see how badly you're hurt."

Her eyes rolled in his direction, widened and then, with a sigh, closed again as she slumped back.

"She's fainted again. Quick, what's the damage?"

Without hesitation, he lifted the torn and bloodied petticoats to expose the foot and ankle. The wound was only just visible under an oozing jean boot, its leather ripped by the prong which had penetrated through to the flesh beneath.

With care, Theo lifted the leg. "Undo the strings and take off the boot."

The gamekeeper deftly began on the task. "Good thing she was wearing boots, your grace. That thing could've snapped her ankle."

"We don't know yet that it hasn't." The panic was subsiding, to be replaced with urgency and a dreadful hollow — remorse mingling with the sick horror of the accident happening within his sight and he unable to prevent it.

"I know the look of a break, your grace, and this ain't it."

"Are you sure?"

"Certain sure." The strings were undone and he was carefully lifting away the boot. "But it's a nasty wound for all that. Reckon she's got one on the back as well."

Theo's guts were already refusing the sight of the nasty gash, still sluggishly bleeding through the torn stocking. He saw Beattock trying to peer under the leg to see the other side and balked. "Never mind that, man! Get to the house as fast as you can! Bring men with a hurdle of some kind to carry her. And have Flint send for a doctor to come directly."

The gamekeeper was already on his feet. "You'll stay with her, your grace?"

Theo was unwinding the neckcloth from about his throat. "I'll bandage it as best I can. Got to stop the bleeding. Then I'll carry her. But I won't manage it all the way to the house without hurting her, I don't think. Hurry, Beattock! Off with you!"

Thus adjured, the gamekeeper hefted his firearm and shot off upon his errand, moving with surprising speed for a man of his years.

Left alone with Hetty, Theo cast another glance at her pallid countenance. Oh, Hetty. Miss Disaster, he'd called her. All too apt today.

A streak of something very like grief attacked him as he set about the task of bandaging the foot and ankle with his neckcloth. He hoped she would not wake yet. Good thing the damn things had so much material in them. He was able to cover the injury fully with the cloth opened out and he wound it tightly several times around Hetty's slim ankle and foot. She emitted a groan as he was tucking in the ends and he shifted to lean over her face.

"Hetty? Can you hear me?"

The dizzying world began to slow, and she tried to open her eyes. Flashes of a face. Trees and sky. And then a griping ache.

"It hurts…"

"It will, sweetheart. Here, let me sit you up."

Sweetheart? Someone was lifting her, setting off the pain. She uttered a sharp cry and a hushing voice she knew spoke in her ear.

"Be brave now. I've got you."

Her head swam again as she was tugged upright and she sank into the supporting arms. "Dizzy … feel sick…"

The arms were shifting. A soft clink sounded and something cold was put to her lips.

"Take a sip, Hetty, come. Open your mouth."

Without will to refuse, she did as he asked and a measure of liquid tipped into her mouth. She tried to swallow. Fire enveloped her throat and she choked.

A muttered expletive was followed by a hand slapping her back. Agony flared somewhere in the region of her feet and she whimpered, catching her breath as tears squeezed from her eyes.

"The deuce! Don't weep, Hetty, please."

The arms captured her close. The embrace was comforting, and the voice crooned in a way she would never have thought it could.

"Hush now, hush, my little Miss Disaster… You're going to feel better presently, I promise."

She responded, muttering into his chest without thought of anything but the unaccustomed tenderness in his voice. "Theo … don't let me go… I'll fall."

The embrace loosened a trifle. "You're not up a tree, Hetty. You're on the ground."

A vague notion of panic in his tone caught at her senses. The confusion began to recede and the pain coalesced into a single point. "My foot hurts."

Theo's face, very close, came into focus. Was it relief there? He smiled and one hand pulled at the strings of her bonnet. "I'm sure it must, sweet. Let's get this thing off."

The bonnet came away and Hetty let her head fall back against his supporting arm. She was more conscious of the discomfort in her foot than anything else, but her breath was still catching in spite of her reviving senses. "I d-don't know what h-happened, Theo. Why does my foot hurt so much?"

He was brushing at her cheeks with a finger but his tone became curt. "Poachers. They've set traps, the fiends. You stepped on one and sprung it."

Sprung a trap? She cast her gaze about but could not see anything untoward. She still felt hazy and weak and the effort proved too much. The exigency of her situation penetrated. "I can't stay here."

Theo's voice became brisk. "I've sent Beattock for help. When you're a little recovered, I'm going to carry you."

"Carry me where?"

"To the house. But I expect the men will get to us before we reach it."

Panic superseded the dull ache that was ever present. "You won't leave me, will you?"

The arm about her tightened. "What, walk away and let you get yourself into even more trouble? I wouldn't dare. Sure as check you'd be injuring the other foot in a second."

The tease in his voice warmed her and she let out a weak laugh, grasping at his coat with one hand. "Rude beast, how can you say so? I can't even walk."

A wry grin came. "No, and that means I've got you at my mercy." He frowned, the light grey eyes studying her face. "You're still devilish pale. Where's that flask?"

Hetty watched in gathering dismay as he found a silver flask he had set aside and flipped open the lid. "No, I don't want any."

Theo brought it to her lips. "I don't care what you want. You'll take another sip. I told you you're at my mercy."

Henrietta tried to push it away. "How can you be so horrid? It's vile stuff!"

"It's medicinal brandy, and you know very well I'm a brute who won't take no for an answer. Now do as I tell you."

The cold edge of the flask was once more at her lips. The fight went out of Henrietta and she sipped. Heat scoured her mouth and she held it there for a second before swallowing it down.

"Good girl! Better?"

"No!" In fact her head was clearing and she was better able to berate him. "It's as vile as you and I have a good mind to spit it in your face!"

Theo's features broke apart in a grin. "You sound more like yourself every second, Hetty. But if you want to spit it at me, you'll have to take another sip."

He proffered the flask again but Henrietta put her hand over his to hold it back. "Please no, Theo. I do feel a bit better. Don't make me have any more."

"Well, all right, but if you feel faint again, tell me."

Henrietta immediately resolved to say nothing if she did. She watched him fit the top back on and slide the flask into a pocket.

"How's the foot?"

To Henrietta's relief, the pain had subsided. "It's not hurting so much."

Theo looked grim. "Well, brace yourself. We've got to move and it's bound to revive it when you shift the foot."

Apprehension claimed her. "Must we move? Can't we wait for a bit?"

"The sooner we get you to safety, the sooner it'll be seen to. I'm sure the doctor will be able to make you a degree more comfortable."

The thought of losing this precious intimacy was anathema, but remembrance was creeping back. It could not last. She would soon be back at Moss House and Theo would be lost to her again.

He was shifting his position, pulling away from her though he kept an arm about her. Her thoughts faded as even this small change of position jogged her foot and the pain increased. She bit her lip, watching Theo fold his limbs into a squat.

"Ready, Hetty?"

She nodded. He slid his other arm under her knees. Her foot changed position abruptly and a sharp jab from the wound made her hiss in a breath.

"I'm going to lift you. Put your arm around my neck."

He sounded curt again. She obeyed, bracing against the coming reminder of her injury as he had earlier instructed. The foot swung as he rose, lifting her with him. For a moment, Henrietta concentrated on not crying out as Theo shifted her body in his hold.

"It's a good thing you're such a little slip of a thing."

Anxiety popped up. "Can you manage? Shouldn't we wait for the men?"

He looked into her face, a wry smile appearing. "But then I'd have to give you up to them, wouldn't I?"

A swell of tenderness attacked her bosom and Henrietta had to fight a prick of tears. He did like her after all. She'd persuaded herself she had imagined it all these weeks.

But her attention returned to her injury as he began to walk, every step sending a jolt through the wound in her foot. She took hold of Theo's coat, kept her eyes on the column of his throat, which was oddly bare, and concentrated on holding back the groans threatening to escape.

A very few minutes of the motion drove the agony to almost unbearable proportions and she bit down on her lip, tears slipping unregarded from her eyes. Her breath began to catch and Theo halted.

"I'm — hurting you."

He sounded remorseful and he was clearly labouring. His words penetrated to the little core where she'd hidden the other kind of hurt, and the long-buried griefs crept through.

"It is all of a p-piece. It m-must be d-d-destined." She caught her breath on the soft sobs that would escape and found Theo's light eyes on her face, the oddest expression in them.

"You may be right at that, Miss Disaster."

For an instant that seemed to stretch into eternity, every hurt receded and Henrietta's world was an island of two.

Then Theo's face changed and he looked away from her. "They're coming. Can you hear it?"

Sounds, previously vague in the background of her immediate discomforts, became abruptly obvious. Feet thrashing through the undergrowth. Many of them. The threat of loss overcame her and she clutched at Theo's coat, her arm tightening about his neck. His eyes came back to her.

"I'll be with you, Hetty. I gave you my word."

He knew. He understood. Tenderness enveloped her and, obeying instinct, she rested her head against his shoulder. His hold shifted and she could swear he dropped a kiss on her hair.

Then there were voices and men. Motion and change. And Theo's voice was back to command and action, the pain reviving so rapidly that it overtook all else. She was only half aware when he released her, feeling a hard surface beneath her and the added agony as someone changed the position of her foot and her heel came to rest, jabbing at her from behind so that she cried out.

"Careful! Wait, has anyone a kerchief?"

Presently, the foot was lifted and laid down again, coming to rest on a cushioning surface. Henrietta sighed with relief, gazing up at the unknown faces around her.

"Take it gently. She's in a lot of pain."

Gratitude swept through her. Theo would not let them hurt her. She looked for him among the faces and could not find him. Bereft, she murmured his name. "Theo?"

"I'm here."

Her hand was taken in his warm clasp and he was there, walking beside the hurdle as the men began to carry her. The jogging was worse than when she'd been held in Theo's arms and she could not keep in a tiny whimper. The clasp around her hand tightened.

"Not far now. Be brave for a little longer, Miss Latimer."

Miss Latimer? Must she then call him Duke? Her mind hazy with the constant pain, her gaze roved the heads she could see, the trees above and the glimpses of the blue sky. It was still daylight. It felt as if hours had passed. And she was Miss Latimer again. No Hetty. No Miss Disaster. But she had his hand still. He said he would not leave her. He must in the end.

Her vision misted and she fought the urge to weep. She felt weak and silly. Why had she to come out today of all days? Why had Theo to be out also? Only if he had not been, what would she have done? What if no one had found her? What had he said? Something about traps. Oh, yes, she had caught her foot in a trap, had she not? She was growing accustomed to the dull ache, but the sharp jabs every so often with a jog in the pace kept pulling her attention back. A certain rhythm in the motion lulled her, making it hard to think. Her fingers moved in the hand and Theo's reassuring voice came again.

"Nearly there. I can see the house."

A murmur of talk grew up among the men and Henrietta's attention faded as a mist crept over her mind.

Voices jolted her out of her semi-conscious state.

"Straight upstairs, your grace. I've had a room readied."

"The doctor?"

"I sent Robert flying, your grace."

"Excellent… No, no, don't all try going up at once."

The hand holding hers was gone. Bereft, she blinked at a high ceiling that seemed to shift in her vision.

"Careful! Try not to tip her too much."

Theo was still here? Henrietta's head swam again as the hurdle's angle shifted. The background murmurs continued, along with grunts. A shrill voice.

"Good heavens! What in the world is going on? Theo, what happened?"

"Hush, Cecilia, not so loud."

The duchess? Hetty heard Theo's voice continue but could not make out the words. The world was turning and she glimpsed a crowd below. Who in the world were all those people down there? Where was Theo? He said he wouldn't leave her. An urgent need, ancient and natural, overtook her and she cried for it.

"Mama… I want Mama…"

"Damnation, why didn't I think of that?"

Theo. Close. Then she saw him leaning over a bannister rail, calling down.

"Hathersage! Go at once to the Latimers. Take the landau and bring Mrs Latimer back here as soon as you may."

The answer came up from below. "Of course, your grace. How much shall I tell her?"

"The truth. You'll alarm her if you don't. Miss Latimer had an accident in the forest and hurt her foot. We have her safe and the doctor is on his way."

How sensible of Theo. Though Mama would never panic. She would come. Silve too. How she wanted her twin now. Because she knew it all. And Papa would be furious. Poor Theo. It was not his fault.

The thoughts came dimly, dropping in between the now constant awareness of the pain in her foot, dizziness and the resurgence of nausea.

"Don't set it down. I'll lift her off." Then Theo was there again, above her. The grey eyes met hers in a look both reassuring and anxious. "I'm going to put you on the bed, Miss Latimer. You'll be a deal more comfortable in a trice."

She was plucked from the hurdle and safe in his embrace. Treasuring the feel of his arms supporting her, Henrietta kept her eyes on what she could see of his face, wincing against the sharp jolt at her foot. But the bliss was over before she could cherish it as Theo set her down on a soft surface. He pulled his arms free and leaned close, his voice a whisper.

"I have to leave you now, Hetty, but I'll be back."

She groped for his hand and it closed briefly over hers. Aware of people still in the room, she withheld the words hovering on her tongue. "Thank you … Duke."

He winced. "Don't thank me. I could wish the thing undone." Then he straightened and threw a curt command at someone standing near. "Make her as comfortable as you can. But don't touch my bandage. Wait for the doctor to see it."

He went out and Henrietta was left with a bevy of female servants.

CHAPTER ELEVEN

The knot of men, two of them bearing the empty hurdle, was still in the hall when Theo ran down the stairs, calling for his gamekeeper.

"I'm here, your grace."

Cecilia, hovering by the parlour door with her usual entourage, intervened. "Theo, what is going on? I insist upon an explanation."

"In a moment, ma'am." He crossed to the men. All were outdoor servants who worked the stables or grounds. "Beattock, take these fellows and get rid of every one of those cursed traps."

"We'll do that, your grace, but —"

"You should be able to scour the forest among the lot of you. For pity's sake don't let anyone else get injured."

The gamekeeper nodded. "No fear of that, your grace. I'll set up an armed patrol."

Theo balked. "Yes, but don't go shooting at shadows."

"No, your grace." He gestured to one of the men behind. "What d'you want Wilf here to do with them things he's got?"

A youthful lad — one of the gardeners? — was proffering a familiar basket, an edge of straw sticking up within it. "It be the leddy's hat and boot, yer grace. I brung the basket and all, thinking as how it must be hers."

"Well thought of, Wilf. I'll restore them to her." He took the basket, thanked the men, assuring them their trouble would be rewarded presently, and sent them off upon their next errand before turning his attention to his aunt at last. She had retreated into the parlour, leaving Swarland behind. To ensure he attended her?

"Her grace is waiting, your grace."

Theo grunted, but found the elderly butler at his elbow. "Yes, Flint?"

"Refreshment, your grace? Is there anything further to be done for the young lady?"

Yes, a great deal. Only he was not competent to do it, much as he would wish to. Instinct bade him return to Hetty and hold her safe until the doctor arrived, soothing her distress with kisses. But that was outside his role and perfectly irrational. "Nothing until the doctor has been, but they'd best be ready to make tea or a tisane or whatever is needed. Oh, and Mrs Latimer will be here shortly, I hope. Supply whatever Miss Latimer requires, if you please, and ensure she is well served. Oughtibridge will no doubt do the honours."

"Of course, your grace. I will confer with Mrs Oughtibridge the moment she comes out of the young lady's chamber."

Within an ace of holding out the basket for the butler to take to the housekeeper, Theo refrained, abruptly realising it presented him with a perfect excuse to visit the sickroom. "Thank you, Flint."

Noting the steward still waiting, he gave an inward groan and went into the parlour, prepared to face Cecilia's agitated questions. She greeted him with a demand to know why he was but half-dressed.

"Half-dressed? What are you talking about?"

She gestured. "Your neckcloth, Theo. You look like a ragamuffin."

Oh, for pity's sake! "I used it for a bandage. I'll change presently."

"Bandage? But what happened?"

She was predictably horrified by the tale he then related. To his annoyance, her mind jumped more to the inconvenience of the disturbance than to Hetty's distressing condition.

"Gracious heaven, how could such a thing happen? Now we will be subjected to an invasion, I suppose."

"Scarcely an invasion, Cecilia. I've sent Hathersage for her mother, as you must have heard."

His aunt sighed. "Yes, I suppose you had to do that." She brightened. "Well, Mrs Latimer will want her home, I expect. I know I should, if it were Ellie."

The notion of losing Hetty from his vicinity when he would not be able to discover how she did was out of count. Theo scotched it at once. "She ought not to be moved so soon. It was painful enough for the poor girl to be brought here on a hurdle. She needs rest. We will keep her here until she is sufficiently recovered to make the journey without ill effects."

Cecilia eyed him with a discontented expression. "I can't think why you are so set upon housing the girl."

"I've just told you. You may as well make up your mind to it to play hostess to Mrs Latimer too, since I imagine she will wish to remain to nurse her daughter."

At this, his aunt looked positively affronted. "You expect a deal of me, Theo. What is it with these Latimers of yours? What in the world was the child doing, wandering about in our woods?"

Incensed, and forgetful of the erstwhile secrecy, Theo abandoned caution. "She was collecting flowers. And before you ask, I gave her permission to roam the woods. I wish I had not now, but I had no notion there were poachers setting these afflictive traps."

"Gathering flowers? But there are no choice blooms in the woods."

"Wildflowers. She gathers wildflowers."

Cecilia was staring at him in astonishment. "What does she want them for?"

Theo hesitated. The devil! He should not have mentioned that. Now what was he to do? Reveal Hetty as the artist of that wretched cat in a tree picture which had led to all the trouble?

But Cecilia's expression was altering. "Good heavens! Never say it is she who made that picture? The Latimer child?"

An inward sigh shook him. Little point in concealment now. "Yes, she's the artist. Your friend Angelica is her godmother."

Astonishment was writ large on Cecilia's face. "Gracious! I had no notion. Well, I must concede she is talented, if nothing else."

Nothing else? What the deuce was that supposed to mean? What the devil else was there to be deprecated? Apart from the wretched father, of course. Plus the fact that, by all dictates of custom, she was out of count for a duke.

Theo fought down the rebellion that threatened to overtake him. He had an inescapable duty and he must abide by the rules. But at least he might indulge his preference while Hetty was tied by the heels — literally, almost. Hetty knew. She understood. She was hurt too, in more ways than one. He couldn't repudiate her. Not now. Not while she was dependent upon him. She'd been injured in his grounds. It was the least he could do.

They must have finished getting her comfortable by now. Theo crossed to pick up the basket he had set down on a bureau near the door. His aunt's voice caught him before he reached it.

"How is it you know all this, Theo? Why did you not tell me?"

He responded without thought. "I've known all along. I ran into her when she was collecting her dratted flowers ages ago and she told me."

"And you never said? Gracious heavens, Theo!"

"Why should I say anything? It was a chance encounter, that's all." Not to say a consequential one, but he had said quite enough. He was not going to say anything about Latimer's accusatory ploy. Not that he was any longer fully convinced of its having been such.

His aunt remained dissatisfied. "Then, when Angelica brought me that picture —"

Theo's temper betrayed him. "Yes, I knew it was Miss Latimer's. And yes, I raised the price for her sake. If you must know, I had heard of the family's reverses — not through the girl, from elsewhere. In fact, it was you who mentioned it, didn't you?"

"So I may have, but —"

"In any event, it seemed to me churlish to be paying a pittance when a little more must help her — them. So it proved, since she got all these commissions through your agency. Though the advantage is now doubtful since it has led to this cursed accident. But it happened on my land and becomes therefore my responsibility. What the deuce Latimer is going to say," he added, recalling that first encounter, "I dread to think. He'll likely kick up the devil of a dust."

This proved a fortunate departure, for it served to distract Cecilia's attention. "But he can scarcely blame you, Theo. You did not know of these poachers and their traps."

"All very well, but you don't know Latimer." He regretted these unguarded words at once, but his aunt thankfully did not pick up the inference.

She became thoughtful. "I see there is more in your desire to succour the girl than I supposed, Theo. Yes, I think we must take up a conciliatory stance. I shall receive Mrs Latimer with every expression of regret, but her spouse I must leave to you."

Too relieved by her change of attitude to cavil, Theo fought down his annoyance at her lack of compassion for Hetty's sufferings. He made for the door.

"Where are you going?"

The deuce! He turned. "To return Miss Latimer's belongings and to find out how she does."

He walked out before Cecilia could detain him further or question his interest. As he went, he heard her bidding Mary Eddleston ring the bell so she might send for Oughtibridge. An excellent turn, if she meant to give order for Hetty's comfort and Mrs Latimer's accommodation. At least he might rely on her company manners when she was playing hostess.

But Cecilia's vagaries faded at the prospect of seeing Hetty. He hoped she was a degree rested. The foot must still be paining her, though, with that ghastly injury. Where in the name of all the gods was that doctor?

He sped up the stairs and made the best of his way to the chamber where Hetty had been taken. It was one of the principal guest rooms on the first floor, presumably chosen by the housekeeper for the sake of speed, but nevertheless convenient.

Reaching the door, Theo listened. There was no sound from beyond. He knocked softly, not wishing to disturb her if she was restful at last.

The door opened a little way and one of the maids poked her head round. Martha, was it? He tried to remember the names of all his dependents. One of the pieces of wisdom his uncle had from time to time imparted.

"They will repay you with their loyalty, my dear Theo, if not their affection too. Remember that, if it comes to it that you must take my place."

Martha's eyes popped at sight of him and she opened the door wider and dropped a curtsy. "Your grace?"

"Is Miss Latimer asleep?"

"No, your grace."

"Well, let me in, then."

The maid hesitated, colouring a little. "Mrs Oughtibridge said as I mustn't let anyone in 'cepting the doctor, your grace."

Incensed, Theo was about to scarify the maid when it struck him how odd it would look to insist that this prohibition did not extend to him. Not that he cared for that, but he had to think of Hetty's reputation. A compromise was called for. "Ask Miss Latimer if I may come in for a moment, Martha." He smiled. "You will remain to play propriety." Which meant he would have to behave. No cuddling. No touching, even. Damnation. He'd become accustomed to the freedom he used with her. The difficulties attendant upon her residing in his house became abruptly acute. He would be reduced to subterfuge. There could be no clandestine encounters here.

The maid, who had gone upon her errand, came back with a positive response. "Miss says you can come in, your grace."

He would wager she did. Hetty must be wondering at his absence. He had promised to return.

Martha gave him access and he looked directly at the bed as he moved into the room. Hetty was lying under a coverlet, but her bandaged foot was exposed, resting upon a pillow. The bloodied stocking was still in place and the edges of petticoat indicated her stained gown had not been removed. Her anxious features were turned towards the door and Theo's heart melted as he crossed to the bed.

He smiled down at her. "How are you feeling? Does the foot still pain you very much?"

Her head moved on the pillow as if she would nod, her fingers shifting where she held the edge of the coverlet. Her voice was unusually breathy. "It still aches, but not as badly as it did when we were coming here."

Theo wanted to take her hand, but he was conscious of the maid, hovering at a little distance. He lifted the basket for her to see. "One of the men brought it. Your hat and boot are in it." He grimaced. "I expect your flowers are ruined again."

"Oh, well…" She plucked restlessly at the coverlet, avoiding his eye, he thought.

Damn the maid. And to hell with the proprieties! He sat on the edge of the bed and set down the basket on the floor near the bedside cabinet. "Have they made you more comfortable, He— Miss Latimer?"

Her gaze met his and a tiny smile hovered. A murmur reached him. "They untied my stays."

He grinned. "Ought you to tell me that?"

Her cheeks, still pallid, threw a trifle of colour. "It's hard to mind my tongue with you."

He leaned a little closer, lowering his voice. "We have to be circumspect, Hetty. I'm sorry for it, but it won't do to flout propriety here."

A shadow seemed to cross her face. "I understand … Duke."

Remorse gripped him. He wanted to catch her up in his arms and tell the world to go hang. But he must not. For her sake. Her reputation was in his hands. A tiny thread at the back of his mind reminded him of her father. He must be careful. But was it for her sake or his? Who knew what Latimer might use against him? What if he chose this situation for his advantage?

He knew Hetty was no such schemer. But he could not be sure of the father.

He got up. "I won't disturb you further, Miss Latimer. I hope the doctor may be here directly. Your mother too."

With inner dismay, he saw the clouds gather in her face and knew she was disappointed at his going. But he dared not stay longer. He could not bear to leave her without hope, however.

"I'll visit you again when the doctor has been, ma'am, if you permit."

Her lips trembled and he saw wet on her lashes. Her voice came huskily. "It is very good of your grace. Th-thank you for rescuing m-me, sir."

Theo had to bite off remarking that coming to her rescue was par for the course. He nodded instead, unable to say anything remotely acceptable in the face of her tears. If they were alone, he would berate her for crying, teasing her into retort, and use his handkerchief to dry those cheeks. Or better yet, his lips.

Ye gods! He had best get out of here before his resolution crumbled.

"Rest well."

Turning his eyes from the sight of her distress, he strode to the door and left without looking back.

Henrietta watched him leave, beset with a yearning for those precious moments in the woods before the men came. The intervening weeks, when she had resolutely put him from her mind — or tried to — had vanished into nothingness. He had been her Theo again, wholly hers.

She had convinced herself she had conjured the notion his teasing was borne of careless affection. But his care of her, the things he said, proved otherwise. Only now he was bound by convention and she was relegated to the status of an unfortunate guest.

She sniffed back the tears, not wishing the maid to know she was crying. But it was hard to control the urge to weep. She felt weak and the dull persistent ache in her foot dragged her down. She closed her eyes, allowing the memories to play in her head, drifting…

A kindly voice, speaking in her immediate vicinity, brought her back to consciousness.

"Ah, this is the sufferer, is it? My poor young lady, what a horrible thing to happen. Well, well, we must do our best to make you more comfortable, mustn't we?"

We? Henrietta could see only the one face. Not one she knew. She had half expected the Latimers' own physician, who was elderly. This man looked to be of middle years. He was dressed much more neatly than old Doctor Grimdale and he wore no wig.

A smile came and he proffered a hand. "I am Doctor Rudchester. Miss Latimer, I understand?"

"Oh! Yes. How do you do?"

"Better than you, I fear, my dear. May I remove his grace's improvised bandage so I can assess the damage? Mrs Oughtibridge will supervise the removal of your stocking, if you permit."

Henrietta had not realised Theo had applied the bandage. For the first time, it occurred to her he must have used his neckcloth. It accounted for the oddity of his bared skin within the open neck of his shirt, its ties gaping loose, though she had hardly taken it in while mesmerised by his presence.

"Yes, pray do so. I don't know how you are to see the wound else."

Doctor Rudchester gave a soft laugh. "How right you are, ma'am. I will try not to revive the hurt too much, though I fear my ministrations are bound to give you a degree of discomfort. However, his grace assures me you are a lady with a deal of fortitude, so we must hope you will be able to bear it."

While he talked with a gentle air, he had moved to the foot of the bed and Henrietta could not see what he was doing. But she felt her foot lifted and fingers unwinding the cloth. Softer fingers drew the stocking down her leg, which stung a little as they pulled it over the wound.

"Dear me, yes, quite a nasty gash," the doctor remarked presently. He was bending, but he rose again and looked across. "You will not object to it if I lift your leg, I hope, for I see your heel has suffered as well."

Henrietta shook her head on the pillow, biting her lip as the pain sharpened with his touch. She felt her leg bent at the knee and laid down again in such a way that the pain subsided a little. She sighed with relief. "That does not hurt nearly as much."

The doctor spoke without raising his head from his examination. "I dare say that is because you are now resting on that part of the foot which is not damaged. I recommend you keep it in this position whenever you can."

He rose again and looked across at the maid. To Henrietta's surprise, she saw the girl was flanked by the older woman who had first supervised the undoing of her stays.

"A bowl of warm water, Mrs Oughtibridge, if you will, and towels. We must clean the wounds thoroughly to avoid any possibility of contamination."

The maid hurried off as the doctor came back to the bedhead, smiling down at Henrietta.

"We will soon have you more the thing, Miss Latimer."

Anxiety gnawed as, for the first time, Henrietta thought of the physical consequences of the accident. "Is it very bad?"

He pursed his lips. "I will not conceal from you that the damage is severe. These traps are designed without a thought of mercy, I regret to say. His grace told me you were to some degree protected by your boot, but the metal teeth nevertheless penetrated your flesh quite deeply."

The matter-of-fact tone made it seem less appalling and she was able to respond with calm and sense. "Will I be out of action for long?"

Doctor Rudchester smiled. "Oh, I think you will be up and about in a couple of days. But walking is bound to be painful until the healing process is well underway. I would advocate resting the foot as much as possible. You will only aggravate the pain if you run around picking flowers too soon."

He knew? Theo must have told him. Well, he had to account for her presence in his woods. She ought to be thankful for the innocuous excuse, but she felt a complete fool.

Fortunately the doctor was distracted by the opening of the door. But it was not the maid returning with a jug. With a mixture of relief and apprehension, Henrietta saw her mother's bespectacled face, creased with worry. Oh, and there was her twin. Her heart warmed and her eyes filled.

"Mama! Silve!"

There came a flurry of greetings, exclamations and fuss. Mama leaning to kiss her forehead. "My darling girl, what have you done to yourself?"

And Silvestre, seizing her hand. "Hetty, Hetty, you gave us such a fright!"

"Oh, it is Doctor Rudchester, is it not? How kind of you to attend my daughter." Then Mama was shaking the doctor's hand and disappearing to look at the wounds as he began repeating all he had said to Henrietta, and more.

Her twin, tumbling down by the bedside, was grasping her hands tightly and leaning close, her tone a very murmur under cover of the conversation going on over Henrietta's foot. "You seem fated to tangle with this Theo of yours, Hetty. How did he find you?"

She gripped her sister's fingers, speaking low. "I don't know, Silve. I fainted and — and when I came to myself again, he was there."

Her twin gave a wry smile. "Ready to rescue you again. How convenient."

Protest rose up. "Don't be horrid, Silve. If he had not been close by, I might be lying there still. Theo took such care of me…" Her voice became suspended.

Her twin's face changed. "Oh, Lord, I'm sorry, Hetty. Now don't turn into a watering pot just because you feel weak and ill. Be strong. You will need to be when you have to face Papa."

This new spectre served to dampen the urge to weep. "Is he very angry?"

Silvestre grimaced, releasing her. "He doesn't know yet. He went off to Reading with Mr Summerhayes a little after you left to go hunting down your wretched flowers."

Henrietta had not before thought of Papa's likely reaction to her being ensconced at Whisley Park. He would want her out of here at the earliest possible moment. What would he say of Theo? "He cannot blame the duke. Surely he will be glad Theo helped me, don't you think?"

"If I know Papa, he will be incensed that Theo allowed traps to be set up in his woods for you to catch your foot in one."

"But he didn't! It was poachers. No one would suppose he meant for me to be injured."

"No, of course not, but you know how Papa is about your Theo. I doubt he will be in a mood to be reasonable."

A lively apprehension superseded all else until the door opened again, admitting the maid, armed with a jug. The prospect of the doctor's coming ministrations served to divert her from the thought of Papa's wrath. The room now seemed overfull of people and she was grateful when the doctor appeared to realise it.

"I think, ma'am, it will be more comfortable for Miss Latimer if we do the business without witnesses. Mrs Oughtibridge may assist me as she knows me of old."

Henrietta watched him as he began to lay out his instruments.

Mama was looking interested, but resigned. "I understand. My other daughter and I will remove until you are done." She came to the head of the bed and Silvestre rose, giving place. "Be brave, my love! I dare say it will be most unpleasant, but the sooner done, the sooner over." She patted Henrietta's shoulder. "We will see you presently, and then we may decide what is to be done for the best."

A wave from her twin and the two were gone, leaving Henrietta unable to decide which was worse: the dread prospect of leaving Theo's house or the sight of Doctor Rudchester's ominous preparations.

CHAPTER TWELVE

"How was it you found her, Duke?"

Theo glanced across at Hetty's sister, so alike in general appearance, but utterly unlike in character if he was not mistaken. His mind elsewhere, he only now took in that she'd been watching him over the rim of her cup as she sipped. Was it speculation in that open gaze? He took the question head on. "Sheer chance, ma'am. I happened to be with my gamekeeper, inspecting evidence of poachers in the area."

"Thank heaven you were there, Duke."

The mother's effusive thanks had already embarrassed him when he met the pair exiting the chamber. He had not exactly been loitering, but having shown them up and knowing the doctor was present, he had lingered, the nagging concern for Hetty holding him there. He had been obliged to invent an excuse on the spot when the pair unexpectedly came out again and Mrs Latimer hailed him.

"There you are, Duke! I am so glad, for I don't think I even thanked you for your care of my poor daughter."

"No thanks are needed, ma'am."

"On the contrary, I doubt I can thank you enough. You cannot imagine how much my shock was dissipated upon hearing what you had already done for Hetty."

"I could hardly do less, ma'am. But pray come downstairs. My aunt is anxious to procure your comfort."

Not that Cecilia's welcome proved more than tepid, but she was at least forced to rise to the occasion when he ushered the Latimer ladies into the family room, saying all that was proper and ordering Mary to ring for refreshments. It had relieved

Theo of bearing the burden of playing host. Cecilia was nothing if not gracious when duty demanded, he had to give her that.

He had found time before the Latimers arrived to repair the ravages to his appearance and had no excuse to leave the room. But at least Cecilia's company manners enabled him to allow his mind to wander where it wanted to be. Except for the cursed proprieties which prevented him from taking his body there as well.

Was Hetty in more pain from the doctor's ministrations? Would Rudchester think to give her a draught of some kind to relieve it? Not laudanum. Ghastly stuff. It would likely make her delirious. A herbal concoction of some kind, then? There were safer remedies. But something was needed. Other than his holding her close and soothing her with…

At which point the wretched sister chose to cut into his thoughts, deuce take the wench.

"For my part, Duke, I cannot be sufficiently grateful for your prompt action," pursued Mrs Latimer. "Without it, I dread to think what might have happened to our poor girl, alone in the woods and so badly injured."

Her dread was no greater than his. The same thought had almost paralysed him several times. But he could not say so. He temporised. "I am glad to have been able to be of service to Miss Latimer. She certainly could not have released herself from the trap, even had she not swooned. Fortunately, Beattock was able to work out the trick of it. I am only sorry he had not found the traps and removed them before Miss Latimer was so unfortunate as to be walking in the area."

Except of course it was conduct typical of her. She could not choose tomorrow, oh no. Little Miss Disaster must needs select this day of all days to go picking her blasted flowers.

He clamped down on the thought as he caught Silvestre Latimer watching him again. What the deuce did she mean by it? Since Cecilia had once more engaged the mother's attention, he had leisure to ponder the girl's intent. For two pins he would demand to know what was in her mind, if the infernal parlour were not so crowded.

At least Swarland had gone off about his business. But the ubiquitous Mary was clucking away in response to Mrs Latimer's remarks, which appeared to be concentrated upon whether or not to remove Hetty. Cecilia, for once obedient to his will, was offering hospitality for as long as was needed. Which effectively relieved him of having to insist upon Hetty remaining. He would if necessary, no matter what anyone thought.

Absently he took in that Silvestre was rising, her gaze fixed upon him. She came across and he got up automatically. She gave him a brief smile. "Pray sit down again, Duke. I am merely exchanging my seat so we may converse with more ease."

Dear Lord, what did the wench want? With deep misgiving he watched her take a seat on the sofa, sitting sideways on. She gestured to his chair beside it and Theo perforce sat down again.

"I had so little time to speak with Hetty, sir, but she appears to be inordinately glad of your opportune arrival."

What the deuce was he to say to that? He stayed silent, meeting Miss Latimer's direct gaze. She pursed her lips.

"You will have noticed our father is absent."

And he was heartily relieved, but it would not do to say so. "He did not desire to accompany you?"

A rueful smile appeared. "He does not know, Duke. He was from home when your messenger came."

Then that ordeal was still to come. Theo cursed aloud. Recalling his company, he grimaced at the Latimer wench. "I beg your pardon, ma'am. That slipped out."

Her lips twitched. "Yes, I rather gather you and Papa do not see eye to eye."

Theo cast a quick glance at the other ladies and found them engrossed. He lowered his voice nevertheless. "How much do you know, Miss Latimer?"

She appeared to consider the question. "I am not perfectly sure I have been privy to everything, sir. Hetty has been unusually secretive."

He let his breath go in a bang. "Damn it to hell!"

A tiny gurgle escaped her, all too reminiscent of Hetty's occasional girlish giggles. "I can readily believe my twin's conduct baffles description."

"It doesn't baffle my descriptive powers, ma'am, as she has no doubt told you. But you need not suppose I think the less of her for it. However, the unfortunate contretemps with your parent remains a difficulty."

Silvestre's voice dropped. "That is just it, Duke. I'm afraid I put Hetty into a quake by worrying her about Papa's reaction."

Incensed, he had all to do not to glare at the wench. "Why the devil did you mention it at all? She's in no condition to be —"

"I know, I know. I did not mean to, but I was so anxious for her and it slipped out. If I know Hetty, she will fret about what Papa may say to you, Duke."

He eyed her in some dudgeon. "You're telling me this because you wish me to placate him or your sister?"

She opened her eyes at him. "Hetty, of course. I imagine you can stand a battering if Papa should choose to cut up rough. Pray tell her so and that you do not mind it."

But he did mind it. Very much indeed. To have the blasted Latimer father ring a peal over him because his misbegotten daughter must needs do what any normal female would not? The image of Hetty's features, white and still, lying among the summer wildflowers, forced itself back into his head. He all but groaned aloud. "Have no fear," he found himself saying on a curt note. "Your sister's welfare is all that matters at present. I will do whatever is needed to preserve her peace of mind."

Silvestre smiled in a more friendly way, reminding him instantly of Hetty's warmth. "I thought you might say as much." She hesitated and he wondered uneasily what was coming. Impatience claimed him.

"Spit it out, Miss Latimer."

Her brows rose. "I was only thinking you are not as black as I had painted you, sir."

"Then she has clearly not told you everything." It was out before he could think of the wisdom of expressing himself so freely. He became the recipient of another speculative look and cursed inwardly. This creature was far more in control than Hetty. She would either agree at once, berating him for all the terrible things he'd said and done, or haunt him forever with one of those wounded expressions that could not but pierce his defences.

"It is possible Hetty's sensibility may have exaggerated your perceived faults, sir."

Had she read his mind? "In my eyes or hers, ma'am? No, don't answer that!"

She laughed. "Poor Hetty feels things too deeply. She takes after Papa in this."

God help him, then! But it would not do. "She does not cherish grudges."

Silvestre made a face. "No, she is far too soft-hearted to do that."

"Don't I know it." Hell and the devil! He must guard his tongue. He drew a breath. "Keep mum for all this, Miss Latimer, I beg of you. I have said too much."

The indulgence in her face vanished under a frown. "You may rely upon my discretion, Duke. However —"

What she might have been about to say was, to his relief, forestalled by her mother's speaking across to them. "Silve, my dear, the duchess and I are agreed that you will remain here with Hetty in my stead."

Theo saw consternation leap into Miss Latimer's eyes. "I will be only too happy, Mama, but are we not to bring her home?"

Was she reluctant to leave her sister in his vicinity? His mind ran rapidly over what had been said as the discussion continued.

"It will cause her too much discomfort to be moved, my love, and the duchess has very kindly offered to keep her here for a day or two. But one of us must remain. I could not reconcile it with my conscience to leave her without our care. Nor to throw the burden upon your household, Duchess."

"Pray think nothing of that, my dear Mrs Latimer," said Cecilia at her most gracious. "I shall be happy for both the misses Latimer to remain for as long as may be necessary."

Silvestre was still looking doubtful. "But are you content to leave her to me, Mama?"

"I must, my love, for I do not know when Papa may return and I cannot have you alone in the house. He may well end by staying with Hugh for the night, if they are very late back from their excursion."

"Very well, Mama." But as Mrs Latimer turned back to Cecilia, the girl dropped her voice and leaned a little towards

Theo. "What she means, of course, is that she had best be the one to break the news to Papa, and I must say that is true."

Consternation hit him at once. "You suppose he will take it amiss? Because she's here?"

A faint grimace crossed her face. "There is no saying with Papa. He will be upset that Hetty is hurt, and likely furious as well." She gave him a direct look. "With you, sir, for allowing traps to be set in your woods." The injustice of this threw a spark of anger into his chest. Silvestre must have seen it, for she put up a hand. "Oh, he won't say so to you, Duke. Mama will see to that. She is the pragmatic one, you know, and she will persuade him that your rescue redeems the fault."

"Fault! I have many, ma'am, but I do not concede that one in particular. The traps cannot have been there more than a day or so. My gamekeeper is assiduous. He and the outdoor servants are engaged in finding and removing them as we speak. Not that I don't wish they had been found earlier."

"It is no good wishing, Duke. One cannot change what has happened."

He eyed her with a mix of amusement and annoyance. "You resemble your mama in character, I take it."

Another of those gurgles escaped her. "Unlike poor Hetty, yes. I am the practical twin."

Irritation swamped him. "I wish you won't keep on saying *poor* Hetty, when you know perfectly well your sister is a walking disaster."

Her brows rose. "A trifle harsh, sir, is it not?"

"It's not harsh at all. She is perfectly exasperating and I should think she would drive any man demented." He caught himself up, moderating his tone. "But that does not mean I am not sorry for her injury."

"I did not suppose it for a moment. She said you had taken excellent care of her."

His chest tightened. "How could I help but do so? I'm not a monster."

"Far from it, according to my sister."

Theo frowned as he eyed her, wondering just what Hetty had told her. He could hear Hetty's voice in his head, berating him for a rude beast, and affection caught in his chest. He spoke low, without either thought or reason. "She's so funny, and so acutely vulnerable. And so very sweet…"

The parlour door opened, admitting the doctor. Theo leapt up and went towards him, only half aware of Silvestre's strange look as she stared at him.

"Rudchester! How does Miss Latimer?"

CHAPTER THIRTEEN

The doctor's ministrations had tried Hetty's fortitude to the limit, and she was glad to be left in peace at last. Her throbbing foot, now bandaged and placed sideways on the pillow, took her whole attention and she could not help the tears that squeezed from her eyes.

"Here you are, miss. Take this."

The unobtrusive maid was holding out a handkerchief. Hetty took it, sniffing on the tiny sobs. "Thank you. I don't m-mean to cry, only it hurts so much."

"I should think it must, miss. Nasty-looking wounds, they are. But not to worry, miss. Mrs Oughtibridge is making up the potion the doctor left."

Wiping her wet cheeks, Hetty regarded the maid's face above her with misgiving. "What potion is it?"

"That I don't know, miss. It's in a little bottle and you're to have some drops in water."

Then it was not laudanum. Mama never encouraged her daughters to rely upon that particular medical aid, except in the worst of extremities. The hope of relief made the tearfulness recede and Hetty held out the handkerchief. "Thank you." She hesitated. "I do not know your name."

"It's Martha, miss, and you keep that. His grace give it me for you. He said as you'd need it."

A wash of tenderness invaded Henrietta's bosom and she had much ado not to burst into sobs all over again. Theo's thought for her warmed her. His voice resonated in her head: *If there's one thing I can't abide, it's a weeping female.* But he'd dried her cheeks nevertheless, even on that first occasion. Oh, Theo…

"When did he give it to you?" The question came out of hope. Was he near?

"When he brought the doctor up, miss."

But then the maid stood back, to be supplanted by the housekeeper. She was armed with a glass containing a small amount of liquid. "Will you drink this, if you please, ma'am? The doctor said it will settle you."

Struggling up onto her elbow, Henrietta took the glass and eyed the yellowish potion with misgiving. "Will it send me to sleep?"

"A trifle drowsy, perhaps, ma'am. But he said it will ease the pain a little."

This thought was so welcome, Henrietta made no further demur. She tipped the glass to her lips and drank the stuff down. The aftertaste was faintly bitter and she discovered the housekeeper was proffering a small sugar lump in a dish. She took it with a word of thanks and popped it into her mouth, sinking back upon her pillows.

"Martha will remain with you, ma'am. You have only to ask if there is anything you need."

Then she was gone and the maid was smoothing the down coverlet over her and advising her in a motherly way to rest while she was able. Henrietta doubted she could for the nagging throb in her foot. Realising she was still clutching Theo's handkerchief, she smoothed it out and found an embroidered set of initials in one corner.

She made it out as TOLD. T for Theodore. D for Devenal. What did the O and L signify? That he had three names reminded her too much of that lofty status which meant she would not do. She crumpled the square of linen into her fist again and allowed her eyes to wander about the chamber. It was not as grand as one might have expected, with a press, a wash stand, a whatnot in one corner and a long mirror in addition to the bed she was occupying. A couple of landscapes adorned the walls and there were two straight chairs, one by the window, the other by the door.

Had not Mama said that Theo's predecessor was used to talk of Whisley Park as his little summer residence? Although he had spent fewer summers in the place since his remarriage. Which might explain why Theo had not been known in the district. Or no, had he not been abroad? He had not wanted to inherit, had he?

She knew so little about him really. How was it she felt she knew him so well? If she counted up the times they had met, there were not nearly enough to claim more than a casual acquaintance. Only those encounters had been anything but ordinary. As for this one…

Remembrance of those precious moments in Theo's care could not but heap coals upon her present distresses. She might be in his house, but she would not see him. Had he not spoken of circumspection? She had been too dazed at the time to take in more than the horrid necessity to lose his company. He had come back, as he promised. But only for a moment. He did not mean to set tongues wagging by visiting her in this chamber. It was almost worse to be here, where she knew him to be close and yet be barred from the intimacy she had come to cherish, than to be at home, where distance must put him wholly out of her reach.

Oh, where had her wits gone begging? She had no right to be thinking of him in such terms. She ought to be glad he meant to hold aloof. Glad of his horrid circumspection. Only she was not. His absence caused an ache that mirrored the real one. The latter would mend in time. The other seemed to yawn into eternity.

The sound of the door opening brought her senses alert. Her eyes flew open, a flurry attacking her heartbeat as she raised her head to see who entered.

"How are you feeling, dearest?"

Silve! Disappointment mingled with relief and she held out her hand towards her twin as she came swiftly to the bed. "I've had a potion to settle it."

Her sister grasped her fingers as she plonked on the edge of the bed. "Well, that's a relief. Does it still hurt?"

"Abominably." There was no need for bravery with Silvestre. "It's throbbing like mad."

"That ought to pass off very soon. The doctor said he left a concoction for the purpose."

"You've seen him?"

"He came down to the parlour to report to the duke."

Henrietta stared at her. "Report to Theo?"

"Your Theo sent to him, remember? He is not our doctor. He seemed a good deal more sympathetic and sensible than old Grimdale, I must say."

Henrietta laughed. "Yes, he would have scolded me dreadfully for being so silly. This one was very kind."

Her twin shook the hand she held. "You were not silly, Hetty. It wasn't your fault. If you ask me, the duke is more upset about it than anyone."

A flurry attacked Henrietta's bosom. "Why do you say that?"

Her twin cast a glance over her shoulder to where the maid Martha had effaced herself by the window and lowered her voice to a near whisper. "We talked a little."

"About me?"

"No, about the man in the moon! Of course about you."

Henrietta shook the hand holding hers, her whisper frantic. "Silve! What have you been saying?"

She would swear her twin looked guilty. "You need not fret. I only warned him about Papa." Silvestre clasped her fingers tighter and leaned close. "He likes you, Hetty. More than somewhat, if I am any judge."

A flood of feeling threatened to overset Henrietta all over again and her voice turned husky. "I know he does. But it's of no use, Silve. Theo can't…"

"Can't what?"

The underlying steel in her twin's murmur dismayed her, but she leapt to Theo's defence. "You know perfectly well what I mean, Silve, and he's not to blame. He is to be applauded, rather. You need not think he has led me on in any way. He's an honourable man, even if he makes me fume sometimes."

"An honourable man would not care who you were. Did Lynchmere care about Felicity's position in life?"

"He isn't a duke." She sighed with frustration as her twin opened her mouth again. "Don't, Silve. Don't say any more."

She watched Silvestre close her lips again, but her eyes were smouldering. It was more than she could bear to have her twin prick at the inner wound, the one she could not see. She jerked her chin in the direction of the maid. "We may be overheard."

The last thing she needed was to set tongues wagging after Theo had made it abundantly clear that was just what he feared might happen. For no consideration could she endure the notion of his hand being forced if he was thought to have compromised her. That would be worse even than the inevitable loss that must come as soon as she was well enough recovered to return home.

Silvestre's frowns vanished and she smiled. "There will be time enough to discuss the matter. I am to remain with you."

Surprise warred with a leaping hope. "Am I not to go home?"

Her sister raised her voice to be heard by the maid. "Not for a day or two. The doctor does not recommend moving you as yet, and the duchess has very kindly offered her hospitality for as long as may be required."

"But what of Mama?"

A significant look came her way. "She does not wish me to be alone at home, for there is no saying Papa will be back tonight."

Henrietta had no difficulty in interpreting this and a faint rise of apprehension at once superseded the pleasurable notion of being in Theo's vicinity for a while longer. "She means to tell him herself."

"Exactly so. There is no need for that troubled look, Hetty. Mama knows just how to broach the matter."

Henrietta breathed more easily. "Yes, she does." She groped for her twin's hand again. "I am glad you will be here. No one can suppose anything untoward has occurred if you are with me."

Her twin gave her a wry look. "That's all you want me for, is it?"

An overwrought giggle escaped. "Of course not, don't be silly."

"Well, you won't be nearly as pleased when I prove a very dragon looking after you. I should not wish to incur displeasure from a certain quarter if I don't ensure your welfare."

Henrietta could not but warm to the implication that Theo cared so much. Yet she hankered for Mama's common sense approach. "Mama has not gone, has she?"

"She would not leave without seeing you, but she's obliged to do the pretty in the parlour downstairs. I escaped on the pretext of checking on you after the doctor had finished with you."

A knock at the door sent the maid tripping across the room and Silvestre rose from her perch on the bed. "This is likely Mama now."

But the voice that spoke outside the room was deeper, and it sent Henrietta's heartbeat into high gear.

"Ask Miss Latimer if I may come in for a moment, Martha."

Even though Theo had expected to find Silvestre Latimer in attendance, her presence could not but irritate. Such words as he might say in her presence could not convey his true feelings. Nevertheless, he smiled as he approached the bed. "I came to ensure the doctor did his best for you, Miss Latimer."

Hetty's wavering smile belied the wary look in her eyes, but her twin, to his annoyance, raised her brows.

"Miss Latimer? Now, that is likely to prove confusing." Was that mischief in her face? "Would not Miss Hetty serve the purpose better?"

"Silve!" The frantic whisper was accompanied by a glare and an apologetic look flicked towards Theo.

He had to laugh. "An excellent suggestion, ma'am. However, *Miss Hetty* has gumption enough to know when I am addressing her specifically, whatever appellation I may use." He glanced at Hetty as he spoke and was gratified to see a faint colour rise in her pallid cheeks. She understood him perfectly. Then he caught the sister looking from him to Hetty and back again. The devil! He must be careful. Shifting to the bottom of the bed, he viewed the bandaged foot, resting now on a pillow at an angle that no longer pressed on the wounds at the front and back. "Rudchester's bandage looks more professional than mine. I wish I had thought of placing your foot like that." He looked towards Hetty's anxious features. "Is it more comfortable so?"

"I can't tell. It's still throbbing, though it does not jab in that horrid way."

Silvestre rose from the bed and came to join him. "I didn't see the actual wounds. Were they very bad?"

Theo did not mince his words. "Hideous. Those traps have sharp teeth." He glanced at the maid, back in her position at the window. "I trust the doctor cleaned these wounds thoroughly, Martha?"

"Oh, yes, your grace." The girl came to the bed and dropped a curtsy. "He bade me fetch warm water and towels and he bathed the foot proper, your grace, and patted it dry, and then he poured on a potion as stung poor miss at first. He said as it were to stop it going bad. And he put a powder on before he bandaged it up."

"Basilicum powder?"

"I don't know, your grace, but he covered it all up so's you couldn't see the blood no more. And he said as he'll put more on tomorrow." The recital over, the maid curtsied again and withdrew.

Theo fastened upon the one point that caught at his imagination and looked at Hetty again. "I would guess it was alcohol that stung. Was it very bad, Het— Miss Hetty?"

She shifted on the pillow. "To say truth, I don't recall. The whole thing was unpleasant and I had no notion he was doing all that. I just know it was hurting."

"Is it hurting still?"

She looked a trifle surprised. "Not nearly as much, thank goodness. It has subsided a good deal."

"That will be the potion, I expect," put in Silvestre. "Are you feeling drowsy, Hetty?"

"Not really."

To Theo's ears, she sounded forlorn. He could not withstand the urge to go around the bed to be closer. He dropped to sit on the spot Silvestre had vacated and set his hand on hers for a brief moment, squeezing it. "Is there anything you need? You have only to name it."

She clenched the hand he had touched, flexing her fingers, her gaze roving his face. "Might I have a drink?"

Theo cursed inwardly. "Good grief, yes. I told them to give you nothing until the doctor had been. You must be thirsty. Lemonade?"

"Could I have tea, if you please?"

"Anything you wish for. Martha!"

The girl was there in a moment. "Your grace?"

"Go and arrange for tea for Miss Hetty. At once, if you will. You need not fear to leave her, for Miss Latimer is here."

The girl hurried out and he turned back to Hetty. "There. Easy as pie."

For the first time since the accident, she twinkled. "You always make things look easy."

"That's the one advantage of being a duke."

"It has nothing to do with you being a duke. You would do just as you chose whoever you were, you know you would, horrid beast." Her expression changed, consternation entering in as she cast a glance at her sister. "I did not mean to s-say that. You've been so kind, Duke."

He could not endure the change. "That's not what you said when I made you drink that brandy," he said in a rallying tone.

He was rewarded with her gurgle of a laugh. "No, I didn't, did I? But you were kind, Theo — I mean, Duke."

"Oh, the devil!" To hell with it. "Don't, Hetty. It's only your sister here now, and she won't betray us." He turned to look at Silvestre. "Will you?"

The twin gave him an enigmatic look. "I cannot imagine what you mean, Duke."

"Oh, can't you just!" He wafted a hand at her. "Retire out of earshot for a moment, will you?"

"Theo, you mustn't!"

"Hush! Miss Latimer, indulge me, if you please."

Silvestre's eyes danced. "Very well, but under protest."

He watched her walk away to stand at the window, looking out. Then he turned back to Hetty and seized her fingers, lifting them to his lips and kissing the soft tips. Leaning down, he dropped a kiss on her forehead for good measure. He lowered his voice to a murmur. "There, my brave disaster girl. Stop thanking me and saying I'm kind. You have no notion how badly I feel about this ghastly business."

"Oh, don't, Theo. It was not your fault." She was grasping at his coat and he covered her fingers with his hand, holding them fast.

"It might as well have been. I saw you and I wanted to escape. I wouldn't listen to Beattock. If I had, and I'd warned you —"

Her free fingers came up and were laid against his lips for a precious instant. "You could not have prevented it. You did right to avoid me. You know we can't be meeting, Theo. It wouldn't be right."

She was whispering and he had to lean close to hear. The temptation to kiss her lips was strong and Theo had to exercise enormous self-restraint not to give in to it. "I don't think I care if it's right, Hetty. To see you lying here like this —" He broke off. Common sense and the memory of Silvestre's presence tapped on his consciousness. Yet he was loath to end the stolen moment. She was regarding him with those expressive eyes of hers and what he saw there drew an answering swell of tenderness within him. "Oh, Hetty. This isn't going to go away, is it?"

A flutter attacked her lashes and the growing shine in her eyes rebuked him. He barely heard the whisper on her breath. "I don't want it to, but it will in the end, if only you will cease to..."

Yes, he must cease, and that right speedily. He was being altogether self-indulgent, unfair to her, as mean a beast as she had ever called him. Releasing her hand, he sat up, raising his voice. "Very well, Miss Latimer, you may return." He shifted his eyes away from Hetty's face, unable to bear the sight of her distress if she should be crying. The sound of the opening door made him shoot to his feet. He looked across, expecting Martha, but it was Mrs Latimer who entered. Thanking providence she had not done so a moment earlier, he forced a hearty note into his voice as he moved towards her. "In good time, ma'am. I came to ascertain how your daughter is faring after Rudchester's ministrations and it seems she is feeling the wounds less."

The words in no way expressed the frustration in his breast and sounded false in his own ears. But the matron appeared to accept them at face value and he breathed more easily.

"Is it so indeed, my love? I must thank you for your concern, Duke."

It was too much. "Pray don't start thanking me all over again, ma'am. Het— Miss Latimer knows I cannot sufficiently regret the incident."

Mrs Latimer had taken his place at the bedside, but she turned with a smile. "Well, I have no wish to embarrass you,

Duke, and I believe we may be sanguine. I have consulted at length with the doctor and he assures me Hetty will be up and about in a day or two."

She reached for Hetty's hand as she spoke, patting it in a comforting fashion. Theo dared to look at her face and found relief there. Was it her mother's presence? She was avoiding his eye. A wash of something all too close to possession seized him, as if he ought to be the only one to pet and comfort her. Ye gods! He had best get himself out of here before he betrayed them both. Bad enough Silvestre had seen that careless moment of intimacy.

Theo took a step towards the bed. "I will leave you, ma'am. My secretary will escort you home as soon as you are ready." He received another of Mrs Latimer's placid looks. With all anxiety past, she appeared to have reverted to the calm manner that appeared to be habitual to her. Unlike that of her spouse, God help him!

"Thank you, Duke. We shall not keep him many moments."

"We?" Theo's gaze flicked to Silvestre. "I thought you were staying, Miss Latimer."

"She is," said Mrs Latimer, still placid, "but she must return to pack a few necessary items, both for herself and our poor girl here. Your secretary will not mind waiting for her, I trust?"

Relief swept through him. "No, of course not. He is at your disposal, ma'am. Take your time here." He glanced at Hetty's still pale features. "Your tea will be here directly, Miss Latimer. Don't hesitate to ask for anything else you require."

"Ah, tea, that is excellent." Mrs Latimer patted her daughter again. "That will revive you, my love. There is nothing like tea to settle the system after being severely shocked."

Except for the comfort of a soothing embrace. But that was out of count. Theo got himself to the door at last, but the thought of Hetty's imminent loss of Silvestre stayed him. He caught the twin's eye and jerked his head. Her brows rose, but she glided across to join him.

"Duke?"

"You'll hurry back?"

"Certainly. I should be able to return within the hour, I would guess."

"And you'll stay with her? In this room, I mean."

The brows climbed higher. "You wish me to remain in here overnight?"

Yes, to prevent him from an overmastering temptation. But that he could not say. "Would it incommode you? I can arrange for the room next door to be prepared, if you prefer it?" Only that would not prove enough of a deterrent to the demon that was residing in his depths.

Silvestre's gaze seemed to inspect his. Did she read his dilemma? She pursed her lips in the way she had before. "Why, Duke? Do you think she will need my services in the night?"

He spoke from the heart. "I think she will be lonely and forlorn, and if I cannot comfort her, you must."

Her expression softened, but her tone was matter-of-fact. "This becomes interesting, Duke. There is much I might ask, but I will refrain."

He cursed inwardly. "Don't ask, for God's sake, Silvestre. And don't trouble Hetty either. You will only distress her, and I can't bear that."

She smiled. "No, I won't distress her, Duke. If she wishes for me, of course I will remain with her."

Would she prefer Silvestre to him? Of course she would. All he ever did was upset her, and for what? Damn it to hell! She had turned him inside out and upside down and the devil of it was, he liked it.

Silvestre was regarding him with an expression akin to amusement. Was he giving himself away? He attempted to master his mind. The thought that Hetty would shortly be alone for a space wrought upon him, but he must not give in.

"I will not come again today. Let her know it."

With which, he slid from the room, closing the door behind him. Heading for the stairs, he bethought him of the decanter in the cupboard in his library. Uncle Oliver had kept it there for emergencies. If this turmoil in his head was not an emergency, he did not know what was. What in Hades was he to do?

CHAPTER FOURTEEN

Sitting up against banked pillows and sipping her tea, Henrietta contemplated the bedpost. She was glad to be able to rest again, for the exertion needed to make use of the chamber pot had exhausted her. It had taken the assistance of both Mama and Silve to manage it, and she was not looking forward to having to change into her night attire. Every motion aggravated the ache in her foot. Silve's exasperated suggestion gladdened her heart.

"It won't do to be putting you through this every time, Hetty. I'm going to ask the maid to find a bordaloo, then you need not squat like this."

Fortunately Martha had arrived with a tea tray before her relatives left and, with their combined efforts, they were able to arrange Henrietta in her current posture and settle the foot again on the pillow in the position recommended by the doctor.

Martha, having supplied her wants, had retired to a chair near the dresser and was seated with her hands folded in her lap, staring into space. So patient. In her place, Henrietta would find doing nothing at all severely tedious. On impulse, she called the girl.

"Martha!"

The maid rose at once, moving to the bedside. "Yes, miss?" She peeped into the half-empty cup. "Do you wish for a refill, miss?"

For want of anything else to say, Henrietta agreed to it. She watched Martha pour from the pot and pop another sugar lump into the cup, stirring vigorously. As the girl set the cup back in the saucer Henrietta was holding, she found her tongue.

"Do pray bring your chair closer, Martha, so that we may talk."

The girl blinked. "Talk, miss?"

Henrietta felt warmth rising in her cheeks. Did one not talk to the maids in a duke's residence? She was so used to treating the servants at home in a friendly way, it seemed odd not to do so here. She recalled the footman's look of surprise when she had thanked him for showing her the way at the party that night. "Are you not permitted to talk to me?"

Martha dropped a curtsy. "I'm to do what you wish, miss."

"Then bring your chair to the bed and sit by me, if you please."

The girl was clearly surprised, but she did as she was asked, plonking into the chair and looking at Henrietta in much the manner of a rabbit eyeing a fox askance.

"Do I seem mad to you? I don't mean to embarrass you, Martha, only it is dull work sitting here mumchance."

A tiny smile flitted across the maid's face. "I'm used to that, miss."

"Are you? I should suppose you are in general too busy to have leisure to sit quiet."

"Well, that's true enough, miss."

It was uphill work, but Henrietta persisted. Anything to take her mind off her injury. Not to mention a certain person who ought not to dwell in her head the way he did, especially since her twin's whispered message that he would not come again today. Said so that she would not uselessly yearn for a sight of him? She swept away a guilty thought that she might learn more of him, of his household and without compromise. What harm was there in talking to this girl? "I suppose you are one of many maids here?"

"Not here, miss. There's only three of us housemaids. Not like at Devenal."

This was of interest. "The castle? Is it very large?"

"Ooh, huge it is, miss, only no one don't live there now for it's a ruin. Nasty, scary place it is, miss," added Martha, becoming loquacious.

Not according to Lady Ella, whose enthusiasm for the ancient building was patent. But she must not give away her secret knowledge. "But the house is also large?"

"It's a fair mansion, miss," disclosed Martha, opening her hands to indicate breadth. "Nor that ain't all of it, not by a long chalk. Lost my way in them long corridors when I first come. I was right glad to be sent down here under Mrs Oughtibridge and Mr Flint."

"Do you not go back with the family when they return to Devenal?"

"Oh, no, miss. We've to keep Whisley Park ready at all times. The other duke was used to come down for a day or two on his way to London, and you never know when her grace might take it into her head to visit. It's only while they was in mourning as she didn't come down. Nor his grace neither."

She must mean Theo. But surely he could not be wholly new to Whisley Park? "Did you not meet the duke before this summer, then?"

Martha nodded fervently, apparently having lost her initial wariness. "Oh, yes, miss, for he'd visited his uncle now and now. Only he were off on his travels mostly. Mister Theo, he was then. Leastways that's what Mr Flint called him, for Mr Flint has known him since he were a nipper, and Lord Lionel Devenal too."

"Lord Lionel Devenal? Who is that?"

"It's his grace's father, miss. Leastways it was, for he died a long time ago, says Mr Flint, or he'd have been the duke now."

"And his mother?"

"Her ladyship, miss? She lives at Devenal Manor, which is where his grace grew up."

"Does it belong to his grace?"

"It does now, miss, for as he's the duke. Mr Flint says as the old duke, which is to say this one's grandpa, give his second son the Manor for a home when he married."

A fleeting wish crossed Henrietta's heart that Theo might have been cut out of the succession like Papa by a son born to the duchess. Theo Devenal of Devenal Manor need not aspire to the hand of a lady of rank. Although of course she would never have met him had he not been the duke and shooting rabbits on his own lands. She thrust the pointless thoughts away along with the empty teacup she handed to the maid, who at once offered to refill it. "I have had sufficient, thank you."

She watched the girl get up and set the saucer down in the tray resting on the whatnot in the corner, tidying its contents as she did so. The urge to learn more of Theo's life was strong and she could not resist resuming her questions.

"Why does the duke's mother not reside with him?"

Martha let out a little giggle. "Her ladyship can't abide Devenal Castle, she says, but Mrs Oughtibridge says that ain't it." She then threw a hand to her mouth, looking conscious and tutted at herself. "I beg you'll forget I said that, miss. That's what comes of speaking so free, as Mrs Oughtibridge has told me often and often."

Intrigued, Henrietta longed to probe. But she could not get Martha into trouble. "It is forgotten already. I am sorry if I made you speak out of turn, Martha. But I'm glad to know all you've told me. Thank you."

"It's no trouble, miss. I've not told you much when all's said. There's a deal Mrs Oughtibridge could tell you, for as she's been with the family nigh on thirty year. Knows it all, she does. Not as well as Mr Flint, for he was a footman when the old duke took the title. Theodore too, he was, and this duke was named for his grandpa as being the first boy born to one of Duke Theodore's sons. Duke Oliver was never blessed with a boy, and his first wife, Mr Flint says, couldn't bring no babies to term at all and in the end she died trying."

Which explained how Theo came into the title and duties he had never wanted to inherit. Although he must have known, since his own father's death, that he might well do so. "When did Duke Oliver marry again, then?"

Martha had come back to the bedside as she rattled off the last and she sat down again, leaning a little towards Henrietta in a manner both eager and confiding. "Well, as Mr Flint tells it, miss, it were our duke as urged Duke Oliver to it after Lord Lionel died. Fifteen or thereabouts, he must have been then. When he knew as Duke Oliver were thinking about getting hisself a new wife, our duke said as he should and welcome. Seemingly his grace weren't suited with being the heir, for as he was one as wished to travel and see the world, Mr Flint says. The minute Duke Oliver was married, off he went. Only it was Lady Ella who arrived and no boys at all."

"But did not Mister Theo — as he then was — come back again?"

"He did, miss, and was living at the Manor until her grace was with child again. Mrs Oughtibridge says as Duke Oliver were certain sure it must be a boy this time and he didn't object to Mister Theo going off again."

Thinking he was safe, of course. "But it wasn't a boy, was it?"

Martha sighed. "No, miss. And after Lady Pru were born and Duke Oliver were ailing, he sent to Mister Theo to come home. That he did, miss, and were obliged to take the title after all when Duke Oliver died and it become clear as her grace wasn't again increasing."

"Goodness, do you say they had to wait for that?"

"Ooh yes, miss. The whole household were on tenterhooks, for if she had been, we'd all have been waiting for the birth to know if there were a new duke to come or no. Mrs Oughtibridge said as it were a mercy in the end as her grace weren't expecting again, for as it would have meant more waiting, and then, if it were a boy, trustees and all. Moreover, his grace would likely have had to run all in any event until the boy were grown."

"Without having the benefit for himself? Yes, I see."

Poor Theo. Although she was sure he would have done his duty without being the duke. And might have pleased himself in matters of the heart, perhaps? *No, Henrietta Latimer. There is no point in thinking like that.* Theo was the duke. There was no getting around it. He had been perfectly clear about his duty. She would not do and that was that.

"Are you hungry, miss? I should think you must be."

With a reluctant sigh, Henrietta turned her thoughts to the needs of her body. "A little, Martha. What do you suggest?"

Mr Latimer had been shown into the smallest of the upstairs saloons. A measure of Flint's judgement? Or had the butler divined the uneasy relationship existing between his master and this particular visitor?

The Green Saloon was in general reserved for those who came on business rather than a social matter. It was a trifle more formal than the bigger rooms, with its green-striped furnishings with a gold trim and plain dull green walls and had been reserved for the card players on the night of Cecilia's soirée.

Hetty's father was standing at the window, looking out no doubt upon the rose garden situated on that side of the house, just now colourful in its summer bloom.

Theo closed the door, the click of the latch sounding loud in the silence. Mr Latimer turned and looked across at him, his expression austere. He did not speak and Theo, bracing against the expected storm, moved into the centre of the room. With a view to diffusing the difficult atmosphere, he began on a mild note. "Good morning, sir. Have you yet seen your daughter?"

Latimer lifted his chin. "I have not."

The tone was far from encouraging. Theo tried again. "You will be glad to know that I received a comfortable account of her from Miss Latimer at breakfast. She slept well, I believe, and the wound is at least no worse."

A nod came, as if this news were of less account than whatever the wretched fellow had come to say. Irritation itched at Theo's breast. Should not Hetty's condition have been his first concern? He tried a different tack.

"I am also able to reassure you, sir, that my people have removed all such traps from my woods." He waited, but no response was forthcoming. "Unfortunately, there is no sign of the perpetrator, but I have ordered my gamekeeper to increase his patrols."

Latimer pursed his lips, but vouchsafed no other sign.

With an inward curse, Theo moved to the mantel and indicated the chair to one side. "Would you care to sit down, sir? It is evident you have a deal on your mind."

Latimer eyed him a moment, looked at the chair and then moved to a position where Theo was obliged to confront him face to face. "You are correct in your surmise, your grace."

The formal address threw Theo into annoyance. Was it to distance him? To belittle his supposed pretensions? He waited in rising indignation for what the fellow might say next. It came, on a note of heavy chagrin.

"I am in the unhappy position, sir, of being obliged to one for whom I cannot conjure the necessary feeling of gratitude."

"Meaning me," Theo snapped, abandoning all attempts to avoid the confrontation. "Then pray don't trouble to try, sir. I neither desire nor expect your gratitude. Anything I did was for your daughter's relief, not yours."

Latimer's eyes, so like Hetty's, filled with sudden satisfaction. "Excellent. Then I need have no compunction in speaking my mind."

"I wish you won't, sir. But I warn you I shall give as good as I get."

"I should expect nothing less from a whippersnapper whose impertinence is already legendary."

Theo gripped the mantel with one hand, struggling to keep his temper. "Are you referring to my refusal to kowtow to the dictates of social etiquette?"

"I refer, *your grace*, to the dismissive attitude you have adopted towards your so-called inferiors, myself included."

The charge, which he could scarcely deny, rebuked him. But it maligned him too. He fought back. "My attitude, as you call it, was not meant for impertinence, sir. If I seem reserved —"

"Reserved! When you have made it your business to hold aloof at all times?"

"That is only because —"

He was ridden over, Latimer's features contorting with rage. "Who are you, sir, to look down upon your neighbours? To place yourself upon so high a form that you may ignore the common courtesies of life? Worst of all, to treat with indignity a genteel girl of a birth evidently too low to command due respect? My daughter, sir, is not a milkmaid!"

So that was it. He was unforgiven for the first misunderstanding. Theo burned with the injustice of it, even while his conscience pricked at his subsequent encounters with Hetty. But treat her with indignity? That he could never do. Or had he? But the frustration engendered by the tirade superseded any effort to examine the question. "You labour yet under a misapprehension, Mr Latimer. If you had allowed either of us to explain —"

"Explain, sir? What is there to explain? Did my eyes deceive me, then? Was the indecorous posture a mirage?"

"I was trying to help her!"

"To do what? Become little better than a lightskirt?"

"Oh, this is impossible!" Goaded beyond endurance, Theo left the mantel and marched across the room, half inclined to walk straight out of the place. He stopped short at the door, glaring at its wooden panels. He could not leave it there, he must not, for Hetty's sake. With an effort, he turned to confront the man again and found Latimer had taken his place at the mantel, resting his head on one hand, his back to the room. A riffle of concern shook Theo out of his fury. He took a couple of steps towards the man. "Mr Latimer?"

His unwelcome guest straightened and turned a haggard countenance upon him. The change was all too reminiscent of

Hetty's mercurial temperament. Latimer's voice was redolent with feeling. "I promised my wife I would not refer to that matter. I had not realised how my blood still boiled on account of it."

About to retort that it was without reason, Theo held his tongue. He might plead innocence upon that occasion. His later conduct would not bear investigation. If Latimer were to know the half of it! He changed tack. "I was led to expect you would take me to task for allowing traps to be set upon my land."

Latimer's head came up, a trace of fire back in his eyes. "So I would have done, had not remembrance of your earlier behaviour overwhelmed my intent."

Impatience claimed Theo. "I wish you will have done with that, sir. It was not what you thought you saw."

The echo of Hetty's eyes regarded him in a fashion as bleak and cool as they had before been fiery. "Indeed? Then what possessed you to throw a despicable accusation at my head?"

That rankled, did it? Theo moved back into the room, willing himself to make an apology he felt altogether disinclined to offer. Instead, he turned it back upon Latimer. "Tit for tat, sir. You came here under protest today. Your misplaced accusations that day drove me likewise into fighting back."

To his surprise, a dry laugh escaped the man. "I'll concede you have brass enough, young man, even if your manners leave a deal to be desired."

Theo eyed him with returning resentment. "You presume too much, Mr Latimer. Is it your custom to make hasty judgements?"

The fellow's brows rose in a fashion that reminded Theo instead of his other daughter. "Such as?"

He set his teeth. "I have my faults, sir, but what you deem impertinence comes not from any sense of superiority. I have seen too much to be contemptuous of my fellow man."

"At your age?"

"I may be young in your eyes, but I am a seasoned traveller and I did not waste my time abroad in hedonistic pursuits. Moreover, I was not groomed for the position I now occupy, nor did I seek it. If you find me aloof, it is because I shrink from parading a false public face."

Latimer's eyes narrowed. "People may take as they find or go hang, is that it?"

Theo gave a short laugh. "In a nutshell."

"Then I have mistaken arrogance for conceit. One is as reprehensible as the other."

"I thank you. Have you any further vilifications you would care to make?"

The brows shot up again. "So haughty? You do not hesitate to come the duke when it suits you, I notice."

Knowing this to be true did nothing to aid Theo's command of his temper. "What do you want of me, Mr Latimer? I am as I am. Have you no faults?"

"Indeed, but I make an effort to overcome them."

"Not noticeably!"

Latimer appeared to struggle with himself. His fiery glance subsided after a moment and his mouth twisted. "*Touché*, Duke!"

Theo let his breath go as the tumult in his breast died down. He moved to the bell-pull and tugged. "I'm sending for wine, sir. I need it, even if you don't."

Latimer nodded, his gaze still fixed upon Theo. "I'll take a glass."

"Will you sit?"

To Theo's relief, he elected at last to take a seat in the chair to one side of the mantelpiece. Theo took the other, feeling perfectly filleted. Mr Latimer's eyes still raked him and the man's first words did nothing for his comfort. "You may embark upon your explanation, Duke."

Theo cursed inwardly. Now that chance offered, he was reluctant to say a word. So much had passed since, the first meeting had become hazy in his mind. He opted for simplicity. "The incident was innocent, Mr Latimer. Your daughter wandered into my woods where I was out shooting. She called out to warn me of her presence. She had become disorientated and we guided her to the lane to set her on her way."

"We?"

"My gamekeeper was with me. He knows the area better than I."

"Ah, yes, Beattock. I know him." Latimer's gaze remained keen and oddly disturbing. "Proceed."

Conscious of inner disquiet, Theo belatedly realised the difficulty in disclosing the rest. It was innocent enough in context, arising as it had out of the teasing banter. Yet the intimacy he'd felt at the time made it questionable. There was no going back. He drew breath. "Miss Latimer was distressed by the wreck of her flowers. I was in the act of drying her cheeks when you came upon us."

Latimer's gaze bored into him and his tone was dry. "Indeed? My daughter is then incapable of performing such an office for herself, I take it?"

The deuce! How was he to answer that? The words left his lips without will. "I have an aversion to seeing a female weep. I wanted her to stop." That damned sceptical gaze! He grew hot and his neckcloth felt tight.

"I see."

At least there was no explosion of wrath. Theo forced himself to meet the man's steady regard. He waited, the tightness in his chest at one with the flitting memories of his far less innocent dealings with Hetty.

The door opened. With perfect timing, Flint entered, Robert at his heels. Theo saw the tray the footman carried and relief swept through him. The butler had anticipated his need. He watched Robert set down the heavily burdened tray and assumed as natural an air as he could.

"Madeira, Mr Latimer?"

"That will be satisfactory."

No word of thanks. Well, what did he expect? He signed to Flint to do the honours as the footman retired. The visitor took a glass from the silver salver the butler presented and sipped. Theo seized his drink and took a gulp, with difficulty refraining from tossing it off and demanding more.

Latimer watched Flint leave the room and then turned his gaze back upon his host. "Your story tallies in general with Henrietta's. Therefore I must accept it."

The tone was grudging and Theo could not bring himself to thank the man. He waited. Would there be more?

Latimer looked at his glass and sipped. "A tolerable wine. Your uncle always kept a good cellar."

Diverted, Theo frowned. "You knew him?"

"We all knew him. A bonhomous type, was Oliver. Easy with his fellow man."

Unlike his nephew, he might as well have said. Reluctant to re-open hostilities, Theo kept his tongue, taking refuge in throwing the rest of his Madeira down his throat.

Latimer likewise finished what was in his glass and set the vessel down. "I may now thank you for your care of my daughter with a good heart, Duke."

Theo felt no urge to respond in kind. "I could scarcely do less than I did."

"My wife assures me you did more than might be expected." The intimidating look was back. "Did you seek to curry favour?"

Taken aback, Theo stared at him. "With you, sir?"

"Or with my wife. She appears to cherish an inordinate faith in your good qualities. I cannot think you might hope to placate me."

Annoyance got the better of Theo. "I had no thought of placating anyone, sir. Nor of currying favour. All I cared for was your daughter's agony and distress. Or is my character too besmirched in your eyes to believe that?"

Latimer's brows rose again. "Here's a heat!"

Theo rose, lost in wrath. "You have impugned me in every way, sir, but this is the outside of enough! If you have more interest in my possible motives than in your daughter's injury, so be it. It is otherwise with me."

Latimer was on his feet. "Now we come to it. You admit an interest in Henrietta?"

"In her comfort, yes."

"And what more?"

Theo's simmering resentment got the better of him. "Are we back to that? Allow me to reassure you, Mr Latimer. I have no pretensions towards your daughter's hand."

"Well for you, sir. I should certainly refuse my consent."

The words were thrown at his head, Latimer squaring up to him, his stance pugnacious. Theo received them with a violence of feeling. Refuse? The fellow would refuse a future so advantageous to Hetty? He stared at the man. "I beg your pardon?"

Latimer barked a mirthless laugh. "Shocked you, have I? Of course I have. You supposed me to be angling for it, did you not? Seduced by rank and position, eh?" He sank back on his heels, looking supremely smug, much to Theo's chagrin. "When I give one of my daughters into the keeping of another man, sir, it will be to one I can respect, one whom I may trust to secure not merely her comfort but her happiness, at the expense of his own if need be. In a word, sir, a husband, not a title."

Theo could not utter a word. What was there to say? His breast was a tumult of conflicting emotion and his tongue balked at letting out even one of the rising thoughts in his head.

Latimer nodded, as if it was just as expected. "I will now visit Henrietta's bedside, Duke, if you will be so good as to show me the way."

Theo had rather throw him out of the window! Such a course was unfortunately ineligible. Seething, he led the way to the door.

CHAPTER FIFTEEN

How Lady Ella had discovered her presence in the house was unknown to Henrietta, but the little girl's chatter was a boon and a pleasure.

She had passed an indifferent night, sleeping only fitfully as each incautious motion of her limbs woke her with the reminding stab of pain in her injured foot and ankle. Beside her, Silvestre had slumbered on, waking only when Henrietta nudged her, beset by a need she could not withstand. Her twin's help with the bordaloo that had thankfully replaced the chamber pot was given freely, but she yawned back to sleep far more quickly than Henrietta, who welcomed the dawn at last.

Too many times her thoughts had wandered to a bedchamber somewhere in this house. What did Theo look like in repose? She found it hard to picture the energy contained, the teasing grey eyes veiled. Yet it was all too easy to imagine the strength of his arms about her and the touch of his lips on her forehead or hair. Henrietta knew she blushed in the darkness, but the longings would not be dismissed.

The morning was balm, bringing the distraction of the difficulties inherent in performing the necessary ablutions and dressing, normally so routine. She relied heavily upon her sister and Martha, although the wounds soon subsided to a dull ache once she was settled.

The maid served her with breakfast while Silvestre, for the sake of politeness, went down to join the duke's family. Henrietta had scarcely finished her rolls and hot chocolate when the door opened and Lady Ella peeped into the room, mischief in her face.

Amused, Henrietta called out at once. "Goodness, is that you, Ellie? Come in, do."

The child skipped up to the bed. "You got grabbed like a rabbit."

Henrietta smiled. "Yes, I did. Horrid it was too."

"Can I see?"

"I'm afraid not, for the wounds are covered up."

Which brought Martha tutting to the bedside. "Now just you behave, young madam. We won't have none of your ghoulish nonsense here, if you please. She's a right one for liking the horridest things, miss. Don't you go plaguing the lady, Miss Ellie."

Lady Ella looked mutinous. "Not plaguing. I'm just asking." She turned a gaze sparkling with excitement on Henrietta. "Did it hurt?"

"Yes, it did. Very much."

"Well, and I should think it might too. What a question! Don't you encourage her, miss, or she'll be asking all manner of silly things, naughty piece."

But the distraction was all too appealing and Henrietta invited the child to sit on the bed. Nothing loath, Lady Ella scrambled up, ignoring Martha's scolding admonitions to mind the lady's poor foot, climbed over Henrietta and plonked down on Silvestre's vacated side in a pose as careless as it was indecorous.

Martha was scandalised. "What would Miss Jurby say if she could see you sitting like that?"

Ellie shook a fist. "Don't go telling her, Martha! I'll get Thomas after you!"

The maid flushed with wrath and Henrietta thought it prudent to intervene.

"Martha, I would dearly love a cup of coffee. Would you mind fetching one while Ellie is here to mind me?"

"Mind you? She don't mind no one, naughty piece. Excepting her governess and his grace."

"I meant Lady Ella may help me with anything while you are gone."

The maid tossed her head. "If she can be made to listen for half a minute 'stead of talking her head off, miss, which ain't nowise certain."

Lady Ella waved a hand, imperious all at once. "Yes, I shall listen 'cos I like her."

"Ooh, it's honoured you are, miss."

Ignoring the maid's sarcasm, Henrietta reiterated her desire for coffee and Martha went off, muttering to herself. Henrietta turned to the triumphant Ellie.

"You embarrassed the poor thing, Ellie. That wasn't very kind. Who is Thomas?"

Lady Ella did not look in the least chastened. "He's the second footman and he likes Martha, only she don't want him and she says he bothers her all the time, 'cept Betty says it's 'cos Oughtibridge won't have any hanky-panky in the house."

It was plain the child ran free in the domestic quarters, although Henrietta doubted she understood the significance of what she heard. Henrietta ignored the disclosures.

"How is it you have escaped your governess? Are you having a holiday?"

Ellie was examining the bandage. "I'm allowed to play more when we're here. Did Theo bandage you? Robert said he brung you with the hurdle."

"Brought," corrected Henrietta automatically, "not brung. And yes, he did, with his neckcloth. But this is the bandage the doctor put on."

"Can we take it off so I can see your rabbit foot?"

"Certainly not. Only the doctor can take it off."

"I want to see! Is it all furry?"

Henrietta laughed. "Of course not. It's just my foot. Where did you get that idea?"

"Robert said the rabbit trap got you and you got a rabbit foot."

"Gracious, did he? I think he must have been teasing you." Or more likely Lady Ella had misunderstood. But she prudently changed the subject. "Are you allowed to play in the woods?"

"Mama won't let me 'cos she thinks I'll drown in the lake. I can go if Theo takes me. I can do anything if I have Theo, only he won't marry me when I'm growed up 'cos he couldn't stand me chattering in his ear all his life. But he has to anyway 'cos he's my garden."

"I think you mean guardian," said Henrietta, in no way averse to talking of Theo.

"Yes, and he's the best guardian in the world 'cos he never shouts and says silly things about girls and he doesn't mind if I have adventures either."

Having seen for herself how Theo treated his wards, Henrietta could well appreciate this point of view. But she ought to deflect the child's bias. "But you are fond of your nurse, I expect."

"Moggy's all right. She don't bother me. 'Sides, she's busy with Pru mostly 'cos she don't think Gatty is fit to look after a worm, never mind Baby Pru."

The prattle was clearly culled from the nurse's lips without any real idea of the implications. It was plain the child had few inhibitions and was apt to glean a good deal of information from her elders that would better be kept to themselves. In a word, she was running wild. Henrietta had a brief vision of how Papa would have reacted had she or Silvestre expressed themselves in the way Ellie did, and her mind boggled.

Lady Ella chattered on, shifting from one thing to another, and Henrietta could not but wonder how the duchess allowed her to be so much in the company of servants. Or was this laxity confined to Whisley Park?

"How do you spend your days when you are at Devenal?" she chimed in, picking a moment when Ellie took a breath.

The child grimaced. "Old Jurby makes me do my letters and all that. I like Bunny best 'cos I'm allowed out riding every day for exercise 'cos Mama says it'll tire me out of my restiss energy."

"Restless, Ellie. Rest-less."

"That's right. She says I have too much rest-less energy and it fidgets her, so she likes me to go with Bunny. I'd rather go with Theo, but he has to do his duking and it takes forever and he don't have enough time for me."

"But you must spend time with your mama every day too, I expect."

"Yes, but it's boring 'cos she wants me to be quiet and sew and listen to a story and I don't like them stories 'cos princesses don't have no adventures. And she says I'm not allowed *Bluebeard* and it's the best story in the book."

Henrietta laughed. "Yes, I suppose it is just the tale to appeal to your bloodthirsty tastes, Ellie. I always found it horrid. I liked *Sleeping Beauty* the best."

Lady Ella made a disgusted face. "But she does nothing but sleep!"

"She goes up the tower. Wouldn't you have gone up the tower to find out where it went?"

"We've got better towers at Devenal, only Theo won't let me up them 'cos they're dangeruss. He took me up once and it did make my heart bump like he said it would and he had to carry me down 'cos my legs got scared and wouldn't move."

A salutary lesson. How typical of Theo. "Ah, so now you know why you must not go up there, I dare say."

"Yes, and Theo is glad 'cos I don't plague him about it, he said. There's lots of things I plague him about, he says, and when he gets rid of them all he's going to stop calling me monkey face. But I like him calling me monkey face 'cos he makes me laugh, so I'm going to plague him forever and ever."

Henrietta could not help laughing, although she dared say this programme would not be to Theo's taste. But did he realise how much the child stood in need of proper guidance? Of course it was the duchess's business to ensure she was instructed, but it seemed Ellie had no example to set her on the right path. Perhaps it was not such an advantage to be surrounded by servants. Henrietta's childhood had been far different, with her twin's constant company and Mama's careful training, together with the precepts inculcated by Papa. Nevertheless, she had grown up as lively as Ellie, but with a far better notion of appropriate conduct.

Her ruminations, punctured by the child's remarks, were interrupted by Martha's reappearance with the requested coffee and tidings that added nothing to Henrietta's comfort.

"Miss Latimer said to tell you your father is come, miss. He's meeting with his grace in the Green Saloon."

Oh, no! Papa and Theo? What in the world was he saying to the duke? He was bound to upbraid him. Theo would not take kindly to that. The possibilities dismayed her as she sipped her coffee, paying scant attention to Ellie. The child had embarked upon an involved story of an adventure she was planning, which seemed chiefly to consist of battling imaginary villains in the castle at Devenal.

When the door opened to admit Silvestre rather than Papa, Henrietta was inordinately relieved. Her twin lost no time in getting upon terms with Lady Ella, who volunteered to escort her when she expressed interest in the rose garden.

"Later, perhaps. For the moment, I must remain with my twin."

This at once caught Ellie's attention. "Are you twins? You ought to look the same, then."

Silvestre laughed. "Don't you think we do?"

The child peered first into Henrietta's face and then eyed her sister closely. She shook her head with decision. "No, 'cos this one is soft and you ain't."

"I hope you don't mean soft in the head," Henrietta protested.

"Just soft, like this pillow."

"How am I to take that, pray?"

But Silvestre was laughing. "She has gauged the matter exactly. Well done, Ellie."

The child grinned. "I'll call you Softy."

"Thank you, but I should infinitely prefer Hetty. Softy indeed!"

"Softy Hetty, Softy Hetty," chanted the girl, giggling the while.

Henrietta threw an exasperated glance at her sister and Martha instantly called the child to order.

"You'll address the lady as Miss Hetty, as is proper, young madam, and no more nonsense or I'll put you out of the room."

Ellie shrieked defiance. "No! I want to stay with Softy! I want to see her rabbit foot when the doctor comes!"

"You won't be allowed in when the doctor comes, so don't you think it. Now be off with you!"

The maid advanced upon the bed, causing Ellie to leap off and scramble around the room to escape. The ensuing chase set Silvestre off laughing, but Henrietta felt obliged to intervene.

"Ellie, come here! Martha, don't excite her so, for goodness' sake!"

The maid seized the child near the door just as a knock sounded and it opened. Henrietta's heart sank as she saw Papa standing in the aperture and glimpsed Theo behind him.

The cacophony within the room held Theo from walking away as he had intended. Peering over Latimer's shoulder, he took in the scene in one comprehensive glance and swore inwardly.

"Give me leave, sir." With which, he pushed past the guest and went in, his eyes on his little cousin. "Ellie, be quiet!" The sharp tone silenced her instantly and she stared up at him in mute question. "That is better. Let her go, Martha."

The maid released her and stood back. Theo held out his hand and Ellie took it at once.

"Theo, I want —"

He lifted a warning finger. "Not a word!"

She peeped up at him, uncertainty in her little face, and he very nearly gave in to the impulse to indulge her. But it would not do. His stock with Latimer was bad enough. The last thing he needed was his ward's impertinence making things worse.

He glanced towards the bed. Silvestre was looking amused, but Hetty was plainly horrified. Was it her father's reaction she feared? He had not seen her since yesterday. At any other time he would go across and let the world go hang. But his castigation at her father's lips was too raw to permit of his doing anything to call attention to the intimacy between them.

"I will relieve you of her presence, Miss Latimer. As you see, your father is here to see you."

Her eyes dulled and she looked down. "Thank you, your grace."

Your grace? Oh, Hetty. But Latimer was in the room and Ellie was tugging at his hand with impatience. He kept hold of the child and walked out of the room, closing the door behind him.

"I wanted to stay, Theo!"

The whine pricked at his sorely tried temper and he released Ellie's hand and swung her up into his arms. "If I was any sort of a proper guardian, I would give you a smacking where it might do some good, you horrible brat."

Her mischief quenched in a look faintly apprehensive. "You won't, will you?"

He could not resist. "Of course not. I'll get Jurby to do it."

"Theo!"

"Monkey face!" Her face puckered and he relented, giving her cheek a peck. "Don't fret, sweetheart. I'm teasing."

She sighed and smiled, catching him about the neck for a cuddle. "I knew you wouldn't really."

Vent his ill temper on the child? Unthinkable. Neither could he blame Hetty for the possession of a father whose attitude had effectively driven the wedge between them he'd been attempting to create himself. But his ward's conduct still called for question.

"What were you doing in there, Miss Nosy?"

Not much to his surprise, Ellie was unperturbed by the scolding note. "I was talking to Softy."

"Softy? Who in heaven's name is Softy?"

"Softy Hetty. I call her that 'cos she's all soft. Not like the other one."

Her perspicacity astonished him. The accuracy of the description caused a flurry of misplaced tenderness in his breast. The deuce! He had to stop this. He set off down the corridor towards the stairs. "Well, you're not to call her Softy, you hear me? It's rude. You'll call her Miss Latimer or Miss Hetty."

"But she is a softy."

"It makes no odds. Don't go plaguing her either."

"She likes me to plague her. She asked me things and I told her about *Bluebeard* and my adventures."

Theo gave it up. He was in no mood to deal with his determined little cousin. He set her down at the stairs and urged her up the second flight. "Back to the nursery, monkey face. And if I catch you snooping down here again while Miss Hetty's here, there'll be trouble."

Ellie had started up the stairs, but she paused at that and turned to frown at him. "Ain't she staying?"

"Of course not. She is only here while her foot mends."

"But I like her. I want Softy to stay!"

"Well, you can't always have what you want, can you?"

"Don't you want her to stay, Theo? I thought you liked her too."

A stab of discomfort affected Theo. Yes, he liked her all too well, that was the difficulty. "Enough! She'll go home again as soon as she's better and that's that."

"But what about her rabbit foot? I won't get to see it."

"Rabbit foot? What nonsense is this?"

Ellie frowned. "Don't she have a rabbit foot? The rabbit trap grabbed her, didn't it?"

"Yes, and it gave her a wound."

"Then she has got a rabbit foot. Rabbit foots are lucky."

"I don't think Hetty would agree with you," he returned on a rueful note.

"I'm going to tell her she's lucky."

Which effectively brought Theo back to reality. "You'll do nothing of the kind. You are not to go sneaking into her room again. Do you understand?" Ellie began to pout and his temper rose. "Don't you dare show me that face!" He pointed. "Upstairs! Now!"

She went, but with lagging steps, looking back. He was tempted to retract, but the interview with Latimer had left him too bruised to indulge Ellie. She was resilient enough to bounce back, and she was perfectly aware he was not really angry with her.

When she reached the landing, he turned and made his way back to his own apartments. He needed a moment to himself before Hathersage plied him with papers. The private sitting-room was his refuge. None but his valet was permitted to disturb him here. The household was aware to a man that any message must be relayed through Gateley if he was in his own apartments. The prohibition did not extend to his aunt, of course, but Cecilia, thank heaven, would not think of bearding him in his own rooms. She was far more likely to send Swarland, who would not have the temerity to gainsay the valet against his express prohibition.

Theo threw himself onto the daybed which overlooked the front lawns and stared out of the window, brooding. The interview with Latimer had provoked him on so many levels he hardly knew where to start. The outcome, he realised, was unpalatable. He was obligated to curtail any private intercourse with Hetty.

Galling as it was, he could not but acknowledge the wisdom of the undertaking. For her sake, as much as his own. Latimer could not have been plainer. His dukedom meant nothing. His character was wanting and that was that. The smart could not readily be overcome.

Was he so despicable a man? When one looked at it, what evidence had Latimer to support his dislike? Or, no. Say disdain, or contempt. Merely because he would not kowtow to the dictates of Society? What, must he grovel to the whims of the gentry roundabout? What had Latimer said? Uncle Oliver was a bonhomous type? Well, and so he was. Did it therefore follow that Theo must be the same because he succeeded to his dignities? It was not his style. He did not choose the life. It chose him. He'd done his damnedest to escape it. To no avail. Had Ellie or Pru been a boy, he would not be in this situation, condemned to the castigations of a man far inferior in station.

No, that was unjust. Unworthy. If anything, he preferred to be treated without those sycophantic platitudes that Cecilia took as her due. He could admire Latimer for ignoring his rank, if only his criticisms had been just.

Was he arrogant? He was accused of looking down on his neighbours. Of thinking himself superior. Neither was true. But he did expect people to take him as they found him. Why should he not? It had nothing to do with being a duke. He had been so always.

"You take after me, my dear one. Your papa was just like Oliver."

His mother's voice in his head, soothing. Yes, his father had been very easy with his fellow men, as far as he remembered. Easy with his son. Lax in discipline, some might have said. But Papa did not believe in coercion, and Theo had taken a lesson from that.

"You will get far more from people if you allow them to think for themselves. I had rather see you a competent individual, Theo, who knows his own mind, than a fool who depends on me and others to know what he must do. Use the brains God gave you, my dear boy, and keep your eyes open to learning."

He had taken the words to heart, and his travels had inculcated a thirst for knowledge of the wider world. What he could not see for himself, he found in books. But nothing taught a man more of humanity than to steep himself in the cultures of other lands. It had given him a distaste for the narrow confines of English society. No, Mr Latimer. He was less arrogant than his compatriots, who mistook their petty lives of leisure and indulgence for real living. If they could only see what he had witnessed! If there was any virtue in his being a duke, it was that his position enabled him at least to remedy some of the ills endured by those less fortunate than himself.

Yet he must be vilified for refusing to partake of the fashionable foibles that so engaged Cecilia and her ilk. Lord, but he did hold them in contempt! In that, at least, Latimer had hit the mark. Was it arrogance?

All at once it occurred to him that he despised them for an ignorance they could not help. But this arrogance, if it was that, did not extend to Hetty. Because he liked her? Because she amused him? Because he knew he had her affection?

The thought stilled in his head. Was that more arrogance? More conceit, as Latimer would have it.

Affection … but not irrevocable. She would forget him when he was absent. When he married, as he must in due course. Cecilia, herself an earl's daughter, was already scanning for potential duchesses to take her place. Some high-born female drilled into conformable behaviour who would drive him to tedium in a week.

Damn it to hell! Why must duty be so unpalatable? What did he want with such a cold creature when he might have Hetty's warmth, Hetty's crazy antics and her appalling sensibility? But he couldn't have them, could he? Latimer would never give his precious daughter into Theo's keeping. He had made that abundantly plain.

As well. It must make it easier to hold aloof — once she was out of his house. Sheer courtesy demanded he at least discover how she did. Especially after her father's visit. Did she know he had first demanded an interview with the master of the house? Hell and the devil! Hetty would be anxious on that account. If nothing else, he must set her mind at rest. Though he could scarcely reveal the substance of the acrimonious discussion. He ran it under rapid review, wondering what in the world he could say to relieve Hetty's apprehension.

CHAPTER SIXTEEN

The doctor's probing fingers caused enough discomfort to drag Henrietta's mind from remembrance of Papa's visit. She had been on tenterhooks throughout, fearing what he might say of Theo, desperate at the thought of what had passed in that interview. Theo's sombre look had chilled her, setting up the horridest speculations in her head.

"It is looking a degree less angry, Miss Latimer, you will be glad to hear."

"Is it?" She felt her cheeks grow warm and hastily amended this. "I mean, I am relieved, of course."

An amused look came her way as Doctor Rudchester raised his head. "You need not pretend, ma'am. I have no doubt it still pains you very much, and I should be surprised if you felt much relief at this juncture."

She had to laugh. "Well, it is true that I feel perfectly frustrated, sir." Papa's dismaying dictum came into her head. "The sooner it mends, the better, however. My father is anxious for me to return home."

The doctor straightened, directing a frowning glance upon her. "I should not advocate a removal quite yet. I would prefer to see you on your feet before you attempt it."

The painful hollow revisited her breast, the one that had opened up when Papa said his piece. "You will not wish to be beholden to the duchess, Hetty. We will bring you home at once. I shall arrange it."

"I'm afraid I must attempt it, sir," she told the doctor, albeit with reluctance. "I may be able to hop, don't you think?"

"No, I do not think!" The doctor came around to the bedside, leaving her unbandaged foot exposed. "Miss Latimer, you have sustained a severe injury, as you will realise the moment you attempt to put this foot to the ground. As for hopping, such untoward motion is liable to bring it on to bleed again. The wounds must have time to close properly."

She stared up at him, beset with conflicting emotions. What was she to do? Papa had been adamant, even when Silvestre had intervened.

"Papa, should we not consult with the doctor before moving her?"

"It makes no matter. Grimdale will attend her at home. I have every confidence in his ability to do as much as this fellow Rudchester."

For herself, Henrietta dreaded leaving Theo's vicinity and yearned for it too. It was torture to be so near and yet not be able to see him, wondering at every moment if he might come in. To be borne out of reach would make it certain she could not meet him. On the other hand, she hated the thought of losing the hope altogether. But to leave without knowing what Papa had said to him!

She dared an impulsive throw. "Well, sir, if — if you think it will not do —"

"It most certainly won't, ma'am, if you don't wish to retard your progress."

"No … at least … well, perhaps you might say as much to my mother? She intends to come today, though I don't know when."

Only Mama could curb Papa's intent. He might listen to her.

The doctor pursed his lips. "If she is not here by the time I have done my best for you, I will leave a message for Mrs Latimer with your sister, if you suppose that may answer."

It might. But Silvestre had seized the opportunity to go down to the gardens.

"If you are able to see her, sir."

He smiled, returning to the end of the bed. "Martha here will go and find her for me, will you not?"

The maid curtsied but stood her ground. "I'm not to leave Miss Hetty, sir. Not as Mrs Oughtibridge ain't here."

"Then ring the bell and we shall get her here." Impatience sounded in the doctor's voice, but he paid no further heed as he bent again to his task. "Now then, a little more of my basilicum is needed, I think."

Her whirling apprehension made it easier to bear his further attentions to her wounds as he applied his powder and began re-bandaging the foot. The housekeeper arrived during this operation and the colloquy between her and the doctor as to the state of the injury left Henrietta free to think.

What if Papa remained adamant? What had been said between him and Theo that caused him to insist upon her instant removal? It could not be but that an altercation had occurred. If only Papa was not so prejudiced! Only she could not tell him how he misjudged Theo, could she? She dared not. He would demand to know how she knew so much. She could scarcely tell him of those encounters between that first one and this.

The rhythm of her pulses went awry and a horrid sick feeling seized her stomach at the thought of Papa's emotions were he to hear how Theo had been obliged to extract her from the tree, or how they had spoken so freely — twice! — in this very house on the night of the soirée. As for the exchanges as he'd cared for her at the accident and since —! No, Papa must never know. Unthinkable. She grew hot with embarrassment at the imagined expression on his face. Such a rage he would be in.

She fairly shuddered, bringing unwanted attention from the doctor and Mrs Oughtibridge at the foot of the bed.

"Am I hurting you, Miss Latimer?"

"No, indeed. At least, only a little." She thrust the thoughts away. "I am very grateful to you, sir, for coming again."

The doctor smiled. "My dear young lady, I am here at his grace's request." He tucked in the end of his bandage. "There, that will serve, Mrs Oughtibridge. I rely upon you to ensure Miss Latimer remains where she is for another day." He threw a minatory glance at Henrietta. "No hopping, if you please, ma'am. I shall speak to his grace on this subject when I see him."

Speak to Theo? And tell him of Papa's insistence, no doubt. As if it was not obvious things were bad enough in that quarter. What should she do? "I should much prefer it if you spoke to my mother, sir."

Rudchester was packing the items he had used into his bag, but he looked up, brows raised. "I shall do so if I can, of course, or your sister. But I must also report to his grace."

Because Theo employed him on her behalf? She dared not say more. She could hardly entreat him not to mention Papa's demand without speaking of the hostility between him and Theo.

To her relief, the door opened to admit her twin, the maid behind her. Silvestre glanced at the re-bandaged foot and approached the doctor. "You wished to speak to me, Doctor Rudchester?"

"Yes, indeed, Miss Latimer." Henrietta kept her anxious gaze on her sister as the doctor repeated all he had said to her, stressing the dangers. "It is imperative, in my opinion, that the foot remains relatively static for another four and twenty hours at least. Pray warn Mrs Latimer that the wounds are yet in danger of breaking out bleeding again. Indeed, the wound on your sister's heel is by no means closed as yet and bled a little at my touch."

"I see." Silvestre sent Hetty a reassuring glance. "I shall certainly convey your remarks to my mother, sir. She will have no desire to go against your advice, I am sure."

She would not, no. But how to persuade Papa? He meant her to remove from this house without delay. If Mama could not deter him, he would have her out before nightfall. Out of Theo's reach. That was his intention, was it not?

A lump formed in her throat and she had difficulty bidding the doctor farewell. Left alone with Silvestre, she hunted under the pillow for Theo's handkerchief.

"Hetty, you goose! Are you crying? For heaven's sake, don't be such a ninny!"

"It's n-not the w-wound, Silve."

Her twin sat on the bed and patted her in a soothing fashion. "I know it isn't. You don't want to go home and I'm not surprised."

Henrietta tried to sniff away her distress but the tears kept coming. "It's n-not that either."

"Well, what is it then?" She glanced to where the maid was busy gathering up the old bandage and making all tidy. "Martha, could you bring tea, if you please?"

The maid bustled up to the bed. "Feeling poorly, are you, miss? I expect that foot of yours is hurting bad now, is it? We'll soon set you to rights. Too many visitors as well, if you ask me. Not to mention that naughty little Lady Ella."

"Oh, she was showing me the gardens, Hetty," Silvestre chimed in, her tone bright and cheery, just as if Henrietta was a child herself in need of distraction. "She talked non-stop. Such an amusing child, she is."

"Yes." Henrietta essayed a dutiful smile. "You m-must tell me all about it."

Martha nodded with enthusiasm. "That's right, miss. And a cup of tea will set you up proper. You'll take some yourself, miss?"

This to her twin, who thanked her and enjoined her to hurry. No sooner had Martha got herself out of the room than Silvestre's tone changed. "Now then, dearest, what is the matter?"

Unable to help herself, Henrietta dissolved into tears again, putting Theo's handkerchief to her eyes and holding it there.

"Hetty, do stop! There can be no occasion for all this misery."

"Yes, there can," Henrietta protested, blowing her nose and crumpling the handkerchief in her fingers. "Did you not see how Theo looked? P-papa must have been horrid to him. I can't bear it, Silve. What did he say to him? You know what Papa is like when he is upset, and he was furious with Theo. He would not be insisting upon my coming home if there had not been an altercation."

"You don't know that. Papa was perfectly amiable."

"To me, yes, for he would never distress me when I'm in this state. But if you think he was amiable to Theo, you must have windmills in your head. I know Theo and he looked perfectly sombre. It's not like him at all. I know Papa said dreadful things to him and Theo would never endure them without hitting back. Oh, Silve, I'm so afraid they quarrelled."

Her twin was frowning a little but she remained as composed as ever. "Even if they did, there is no occasion for you to look so woebegone. Theo likes you too well to be put off, I'm sure."

"Put off what, Silve? There is no question of … of…" She faded out, unwilling to embark upon explanations that must inevitably lead her to reveal her secret knowledge of Theo's repeated insistence there could be nothing between them. Nothing for the future, at least. At this present, there was the balm of his affectionate treatment of her. But Papa, she was convinced, had ruined all hope of that continuing. Theo had given her such an alienating look.

To her relief, Silvestre did not pursue the matter, although she was wearing her enigmatic face. "Well, you may cease fretting. Mama will see to it you remain here at the doctor's behest."

A faint riffle of hope slid through Henrietta's breast. "Do you think so indeed?"

"Come, come, Hetty, you know as well as I that Papa is as wax in Mama's hands. Moreover, I am very sure she does not want you leaving this house in a hurry."

This was said with a significant look that set up a flurry of a different sort and caused Henrietta to regard her twin with suspicion.

"You need not look at me like that," said Silvestre, laughing. "Mama has your best interests at heart. I suspect she did not accompany Papa because she has gone off to confer with Aunt Angelica."

Suspicion turned to foreboding. "Confer about what?"

"Well, Aunt Angelica is friends with the duchess, isn't she?"

"What has that to say to anything?"

"She will be able to advise Mama."

"Advise her about what?"

"How to deal with the duchess, of course."

Henrietta drew a breath, all desire to weep gone. "Silve, tell me what is in the wind, I charge you."

Her twin raised her brows. "Why, nothing. Mama feels indebted to the duchess and she wishes to know how she should show her appreciation."

"I have lost the use of my foot, Silve, not my wits! Mama needs no assistance to know how to treat the duchess. Or indeed anyone else."

"You need not bite my nose off. Gracious, Hetty, you are being perfectly ridiculous."

Was she indeed? If this portended what she suspected, heaven help her! But neither Mama nor Silve could know Theo's determination. Nor could she tell them. She had not before thought of it, but it was quite as dangerous for Mama to know of the intimacies she had shared with Theo as for Papa to hear of it.

A dreadful thought occurred and she gave it voice at once. "Silve! Did you betray us — me — to Mama? Did you tell her —?"

"No, I did not," snapped her twin, becoming indignant. "How dare you suggest I would do such a thing?"

"You must have said something!"

"Oh, for heaven's sake, Hetty! Mama has eyes in her head, you know. All I told her was that I believe Theo likes you. Which, before you ring a peal over me, was in answer to her asking me if I did not think so."

"She asked that?"

"Why would she not? One would have to be a ninnyhammer not to recognise how much your Theo cared for your welfare, and Mama is not a ninnyhammer."

By no means. No one had more common sense than Mama. Her powers of observation were superior. But if she supposed there was the slightest chance of fostering a match between the duke and her daughter, she was in for a rude awakening. Yes,

Theo liked her more than a little. But duty came first. And Henrietta Latimer could not fulfil his duty.

Curiously, this thought strengthened her. Even were it possible, she cared too much to swerve Theo from the path of right. She would not do. He knew it, had said it from the first. She was not going to thrust herself in where she did not belong. She had rather suffer the heartache of loss than endure such humiliation.

Scarcely had she settled this determination in her mind than a knock at the door produced the man himself, poking his head around it.

"Are you chaperoned? May I come in?"

Silvestre rose at once and went up to him, speaking with great affability. "Yes, do come in, Duke. We are awaiting tea. Will you take a cup?"

Heavens, what was Silve about? Theo looked taken aback, and no wonder. He glanced at her and her heart sank as she took in the frowning severity of his features.

"I only came in for a moment."

"Well, sit down and talk to Hetty. I will catch the maid as she comes and ask for another cup."

She was at the door, but Theo stood his ground. "You are not leaving?"

"I'll just be in the corridor." She threw a saucy look at Henrietta. "Don't fret, Duke. We will leave the door open."

Then she was gone, setting the door wide as she went.

Her heart behaving like a startled frog, Henrietta watched Theo hesitate. Then he shrugged, picked up the straight-backed chair the maid had used yesterday and set it down near the bed. He did not sit at once, instead clearing his throat and looking rather at her bandaged foot than at Henrietta.

"How is it today?"

She had to swallow before she could answer. "Better, thank you."

He hesitated, and then sat, looking briefly at her before dropping his gaze to his clasped hands. "Rudchester says you are wishing to go home."

She wanted to cry out that it was no wish of hers. But this was a new Theo and her tongue was frozen. Distance yawned between them and it chilled her. But she must say something. "P-papa thinks it b-best." His head came up and the burn in the grey eyes convinced her she was right. The words escaped before she could prevent them. "Oh heavens, but you did quarrel!"

He shot up, shifting away into the room. Henrietta watched him, misery engulfing her. What had Papa done?

He turned, looked at her, the frown pronounced. "Hetty…" A grimace crossed his face and he came to the end of the bed, looking down at her foot. "Don't trouble your head about it. Concentrate on letting this foot mend."

She could not speak. How in the world did he suppose she could think of anything else? He was so horribly distant, nothing like the Theo she knew and…

The word whispered in her heart, but she refused to give it voice in her head.

He was looking at her, the grey eyes softening. "Don't look like that, Hetty."

"I don't know how I look."

"Wounded!" There was an ache in his voice that went straight to her heart and her throat tightened. Theo swung away, as if he could not endure the sight of her. From the window, he spoke again. "I hope you will think better of going too soon."

She wanted to reassure him, to say that Silve planned to give Rudchester's messages to Mama. But the impersonal note made her shrivel inside and the urge to weep receded. "I cannot please everyone." She hardly knew what she said. "I understand the doctor's concern."

He nodded as he turned. Then he glanced towards the open door. "Your sister ought to be in here." He crossed to the door and then stopped, turning there. "I meant to apologise for my ward's earlier importunities."

Welcoming the innocuous subject, Henrietta leapt upon it. "Oh, no, it was a pleasure to have her here."

A faint disbelieving smile crossed his face. "You jest."

"No, indeed, I like her." A half-acknowledged desire to keep him there made her babble. "She is an intelligent child, sir, although I guess she is running rather wild. Someone ought to give her a better example." That was hardly felicitous. What was she saying? "I don't mean —"

"Yes, what do you mean?" He was frowning, the grim look pronounced.

Henrietta blenched. "I should not have spoken. It is none of my affair, after all."

But he came to the bed, staring down at her. "No, say it. Running wild? Is that what you think?"

A demon leapt in her breast. "Yes, it is, if you wish to know. If you insist upon my saying what I think, then know that I suppose her to be too much in the company of servants who do not scruple to speak of matters to which she ought not to be party. Nor does she appear to have anyone who may demonstrate the sort of conduct she ought to learn merely by example." She drew a breath. "I do not mean to criticise, sir. It is merely an observation."

"From your brief acquaintance, no doubt."

Henrietta bridled. "You need not be sarcastic, Duke. I have been in Society for some time and I was brought up to a very different tune."

"I'll warrant you were, under the aegis of your abominable father!"

She gave a gasp, staring at him in shock, her bosom writhing all over again.

Theo appeared to recollect himself. He threw out a hand. "I beg your pardon. That was uncalled for. I did not mean to speak of him at all."

"That is evident."

"Oh, the deuce! Forget it. Forget I even came in here!" With which, he stalked to the door and thrust through it. But a second later, he reappeared, stomping back to the bedside and glaring at her. "Hopping! I forgot the blasted hopping business and that's what I came to say." He wagged a furious finger. "No hopping, do you understand me?"

Incensed, Henrietta sat up in a bang, jogging her foot painfully. She ignored it, too intent on hitting back. "How dare you? I shall hop if I choose!"

"Not in this house you won't!"

"I shall! You are not the arbiter of my movements!"

"I am while you're here."

"Well, that won't be for long, my lord duke, you may be sure."

To her mingled astonishment and apprehension, he plonked down on the bed and seized her by the shoulders, the grey eyes blazing. "You are going nowhere until that foot is better. I don't give a tinker's damn what your father wants. If he cares more for dragging you away from my vicinity than for your welfare, I don't, and he knows it. You are my responsibility and I won't have you hurt by a premature move."

Every vestige of fury had left her. She could only stare at him, the whole ghastly truth of his interview with Papa whirling in her head.

Theo's face changed. The stern and alienating look died out of his eyes and the grip on her arms loosened. He lifted one hand and his fingers stroked her cheek. "Hetty…"

It was that tender whisper all over again, the one that had got them into trouble in the first place. Instinct caused Henrietta to pull away. Her voice came huskily and she knew her eyes were wet. "You are not r-responsible for me, Theo. You m-mustn't think it. You have to l-let me go."

His hands dropped. Was it anguish in his eyes? "But not yet. Not before you are better. Give me that, at least. It's my honour at stake, Hetty."

The tears spilled over. "And what of mine? I have honour too, Theo. I w-won't be the m-means of — of turning you from your d-duty."

"Hang my duty!"

Before she could protest, her hand was in his and he lifted her fingers to his lips and kissed the tips as he had done before. Henrietta's heart was in pieces. "Please don't, Theo. It hurts enough already."

He set her hand down, his eyes meeting hers. "That's the last thing I want."

Then he rose and turned for the door. He did not look back and Henrietta listened to his hasty steps vanishing down the corridor.

CHAPTER SEVENTEEN

The day dragged. Henrietta had remained mumchance when her twin demanded to know what had passed. Martha's presence, however, prevented Silvestre from achieving her purpose, which relieved Henrietta. She was no match for her sister, but the distress of the exchange with Theo was too raw to be touched.

The tea helped to keep her from weeping her heart out, but nothing served to lighten the feeling of desolation. Whatever had been said in that fateful interview, Theo had come out of it an enemy to Papa. As well there could be no future to be dreamed of, for Henrietta could not conceive of being estranged from her family if her loyalties were to be shifted to Theo.

The tiny thrust of rebellion that protested they already had shifted thence was crushed on the instant. She had known Theo but a few short weeks. A lifetime of affection and care could not be set aside on his behalf.

Yet the consciousness of his presence somewhere in this house could not but impinge, and Henrietta found herself unexpectedly disappointed with Mrs Latimer's dictum when she finally arrived in the middle of the afternoon.

"Gracious, my love, no indeed. There can be no question of your removing from here for a day or two yet."

"But Papa said —"

"I knew you would have calmed him down, Mama," Silvestre broke in. "Is he in agreement?"

Mrs Latimer, who was busy setting a light shawl she had brought about Henrietta's shoulders, laughed out. "Well, of course he is, my dear Silve. He is far more concerned for Hetty's health than anything else." She patted Henrietta's cheek. "You must not take your poor papa's strictures to heart, my love."

"But he did not scold me at all, Mama." Not as he no doubt scolded Theo. "But he was adamant I must go home today. I thought you had come to fetch me."

"Nothing of the sort." Her mother's bespectacled face looked perfectly complacent. "It is true Henry had that notion, but he had not seen your wounds for himself as I had. When I told him just how badly you were hurt, he very quickly realised it would not do to be jogging you in any sort of conveyance."

Silvestre, who was leaning against one of the bedposts, broke in again at this point. "That is just what Doctor Rudchester said, Mama. You may tell Papa the wound on Hetty's heel broke out bleeding when the doctor was here."

"I am not at all surprised."

As her twin went on to relay all the doctor's messages, Henrietta recalled the oddity of her utterances this morning and a flutter of dismayed apprehension went through her. Dared she ask about the visit to Aunt Angelica? Not that she wanted to hear, if the subject of the conference was what she suspected. But presently she was saved the trouble as Mama turned to her again.

"Angelica plans to visit in a day or two, my love. She has not seen the duchess for an age and she feels she ought to confess her subterfuge about your skill with flower pictures."

"Oh, no, Mama, why? It is supposed to be secret."

"Ah, but when you are unable to fulfil the commissions as quickly as you hoped, it will fall to Angelica to explain. She thinks the duchess ought to know, as it is her influence that brought you so many requests."

Or was it that Mama and Aunt Angelica hoped to present Theo's aunt with the one talent she possessed in hopes of making her look kindly upon a possible union? But she must not say so. Mama must not know she had divined what was afoot. That would inevitably involve her in explanations she could not possibly make. As long as Silve did not betray her.

She cast a glance at her twin and found her wearing her enigmatic face, but with a tease in her eyes as she caught Henrietta's gaze. "Very true, Mama. In that connection, I do hope you have a good stock of flowers already drying in Papa's library, Hetty, or I shall be obliged to go hunting wildflowers for you."

This was a much safer topic and Henrietta embraced it with enthusiasm. "I have enough for a few of the pictures. By the time I need more, I must hope to be able to walk freely again."

Mama got up from the bed. "I think you must resign yourself to a period of inaction, my love. I dare say it will be some time before you are comfortable setting your foot to the ground." She leaned down and pecked Henrietta's cheek. "I must go and pay my respects to the duchess, Hetty, and then I will come back. Will you arrange for coffee here, Silve? Then her grace need not trouble to entertain me."

"What she means," said Silvestre the moment their mother was out of the room, "is that she needs Aunt Angelica to smooth her path."

"Why? Mama is easy with everyone."

Her twin was at the bell-pull, tugging on it. "So too is the duchess, in company. But Aunt Angelica says she is unpredictable and apt to go off at half-cock without warning."

Which was to say she would not welcome any hint that the Latimer ladies were setting their sights on the Duke of Charlton. Despite all her careful reasoning, Henrietta could not withstand a burgeoning resentment. To be thought to be setting her cap at Theo was bad enough. But it was equally galling to know she must be unacceptable to the duchess.

It occurred to her for the first time to wonder if Theo's sense of his duty in this regard had been instigated or instilled into him by his aunt. She had not thought of it before, but it did not sit well with what she knew of his character. For one who was accustomed to going his own way and doing just as he chose, to be swayed by another's notions of what was right seemed out of place.

No, she was grasping at straws. Theo knew his own mind. That he was fighting his inclination she could not doubt. But he was fighting it for a determination of his own, not to please the duchess. He was abiding by the dictates of convention because he knew he must. He had no choice. Just as he had no choice in the path life had set him on by an accident of birth. And Henrietta did not belong on that path.

Aunt Angelica and Mama might scheme, but it would avail them nothing. Besides, in this regard she could not believe even Mama would prevail with Papa's obvious dislike of Theo. He would never permit such an alliance, even were Henrietta's happiness at stake.

On this gloomy note, she sank into her banked pillows with a sigh. Silvestre, who had been gazing out of the window, came across and perched beside her.

"Are you ever going to tell me what passed between you and your Theo?"

"He's not my Theo."

Her twin ignored the agitated interjection. "I heard raised voices, Hetty. Now what occurred?"

Henrietta fiddled with the edges of her shawl, gazing at the sprigs on her gown. "It was too stupid to talk of."

"That won't do, my recalcitrant twin. Tell me!"

Henrietta capitulated. "Oh, we fell into argument about Ellie, but that was nothing to the purpose. Theo was stiff with me, and awkward." The need to unburden herself loosened her tongue. "It is all Papa's fault! I don't know what was said because Theo would not tell me, but he called him *abominable* — Papa, I mean — and I was furious, and we exchanged more words and then… Oh, I don't know, Silve. It all went awry and Theo said things he shouldn't and I told him…" Her overfull bosom heaved and the despair came tumbling out. "I t-told him he m-must not k-kiss my f-fingers like that b-because it hurts, Silve. It hurts even more badly than my f-foot."

Then her tears were flowing and she was weeping in her sister's arms, unable to stop. In the background of her mind she heard the balm of her twin's loved voice, murmuring words meant to soothe which had no real meaning for her while the image of Theo's face as he left her hovered in her mind. She'd hurt him! In her anxiety to save herself, she had rejected his affectionate gesture. Yet in her heart of hearts it was all she wanted.

"Gracious me, what in the world is all this?"

Mama! Henrietta pulled herself free of her sister's embrace and dashed at her cheeks in a futile effort to hide her distress. Silvestre backed her up loyally.

"She is feeling low, Mama, that is all. You were very quick."

Mrs Latimer was at the bedside. "The duchess is resting. I am told she invariably does so before she must dress for dinner. I sent a message by her companion instead."

Henrietta had found Theo's maltreated handkerchief and was drying her cheeks, aware of Mama's concerned regard. She was saved from further question by Martha's entrance.

"Did you ring, miss?"

Silvestre took charge. "May we have coffee, Martha, if it will not incommode them in the kitchens? Our mother would like to take a cup before she goes home."

The maid curtsied to Mrs Latimer, but her eagle eye was on Henrietta. "It's no trouble, ma'am, but is Miss Hetty poorly again? You do look ever so peaky, miss. That there handkerchief will be in shreds soon. I'll find you another, miss."

"Yes, do, Martha." Silvestre ushered her towards the door. "But the coffee, if you please."

"Ooh, yes, I'll fetch it straight, miss."

She hurried out and Henrietta found Mama sitting in her twin's place. She reached for her daughter's hand and held it, squeezing gently.

"Try not to give in to melancholy, my love. Remember what I've told you often and often. Things are never as bad as they seem if you will only look for the silver lining."

"Yes, Mama." Only where was it? She could scarcely tell Mama what was really upsetting her. "I dare say I shall feel happier when I can get up. I would try, but hopping is forbidden." She closed her lips, at once recalling Theo's violent prohibition. So typical. Only she had fought back because she was already fuming. So stupid.

But Mama was laughing. "Hopping? I should think so indeed. But I shall bring you one of Papa's canes next time I come and you may try leaning on that to support your foot." She put up a finger. "But only once the doctor permits."

Henrietta sighed again. "I feel as if I've been lying here forever."

"You are bored, I expect. But don't despair, my love." She rose and went to pick up the valise she had brought. "I packed a volume I found in the old nursery as well as a pack of cards. I could not well bring the backgammon or chess board, but I dare say there are sets in the house, if you wish to play." She produced the book as she spoke, setting it aside and rummaging further. "Ah, and your sketching pad and pencils too, in case you should feel up to designing one of your pictures."

"Excellent, Mama." Silvestre took the items from her and set them on one of the shelves of the whatnot. "I shall keep her entertained, never fear." She cast a teasing glance at her afflicted twin. "Anything to stop her brooding."

Henrietta flashed her an indignant look. Although she must confess to needing a distraction to turn her mind from her troubles. Especially if Aunt Angelica meant to stick her oar in where it could only make matters worse.

The strains and stresses of her situation caught up with Henrietta upon the following day, leaving her exhausted once she had washed, been assisted to dress and partaken sparingly of a breakfast far too substantial for an invalid. Afterwards, she was disinclined to do anything but lie abed, drifting. She felt as if her mind had closed down and listened with only half an ear to Silvestre's voice as she read to her from Mrs Fossebridge's extravagant gothic tale, the book brought by Mama. Her twin had borrowed it from the circulating library at Reading.

"To give me an idea of how it is done." Silvestre twinkled mischief. "It is a deal more bloodthirsty than *The Old Priory*, I warn you."

"Is that what you are calling your story?"

"For want of anything better. But let me entertain you with *The Dastardly Deeds of Baron Bolsover*. You may laugh, but Greta Fossebridge has created a most villainous creature, I assure you."

The story proved altogether ludicrous in its ghoulish ramifications, but it served to lull Henrietta's troubled bosom. There was nothing she could do to change anything at this present in any event. She might as well rest, as she had been bidden to do by everyone around her, including the person whose opinion mattered the most. Not that she had seen hide nor hair of him since the previous day's débâcle.

Doctor Rudchester came again and pronounced himself well satisfied with the progress of the wounds, but a message was received from Moss House that Aunt Angelica was delayed and neither Mama nor Papa were free to come over today. Henrietta breathed more easily and fell into a light doze after drinking down most of a sustaining broth.

Some instinct pricked her awake. Her eyelids fluttered open and her gaze shifted about the quiet chamber, coming to rest upon a familiar figure seated in the chair by the bedside. Her heart leapt.

"Theo!"

He put a finger to his lips, indicating the maid Martha, slumbering in her accustomed chair near the press. A whisper reached her. "I heard you are fatigued today. I had to come and see for myself."

She could not help smiling at him. "I am a little weary."

"Hardly surprising after all you've gone through. Rudchester says he expected you would succumb. That's why he vetoed your trying to leave."

"He told you?"

"His orders are to report directly to me when he's seen you."

She gave a little sigh. "Responsibility."

"Yes. And an ardent desire to see you again … after what passed between us yesterday, I mean." He let out a heavy breath, the grey eyes dull. "Hetty, I never meant to hurt you."

A flitter of warmth went through her. "I know, Theo."

He cast a quick glance towards Martha. "She's well away, thank the Lord. I seized my chance when your sister said she was going out for air."

She knew she ought to reproach him, but she was too listless to be capable of going against everything her heart desired. He reached for her hand and she turned hers so that their fingers laced. It was balm, and she had no strength to resist the promptings of her bosom. "I'm glad you came. I missed you."

A gleam entered his eye and he leaned in, lifting her hand to kiss it. "Let's pretend, Hetty. For just a little while."

Pretend what? But she did not ask. Grateful, in her debilitated state, for even this little crumb, she lay quiescent, letting her gaze rove his features. His thumb caressed her flesh and the bliss of it swelled in her chest. If only it could be like this…

From somewhere in the recesses of her memory, the question came. "What do the O and L stand for?"

His face changed, the old teasing gleam returning, though he kept his tone low. "What are you talking about, you nonsensical female?"

"TOLD. It's on your handkerchief."

Theo's face cleared and he grinned. "Ah. An extremely pompous set of names: Theodore Oliver Lionel Devenal, for my sins."

Remembrance floated into her mind. "Oh, yes, Martha told me. Theodore for your grandfather, Oliver for your uncle and Lionel for your father. Isn't that it?"

"You've been pumping the maid, have you? I'm flattered."

She squeezed his fingers. "I wanted to know. Oh, and why does not your mama like to live at Devenal?"

"Because she can't endure Cecilia's prattle, as she calls it. My engaging mama is decidedly eccentric. She hates formality. She refuses to conform and she always does exactly as she wants, regardless of what anyone says."

Henrietta had to laugh. "Well, that accounts for you being so dictatorial and independent."

"Dictatorial? That's what you think of me, is it?"

"Yes, it is. You're horridly bossy and a brute besides." But then the altogether different side of him came to mind and she caught her breath on a sudden sob. "Not all the time. Oh, Theo…"

His grip tightened and he leaned in close, whispering, "Don't! You know I can't endure it when you weep, Hetty."

She sniffed and shook her head on the pillow. "I'm not weeping. You shouldn't be tender if you don't want to set me off."

"But I didn't do anything. I was sitting here, minding my own business…"

Releasing his fingers, she slapped at his hand. "Stop it, horrid beast!"

To her consternation, a snorting sound came from the maid. She cast an anxious glance towards the chair by the window as Theo sat up in a bang. Just in time. Martha yawned and opened her eyes. They sprang wide as she spied the duke.

"Your grace!" She leapt up. "Ooh, I'm that shamed, your grace. I fell asleep."

Theo was already on the move, rising and shifting the chair away from the bed. "No matter, Martha. I just popped in to see how Miss Latimer does. The doctor said she is tired today."

"That she is, your grace, and no mistake," said the maid, coming to the foot of the bed. "Nor she ain't ate enough to feed a kitten."

Fearing Theo's strictures, Henrietta hastened to contradict her. "Not at breakfast, but I drank the broth you brought up, Martha."

"Well, and I should hope so, miss. It were made special by Cook on Mrs Oughtibridge's say-so, and I make no doubt it done you good."

Theo put up a hand. "Enough, Martha! Miss Latimer must be the judge of her own appetite." He looked back at Hetty. "I dare say she could do with a cup of tea, couldn't you?"

"Yes, if you please."

"There. Off you go and procure some, Martha." The girl hesitated, looking disapproving. "I'm just going. You've no need to concern yourself. Leave the door open."

Muttering under her breath, Martha did as she was told, clearly unwilling to refuse a direct order from the master of the house. The moment she had left the room, Theo sat down on the edge of the bed and caught Henrietta up, seizing her into a comprehensive embrace.

Warmth swept through her and she nestled her head under his chin, wholly unable to find it in her to pull away, so great had been the yearning to be held in his arms again.

It lasted but a moment. He laid her down gently and sat up, the light eyes roving her features. "I'll have to stay away, sweet, or I won't be able to resist you. Not when you're so helpless and vulnerable. It's more than flesh and blood can stand."

She could not utter a word, her voice trapped in her throat. She was aware of a tremor at her lip and at her fingers as she lifted them up towards him. He caught them, pressed them to his mouth, turned them and touched them to her lips. Then he let her go and spoke in the harshest tone she had ever heard from him.

"Get better fast. I can cope when you're strong enough to rail at me."

A moment later, he was gone. Henrietta set her fingers back to her lips and held them there awhile, her heart fluttering in her breast.

CHAPTER EIGHTEEN

"If you will sign this authority, your grace, I can see Wheldrake and settle the matter once and for all."

Theo stared in an abstracted way at the paper Hathersage had set under his hand, reading words that made no sense. The image hovering at the back of his mind was interfering with his ability to concentrate.

"Your grace?"

He blinked. What was he doing, sitting with his pen poised like a brainless schoolboy? He read the words again, forcing his mind to action. An importunate tenant, yes. Hathersage was dealing with local matters now, was he not? He proposed a compromise in this case. "Will this content him, do you suppose?"

"I think so, your grace. It allows him access to his field without having to tramp around the edge of the lake. Your predecessor's agent would not allow him to cross the land, fearing the precedent might make others think it a public footpath."

"So what if they do? Does it encroach too nearly?"

"I don't think so, your grace. It's a shortcut across a corner. I can't imagine it would cause any disturbance in the woods."

Unlike the disturbance the other day, the cause of which was still languishing in a spare bedchamber upstairs. He had kept to his vow. Stayed out of her chamber, though he had received a comfortable account from Rudchester this morning. Hetty was brighter today, it seemed. Yet he dared not venture. He had said too much. Done too much. It was altogether dangerous to be anywhere near her.

Theo brushed the thoughts away, dipped his pen in the inkpot and signed the document. He watched his secretary shake sand over it, reflecting that his determination to throw himself into work had proved an inadequate distraction.

Hathersage was efficient and had few matters on his plate that needed his employer's personal attention. He was aware of enquiring into things more than was necessary, just to keep from thinking about Hetty. A fruitless exercise, since her presence in the house shadowed his every waking moment. His sleep too, if it came to that. He was aware of vague dreams wherein he was obliged to rescue the wretched girl from the Lord knew what scrapes. The sooner she recovered and was removed from his vicinity, the better for his peace of mind.

Hathersage leaned close as he picked up the document, and a low murmur reached Theo. "Swarland is here, your grace."

The deuce. What did Cecilia want now? He had already endured a litany of complaints concerning the Latimer invasion. She had broken out the moment Silvestre left the breakfast table this morning.

"When I agreed to house the girl, Theo, I did not expect the entire family to be marching in and out at all hours and treating the place as their own."

"An exaggeration, Cecilia. No one even came yesterday."

"The wife was here the day before, much too close to the dinner hour. I denied myself, of course. Why could she not have come with her husband earlier? Not to mention the constant demand for trays of tea and coffee," she went on, giving Theo no chance to respond, "at any time of the day or night. The servants seem to do nothing but wait upon those dratted twins and the household is falling apart."

Theo had cast a swift glance towards Flint and caught him rolling his eyes. He resumed his butlerian mien on the instant, but it was enough to reassure Theo his aunt's assertions were nonsensical. "Do stop making such a fuss, Cecilia. It's not an imposition. Martha is the only servant taken off her normal duties. If you don't think the staff can cope with a little extra work, you had better not hold any more parties."

He might as well have spared his breath. Cecilia paid not the slightest heed.

"What is more, Jurby tells me Ellie has been sneaking out to hobnob with the other one in the gardens instead of looking to her letters."

"I've already told Ellie she's not to disturb Miss Latimer."

"I won't have them encouraging the child to run wild, Theo."

It was on the tip of his tongue to hit back with Hetty's earlier criticism that had provoked a quarrel the other day, but he refrained. It would infuriate Cecilia, as it had annoyed him. But upon reflection, he had been obliged to admit there was truth in it. Ellie did not have a suitable example to follow. Her mother paid her scant attention and she was always escaping from her governess. Did she run tame in the domestic quarters? He ought to do something about it, though how Ellie was to be curbed he knew not.

He had abandoned the attempt to bring Cecilia out of her ill mood, claiming Hathersage needed him. Now here she was again, no doubt demanding his immediate attendance.

With a sigh, he turned to confront her steward. "Yes, what is it, Swarland?"

The fellow was standing just inside the door, looking decidedly embarrassed. What in the world was going on now? "Her grace requests your grace to join her in the family room."

"Does she now? Upon what occasion?"

Swarland reddened a trifle. "I could not say, your grace."

"Oh, couldn't you? I'll warrant you know exactly why she wants me."

In the periphery of his vision, he noted Hathersage's faint sly smile. Damnation, he was being indiscreet. He rose. "Very well, I will come directly."

The steward's relief was patent. "I will inform her grace at once."

Theo waited for the fellow to leave the room and turned on his secretary. "You can take that smirk off your face, Hathersage."

"I beg your grace's pardon." The man assumed a suitably solemn mien, which did not fool Theo in the least.

"Don't pretend you don't know what this is about."

He cleared his throat. "I may have an inkling."

"Well, inkle it out of that mouth of yours, if you know what's good for you."

It was plain his secretary was having trouble keeping a straight face. "It — er — it really ought to come from her grace, sir."

"Forewarned is forearmed. Spit it out, man!"

"As I understand it, your grace, there is a suspicion in some quarters that perhaps Miss Latimer trod upon that trap on purpose."

"*What?* No one in their right mind could suppose she would do such a thing deliberately."

Hathersage was openly grinning now. "Exactly what I told Swarland, sir."

"Did he concede the point?"

"Not precisely, your grace. He felt it to be unlikely, if not for the — er — invasion. It is thought that Mr Latimer's entry into the proceedings is significant. Now it appears Mrs

Summerhayes is also becoming involved. She is Miss Latimer's godmother, your grace."

Theo's mind was leaping with conjecture, and none of it pleasant, but he could not let this pass. "How the devil do you know all this?"

Hathersage raised his brows. "In the usual way, your grace. Servants talk."

"And listen at doors, no doubt," returned Theo, wrathful. "Damn it to hell and back!"

From the servants to Oughtibridge and thence to Mary Eddleston. The rest was inevitable. The whole blasted household was likely discussing it. So much for discretion and his efforts to keep within the bounds of propriety. He groaned in spirit. Why could Cecilia not have borne a son in the first place and spared him this intolerable existence? He might as well be living in a fish bowl.

The deuce, but it had to be faced. He turned for the door.

"Good luck, your grace."

"I'll need it."

He found Cecilia pacing. She was alone, thank the Lord. At least he would not have a witness to this row.

She turned at his entrance, showing him a countenance suffused with passion. She flung out a hand. "At last! Theo, it is all a plot. You must be rid of the girl without delay. Angelica has been here and —"

"She's gone?"

"She has gone up to visit her god-daughter, but she promised to return, which is why I sent for you so urgently. We have not much time, Theo."

He put up a hand. "Cecilia, be still! There is no need to fall into a distempered freak."

"There is every need." She paced away from him to the fireplace and turned there, her tone becoming tragic. "Cannot you see what is going on under your nose? They are determined, Theo. She and that Latimer woman. Oh, I should have seen it coming. Bringing me that picture, seducing me into an interest but creating a mystery of it withal. Only now does she confess the truth! Of course I pretended I did not know it already. What would you? If I had said you told me that girl made the picture it would have supplied her with additional ammunition, of which, like a fool, you have already given more than enough."

Theo cut in swiftly. "I wish you will not be absurd, Cecilia. I collect you mean to imply the Latimers are looking for a bridal?"

She could not be more wrong, but he was not going to reveal the substance of his argument with the father. Cecilia stared at him as if he was a halfwit. "Are you blind, Theo? I should have realised what was in the wind the moment you brought that girl into the house. Such a convenient accident indeed!"

It was too much. "Don't be ridiculous. Whatever else, it is utterly absurd to suggest Hetty intended to step on a rabbit trap. In the first place, she didn't know the things were in the wood. In the second, she wasn't even aware of my presence."

Cecilia seemed not to have heard him. She was staring at him with a look of shocked surprise. "She has taken you in! *Hetty*?"

He felt his face grow warm, but he turned it off in haste. "That is nothing to the purpose. I've been calling her by name from the start."

Cecilia came to him, consternation in her eyes. "The start? Oh, good heavens, Theo, what in the world do you mean? I thought you knew too much. Don't say there is enough to compromise you?"

Ten times over, but he was not going to admit to that. "It's neither here nor there, Cecilia. There is nothing to alarm you. Even were there such a plot — which I don't for a moment believe — it would not work on me. I am my own man."

She threw up agitated hands. "All very well to say, Theo, but you do not know these matchmaking women. They are as cunning as can be, and Angelica is a schemer. Yes, yes, I know I have counted her a friend, but if she is determined to stab me in the back, I can call her so no longer."

"Oh, for the love of God! Cecilia, will you stop this? I'm in no danger from Henrietta Latimer. And if I were —" He broke off. He was, of course, but not because of any scheming matchmaker. Yet Latimer himself was the main barrier. One he could not get past, if he wanted to. But there was no revealing that to his aunt. She would make a meal of it, and it would lead to confessing all.

But Cecilia was not appeased. "You are a fool, Theo, if you suppose any girl would not jump at you if opportunity offered. How many eligible dukes do you suppose there are in our circle? No, you must be on your guard. They think to steal a march on those ranked females we had rather consider, only because she is on the spot. Vulnerable too, in her injured state. They will suppose your compassion may lead you to look kindly upon her. Don't, I charge you, visit her again."

All too conscious of his indiscretions in this regard, he nevertheless fought back. "I have only done what might be expected of a conscientious host."

"Nonsense! A man has no place in a sickroom."

But a man whose affections were somewhat engaged had difficulty keeping out. He crushed the thought, setting himself to soothe. "You need have no fear, Cecilia. Nothing will come of it. Rest assured, when I marry, it will be on my own determination. You know well I am not a man to be coerced."

She let out a sigh. "I trust it may be found to be so, but my heart misgives me. I will speak to Rudchester."

Alarm leapt in Theo's breast. "You'll do no such thing! Enough, Cecilia. Leave well alone, or you will have me to reckon with."

She looked utterly dismayed, but Theo was beyond caring. Bad enough that she thought so badly of Hetty as to believe her capable of the kind of duplicity required to carry out such a plot. He was not going to have her interfere with Hetty's recovery.

He would have left the room there and then, but the door opened to admit Mrs Summerhayes. She paused on the threshold, flicking a glance from one to the other.

"Am I interrupting?"

He quashed his rising spleen. "Not at all, Mrs Summerhayes. I trust you found your god-daughter in better frame?"

She hesitated, casting a doubtful look at Cecilia, who had not quite managed to conceal her chagrin. No doubt she would produce her gracious front in a moment. "Hetty is better, yes, so Silvestre tells me. Although she is insisting upon trying to walk today, which I think is a trifle foolish."

This intelligence had a powerful effect upon Theo. Trying to walk? Heaven send she did not fall! Forgetful of everything that had just passed, he excused himself without ceremony and left the room.

Taking the stairs two at a time, he made it to the gallery with speed and came upon Hetty in the corridor, leaning against the wall and panting, her countenance perfectly white.

"For pity's sake, Hetty! What do you think you're doing?" Without hesitation, Theo swung her up into his arms, ignoring a half-hearted protest.

"Theo, you mustn't!"

The pent-up wrath escaped. "You idiotic female! What possessed you to go waltzing about like this?"

Her expressive eyes flared. "I'm scarcely waltzing. I was just trying —"

"Where is your sister? Why didn't she stop you?"

"She went for a breath of air while Aunt Angelica was with me."

He was moving, heading for her bedchamber. "If I don't give her pepper for leaving you, she may count herself fortunate."

"Don't you dare be horrid to Silve, you beast!"

He paid no heed, still seething. "What about Martha? Where the deuce is she when you insist on behaving like a ninny? Not that I should have expected anything else. Didn't I say at the outset you can't be trusted to put one foot in front of the other?"

Hetty wriggled in his arms and he received a blow in the chest. "How dare you say that? Of course I can't put one foot in front of the other, but it's not my fault this time."

"Aha! You knew you couldn't, but you must needs try. If ever I met such a —"

"Don't you dare call me names! Put me down! Horrid creature! Rude and vile beast, I hate you!"

She was kicking and wriggling so that Theo had the greatest difficulty holding her and was obliged to stop walking. "*Will* you keep still? Do you want me to drop you?"

"I want you to set me down at once!"

Her cheeks were pink, her eyes bright with fury as she glowered at him and the oddest sensation of déjà vu attacked him. He stared into her face, the violence of feeling draining out of his chest. The murmur escaped him without thought. "What in heaven's name am I doing?"

Hetty's expression altered in a bang. Consternation? And then consciousness. Her voice dropped to a plea. "Set me down, Theo. Let me go."

A twist in his gut. A thrust of rebellion in his breast. He clutched her closer. "No!" Looking about, he found he had taken a route past her bedchamber and beyond, closer to his own quarters. He glanced swiftly back down the corridor. It was clear of any servant. They were alone, but it could not be for long. At any moment, Martha might come into sight. Or Silvestre. Theo made up his mind. Shifting Hetty in his grip, he took the few steps between them and his goal. "Can you open that door?"

She looked to the handle, which was within her reach and then back to his face. "Theo, where are we going?"

"Just open that door!"

She looked worried, but she did as he asked. He manoeuvred his way into his sanctum and kicked the door to behind him.

CHAPTER NINETEEN

Dumped on the daybed in considerable disorder, Henrietta made haste to pull her gown straight and brush at her tumbled locks. She leaned back against the scrolled end of the bed, only half aware of the familiar ache in her foot, and glanced about the chamber.

She took in the inlaid escritoire, the bookcase and a leather-backed pair of chairs either side of the fireplace. The room had an indefinably masculine atmosphere that gave her an uncomfortable feeling of intrusion.

She looked up. Theo had retired a few paces, somewhat out of breath. He was regarding her with an expression she could not fathom. She spoke, her tone instinctively hushed. "What is this place? Why have you brought me here?"

He looked away, shifting to the window. "I'm not sure." He sounded brusque again. "This is my private sitting-room. Only my valet is permitted to disturb me here."

Henrietta's discomfort became acute. "I should not be here."

He looked round. "True."

"Then why did you bring me?"

A faint smile touched his lips. "A good question."

An urgent need to be gone from here possessed Henrietta. She pushed up, making to set her feet to the ground. In an instant, Theo was there, pushing her legs back.

"Don't be a little fool, Hetty! Stay where you are!"

She did not relax, looking up at him in a good deal of perplexity. And not a little trepidation. "Theo, this is just what you said you must not do, don't you see? You've kept away, you must not spoil it now. We can't be alone like this."

"I know that." He dropped to perch on the edge of the daybed and his nearness at once felt stifling. "I just — needed a moment with you."

"A scandalous moment?"

"No one need know. I will carry you back and say I found you walking. Which is true."

Her breath was tight, but she could not let this happen. "Take me back now. Please!"

He grinned suddenly. "If anyone questions it, you may complain that I kidnapped you."

A breathless laugh fluttered out of her, accompanied by a rush of tenderness at the warmth of his smile. "Well, you did, you beast."

He caught her hand and held it and the amusement died out of his eyes. "Hetty, we're in trouble."

Her heart stilled. "How?"

His grip tightened. "This is wholly unorthodox and I ought not to do it, but we've been too close for me not to be truthful with you."

She was aware of a tremble inside her, but she managed to speak without showing it. "You have always been truthful with me, Theo. You never pretend."

"And I won't now." He drew an audible breath. "Cecilia is on the warpath. She is convinced your female relatives are bent on making a match between us."

Henrietta did not hesitate. "I thought that too!" Anxiety attacked her and she voiced it at once. "You can't believe I'm a party to it, can you?"

To her relief, his face softened and he raised her hand to his lips, kissing it briefly. "I know you better than that, Hetty. You've been just as truthful with me."

"Then we need not regard it, Theo. You should pay no heed to the duchess."

"I didn't. But what she doesn't know, nor you either, my sweet Hetty, is that your father has forbidden the banns, as it were."

Aghast, she stared at him, her world tumbling about her. "Wh-what did he say, Theo?"

"He accused me of having an interest in you. When I assured him I have no intentions towards you — don't look like that, Hetty!"

She managed a tremulous smile. "It's all right, Theo. I knew it. I have known from the first. You are perfectly aware of that."

He blew out a breath that sounded overwrought. "So I may be, but that doesn't make it any easier when I know how I've wounded you."

But that would not do. "It's not your fault, Theo. F-feelings happen. Life d-does not always work the w-way it should."

She would swear Theo now looked wounded. He released her hand and reached to wipe away the tears she had not known were seeping from her eyes. She sniffed.

"I'm sorry. I know you h-hate a weeping female."

"I hate a weeping Hetty!" He dove a hand into his pocket and brought out a handkerchief, passing it across with a rueful grin. "I dare not wipe your cheeks for you, sweetheart. Your dear papa was scathing of my efforts in that direction."

Henrietta rubbed at the damp. "I knew he had been horrid to you. Poor Theo. Was he very angry?"

He shrugged in a dismissive fashion. "Oh, he rang a fine peal over me, but in the end he believed my story."

"Which story?"

Theo threw up his eyes. "Of that first day. You don't think I gave him any hint of the rest, do you?"

Henrietta sighed. "No, but I don't believe you tamely let him berate you either."

"Of course not," he said, grinning. "I warned him I would give as good as I got. I don't think he cared for that." The disgruntled look returned. "But he considers me a far from satisfactory suitor. My rank means nothing. Even were it possible, Hetty, he wouldn't give you to me."

Her heart was squeezing unpleasantly, but there were no more tears. "Then it's a good thing it isn't possible."

He frowned suddenly. "I would have to compromise you."

The look in his eyes became abruptly sultry and Henrietta felt uncomfortably hot all at once. She crumpled the handkerchief in her fingers.

His voice turned husky. "It wouldn't be hard to do, my sweet Disaster."

Henrietta could not move. She knew it was imperative she stop him. The intent in his eyes shot through her like an arrow, straight to a secret place she'd never felt before. It burned. The room became airless. She could not look away if she died for it. Time rolled into forever.

Theo's face came closer. He bent his head and she knew he was seeking her lips. Frozen, her breath stuck in her chest, she waited for the contact.

It did not come.

Instead, a soft whispering curse left his lips. "Hell and the devil and damn me too!" Then he was on his feet, brisk and back to his usual uncompromising self. "Come, get up! I'll help you." He pulled her legs around and settled them ready for her to rise. His arm slipped under her shoulder and he lifted her. "Keep that foot off the ground and use me for a crutch."

Too dazed with the aftermath of what had so nearly happened, Henrietta could only obey. She set her good foot to the ground and then placed the other tiptoe as she had done when she tried to walk.

"Don't put weight on it. Use me to support you."

She leaned into him and felt him take her weight, lifting her slightly as she put her good foot forward.

"There, you see. Is it hurting?"

He sounded too normal to be true. Henrietta did not think she could match him, but she tried, still feeling breathless. "No, it — it is easier."

"Good. Another step."

Slowly she made it to the door. Theo opened it and guided her through into the corridor. She was beyond wondering why he did not carry her, the effort involved in walking taking all her attention. Until her twin's voice hailed them.

"There you are! Gracious, Duke, whatever are you doing with her?"

Henrietta's heart sank, but Theo's voice came, cheerful and horridly impersonal.

"I found her trying, so we decided to let her practise. She is doing very well, Miss Latimer, as you can see."

"Yes, I do see. Hetty, that is excellent. Although I suspect it is a great deal easier with someone there to hold you up."

"She will manage with a cane, I expect, now she knows how to shift her weight so she does not put it on the bad foot."

Oh, did she? In fact, Henrietta was only half aware of what she was doing. With Theo so close beside her, she could not think of anything but the hardness of his limb and the strength of his arm around her back. Not to mention the warmth engendered by the whole proceeding. It was not, thank goodness, as bad as the recent unmentionable furnace, but it was quite bad enough to prevent her from concentrating on how she was walking. Her twin's voice brought relief.

"I should think that is enough practice for one day, Duke, don't you?"

Theo brought her to a standstill beside him, looking down. "Have you had enough, Miss Hetty? Shall I carry you to your room?"

The incongruity of his speaking like a stranger after what had passed in his sitting-room affected her profoundly. How was he able to act a part? It must be pretence. She tried for a natural manner. "It is not far to my room, is it? I should be able to manage." But as she tried another step she became abruptly aware of her lack of strength and started to sink. Theo must have felt it.

"No, you're spent!" He picked her up again and the swooping sensation made her clutch at his shoulder. She dared to look at him and he gave her a reassuring smile. "Hold on. One moment more and you'll be safe in your bed."

Safe from him? The enormity of the danger she had been in came home to her. Being held in his arms like this could not but revive the conflicting feelings he engendered within her. Had he truly meant what he said?

The effort involved in maintaining a semblance of normality was beginning to tell. Theo was relieved to reach the bedchamber and set his burden down again. Not that he didn't enjoy the feel of Hetty in his embrace, however purposeful. But the hideous discovery he had made in his sitting-room was itching to be explored.

"There now, Miss Latimer. I will leave you to your sister's ministrations."

He was aware of Hetty's confusion. He blamed himself. She was too innocent to be able to read his vile intent. Was it vile? She might call him so with impunity today, might she not? Thank heavens he had recollected himself before he took that fatal step.

He glanced about the chamber. "No Martha? Ring the bell, Miss Latimer. I imagine your sister is gasping for tea." He glanced back at Hetty as he spoke and saw an obviously forced smile come to her lips.

"Yes, thank you, Duke. I am indeed."

Well done, Hetty. Good girl. She was wholly reliable. And utterly adorable, damn it to hell. He was a villain and ought to be shot.

He had no real notion of how he got himself out of the room. As of instinct, he turned for his apartments and stopped short. Not there. It was tainted now. Retracing his steps, he passed Hetty's closed door and headed for the stairs, intending to go and cool his heated head in the gardens.

He reached the bottom of the stairs and found himself intercepted.

"I beg your pardon, your grace."

"What the deuce is it now, Swarland?"

The steward's mien was deprecating and he threw a glance towards the door of the family parlour. The sounds of an altercation penetrated to Theo's ears. Locked in his own thoughts, he had remained unaware of it until now.

"I fear her grace is distressed, your grace."

"Distressed? She's fuming, man!"

All the natural male anathema to a feminine-driven scene rose up. And Cecilia could enact a tragedy with the best of them. Was the fellow expecting him to intervene?

"Who is in there? Mrs Summerhayes?"

"Yes, your grace, and Miss Eddleston is supporting her grace."

"Then she doesn't need me."

Swarland coughed. "It is attracting attention, your grace."

He cast a significant glance towards the back of the hall. Theo shifted away from the stairs and saw a bevy of servants, who scattered at sight of him. He lifted an eyebrow at the steward. "Well, that seems to have taken care of that."

The voices in the parlour were growing louder and Swarland became anxious. "It is not good for her grace to be upset, your grace. She will be obliged to retire with a sick headache."

And sulk for days. Didn't he know it? But he was damned if he was going to put himself in the firing line. If the steward knew what had passed between them, he would be less keen to have him interfere. "Well, so be it, my friend. I'm not going in there to give my head for washing, I thank you."

The fellow sighed deeply. "I was hoping —"

"I know you were, but I can't think why. You know perfectly well I have no influence with her grace when she's in this mood."

"I venture to think she values your good opinion more than you realise, your grace."

Not noticeably. Unless he chose to come the duke, which he ought to do, he supposed. At least, he could stop the row, but it would not save him from Cecilia's whining complaints afterwards. He ought to save Mrs Summerhayes, though from the sound of it she was holding her own. He was not much surprised Cecilia's gracious façade had broken down.

He listened a moment, but could not make out words within the shrill to and fro of the battle. To hell with it. He was not going in there. Besides, he was itching to get away and sift the turmoil in the back of his mind.

Obviously the gardens were not now far enough. He could still be got at. Theo made up his mind. "Swarland, make yourself useful and tell my valet to attend me in my chamber, will you? Immediately."

The steward bowed, evidently accepting defeat. "As you wish, your grace."

Theo called after him. "Ah, and have Flint give order to my groom to get Columbus saddled and ready for me in ten minutes."

Then he was running up the stairs, escape at the forefront of his mind.

The gallop across the common land that abutted the woods had been both exhilarating and efficacious. As he reined in to a walk to give Columbus a breather, Theo felt a good deal refreshed in mind as well as body.

He had not taken that fatal step, and he must be glad. The complications would have been disastrous. Yet the guilt at having embroiled Hetty would not be wholly contained. Except that having done so, he could no longer fool himself. He wanted her, in every possible way. In the worst way. Yet in the best too. And she! The thought of how she had reacted fairly took his breath away.

Not a word of censure. Not an inkling of blame. She ought to have called him a beast in earnest, but she did nothing of the kind. Instead she insisted it was not his fault, admitted freely what was there between them and accepted without question that it could not be. Really, she was too good to be true.

No, she was not. She was hurt, and she did not scruple to say it. Rightly. Yet she it was who moved to stop it. Every time. Except that once: yesterday, when she was too weary, too vulnerable, to withstand his embrace. If she had been herself then, she would have pushed him away. She was too honest for subterfuge. Her innate integrity shone through.

Was it her father's doing? Had he inculcated this sense of right, of justice? If so, he must be respected for that at least.

For the first time, Theo looked at his conduct from the viewpoint of the man who must guard Hetty from harm. Just as he must guard Ellie, and Pru as she grew older. How would he feel if he were to see a man all but kissing Ellie? Treating her like a milkmaid? Well, he would likely administer a judicious blow to the fellow's jaw. If he didn't kill him outright.

He had been deservedly scolded, had he not? Mr Latimer had every right to his objections, to his fury. More than he knew indeed. Remembrance of his actions this morning drove in remorse. If Latimer had seen this? Ye Gods! But what the fellow did not realise was that he *loved* Hetty.

Shock froze his mind. His hands on the reins became slack and Columbus halted, taking opportunity to crop at a bank of thistle.

How blind could a man be? A careless affection he had thought it. But it was more. Much more. He could not have bestowed it upon a more worthy object. Indeed, it was he who was unworthy. Latimer had it down pat. He did not deserve Hetty. He had no business desiring her goodness, her unconscious charm and her unspeakable and endearing sensibility.

It went without saying that he desired her in the other way too. He had from the first. She was adorable, yes, but so innocently seductive. Without the least idea of it. The way she looked at him with those giveaway eyes. Incapable of duplicity, they said everything that was in her mind. How had he ever managed to resist the urge to kiss her?

His loins kicked at the very thought. Then the mountain of difficulties in his way crashed down on him.

Impossible. It was impossible. Latimer would never consent. Cecilia would have the vapours at the thought. Worse yet, there was duty.

His aunt supposed his acquiescence in her scheme to find him a high-born bride was due to her persuasions. She had no notion of the truth and Theo would never tell her. His uncle's words had been scarcely flattering.

"She's a bit of a nag, my boy, but she's been well trained. Knows how to behave in company and understands the duties. That's what you want, Theo. It's why you must look high. Conjugal felicity is secondary when you've this much responsibility on your hands."

Theo had wanted to ask how his uncle bore with his wife's less than satisfactory traits in private but Oliver was labouring in his final illness, insisting on using what time he had left to guide Theo for the future. He worded it in a different style.

"Have you never wished for conjugal felicity, Uncle?"

Oliver had wheezed as he laughed. "Frequently. But there are compensations to be had, my boy."

Theo had no difficulty interpreting this. Everyone knew about the then duke's kept woman, conveniently placed for Devenal. Cecilia too? His uncle divined the question.

"A female of the right stamp understands these things, my boy. You perceive the advantages, I hope?"

"Yes, sir. But I can't say I care for the idea of such a bargain."

Oliver's laugh had made him cough. "Just like your father. You're Lionel all over again, Theo. Or he's inculcated you with these free and easy notions. But he didn't have to bite the bullet. I did. Likely you will too. If I've not managed to get another babe on Cecilia — not for want of trying, mark you, I did my best — you're for it, Theo. I'm sorry, my boy, I know it's not what you wanted, but nothing more I can do now. And if you have the dukedom, you've got the package. You'll do as you must, I know that. But get yourself the right sort of wife as speedily as you can. One who knows the rules and can do you proud." He had grasped Theo's hand and squeezed it, his grip still surprisingly strong for one so weak. "Need your word you'll do what's right."

Theo had given it. Not with reluctance at the time. He had wanted Oliver to go in peace, reassured he had left his legacy in good hands. Only he had not bargained for losing his heart to a female as unsuited to the role of duchess as she could be.

Hetty had few graces. She was hopeless at hiding her feelings. She was as likely to fly into a passion as to dissolve into tears. Moreover, she could not be trusted to remain out of trouble for a single day. Adorable, yes. Funny and sweet and true. Infinitely desirable. But a disastrous duchess in every possible way.

He was mad even to think of it. It would be breaking his word to marry Hetty. In the teeth of opposition too. Yet the yearning to have her, to keep her, to make her irrevocably his, would not be dismissed.

He had joked about compromising her, and on the instant discovered how desperately he wanted to do exactly that. Only he cared too much. Hetty was too innocent, too vulnerable, and it would be nothing short of an insult even to kiss those tempting lips. Or do more? Had he tasted her sweetness, could he have stopped? Why ponder? It was enough to ruin her reputation merely to be alone with him in his sanctum.

Even were marriage the object, he would not force the issue that way. No, Hetty must be deservedly wooed in form, given willingly by those who had her interests at heart, and cherished to the end of her days. Theo could offer none but the last. He was the wrong man for Henrietta Latimer.

He urged Columbus into a walk and then a trot, heading for Whisley.

There was nothing for it but to bite the bullet as his uncle put it. No matter that his chest felt leaden. At least he was no longer living in a limbo of uncertainty. He must learn to live instead with the heaviest of disappointments. He would do it. Had he not learned to bear the burden of the dukedom? He might kick against it now and then, but he had embraced the duty. This was merely an extension. He would leave the thing to Cecilia and abide by her choice. It mattered little whom he married, if he could not marry Hetty.

His mood must have communicated to his mount. Columbus broke into a canter. Theo let him have his head, finding the faster pace in keeping with the core of dissatisfaction within.

Presently, he was cantering down the drive and had to curb the horse to a trot as they reached the curve that led around the house to the stables. Aaron came out to greet him, casting an experienced eye over the stallion as Theo dismounted.

"You been letting him run you ragged, your grace, that you have. Sweating, he is. Best I rub him down before he goes after his hay."

Theo patted the horse and ran a hand down his damp flank. "He's already munched half a peck of thistles. He needed the canter to work them off."

Aaron snorted. "Don't tell me, your grace. Riding with a loose rein, you were, that's what."

"All right, there's no need to scold. I'm no longer five."

"Not much more sense than Lady Ella when all's said. She needn't think I'm a-going to stand in for Bunn. Too hot at hand for me, she is, your grace."

Theo ignored his groom's customary grumbling, knowing perfectly well he took Ellie out at Cecilia's orders, and was happy to do so. His attention snagged on the absence of the coach that had been standing in the stable yard when he'd left. "Has Mrs Summerhayes gone, then?"

Aaron was communing with the horse, but he turned his head at that. "Near an hour since, your grace. And them Latimer ladies with her."

"*What?*"

His groom frowned. "Aye, your grace. Took the one as we brung back on the hurdle, she did, and all. Mrs Summerhayes' man were detailed to carry her to the coach."

Hetty was gone? But she was nowhere near well enough to be taken home. He recalled the altercation in the parlour when he'd refused to intervene. This was the outcome.

Wrath enveloped him. Cecilia! This was her doing. By heaven, she had some explaining to do!

CHAPTER TWENTY

The hasty departure and its attendant discomfort, combined with the thankfully short coach trip to Moss House, left Henrietta weak and aching. She was grateful it was their own Frank who carried her in rather than Aunt Angelica's flustered footman.

The commotion brought Mama out of the back parlour at once.

"Gracious, what in the world has happened?"

Aunt Angelica, the angry spots of colour reappearing on her cheeks, swept across the hall. "I will tell you, my dear Margaret, but first we must settle poor Hetty. I fear even this short journey has fatigued her unduly."

Mama came up in haste, peering through her spectacles at Henrietta. "Dear me, you are perfectly white, my love. We must get you to bed."

"Let her recover in the parlour first, Mama," said Silvestre, trailing in the rear with the two valises into which she had stuffed their belongings.

Under a barrage of instruction, Frank bore his burden into the parlour and Henrietta found herself on the sofa, in considerable discomfort from her injuries and with a heart reduced to a misery too deep for tears. She allowed the cacophony to wash over her without paying much attention.

"Set another cushion behind her, Silve, my love. There, is that better?"

"She needs one for her foot, Mama."

"Her foot is the least of her worries. Only wait until you hear what passed, Margaret."

"Presently, Angelica. Silve, set her foot sideways as the doctor did."

"I declare, I could murder that creature! And she called herself a friend!"

"I'm going to lift your foot, Hetty. Tell me if I hurt you."

"She may count herself lucky to have missed Cecilia's condemnation or she would hurt twofold."

"Hush, Angelica, do. Let the poor girl rest in peace. Come, we will leave her to Silve and talk in the library."

This penetrated and Henrietta, at once beset with apprehension, started up. "Where is Papa? Oh, he will be so angry!"

"With good reason," declared Aunt Angelica, evidently still consumed with her wrongs.

Mama was quickly by the sofa, taking Henrietta's hand and squeezing it. "But not with you, my love. You may be sure Papa's care for your condition will shield you from his wrath."

But not Theo, for whom he would reserve it. The duchess too. All contact between the Latimers and the inhabitants of Whisley Park was at an end. Papa would never again allow them to visit there after this.

"Henry is out walking," Mama told Aunt Angelica, "so we may commandeer the library with impunity."

Hetty watched Mama usher her friend out, still talking of the duchess, but in muted tones now. Blowing out an overwrought breath, Silvestre plonked down into a chair.

"Heavens, what a shambles! I wish we had not had to leave in such a rush, but there is no withstanding Aunt Angelica when she is on one of her crusades. She's like a whirlwind."

Henrietta was in too much pain, both of body and mind, to be able to enter into the spirit of this. She tried to smile, but it went awry. "Oh, Silve!"

Her sister leapt up. "Now do not be falling into melancholy, Hetty, or I shall scream. I'm finding it difficult enough to maintain my sanity as it is."

That did produce an involuntary smile. "You have borne so much on my behalf, Silve. I'm sorry for it."

"Don't be, you goose. I could wish things had turned out differently for your sake, but —"

"They would not have turned out differently, Silve. There never was a chance for me, and I know it if you don't."

Her twin dropped to her haunches by the sofa, grasping Henrietta's hand, her eyes anxious. "You love him, don't you?"

Henrietta returned the pressure of her fingers. "I've not said so."

"To Theo? I should hope you would not."

"To myself. To anyone. It's better left unsaid."

Her twin cocked an eyebrow. "Better for whom?"

There was no answer to that. It was too painful to discuss. "Do you think Cook will mind if we ask Dinah to bring coffee?"

Silvestre released her, rising and crossing to the bell-pull. "She can mind all she likes. This is an emergency." She tugged on the bell and then picked up one of the straight chairs and returned to sit by the sofa, mischief in her face. "I wish Mama and Aunt Angelica had gone into the front parlour instead. We could have opened the hatch and heard everything."

Henrietta had to laugh. As children, she and her twin had managed to be party to many an adult conversation. "We were so naughty, Silve. If Mama had known, she would not have allowed us to sit to our lessons in this room."

"Ah, but she set us to work in here because it was easier for her to keep us under her eye when she was busy. She knew we might get up to all sorts of mischief in the nursery if her back was turned."

Henrietta welcomed the change of subject. Anything to keep her mind from dwelling on Theo, and what he might say or do when he found her gone. "Mama must have forgotten the hatch."

The history of Moss House had been eagerly embraced by the twins, its use as a haven for royalists leading them to seek for a secret passage. But the small spy-hatch, high in the panelling behind a false painting on the other side, proved to be the only relic of the time. Silvestre had been obliged to climb on a chair to open it in the days of their girlhood. Many a time had she almost been caught when she'd had to close it in a hurry. But her twin's mind proved to be concentrated not on memories but upon the events at Whisley Park.

"I don't believe I've ever seen Aunt Angelica so angry."

Recollection made Henrietta shudder. "She said the duchess was insulting."

"As far as I can make out, it was an all-out cat fight. She accused Aunt and Mama of making a play for the duke."

"Which they were doing," Henrietta interpolated on an irritated note.

"Not overtly. Nothing was said. At least, I don't think it was."

"Well, she must have said something to make the duchess fly into a fury."

Her twin eyed her with a sudden frown. "How do you know she flew into a fury?"

Conscious, she felt her cheeks grow warm. "She must have done. Aunt Angelica obviously did."

"Yes, but she only said the duchess was insulting." A warning note entered her sister's voice. "Hetty, what do you know?"

For a moment she hesitated. But Silve already knew so much. She sighed. "Theo told me. He said she was on the warpath. Aunt Angelica must have said something to make her realise she and Mama were scheming."

"They were not. Not really. All Godmama told her was that you are the flower artist. Mama said she was going to because you are in no condition to fulfil the commissions, remember?"

"It can't have been all. Why should that make the duchess think…?" She faded out, unwilling to put it again into words that could do nothing but stab at her inner wound.

"According to Aunt Angelica, the duchess said she had put two and two together. She coupled it with the stupid notion that you'd had your accident on purpose. That put Godmama into a flame, as you may imagine."

Undoubtedly. A ludicrous notion which gave her a poor opinion of the duchess's understanding.

Dinah's entrance put an end to the discussion. Upon being applied to for coffee, the matronly maid gave immediate notice that word had spread. "Not as it matters, for as the whole household will take your part, as you ought to know. Don't you fret none, Miss Hetty. It's glad I am to see you home safe, and Cook has the coffee boiling on the stove already, for your papa likes a cup when he comes back from his walk." She went off and returned swiftly with a full pot and a tray loaded with all the trimmings and a dish of macaroons. "Cook did them fresh this morning. Be sure and eat a couple, Miss Hetty, or she'll take it unkind and we'll never hear the end of it."

Supplied with coffee and a couple of the soft almond biscuits, Henrietta was glad to be left alone for a space, her twin, armed with her own cup, electing to go and listen at the library door.

Though her heart was heavy, Henrietta could not prevent a sneaking question arising in her mind. Where had Theo been when they made that hurried exit? She found it hard to believe he would not have intervened if he'd known. Surely he must have heard the bustle from that private room of his? She ought never to have been in there, but at least she knew it was close enough for the noise to have penetrated therein.

Could he have remained there, resolving not to interfere? After what had passed between them? Oh, not Theo. She wronged him even to suspect it. He must have been elsewhere. Having scant knowledge of the layout of Whisley, she could not begin to guess where he might have been within the house to be ignorant of what was going forward. Enough servants had contrived to witness the event, if she was to go by the inordinate number who appeared to have business in the gallery and hall. No, he could not have known. What would he do when he found out?

Recalling some of his more trenchant commands, Henrietta shivered a little. He was bound to be furious. Should she have resisted? Yet how could she? Silve was right. Aunt Angelica was unstoppable. As bad as Theo himself.

A tiny flutter riffled through her at remembrance of the way he had swooped to pick her up, scolding the while. Deaf to all her entreaties. As ever, he did precisely as he chose and paid no heed whatsoever to her protests. So typical of Theo.

A rush of affection went through her. Why this side of him should be endearing she could not fathom. He had made her fume so often with his high-handed conduct. But he changed in an instant if she became distressed. Oh, he was a dichotomy indeed. Bombastic, teasing and yet so very gentle, so kind, and all too tender.

Then she recalled the unprecedented look in his eyes when he almost kissed her. Even in memory, it had the power to reawaken an echo of its effect in the deep reaches within. She felt her limbs weaken and her mind went fuzzy, as if she might swoon.

A hasty footstep sounded without, dragging her back to reality. Silvestre slipped through the door and closed it, leaning against it, lively apprehension in her face.

"Papa is back!"

Theo paced to the rug laid before the fireplace and then back again to the window, his steps sounding loud on the polished boards. The room was cold, dark from its panelled walls, their severity relieved only by a badly executed portrait on the inner wall of a gentleman in the habit of a cavalier of the previous century, with an abundance of lace on his collar and feathers in his hat. The eyes were particularly inartistic, seeming to be hollow rather than properly painted. The whole atmosphere of the place was decidedly unwelcoming.

Not that he expected a welcome. It was galling that Latimer kept him waiting nevertheless. The fellow who had shown him into this dour parlour had seemed doubtful of his reception.

"I will inform Mr Latimer, your grace."

Theo had asked for Miss Henrietta and been denied. She was indisposed. Miss Silvestre was unavailable. Mrs Latimer was engaged. His temper lacerated beyond endurance, Theo came the duke.

"I'm not leaving until I see someone. Go and tell them the Duke of Charlton is here."

The servant's eyes had widened a trifle, but at least he allowed Theo to enter, throwing open the first door leading from a square dark-panelled hall, sparsely furnished with a chest and a couple of straight chairs, cluttered shelving over to the back where a corridor led off and a wide wooden stair leading to the upper levels.

The footman's decision to apply to the master of the house was responsible for Theo's growing agitation. Latimer was the last person he wished to speak to, beset as he was by conflicting feelings towards the fellow. While he had perforce acknowledged the man's right to chastise Theo for his dealings with Hetty, his criticisms rankled. And Cecilia must needs make bad worse. He was here to make right a wrong, but his concern and fury were on Hetty's behalf, not her father's.

Through the leaded pane of the window, he could see Aaron walking the horses. He would have remounted Columbus there and then when he'd found out Hetty was gone. But his groom's representations could not but stay him.

"He's done enough for one day, your grace. I'll not have you riding him hell for leather like you will if you go off in this mood. I'll fig out the chestnut pair and they can draw you in the phaeton."

He had agreed, racing into the house to confront Cecilia meanwhile. He found only Mary Eddleston. True to Swarland's prediction, his aunt had retired to her chamber with a sick headache. Thoroughly deserved, if her companion's account was anything to go by. Not that she blamed Cecilia.

"Oh, it was terrible, your grace. That Mrs Summerhayes said such things as I should never have thought she could say. My poor dear Cecilia was so distressed. To be spoken to in such a fashion! It is no wonder she was obliged to speak harshly in response. I did my best to support her, but I could scarcely edge in a word."

No doubt. Balked of his prey, impatience claimed Theo and he did not even stop to change his dress, dashing back out to the stables and yelling at Aaron to hurry.

He regretted it now. He was hot and sticky and aware the aroma of horses still hung about him. Latimer was bound to think worse of him for coming into his house in all his dirt, let alone being dressed inappropriately. As well the ladies had been denied after all.

The click of the door brought his head round. Latimer stood in the aperture, regarding him with an unreadable expression.

Theo's neckcloth felt tight all at once. He gave a slight bow. "I am obliged to you for seeing me, sir."

The elder man came into the room and shut the door. He did not speak as he trod across the room and then turned at the mantel.

Theo felt all the disadvantage of his position in confronting the man in his own domain. He fought down the dismay. "I imagine you must know why I have come, sir."

Latimer's chin lifted and the look in his eyes was bleak. "I am waiting for you to tell me."

That was it? No appellation at all? No greeting? The pent-up frustrations began to bubble in Theo's chest. It would not help matters to lose his temper. He struggled for calm. "I regret very much what occurred in my house this day, sir."

Latimer's brows rose. "In which particular? To my understanding, there were a number of occurrences."

"Yes, and all related. The quarrel, however, was not of my making." Conscience intervened here. "Although I might have stopped it."

"Indeed?" Coldly said, and clearly without any intention of assisting.

Theo set his teeth and tried again. "I heard the altercation as I was leaving the house. I knew my aunt was … unhappy, shall we say?"

"Unhappy?" A trace of fire showed in Latimer's gaze, but he said no more.

Theo drew a breath. "Very well, if you insist. Angry. Upset. Without, as I believed, reason to be so."

Latimer shifted his weight. "You suggest she was mistaken in her ideas?"

Damn it to hell! He knew from Hetty there had been some scheme afoot, but he could not say so now. "She was, sir."

No response. Latimer continued to regard him with an unblinking stare. It was singularly unnerving. He had no choice but to push on through.

"I did not stay to intervene, Mr Latimer, for which I am sorry. I might have prevented the duchess from expelling your daughters."

Latimer held up a hand. "One moment. You are misinformed, sir. The departure of my daughters from your establishment was entirely voluntary. Mrs Summerhayes rightly believed Henrietta's best interests would be served by bringing her home directly. That is all."

Incensed, Theo threw caution to the winds. "It is not all! Do you seek to pretend Hetty left my house in so precipitate a fashion because she chose to? She had been practising walking, for pity's sake! She was exhausted. She —"

"Be silent, sir!" The reins were loose and Latimer's gaze threw fire. "How dare you presume to tell me my daughter's mind?"

But Theo's temper was too far gone to be recalled. "Because I know it, Mr Latimer, as you do not. You came once to see her, and spent your time vilifying my character rather than discovering your daughter's condition. Nor did you soothe her alarms. No, instead you told her she must leave that same day when she was in no state to do anything but endure the pain of her wounds."

Latimer gave him an unfriendly look. "You presume too far, Duke. You are not the arbiter of my daughter's actions, nor will you ever be."

The words fell on Theo like a douche of cold water. How had Latimer divined his secret hope? Or had he? Was it bluster? Before he could think how to respond, his host was off again.

"Perhaps it has escaped your memory, Duke, but I have not forgotten you made the self-same accusations of me as your aunt has made of my wife and Mrs Summerhayes. Allow me to make it clear once and for all. No one in this household — and I stress that, sir, *no one* — has the faintest interest in regarding you as a matrimonial prospect."

"I did not suppose it, sir." But Theo's mind was ringing with the implication of that *no one*. "Nor have I forgotten your expressed views upon the subject."

"I am glad to find you understand me so well."

Resentment threw Theo into rebellion. "Oh, I understand you, Mr Latimer. I perceive your prejudice. I perceive also that you value your prejudice above your daughter's comfort or happiness."

The flare at Latimer's eyes became pronounced. "I beg your pardon, sir! How dare you?"

Theo gave a mirthless laugh. "What have I to lose in speaking free? You are determined against me. So be it. Yet I will venture to say you know less of your daughter than I. And care less too."

The man's cheeks suffused with colour, but the smoulder at his eyes did not abate. His voice, when he spoke, shook with fury. "I will pass over your insolence, my lord Duke. Your loyalty, if it be so, is misplaced. You would do better to reserve it for your own."

Past caring, Theo hit back. "Loyalty over justice, sir? You would have me back my aunt in this fracas? When Hetty's welfare is in question?"

"Hetty's welfare is not your concern, Duke. It is mine and her mother's. Get that into your head, if nothing else."

"You are beyond reason, Mr Latimer! I cannot talk to you."

"I am glad of that at least. Be assured that henceforth all intercourse between my family and yours will cease. I bid you good day, sir."

For a despairing moment, Theo regarded the unyielding countenance, a tumult of feeling boiling in his breast. He wanted to hit the man. He wanted to find Hetty in this ghastly place and carry her off, away from the implacable enmity of her father. He did neither. Corroding disappointment was seeping into his breast, dictating his words. "I hope you will not have cause to regret this day, Mr Latimer. Despite everything you have said of me, I would not wish on you the depth of my remorse. Tell your daughter. She will understand, if you do not."

Latimer returned no word. He might as well have been stuffed for all the notice he gave.

With a small bow, Theo made for the door. Latimer's voice stopped him as he reached it.

"I would have thought the better of you, my lord Duke, had you fought your aunt's battle rather than your own."

Theo swung around. "Then we differ, sir. Blind loyalty is as mistaken as prejudice."

He waited, but Latimer evidently had no more to say. It was hopeless. The man was as pig-headed as a baboon. And as vengeful.

He opened the door, went through and closed it behind him. He stood for a moment in the hall, but no sound penetrated from elsewhere in the house. Where was Hetty? The realisation that he would never be permitted to see her again began to dawn. Or only at a distance. In church, perhaps. Oh, God, unbearable! For an instant, he thought of tearing round the house to find her. For what? So Latimer could have him bodily thrown from the premises?

Without any real attention on what he was doing, he moved to the front door and let himself out of the house. Aaron, waiting with the phaeton, took one look at his face and closed his lips tightly together. Thank the Lord for a servant who knew him through and through. He swung himself up into the phaeton and took the reins.

Some instinct made him glance towards the window of the room he'd left. Latimer was standing there, watching. To make sure he had gone, no doubt.

Theo lifted his hand to his hat in a mockery of a salute and then gave his horses the office to move off.

CHAPTER TWENTY-ONE

"I will ask you again, Henrietta. For what concerning you should the duke feel remorse?"

Papa's tone, deeply inlaid with an implacable note Hetty recognised from childhood, caused her heart to batter in her chest. She had stared at him, mumchance, when he asked the question first. Coming directly after the overheard interview in the front parlour, which had induced so much agitation, it threw her into dismayed silence.

What could she say? How to answer him without throwing Theo to the wolves? She struggled for breath and glanced at Mama, standing by the door and looking anxious, and then at Silve, still at the wall where she had thankfully closed the hatch before their parents came into the room.

She hesitated too long. Papa took another step towards her and his eyes grew angry.

"Henrietta, I will be answered!"

Mama came swiftly to the sofa, putting out a hand. "Henry, pray! This is too harsh. The child is already overwrought."

But Papa did not relent. "My dear Margaret, I am not going to add to her ills, I assure you. But this matter will brook no delay."

Henrietta found her tongue, though she could not control the jumping of her voice. "Papa, it — it is not what you s-suppose."

His eyes, narrowed and questioning, came back to her. "What do I suppose? Do you presume to read my mind?"

"Henry!"

Mama's intervention only made things worse. Papa reared up, glaring at his wife. "I will not be silenced, Margaret! Allow me to question my daughter in my own way. And alone, if you please. You and Silvestre may wait elsewhere."

Henrietta's eyes pricked. When Papa was in this mood, even Mama could not save her. She did indeed look from her husband to Henrietta and back again, but following her custom, she did not choose to argue the matter before her daughters. She turned for the door.

"Come, Silve."

Her twin darted to the sofa and leaned to give her a reassuring hug. An urgent whisper reached her. "Confess everything, Hetty. It's your best hope."

Then she swiftly followed their mother, leaving Henrietta oddly strengthened by her words, the urge to weep receding as she looked up at Papa's stern countenance. Confess all? Force the issue in order to gain her heart's desire? Put Theo to the necessity of doing what went against his conscience? Never!

She watched her father sit in the chair Silvestre had been using before they both recognised the voices in the front parlour and Henrietta had urged her twin to open the hatch.

Settled, Papa crossed his legs and leaned back, eyeing her the while. "We will remain here, my child, until I know why Charlton specified that you would understand his remorse, such as it is."

The sceptical note was not lost on Henrietta, but she was already determined. Not a word of Theo's dealings with her should pass her lips. Yet she could not help their trembling as she spoke. "I b-believe the duke feels b-badly that — that the traps were s-set in his w-woods."

Papa's penetrating gaze remained on her face, and his brows rose. "Indeed? Yet he professes to know you better than I do. Why is that?"

Oh, heavens! If only Theo had not lost his temper. How was she to deflect this turn? Something she must say, and quickly. "You s-see, he — he made it his b-business to — to see to my comfort." Yes, that would serve. Her voice grew stronger. "While I was in his house, he said he felt responsible for my welfare."

"He visited your room?"

"Only when the maid or Silve was there, sir." Which at least was true, even if there were moments of intimacy therein. "It was only to see how I did. After all, he had rescued me, for which I was glad of the chance to thank him." She warmed to the theme. "Indeed, I scarcely know what would have become of me if he had not happened by that day." Was she having an effect? Did he believe her? He still looked dissatisfied. Her heartbeat became flurried again, but she dared not say more, fearful of making a slip and giving herself away.

"Your mother told me the story. Yet I wonder, Hetty, if your account is to be relied upon."

At least he had reverted to using her pet name. She endeavoured to look innocent. "Why so, Papa?"

The bleak look she loathed came into his eyes. "Because this duke, who claims a more accurate knowledge of you than your own father, appears inordinately concerned with your health. In addition to, as he would have it, your happiness. Why do you suppose that is?"

"Why, I suppose because he is at heart a kind gentleman, Papa." The lie came more easily than she could have dared to hope. "He — he can be terse and autocratic. At least, so I have noticed once or twice," she added hastily. "But in the main, he has treated me with kindness."

Her father's lip curled. "You profess to know him, then, as well as he knows you."

Her pulse leapt with shock. Had she blundered? Her mind twisted this way and that, trying to hit upon a satisfactory response. She found it. "I imagine so, sir. But that is not very much, I admit. I cannot think we have spoken above half a dozen times. It is just that the circumstances were more dramatic than in the normal course of events. Would you not say so, Papa? One is forced into a better understanding. Or so I have discovered." She was astonished at her own invention. There was truth in what she said, of course, but not all the truth.

He was frowning now. She must not crumble. She must look him boldly in the face. Where the strength to do so came from she knew not. Sheer necessity? The determination to shield Theo took precedence over everything.

"One thing more, my child." He put out a hand with finger poised. "I enjoin your utmost truthfulness, Henrietta, when you answer me now."

Conscious of how much she was keeping from him, she was swept with guilt. She forced it away, registering in a tiny corner of her mind that her loyalties had swerved. Dreadful that it was so, but she could not help it. Papa no longer commanded her unquestioning obedience. She would lie, if necessary, and endure the pangs of conscience rather than betray Theo. "Of course, Papa."

"Very well." He paused, as if to drive in the portentous nature of the coming question. "Has there ever been anything in the duke's dealings with you which could compromise you in any way?"

Henrietta looked him in the eye, lifting her chin. "No, sir, there has been nothing of that nature."

God forgive her! For Papa never would if he knew. She waited, a slow thump in her chest.

Her father's gaze searched hers. She must not fidget. She must remain apparently calm, despite the tumult rising in her bosom.

Papa's features relaxed. There was no smile, but at least the sternness of his stare abated. "I accept your word. We will speak no more of this."

He leaned forward and touched his lips to her forehead. Henrietta watched him rise and cross to the door, her teeth tightly clenched. The moment he was out of the room and the door shut behind him, she let her breath go and threw her hands over her face. Oh, but she had learned duplicity now! *And all to be laid at your door, Theo.*

He had said often how she gave away her thoughts so readily. What would he say if he could have seen her just this moment past? A bare-faced lie. She had carried it off. But the triumph was short-lived, vanishing with the inescapable realisation.

It was over.

Only now did she perceive the unacknowledged hope that had been dwelling deep in her heart. Despite all, she had held to the possibility Theo's affection might overcome his determination. But this final fracas must finish it. Whatever he felt — and that discussion to which she should not have been party argued strongly in her favour — the breach could not be mended.

Henrietta marvelled at the dryness of her eyes. She did not even feel the urge to weep. Instead she was aware of a sort of numbness, a dead feeling, as if life as she knew it had ended.

Indeed the only feeling was in her foot, which began to ache in earnest. A compensation for the lack in her bosom? What did it matter now? It would mend in time. And she was home. She could resume working on the flower pictures. The fact she had no slightest interest in so doing was irrelevant. She must do something, and that occupation was as good a distraction as any.

The dull mood held until her sister came into the room, anxiety in her gaze.

"Was it very bad, Hetty?"

She tried to smile. "I managed to convince him."

Silvestre's countenance took on exasperation as she came to the sofa. "You should have confessed it all as I told you. You are a goose, Hetty. Papa would have had to make Theo marry you."

The tears rose up from nowhere. "How could you suppose that would satisfy me? I would not have him forced to it, Silve. Do you think I could be happy, knowing he had gone against what he knew he must not do?"

Her twin took Papa's vacated chair, her brows lifting. "He was within an ace of doing just that from what we heard."

Henrietta sniffed and dashed the drops from her cheeks. "I did not take as much from what Theo said. Besides, I know his mind too well."

"Minds can be changed, Hetty."

"Oh, don't, Silve. It is useless to say so. In any event, I could not buy my happiness at the expense of being estranged from you all."

"Poppycock! Papa would come round in time. Mama would see to that." Her twin grabbed her hand and squeezed it. "I would never abandon you, whatever Papa might say." Mischief leapt in her eyes. "Though how you managed to withstand his probing I can't imagine."

Henrietta regarded her with suspicion. "Were you listening at the keyhole?"

"Of course. At least, I did not hear all, for I had to find an excuse to leave Mama with Aunt Angelica."

"Is she still here?"

"She's gone now, but she is as mad as fire that her schemes have gone awry and she blames Papa for it. In spite of all, she insists she could have managed the duchess if he had not repudiated your Theo in that horrid way."

Curiously, this afforded Henrietta no satisfaction. It did not change the essential difficulty. "I doubt Mama would agree with her. She would not speak against Papa."

"Of course not, but she is disappointed nevertheless, I could tell. It did look so promising for a while."

Henrietta did not trouble to reiterate her doubts. It never had been promising. Theo's honesty had made that clear at the outset.

A pressing need forced her to the realisation that life, regardless of circumstance, went on. "Silve, I need the chamber pot."

"One more signature, your grace."

Hathersage set a neatly written document on the desk. Theo ran his eyes down the sheet. Another set of tenants to be satisfied? He forced his reluctant mind to concentrate. The authorisation would allow his agent to set in train a raft of alterations to the cottages inhabited by farm labourers.

"I trust we can afford this work?"

"I should not otherwise have sanctioned it, your grace. It is necessary. I inspected the cottages myself."

Theo dipped his pen in the inkpot and signed with his usual flourish. He looked up as his secretary shook the sander over the wet ink. "That's all you have for me?"

"Everything else I can manage without applying to your grace."

Must the fellow be so deuced efficient? He needed distraction. On the other hand, his ability to focus appeared to have deserted him these last days. Ten days. No, it was more. Two weeks? Was it twice Cecilia had complained when he refused to attend at church?

He became aware that Hathersage, having disposed of his document, was hovering. He coughed when Theo looked enquiringly and picked up a batch of cards and notes. "What would your grace wish me to reply to these invitations?"

Theo snatched them out of his hand, barely glanced at each and threw them down one by one. "No, no, no, no, no, no and no. Suitably worded in your inimitable style."

His secretary's countenance registered faint disapproval, but he said nothing.

Impatience seized Theo. "Spit it out, man! You think I ought to go to these damned events, do you?"

"If you will forgive me, your grace, I believe your disinclination to participate in the life of the county is coming under a degree of notice."

Theo curled his lip. "You mean my neighbours think me an ill-mannered whippersnapper? Tell me something new."

His secretary went to his chair on the other side of the desk and sat down, collecting up the disordered invitations and tidying them in his fastidious fashion. He held them between his hands where they rested on the desk and raised his eyes, regarding Theo with a look both deprecating and, if he read it right, sympathetic.

"You need not look at me like a disapproving uncle, Hathersage."

"I should not so presume, your grace."

"And don't feel sorry for me either!"

A faint smile crossed the man's face. "I am unable to help that, your grace."

Theo threw himself out of his chair and flung over to the window. He spoke without turning around. "I take it the servant gossip machine has been at work?"

"I have eyes in my head, your grace."

The words were said in a tone that told Theo he had failed to conceal his state of mind from one person at least. It was not as if he tried very hard. He knew he had been terse to the point of rudeness with Cecilia. He could barely bring himself to speak to her, if truth be told. Had she not precipitated a crisis…

No, enough. No more going over it. A useless exercise. As useless as the unquenchable parade of images that prowled ceaselessly across his memory, no matter how much he tried to banish them. *Hetty, Hetty, Hetty.*

He must stop this. What if he repaired to Devenal? He had thought of it more than once. Yet it smacked of ignominious retreat. He would not give Latimer the satisfaction. Nor, if he was honest, could he endure the thought of going so far away from Hetty. He had avoided church in dread of the agony of being in her vicinity and unable to reach her. Fearful also of falling into an urgency so fierce that he snatched her up before everyone and carried her off to Gretna.

In those first hideous hours, he'd toyed with the notion of doing just that. If her injury had not been a deterrent, he might have found means in truth to kidnap her and make her his own. And to hell with Latimer!

But his saner self knew it would not do. He loved her too well to force her to so ruinous a course. Besides which, the objections rudely represented to him by Cecilia still obtained.

"A girl with next to no portion, and of no rank whatsoever? Those women actually dared to conceive of her snaring a duke. I declare, if I had not been so angry, I should have laughed in Angelica's face!"

He had remained tight-lipped and silent, refusing to be drawn into argument. If he spoke at all, he would have blasted her where she sat. Thankfully, her sycophantic companion was ready with agreement and sympathy, sparing Theo's tongue.

But when she'd had the temerity to demand to know what he'd said to Latimer, he had not been able to withhold himself.

"Rave all you wish, Cecilia, but don't enquire into my affairs. If you will refrain from speaking of the Latimers or Mrs Summerhayes in my presence, I will be the better pleased."

Which, as he might have known, she had taken for agreement with her views. "I do not blame you, my dear Theo. I must suppose you to be sick to death of the whole lot of them, as am I, I assure you. As for that girl —"

"Don't say it, aunt! Whatever you have on the tip of your tongue, keep it there. I cannot answer for my temper if you say one word of —" He had cut himself off without saying her name before he spilled the truth. Cecilia had gazed at him in astonishment.

"Well, really, Theo. I can't imagine why you should turn on *me*. Anyone would suppose it is my fault the wretched creature was hustled off. Not that I am sorry for it, for —"

He could not contain himself. "It is your fault, Cecilia. You had no business taking your Angelica to task. I told you to leave well alone, but no, you could not refrain from kicking up a dust as you always do."

She was predictably affronted. "How can you say so? How dare you speak to me in that tone, Theodore? All I did —"

"All you did was more than enough to turn a contretemps into a catastrophe. You've made it impossible for me to see Hetty at all, and I can't even discover how she fares. So pray don't prate to me of snares and go on as if you are hard done by. You were not injured. Hetty was. Thanks to your meddling she's been subjected to discomfort and the Lord knows what else."

He had left Cecilia staring, her mouth at half-cock, and slammed from the parlour, retreating to his sanctum to rage and brood. It availed him nothing. He had later apologised perforce, but his aunt was still in the sulks, addressing him with pointed reserve. He'd been glad of it, for he was at least spared having to listen to her complaints upon a subject that could not but touch a nerve at the slightest hint of criticism of his sweet Disaster.

Hathersage's cough brought him out of the painful reverie. He turned back from empty contemplation of the rose garden outside the library window, its blooms sparser now with the approach of August.

"What is it?"

His secretary jerked a head towards the hall. "There are sounds betokening an arrival, your grace."

Theo frowned. "And so? It's probably another visitor for my aunt. You don't suppose I wish to present myself in the blasted saloon, do you?"

Hathersage was at the door, which was open. "I think it is more than that, your grace. I can hear both Flint and Mrs Oughtibridge exclaiming."

This was sufficiently intriguing to catch Theo's interest. He crossed to the door, following his secretary down the corridor and into the hall, where the commotion indeed betokened an unusual arrival.

The housekeeper was bobbing about like an excited chicken and Flint was beaming all over his face. A gaunt female Theo knew well was haranguing two of the footmen into following her to the coach outside to fetch in her ladyship's luggage. In their midst stood the tall and laughing woman with that mass of curling locks of pepper and salt escaping from under her hat, whom Theo had no difficulty at all in recognising. His heart lifted and he strode forward.

"Mama! What in the world brings you out of hiding?"

Theo surveyed his mother as she arranged herself on the daybed, seeing in his mind's eye a very different female in that very spot. Whom he had brought here. Wanted here. Very badly. Much as he adored his mother, her presence in his sanctum was distinctly unwelcome. But Lady Lionel Devenal had never paid the slightest heed to her son's prohibitions, had she? Assuming, with some justice he must admit, they did not apply to her.

"You do realise everyone else in the world knows I never allow anyone in here save my valet?"

His mother waved this away with an airy hand. "All very well, darling boy, and I perfectly appreciate the necessity for an eyrie to where you may escape —"

"Of course you do, mother mine, when you are ten times the recluse I am."

"— but I happen to wish to talk to you," she finished, ignoring the interjection.

He sighed, leaning back against the window frame and setting his elbows on the sill behind. "Cecilia wrote to you, didn't she?"

He'd known it the moment his aunt came hurrying down the stairs to greet her sister-in-law.

"Isobel! You came! I am so very pleased."

The flurry of greetings and enquiries took some time. His mother was ushered into the parlour, the ever-disapproving Miss Melmerby snatching her pelisse and hat from the floor as Lady Lionel threw them off in her customary careless fashion. Time enough for Theo's pleasure to be tempered by the realisation she was here because of recent events.

"Nothing short of a cataclysm would bring you out of your so-called retirement, ma'am, so you may as well admit the truth at once," he told her now on a note of severity.

The well-known dance began in the large dark eyes that had captivated his father, as he'd told his son time and again. "Must I confess it?"

He threw up his eyes. "Spit it out, Mama. How much do you know? Not that I have the slightest doubt Cecilia told you a barrel of nonsense."

She laughed. "She did, of course, but I know her well enough to be able to read between the lines." She patted the cushioned seating beside her. "Come and tell me all about her, my precious one."

A shaft went through him. She had guessed it, then. He remained where he was, the turmoil rising in him all over again. He strove for calm. "Tell you? About whom?"

She gave him one of those withering looks of hers. "Don't be silly, my darling boy." Again she patted the daybed, with more force. "Come and sit here and stop being a stubborn mule. Really, you are just like your grandfather."

With reluctance he obeyed, the retort automatic as he sat beside her. "Papa would have it I am too much like you."

"In many ways you are."

Her fingers fluffed at his hair as they'd done from his childhood. He jerked back. "Must you?"

Laughter trickled from her. "It's that or smack your face for you, horrid boy. Give me a kiss at once!"

He complied, planting one on her cheek. But the Lady Lionel Devenal was having none of his chaste salute. She seized him in a ruthless hug, holding him tight until he was obliged to reciprocate, his stiffness relaxing as the familiar embrace brought balm and warmth to the cold regions of his breast. His mother never would brook distance from those she loved. Forcing an embrace was typical. As she released him at last, it occurred to him he was more like her than he'd realised. He'd been as ruthless with Hetty more than once, overbearing her resistance.

"That's better." His mother patted his cheek and turned his head to face her. "Let me look at you." She studied him, a half-smile on her lips, but with question in her eyes alongside the affection Theo knew she cherished towards him.

"If you are planning to read my mind, I wish you won't."

Her brows arched. "Do I need to? Talk to me, Theo."

He let out an overwrought breath. "What do you want me to say, Mama? You've come here hotfoot and you won't tell me why."

"You know why, darling." She paused a moment, but he was reluctant to yield, fearing the question he knew would pierce his armour. It came. "Have you fallen in love with her? Not that I need ask."

"Is it so obvious?"

"Not to Cecilia. She thinks you've been taken in by a hussy. But she did suspect you might have a slight *tendre*."

"She's not a hussy!" Restless, he got up and went back to the window.

"Then tell me what she is, Theo."

He threw up his hands as he turned. "Everything that makes her utterly unsuitable. And more that is much too endearing." His tongue loosened before the one person he trusted most in the world and it came tumbling out. "She's utterly hopeless, if you wish to know. I tell her she's a disaster and she is. She can't be trusted to do anything without creating some kind of shambles. Climbing trees, for God's sake! All for a stupid cat. And she must needs step on a blasted rabbit trap. All very well to say it's not her fault and I know that, but it's typical. If there was a table in her way she'd fall over it!"

"Is she so clumsy?"

"She's not clumsy. She's just got too much sensibility for her own good. She weeps at the drop of a hat and she never has a handkerchief to hand. I've had to rescue her from her own idiocy far too many times and all I get for it is to be called a rude beast." He drew an overwrought breath. "She's the worst possible candidate for a duchess, Mama, and I want her so desperately I can't think of anything else!" He threw his hands over his face, fighting for breath. Why had his mother to drag it from him? Bringing back the agony he had been tamping down.

She did not speak and the silence enabled him to regain control. He let his hands fall and looked across at her. Was that a trace of a tear on her cheek? It glistened, but when he looked into the dark eyes they were smiling.

"You've fallen harder than I could have supposed possible." A wry look entered her face. "But tell me, what of the girl? Does she return your regard?"

His heart kicked with the memories and he did not hesitate. "Yes. She won't say so, but she does."

"Then where is the difficulty?"

"Haven't you been listening?"

"So far I've heard nothing to stop you following your heart." His mother stretched out a hand and he went back to the daybed, sinking down again with a heavy sigh. She tucked her hand in his. "What makes you so certain this impossible girl of yours would make a poor sort of duchess?"

The appellation rankled. "Hetty. Her name is Hetty."

"Hetty, then. Why is she impossible?"

He turned his head, fairly glaring. "Have I not just said?"

She opened her eyes at him. "You've ranted a good deal, Theo, but that does not tell me very much. Except that you're smitten with your Hetty."

He flinched. "That's irrelevant."

"On the contrary, it's the most important aspect of the business."

"Listen, Mama. It doesn't matter what I feel, or what Cecilia thinks. Latimer won't give her to me at any price. I blotted my copybook with the man at the outset and he's adamant."

His mother was frowning now. "You've asked him?"

"For Hetty's hand? Of course not. I've assured him more than once that I've no matrimonial intentions towards her."

Lady Lionel released his hand, letting out an exasperated snort. "Gracious heaven, what sort of an idiot have I brought into the world?"

Theo hit back. "I may be every sort of an idiot, ma'am, but I know my duty."

"Duty!" She blew out an impatient breath. "Oliver's work, I collect?"

"Yes, if you must know. He told me what sort of female I ought to marry and I gave him my word I would."

"Then you'll have to break it, you ridiculous boy. Gave him your word indeed! On his deathbed, no doubt?"

"Yes! What would you?"

His mother's tone changed and she patted his hand. "Deathbed promises are made to be broken."

Theo gazed at her in growing annoyance. "If that isn't just the kind of remark I might have expected from you."

"Of course you might. You know I have no opinion of the male obsession with honour. It is a blight upon the world and ought to be eradicated. Too many promising young men have lost their lives on account of it. Besides, one ought never to be obliged to make promises to people who are dying. Circumstances change. One cannot possibly know what may befall, and to be held to a foolish notion merely to comfort a person who is leaving it all behind is the most ridiculous thing I ever heard."

Curiously, his mother mounting her favourite hobby-horse had the effect of soothing his lacerated senses. He did not trouble to argue with her. It would be useless. As useless as the hope of making Hetty his duchess.

"Cecilia would not agree with you."

"Don't talk to me of Cecilia! She's an empty-headed muffin!"

He had to laugh. "She's not a fool, Mama. Uncle Oliver knew her worth to him."

"Yes, because he imbibed the nonsense your grandfather inculcated. Thank the lord Lionel was different. He brought you up to think for yourself. We both did. What business have you kowtowing to the opinion of a creature who can't see beyond her own prejudices? Oh, it's not Cecilia's fault. She can't help it."

"You're even more intolerant of her than I am, Mama, you wretch."

She laughed. "I don't know how you can endure living in the same house. I can take her in small doses, but I'm not going to allow her to dictate your future, so don't think it."

"She's not dictating my future, Mama. But she does know the sort of female I ought to marry."

"Ought!" She seized both his hands and held them fast. "Listen to me, Theo. You've sacrificed your life to this dukedom. Yes, I know you had no choice. But do you truly wish to sacrifice any chance of happiness? Won't it make the burden easier if you have a helpmeet by your side whom you can truly love and cherish? The marriage vow should never be taken lightly."

The constriction in his chest became almost too much to bear. He could not hear such words unmoved. "I have thought of it, Mama. Of nothing else these last days, if truth be told. But then I remember what it means to be a duchess. Hetty would flounder. She's not like Cecilia."

"Well, that is to her credit. You say she has sensibility. Isn't that an asset too? Why not a duchess who will look upon those less fortunate with sympathy? Why not one who is natural and does not put up a gracious façade? So what if she stumbles? You will be there to pick her up, will you not?"

He drew a shaky breath. "Don't make it look so tempting." A memory made him smile. "Ellie called her Softy. She took her measure at once."

"Ellie likes her?"

"Inordinately. I think it was mutual, though Hetty spoke of her running wild and needing an example to guide her."

"Well then, what could be better? Your Hetty could not be a worse influence than her own mother."

For a few precious moments he dwelled upon the dream. Then reality crashed back. "It's of no use. Even if I break my word to Oliver, there is Latimer in the way. The man's a human bulwark. I had as well attempt to scale a castle wall."

CHAPTER TWENTY-TWO

The visitor bore little resemblance to Theo. Henrietta found her charm and manner a trifle overwhelming. Or perhaps that was due to the inescapable flutter in her bosom the moment she announced herself to be Theo's mother.

She had entered the back parlour like a whirl of sunshine, wafting Frank aside with an airy gesture. "Pray do not trouble to announce me, dear man." Her gaze swept the occupants, passing briefly across Silvestre, dwelling for an instant on Henrietta and then fastening upon Mama. "My dear Mrs Latimer, how lovely to see you again! It has been years, I am persuaded."

"Lady Lionel!" Mama looked utterly taken aback, rising as she blinked at the apparition through her spectacles. "Gracious, is it you indeed?"

The creature emitted a laugh, catching at Mama and actually embracing her, much to Henrietta's astonishment. "You do recognise me! I am so glad. It would have been tedious to be obliged to remind you."

"Yes, indeed," agreed Mama, clearly flustered as she peered up into the taller woman's face. "You have changed very little."

Mama cast a glance through her eye-glasses at Henrietta, which she took to be unusually anxious. Upon which, Lady Lionel turned lustrous dark eyes on her, sweeping at once to Silvestre and then back again.

"And these are your daughters, all grown up. Twins, as I recall, no?" A smile of great charm encompassed them both as Mama hastened to perform the introductions. Henrietta stood up as of instinct, wincing as she still did when her foot touched the floor.

"This is Silvestre."

Her twin rose, receiving the lady's hand as she put it out and at once clasped Silvestre's with both her own, smiling.

"I do remember you had an unusual name."

"I was named for Lord Horwood, ma'am."

Lady Lionel's eyes grew sympathetic. "Ah, yes. A wasted compliment, I gather." Without waiting for a response, she turned to Henrietta, seizing both her hands in a warm hold and smiling, although her eyes ran over her in an appraising way. "And you are Hetty. My son has told me all about you and I am enchanted to meet you."

Henrietta could not utter a word as the implication of the lady's identity hit her. Theo's mother! She knew! The rhythm of her pulse went awry. As of instinct, she glanced at Mama and found her for once at a loss. She looked both disconcerted and concerned. And Silvestre's mouth was at half-cock.

Lady Lionel released Henrietta and turned to Mama. "Dear Mrs Latimer, do forgive me. I never stand upon ceremony, for I can't bear formality. May we all sit down?"

"Oh, yes, pray do be seated, ma'am." Mama was rapidly regaining her composure. "Ring the bell, Silve. You'll take a glass of wine, Lady Lionel?"

"Oh, Orgeat or lemonade, if you have it. Or coffee will do. I never touch liquor in the day." She had not yet taken a seat and she turned back to Henrietta. "Should you not sit down, child? I see you have a footstool there. How is your injury? Do you feel it still? That's right, put your foot up again, my dear."

Henrietta found herself willy-nilly back in her place on the daybed, her foot on the stool, with Lady Lionel settling beside her. She was reminded irresistibly of Theo's equally forceful manner, although his mother appeared to accomplish her intentions in a fashion decidedly insouciant.

Once everyone was seated, Lady Lionel reached for Henrietta's hand and turned her gaze upon Mama. "Now, Mrs Latimer, what are we to do about this little waif of yours?"

Mama's brows drew together. "Waif? What in the world do you mean, ma'am?"

Lady Lionel dropped Henrietta's hand and threw both her own into the air. "Oh, let us not engage in pretence, if you please. It is of all things what I most abominate. Where is your husband? I must tackle him, of course, but let us females all be clear at once."

The mention of Papa sent a wave of apprehension through Henrietta and she found her tongue. "Ma'am, pray! What do you intend? Why have you come?"

"Yes, I should like to know that too." Mama was looking rather grim. "Perhaps you are not aware of the breach between our two families?"

Lady Lionel leaned towards her. "I am very glad you mentioned that. So ridiculous. All this taking umbrage for nothing is what I have no patience with." She held up a hand as Mama opened her mouth to speak. "Yes, I know Cecilia began it. Such a silly creature she is sometimes. I might forgive her if she had not done her best to inculcate my boy with her stuffy notions of what sort of a girl he should marry. Not that Theo bears no share of blame, and you may be sure I scotched his absurd notion of duty. Duty! Really, men are so stupid. As if duty matters a jot when one's happiness is in question."

Utterly bemused, and conscious of a snaking curl in her bosom of the hope she had deemed dead, Henrietta stared at the creature's profile as she discoursed on the idiocy of the male sex. Could this mean Theo had changed his mind? Yet if he had, there was still Papa.

The entrance of Dinah put an end to Lady Lionel's monologue. Mama, who had sat mumchance throughout, apparently dazed, started and put in a request for coffee. "Also, pray bring any little sweetmeat Cook may have prepared, Dinah."

The matronly maid fairly gawped at the flamboyant visitor, dressed as she was in a green tiger-spotted pelisse that hung open to reveal a round gown embroidered in bright thread, her black and grey locks flowing from beneath a wide hat ornamented with feathers, colourful flowers and a green gauze veil.

"Dinah?"

The maid started. "Yes, ma'am. Coffee, ma'am." Forgetting to curtsy, she withdrew.

Henrietta felt as if she mirrored Dinah's stupefaction. Glancing at her twin, she found her evidently struggling to suppress a bubble of amusement, her eyes dancing and her lips firmly closed together.

"Lady Lionel," Mama began in a determined voice as the door closed, "I fear you go too fast for me. As far as I know, your son has made no offer."

Lady Lionel took this without a blink. "No, I know he has not, foolish boy. But he is, I can assure you, highly desirous of marrying your daughter."

"Then why has he not said so? He told my husband he had no —"

"No intentions in that direction. Yes, he told me he said as much and I gave him pepper for it. Heavens above! What is poor Mr Latimer to think when he insists he does not wish to marry your Hetty?" She turned and seized Henrietta's hand again, the dark eyes warm. "But he does, you see, very much indeed. The question is, child, whether you wish to marry him? Do you love him?"

The direct question threw Henrietta into confusion. Her heart leapt and then thumped horribly as her gaze shot across to her mother. Mama was regarding her with an intent look, a trifle of distress within it.

"Do you, Hetty, my love?"

She could not say it. Devoid of hope, she had crushed the knowledge too long. Unless Theo was to ask her, she dared not speak the words.

To her relief, her twin cut in. "She has never admitted as much, Mama. And I believe she won't. Not while she knows her Theo thinks her unworthy."

The word brought it all back and Henrietta struggled with the lump in her throat and the pricking at her eyes. Lady Lionel was still looking into her face, and she sighed at this.

"My poor child. Can you truly wish to be saddled with such an idiot as my son is proving to be?"

A gurgle escaped Henrietta and the desire to weep faded. "He's not an idiot, ma'am. He's perfectly horrid at times, and dreadfully stubborn —"

"Don't I know it!"

"— but he's kind too and he would never wilfully hurt anyone. I know he — he regrets having s-said some things to me, but he was honest with me from the first."

"So I should hope. His father and I brought him up to be truthful, for I can't bear duplicity. It is what mars Cecilia's character, I'm afraid. She is apt to wear two faces in a foolish notion of maintaining the dignity of her rank. *You* will never do so, I am persuaded, Hetty."

A sob caught in Henrietta's throat. "But I am not going to be a d-duchess, ma'am. Papa will n-never l-let me marry Theo. He t-told him so and he meant it."

She came under unexpected fire from Mama. "How do you come to know as much, Hetty? You cannot have heard —" She broke off, her eyes flying to the hatch in the wall. "Oh!" Her gaze returned to Henrietta, unusual anger in it. "You were listening? Silve too?"

Her twin rescued her. "Well, of course, Mama. What else could you expect, with the hatch so handy? Poor Hetty was nearly concerned in that conference, and she had a right to know."

Mama arose in wrath. "She had no right to eavesdrop upon Papa. Nor had you, Silve. I am ashamed of you both!"

Relief came from an unexpected quarter as Lady Lionel broke into laughter. "Oh, tut, Mrs Latimer. Do you tell me there is a spyhole in the wall? Left from Cromwell's day?" She was up, moving to examine it as Silvestre went across and stood on tiptoe to open the hatch. "How quaint! And so useful too." She whirled on Mama, seizing her hands. "Come now, Mrs Latimer, don't scold them. Has there not been quarrelling enough? We must move forward, must we not? I think, don't you, that you and I had best put our heads together. If we leave it to this foolish pair of lovers, matters will never be resolved."

Before Henrietta's amazed eyes, Mama was swept from the room by Lady Lionel, pausing only to instruct her daughters to send the coffee to her sitting-room above stairs.

Left alone with her sister, Henrietta collapsed against the back of the daybed, letting her breath go in a whoosh.

Silvestre, who was closing the hatch again, turned upon her a face brimful of mirth. "She is an original, is she not? Heavens, Hetty, what a mother-in-law you will have!"

Henrietta fluttered agitated hands. "Oh, don't, Silve!"

"Why not?" Her sister came to perch beside her. "It is evident your Theo is too much in love with you to hold to whatever notion of duty he has."

Her bosom palpitating uncomfortably, Henrietta twisted her fingers together. "She is forcing him into going against his conscience. He would never do so otherwise."

"Well, I don't believe it. If Papa had not been so very much against him, I am persuaded Theo would indeed have offered for you that day."

Henrietta shuddered. "Don't remind me. I defied Papa too. If he learns the truth, Silve, he will be furious with me."

"Why should he learn it, you goose?"

"Because Theo's affection could not have been formed without those clandestine meetings. He is bound to question it."

"If he questions anything, I suspect it will be Theo's intentions. Lady Lionel was right. Papa won't readily accept his change of heart as far as that goes."

This prognostication could not but throw Henrietta into gloom. She could almost wish away Lady Lionel's advent. The episode had revived all the painful hankering she had been trying to dismiss. In vain. No amount of stern lecturing to herself had served to quieten the yearning. Nor the images that plagued her, of Theo in all his guises. The best she could say was that she was learning to endure the knot of agony deep within.

Now it had flared all over again, reviving hope and thrusting her into a frenzy of turmoil and doubt.

CHAPTER TWENTY-THREE

Two days later, Theo was back at Moss House. At least this time he had not been kept waiting in the gloomy front parlour, the footman showing him directly into a library which caught the daylight through a bank of windows in between the loaded shelves. Latimer was seated at his desk, apparently studying an open tome. He did not look up when Theo was announced.

The silence ticked by for what felt like an eon. Dear Lord, it was as bad as being back at Eton. He already felt shredded, his customary command of himself deserting him at the thought of what lay ahead as he drove over. He had rehearsed what he might say but the entirety had gone out of his head.

This treatment was no doubt deliberate. Meant to unsettle him. He stiffened his spine. If he wanted Hetty, he must get through this.

"Mr Latimer?"

The wretched fellow would not look up. "I am he."

Damn the man! Theo set his teeth. He would not lose his temper. "I owe you an apology, sir."

At last Latimer flicked him a glance, but it was fleeting. "Only one?"

Ye Gods! He did not intend to make this easy, did he? So much for his mother's sanguine hopes.

"I have paved the way, darling boy. The rest is up to you."

He'd balked. "What do you mean, you've paved the way? You spoke to Latimer?"

She had looked mischievous. "To some purpose."

A faint thread of hope had struggled through his pessimism. "Are you saying he will listen to me?"

His mother's vague wafture was accompanied by a gurgle of mirth. "Oh, you have some work to do, but I am confident Mrs Latimer — such a sensible female — has a good deal of influence with her husband."

"Mama, I wish you won't be so cryptic!"

But say more she would not. Nor did she speak of Hetty beyond saying she believed his feelings were reciprocated, which he already knew. He had never doubted Hetty's affections. They scourged him rather.

Now here was Latimer, twice as cryptic and giving no clue as to his current thinking. Although he had agreed to see him. He could not be wholly set against him. A little heartened, Theo tried again.

"I hope my apology may serve for all, Mr Latimer." No response. He drew breath and kept his tone as even as he could. "I have not behaved towards you as I ought, sir, and I've said much that I regret."

Latimer raised his head at last, in his eyes the horrid bleak look Theo remembered. "You do not stand by your words, then?"

Theo met his gaze and held it, opting for truth. "I stand by them, some of them. I should not have said them."

Some of the hardness left the other's gaze. "An acceptable amendment. Which of your words do you not stand by?"

Now was his chance. "Those that concern my intentions, sir."

A curl of the lip and a dry note came. "Now we come to it."

Theo took a couple of steps towards the desk, keeping his gaze on Latimer's. "I will make no attempt to flummery you, sir. It's not my way and I feel sure you would see through me."

Latimer inclined his head but he did not speak. So far, so good.

"My affection for your daughter notwithstanding, I have been holding to a promise made to my uncle. He advised me to marry a female of rank who would understand the duties required of her."

Still no response. Though was there a flicker in Latimer's eyes? Theo tamped down the inevitable rise of frustration.

"My mother —"

At that, Latimer's head reared up. "Yes, I am aware of Lady Lionel's opinion, I thank you."

"But not perhaps of what she said to me, Mr Latimer," Theo said in haste.

A measured pause. Then, "Say on."

"My mother pointed out a flaw. Circumstances change. What was appropriate in the past might not suit the present." He let out a tight breath. "It struck me with some force, Mr Latimer."

The man pursed his lips. "I am at a loss to understand you, Duke. How does this concern my daughter?"

Theo's distresses got the better of him. "Because I love her, Mr Latimer! What sort of man would I be to be offering marriage to a female to whom I could not also offer my heart? Merely for the sake of a way of life with which I have little patience and less interest. I never wanted this dukedom, sir. But I have it and I must find my path through it somehow. I was determined to sacrifice myself on this particular altar, and that was both stupid and selfish." His voice was shaking, he knew, but he pushed on through. "Because I have no right to sacrifice Hetty too."

For the first time, Latimer's lip relaxed into a faint smile. "For once, Duke, you have uttered a sentiment with which I am in the fullest agreement."

"Then you will —"

He stopped as Latimer held up a hand. He glanced down at the large open book on his desk, tapping it. "I have been studying your credentials. The Peerage is most informative."

Too overwrought to respond to a remark which appeared to him utterly irrelevant, Theo merely stared at the man.

Latimer's smile grew, though it was more caustic than friendly. He rose and crossed to the near window, standing with his back to Theo and looking out across the terraced lawns beyond. "I have been guilty of a similar fault." He threw a glance over his shoulder. "You mentioned it yourself, Duke. Prejudice."

For several moments he said nothing further. Theo was left to skim their previous encounter and to wonder how any words of his regarding prejudice could have rankled with the man.

Latimer turned at last and came to where Theo stood. His lip curled again. "Do not run away with the notion your scolding changed me, Duke. Nor, I may add, was I moved by Lady Lionel's forthright views upon the subject of matrimony and, in her words, the general stupidity of the male sex."

Theo experienced a brief instant of embarrassment at the thought of that unknown interview with his outspoken parent, but he was too anxious to dwell on it. "What then, sir?"

To his surprise, Latimer's features softened and there was a look in his eyes Theo had not previously seen. "I will confess your mother did make one comment, inadvertent, I am persuaded, which caused me to look at my own conduct. She spoke of the virtue of mutual affection."

"That she holds the marriage vow should never be taken lightly?"

"Something of the sort, but that is by the way. There is more than one kind of affection, Duke. You say you love my Hetty.

So do I, and I have used her too harshly through this business. That is my regret, sir."

Theo was so much in agreement with the sentiment, he dared not open his mouth again. He must not antagonise the man at this point, just when it began to seem as if there might after all be hope.

Latimer's tone hardened again as he looked Theo over. "I do not like the match. I will not pretend otherwise."

It was too much. "Yes, you've made that clear enough, Mr Latimer."

His brows rose. "And I stand by it, sir. If I yield, it is not for any change of heart towards you, be sure. I hold to my opinion."

"That I'm a worthless whippersnapper?"

A mirthless laugh escaped the man. "I do not believe I ever said *worthless*."

"You implied it," Theo snapped. "I have my faults, as I've before confessed, but —"

"Oh, I'm aware of your good qualities, boy, you need not poker up."

Theo blinked. It was the first time Latimer had ever addressed him in so light a fashion. Or admitted that he might not be uniformly despised. Hope burgeoned more strongly. Urgency engulfed him. "Mr Latimer, I must beg you to put me out of my agony. Will you or will you not give Hetty to me?"

His brows flew up. "As far as I am aware, Charlton, you have never yet offered."

Impatient of this pedantry, Theo flung up his hands. "Then I do so now! Will you permit me to marry Hetty?"

The brows rose again. Would the wretched man still prevaricate?

"It is more a case of whether I will permit Hetty to marry you."

"Must you quibble, Mr Latimer? The cases are the same!"

"No, they are not. They are quite different." Again the look in his eyes became regretful. "You do not understand me, I see that. Strive for a little patience, if you please."

Theo drew an audible breath, struggling not to hit the fellow. Was this what he could expect from a future father-in-law? Ye Gods! If he got Hetty at last, he would keep well away from the fellow. Not that he supposed Latimer would welcome his presence. "Very well, sir, we will play it your way."

Latimer nodded. "I thank you." To Theo's intense surprise, he reached out. "Give me your hand, boy."

Frowning, Theo held out his hand and felt it gripped so strongly that it hurt a little. He winced, but did not speak.

Latimer's gaze became intense and he leaned forward. "Theodore — yes, I will call you by name, for I need you to hear me. In your heart, Theo!"

What came now? Despite his dislike of the man, he felt compelled by a note of passion in his voice that was all too similar to one he had heard in Hetty's. "I am with you so far, sir."

A nod, and then Latimer's other hand came about the one he held, increasing the grip. "Do you swear, Theodore, that you will cherish my girl and keep her safe, even unto your own detriment?"

Theo's inner vision filled with Hetty's image and he had no difficulty whatsoever in giving the required promise. "I will guard her with my life, sir. And cherish her always."

Latimer's gaze became luminous. He dropped Theo's hands and seized him in a stifling hug. Theo endured it, but was relieved when it was quickly over and Latimer stood back.

His voice was husky. "I am glad we understand each other so far. You found me out. I was indeed ready to sacrifice my daughter's happiness to my own prejudice, Duke. In a calmer frame of mind, I came to realise such a course was unworthy. Henrietta has not deserved it of me. I am prepared to give her into your keeping, but I hold you to your given word."

Theo could barely get the words out to thank him. Latimer waved them away, crossing to the desk and picking up a hand bell there which he plied with vigour. Then he turned back to Theo.

"I will have Frank direct you to the front parlour and bid Henrietta to join you there."

Henrietta stared at her father, every faculty suspended. She could not think, speak or move, though her heart felt in danger of jumping out of her bosom, so violent was its beat.

A rueful smile curved Papa's lip and the softened look in his eyes caused a pricking at Henrietta's. "I appear to have deprived you of breath, my child."

"Of everything, Papa," added Silvestre in a tone of amusement, "if I am any judge. It is wonderful news, Hetty, you goose."

Papa held out a staying hand. "Hush, Silve!" He came to the daybed and took Henrietta's hands, pulling her up. "Come, stand upon your own feet, my child. They will hold you now."

Henrietta very much doubted this. Though her foot was sturdy enough, her knees seemed ready to give way beneath her. Papa let go and she managed to remain upright, her mind yet cloudy with the wholly unexpected change. Theo had offered and Papa had given his consent? It could not be true, could it? "D-did you m-mean it, Papa? Truly?"

"I have said it, and I stand by it. I do not pretend to like it, as I told Charlton to his face. But I have eyes in my head, my child. Your demeanour in these past days has convinced me your affections are engaged."

Henrietta dragged in an overwrought breath. "I am s-sorry, Papa. I t-tried n-not to show it."

"You have endured much distress without complaint, Hetty. I honour you." He saluted her forehead with his lips and then gave her a little push. "Your suitor is waiting in the front parlour. Go to him. I must find your mama and make my peace there too."

From which Henrietta understood that Mama must have championed her cause. She must find out how and thank her. But her attention veered as she limped to the door. How had Theo come to this extraordinary change of face? Was it his mother's doing? She trembled to think he might have been coerced.

Outside the parlour door, she hesitated, struggling with the flowering of hope against the plaguing doubt. Papa's abrupt about-face was hard enough to take in. But Theo's? The need to know overtook her and she seized the door handle and turned it, pushing into the room.

She saw him at once, standing at the mantel, his gaze riveting upon her, anxiety within it. Henrietta slid into the room and closed the door, sinking back against it for support, her limbs shaking.

For a breathless moment she could say nothing at all, the very sight of him throwing all her senses awry.

Theo was equally silent, his gaze seeming to devour her. And then an expletive left his lips and he crossed the room in swift strides. Henrietta found herself enveloped in an embrace so powerful and intense her feet left the floor. His voice came huskily in her ear. "Hetty, Hetty! I've missed you so much!"

Everything went out of her head and she was suddenly sobbing into his chest. His hold loosened and his eyes were tender as his fingers came up and brushed at the tears.

"Don't cry, my sweet Sensibility. Please don't."

"I c-can't h-help it, Theo. I d-don't understand…"

He whisked out a pocket handkerchief and gave it to her, one arm supporting her while she made use of it, hiccupping on her tears the while. "What don't you understand, my precious girl? Why your father capitulated?"

She gazed up into his face, unable to think straight at the sheer presence of him, so close, so tender and attentive. But the protests came nevertheless. "That, yes, b-but why did you offer, Theo? Did they make you? You c-can't m-marry me, you know you c-can't."

A faint grin appeared. "I know I can't, but I must."

All her doubts rose up again and she thrust him off. "I knew it! You let them force you, didn't you? Was it your mother?" A horrid thought attacked her. "You did not tell Papa all that happened between us?"

His smile was fading. "What do you take me for? Of course not. As for my mother —"

"Then it was she! Theo, you should not have listened to her!"

"I didn't! What is this, Hetty? Don't you want to marry me?"

"No! I mean, yes, of course I do, but —"

"Then why are you —?"

"Will you let me say it, you beast?"

He closed his mouth and a slow smile burgeoned. "I should have known it would not be long before you began to berate me."

"Well, it's your own fault!" But her spurt of annoyance crumbled and she set a hand to his chest. "Theo, tell me the truth. Why have you yielded? I cannot bear it if you have abandoned your duty because of compromising me."

"Nothing of the kind." His hand closed over hers and he took the handkerchief out of her hand, dabbing at her wet cheeks. Then he caught her by the shoulders. "Hetty, no one forced me, though I confess it was some words of my mother's that made me realise how stupid I was being."

Anxiety was riding her, and longing too. "Stupid how?"

His mouth twisted. "In thinking I could bear to sacrifice us both to convention. My life is burden enough, my sweet one. Without you, for this appalling age since you were taken from me, it became unbearable."

The echo of this last could not but resonate in her own heart. Her life, during these last days without a vestige of hope, had lost all meaning. "Oh, Theo…" The sigh fluttered out of her and his gaze became intense.

"Does that mean you understand? Or was it supposed to be despairing? I can't blame you for doubting me. I've been every kind of fool. Hetty?"

She still felt tremulous as she smiled. "You know very well I love you, Theo. Of course I'm desperate. I want to be with you always, only…"

"Only you are afraid of interfering with my duty? Of being a duchess? What?"

"Yes to both, but that's not it, Theo."

"Well, what is this *only*? You're driving me to distraction!"

Henrietta tugged away, fuming. "Only you've said I don't know how many times and from the first that it won't do, Theo. Now suddenly I am worthy? I'm still the same! I won't stop doing things that will make you mad."

"I don't want you to. I want you just as you are — idiotic and full of sensibility and apt to fall into disaster every other minute. Who do you think I fell in love with, you silly female?"

Henrietta's mind hushed and her eyes filled all over again. "You n-never s-said that b-before."

"Nor did you. But I'm saying it now." She was seized in a comprehensive embrace. "I love you, love you, love you, my darling Disaster!" Then his lips were on hers and he was kissing her with a fierceness that was so in character she forgot to be angry.

As Theo released her, he was regaled with a familiar protest, albeit murmured for a change.

"Rude beast … brute…"

His laugh was shaky as he caught her up again, smiling into her eyes. "But you know I can be tender too." With which he sought her lips again, mouthing them gently, the exquisite pleasure of it throwing the want into his loins. As of instinct, he began to draw away, just as he had done through every encounter when he must not give in to temptation, however overmastering.

Hetty stiffened in his arms and then wrenched out of his embrace, staring at him with dilated eyes. Had she felt his withdrawal?

"What is it, dear heart?"

"I don't know." She was breathless. "You m-made me f-feel as I did *that* day, in your room."

He recalled it vividly, had done over and again in her absence. "Yes, but I didn't do anything then."

"You wanted to c-compromise me." Colour crept into her face and a whisper came. "I'm a terrible female, Theo. I wanted you to, and I know I could not have stopped you. I wouldn't have tried."

The guilt in her face proved too much for him and he could not hold back the laughter. "As well I stopped us both, then, my adorable little wanton."

Indignant, she made a fist and hit him. "Don't say that! How dare you laugh at me, you beast? I'm serious."

He caught her back into his embrace, still smiling. "You're a delight, my sweet, and you need not fret. We're betrothed now. You're allowed to be moved to passion." A special hunger woke in him and he tightened his hold. "And so am I, by God! I was in danger of forgetting it myself." He made to kiss her again, but she held him off, leaning her head back.

"Theo, wait!"

Faint alarm ran through him as he took in the distress in her eyes. "What is amiss? Do you doubt me still?"

A rueful look crept into her face. "No, it's just … I've been standing too long and my foot is killing me."

"Hell and the devil, I forgot!"

Henrietta cried out as he let her go abruptly. But in an instant he had swung her up bodily and the familiar sensation of helplessness engulfed her. This time it proved more than welcome, and she threw an arm about his neck and snuggled into him. "Oh, Theo, I did miss you looking after me."

He dropped a kiss on her hair and a tingle of delight invaded her breast at the thought he might carry her with impunity, without any excuse at all. "Where can I take you? I hate this blasted parlour."

She smiled up at him, free and clear. "The gardens, if you wish."

He frowned down at her as he headed for the door. "I don't wish to be overlooked by your father if he's in his library."

She reached down her free hand and opened the door. "If we go out of the side door, there's an arbour. We will be as private as you please."

"Excellent."

He manoeuvred his way through into the hall and Henrietta directed him along the corridor to the door leading outside. At his command, she turned the handle and pulled it open, just as if they had been doing this every day for years.

Theo took her through into the bright, fresh air and leaned against the door, which clicked to behind them. He shifted her weight in his arms and grinned down at her. "I'm kidnapping you for the last time, Miss Latimer."

Happiness flooded her and she smiled mistily up at him. "I thought it was another rescue, not a kidnap."

Theo's laughter rang into the air and he leaned his head down to kiss her lips quickly. "Rescuing you is henceforth the business of my life, Miss Disaster. Now, where's this private arbour of yours?"

A NOTE TO THE READER

Dear Reader,

One of the aspects that affects me strongly with writing a Regency is the importance of the mores of the time. One can't simply ignore these and have the hero and heroine behaving in a fashion that would be acceptable today but would then have resulted in scandal and much trouble for both parties.

The shibboleths surrounding female behaviour arose primarily from the practice of primogeniture. Titles and estates had to pass from father to son, or failing a son, to the next available heir by way of family connections. We see this in the present day in Royal Families, in particular in Britain. It's only since the Princess Charlotte was born that the rules were changed to accommodate a female not giving place to her brothers in the line of succession. So it was with peerages in the Regency.

The higher the title, the more important it became that the line was "pure". Thus, debutante potential wives of peers, marquises and dukes had to be innocent. That meant, in essence, that there was no possibility of a child being conceived from any other man than the prospective husband. Virginity was therefore at a premium. So no young girl could risk being alone in company with a man, unchaperoned, in case of any hanky-panky!

Once married, the rules became a little more relaxed. There was an unwritten acceptance that a wife could not take a lover until she had provided her husband with "an heir and a spare", though it was still a risky business. Needless to say, the *Ton* was littered with scandalous tidbits and the latest "crim cons" (meaning criminal conversation, the legal term for adultery).

Writing in the period then means one must take these prohibitions into account and, as it turned out, this formed the principal dichotomy for Hetty and Theo. They break the rules left and right, but it was impossible to allow them to do so without consequences. Hetty is undoubtedly compromised, and if their unconventional behaviour had been seen or found out, Theo would have been obliged to offer marriage to save her reputation.

That, a common trope, would have given rise to a completely different story. I wanted my heroine's integrity to shine through and my hero's chivalry to take an unusual path. I hope the resulting sweet story has engaged and entertained you.

If you would consider leaving a review, it would be much appreciated and very helpful. Do feel free to contact me on **elizabeth@elizabethbailey.co.uk** or find me on **Facebook**, **Twitter**, **Goodreads** or my website **www.elizabethbailey.co.uk**.

Elizabeth Bailey

Sapere Books is an exciting new publisher of brilliant fiction and popular history.

To find out more about our latest releases and our monthly bargain books visit our website: **saperebooks.com**